Love at Fourteen

Fuka Mizutani

11

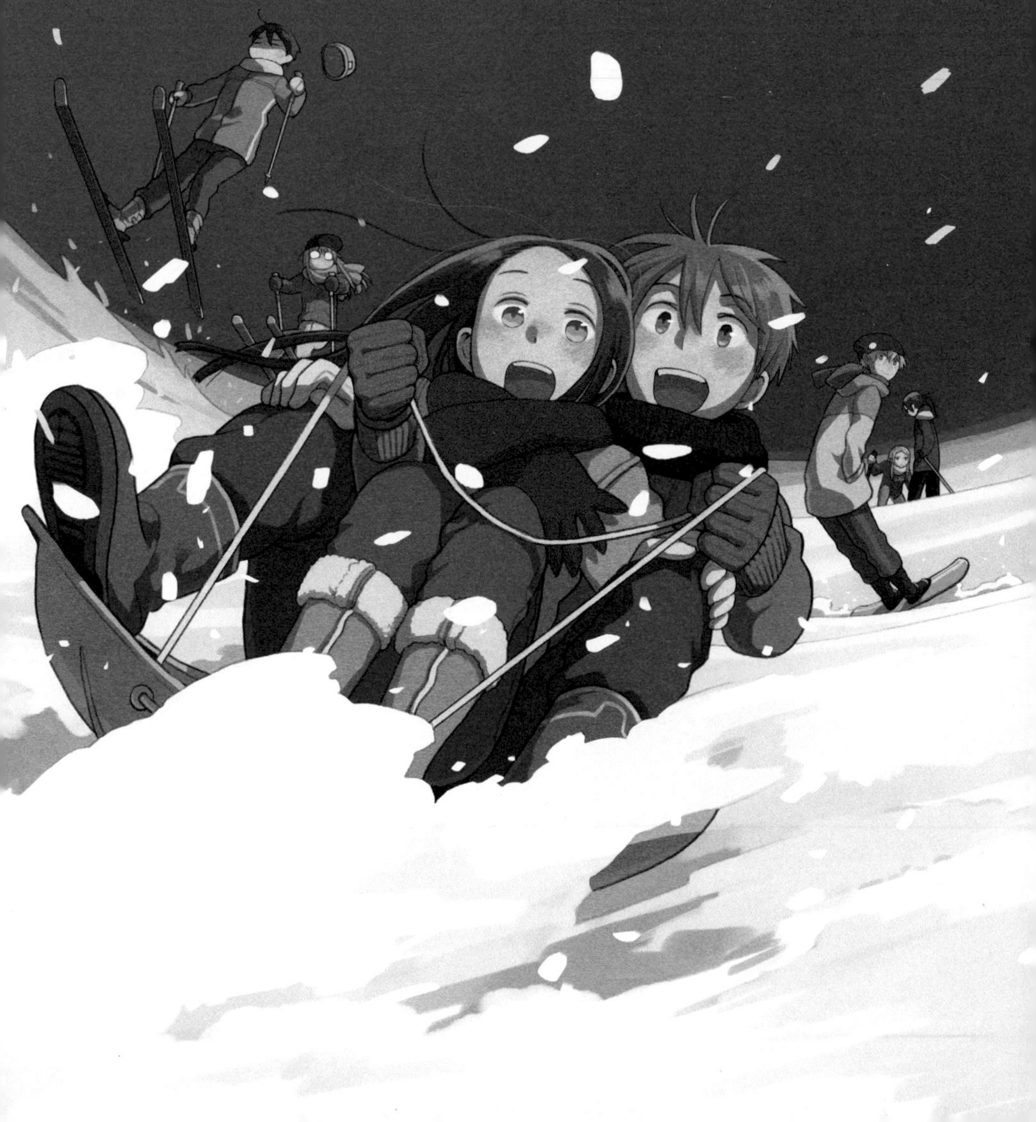

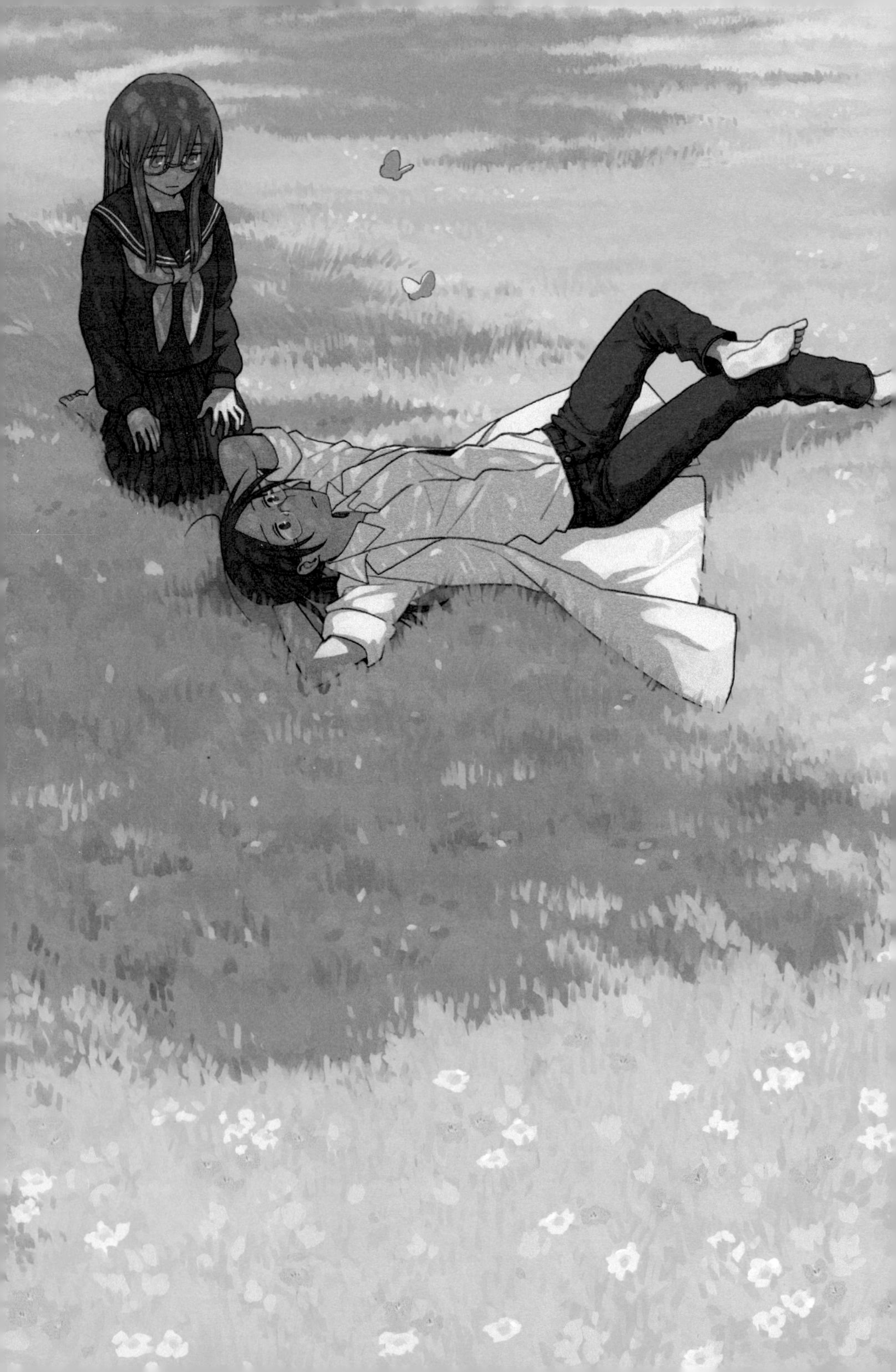

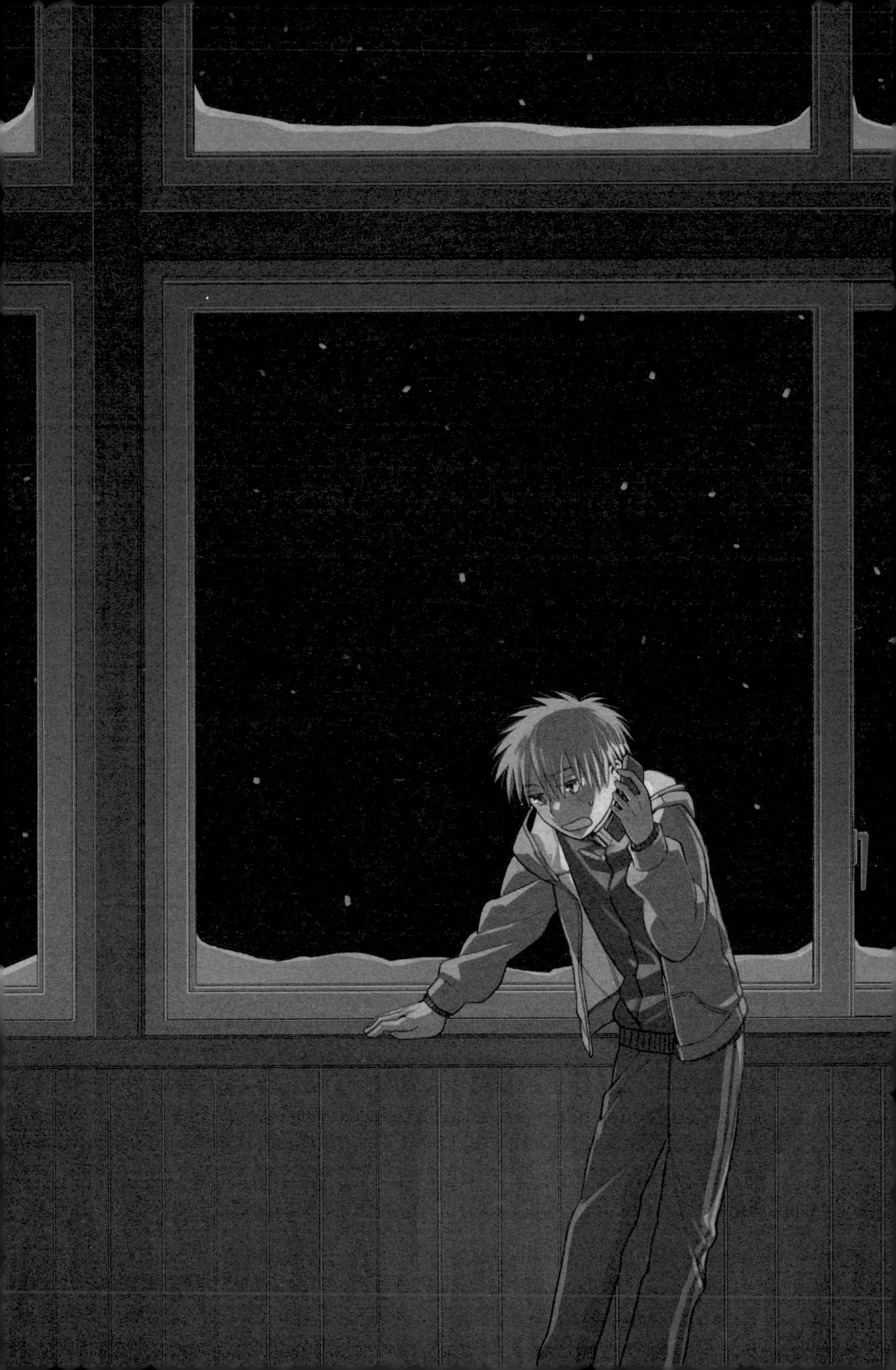

Contents

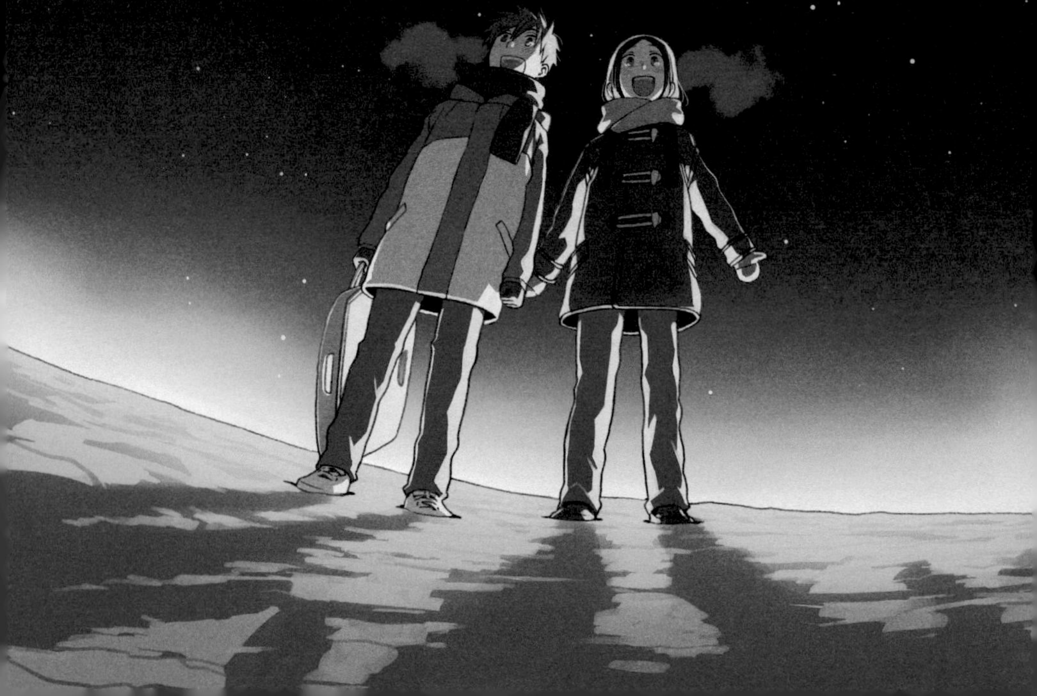

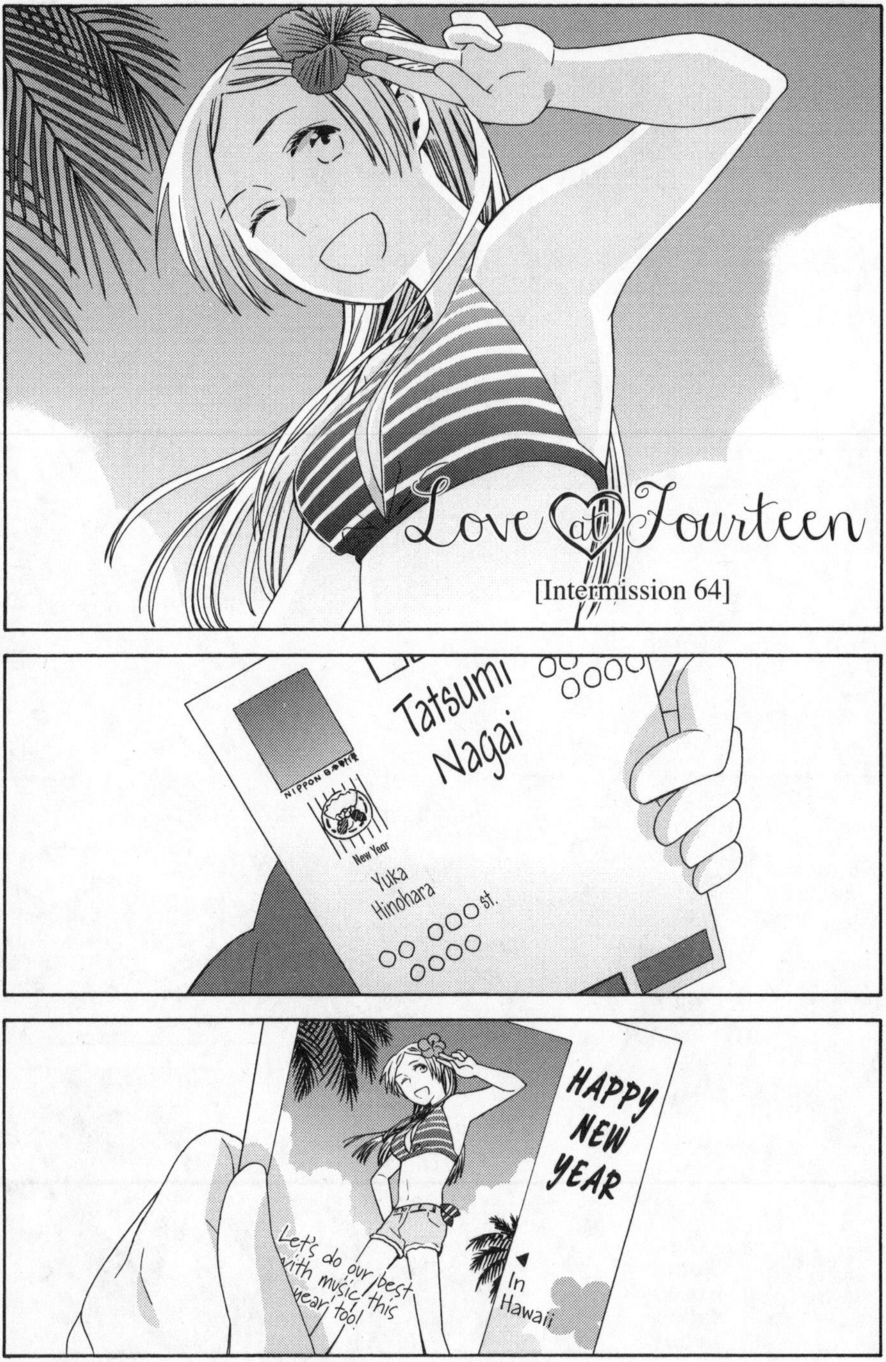
Love at Fourteen
[Intermission 64]
Tatsumi Nagai
NIPPON
New Year
Yuka Hinohara
st.
HAPPY NEW YEAR
In Hawaii
Let's do our best with music this year too!

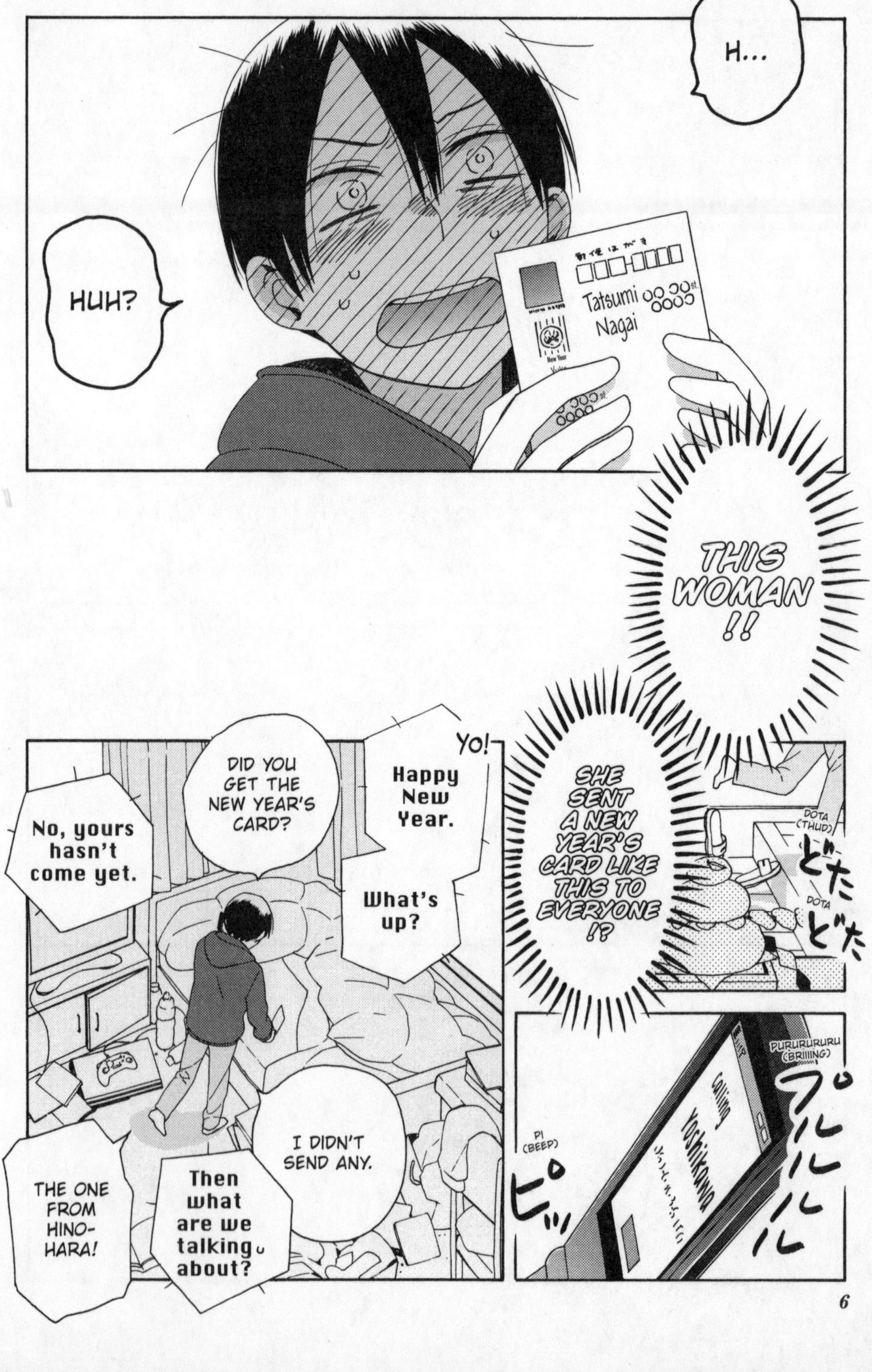
H...
HUH?
Tatsumi
Nagai
New Year
THIS WOMAN !!
SHE SENT A NEW YEAR'S CARD LIKE THIS TO EVERYONE !?
DOTA (THUD)
どた
DOTA
どた
PURURURURU (BRIIIING)
プルルルル
PI (BEEP)
ピッ
Calling
Yoshikawa
YO!
Happy New Year.
DID YOU GET THE NEW YEAR'S CARD?
No, yours hasn't come yet.
What's up?
I DIDN'T SEND ANY.
Then what are we talking about?
THE ONE FROM HINO-HARA!

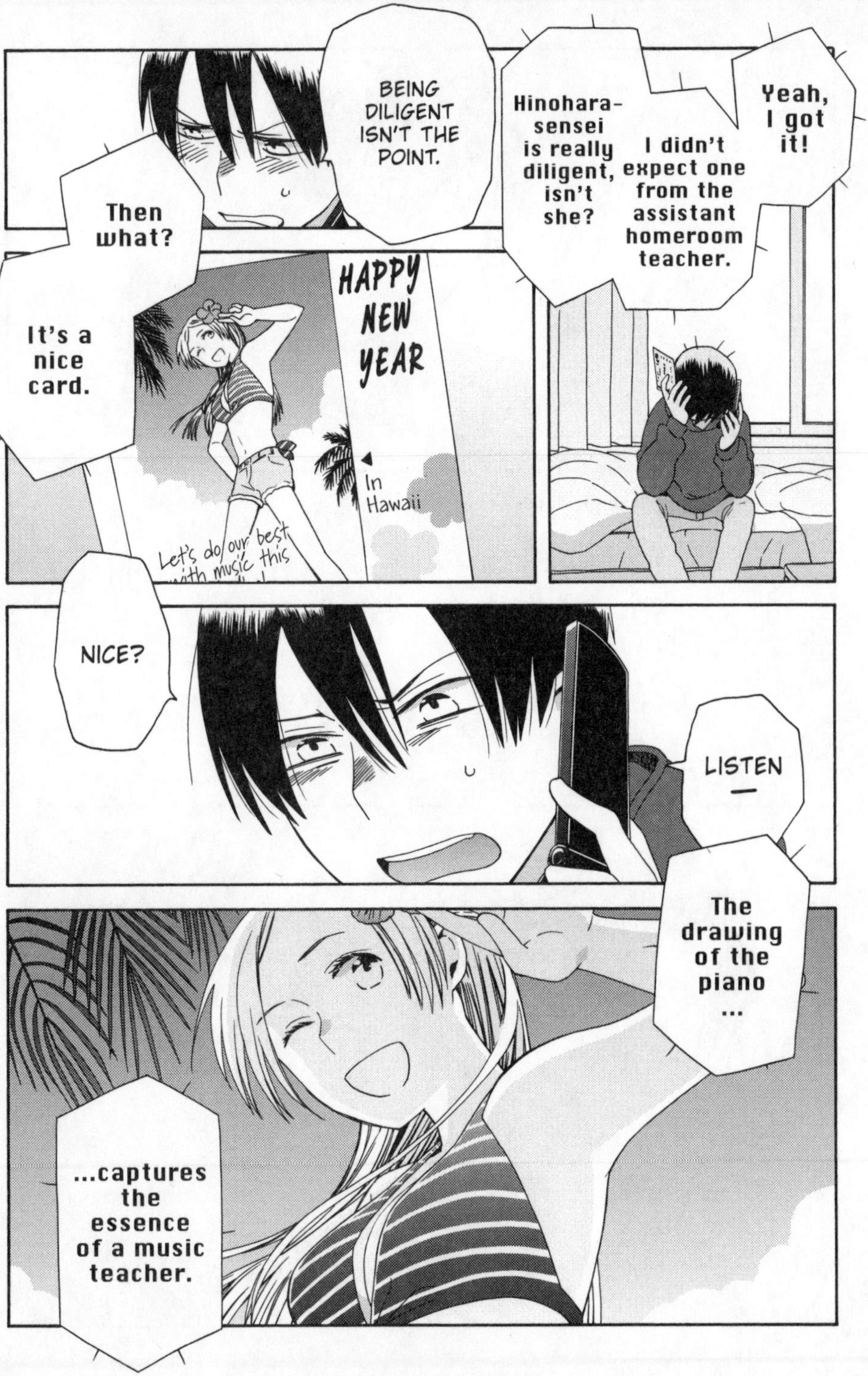
Yeah, I got it!
I didn't expect one from the assistant homeroom teacher.
Hinohara-sensei is really diligent, isn't she?
BEING DILIGENT ISN'T THE POINT.
Then what?
HAPPY NEW YEAR
In Hawaii
Let's do our best with music this
It's a nice card.
NICE?
LISTEN —
The drawing of the piano ...
...captures the essence of a music teacher.

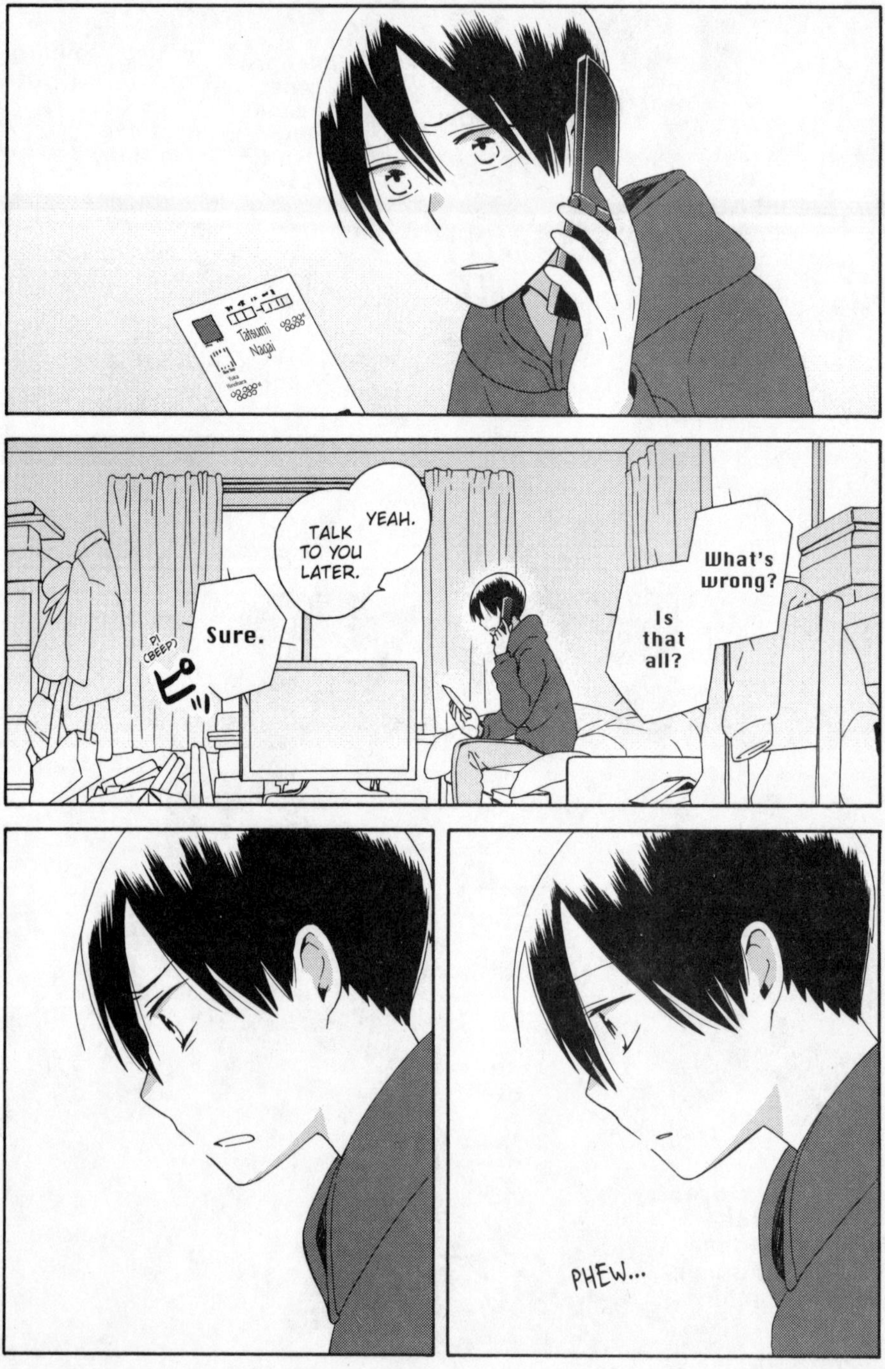
Tatsumi
Nagai
What's wrong?
Is that all?
YEAH.
TALK TO YOU LATER.
Sure.
PI (BEEP)
ピッ
PHEW...

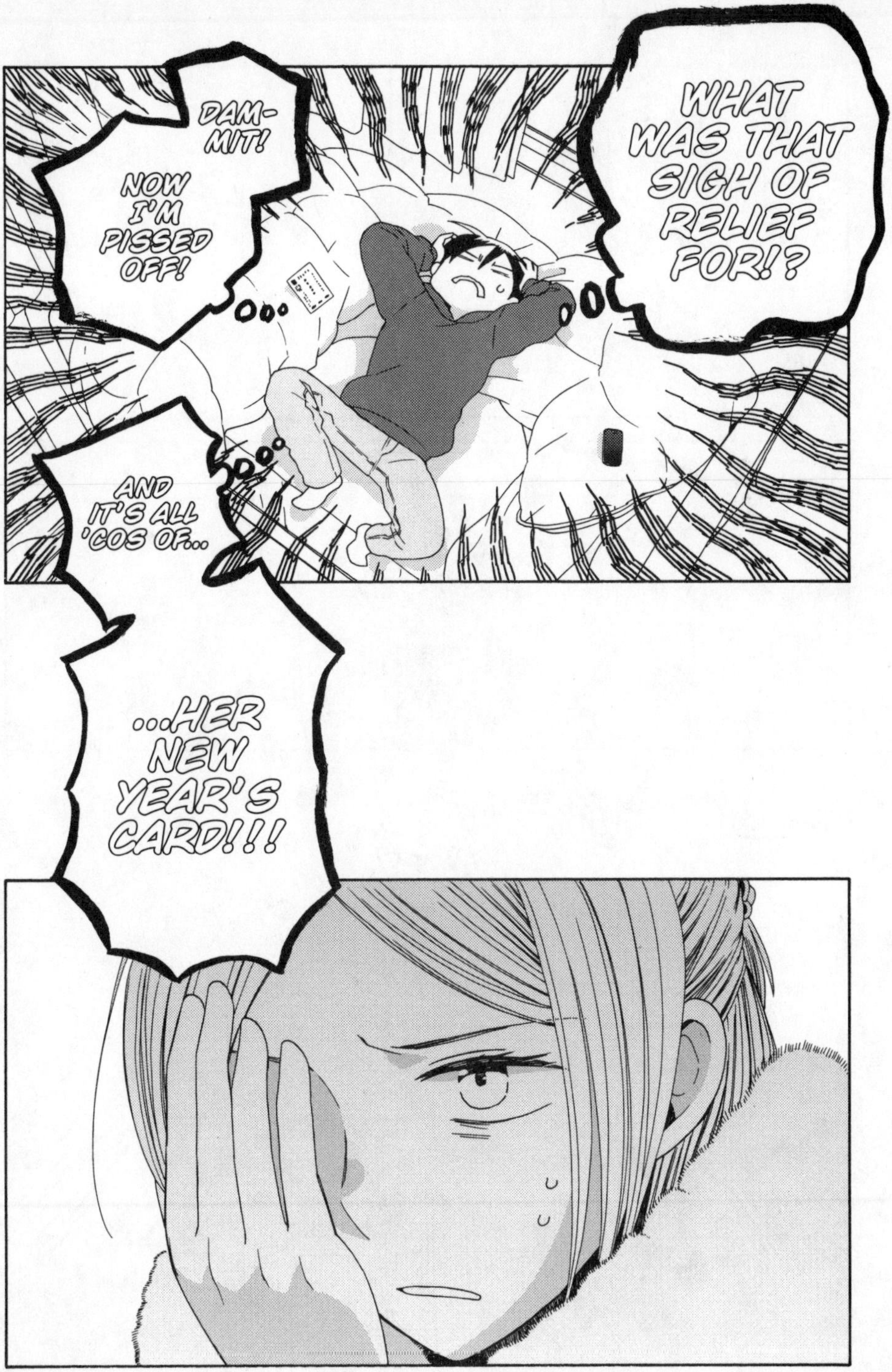
WHAT WAS THAT SIGH OF RELIEF FOR!?
DAM-MIT!
NOW I'M PISSED OFF!
AND IT'S ALL 'COS OF...
...HER NEW YEAR'S CARD!!!

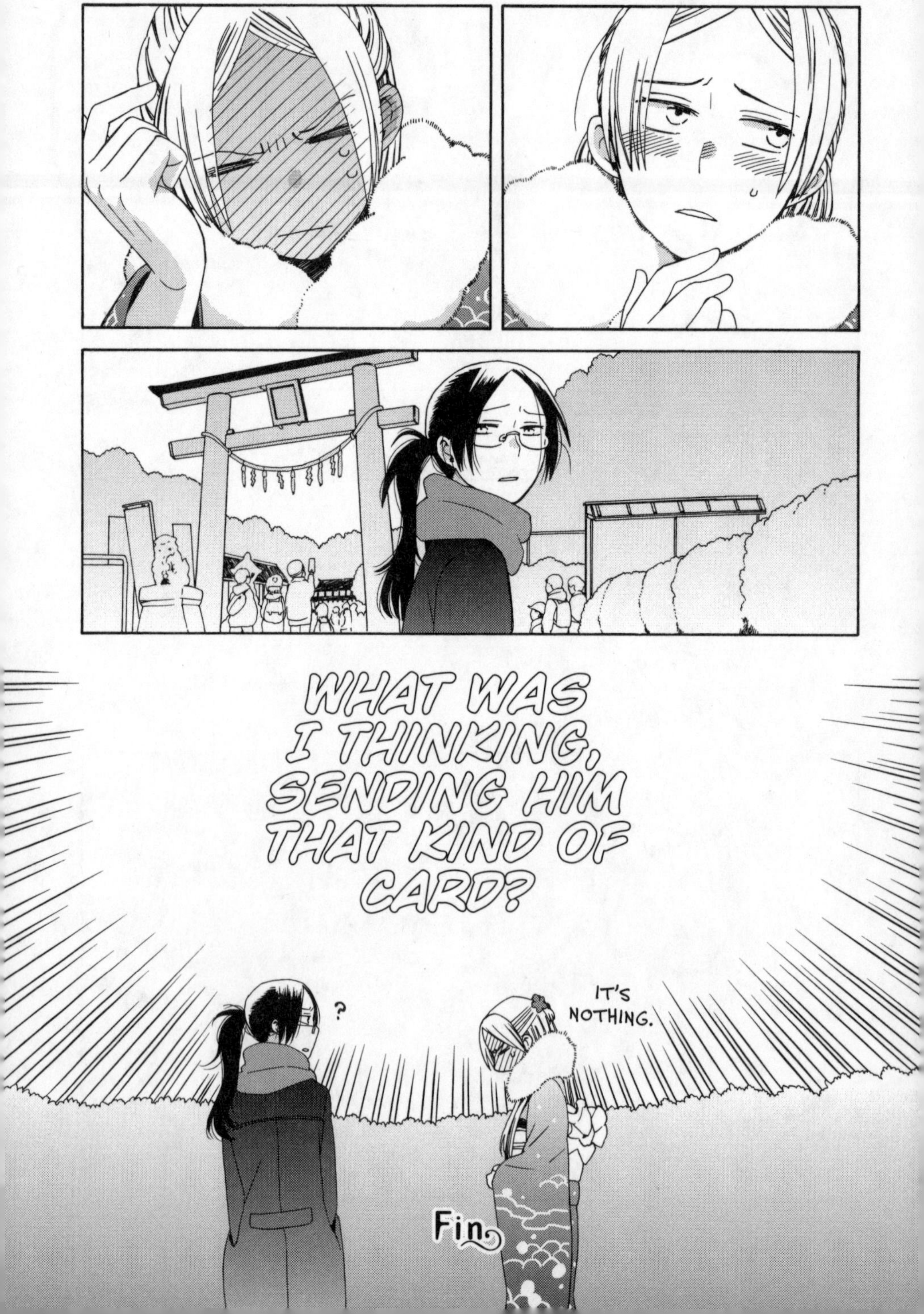
WHAT WAS I THINKING, SENDING HIM THAT KIND OF CARD?
IT'S NOTHING.
?
Fin

Love at Fourteen

[Intermission 65]

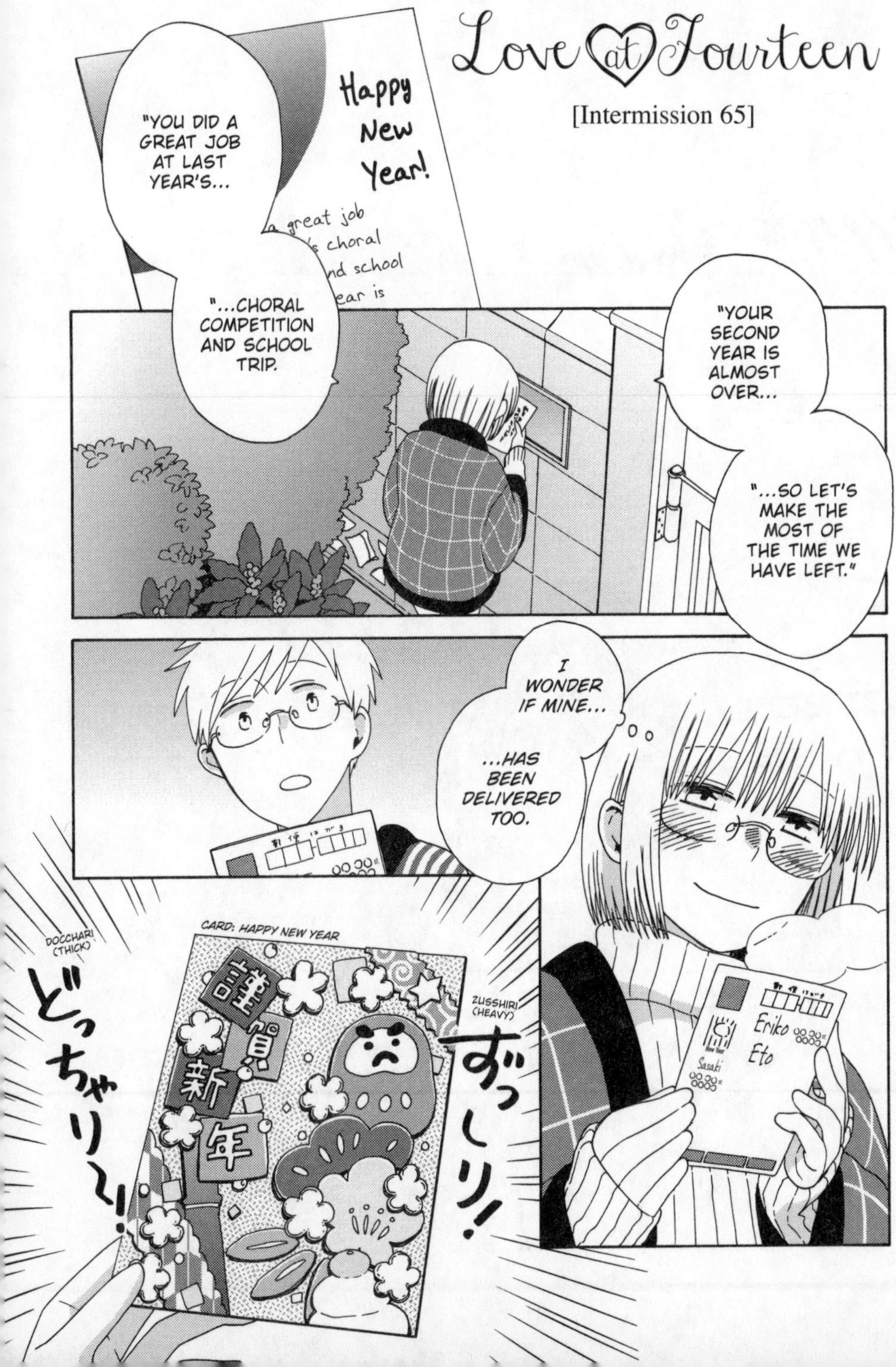
Happy New Year!
"YOU DID A GREAT JOB AT LAST YEAR'S...
"...CHORAL COMPETITION AND SCHOOL TRIP.
"YOUR SECOND YEAR IS ALMOST OVER...
"...SO LET'S MAKE THE MOST OF THE TIME WE HAVE LEFT."
I WONDER IF MINE...
...HAS BEEN DELIVERED TOO.
Eriko Eto
Sasaki
ZUSSHIRI (HEAVY)
ずっしり!
CARD: HAPPY NEW YEAR
謹賀新年
DOCCHARI (THICK)
どっちゃり~!

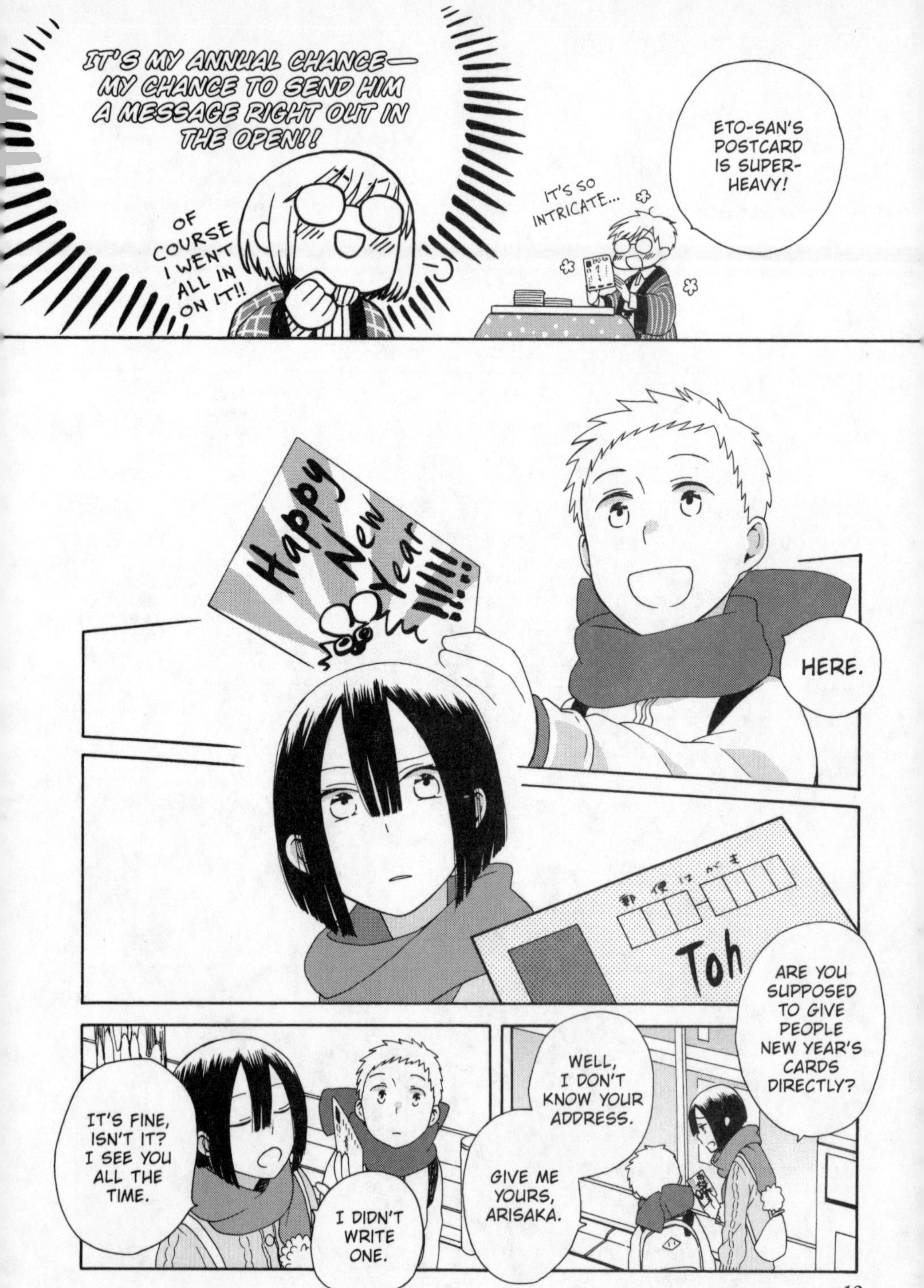
ETO-SAN'S POSTCARD IS SUPER-HEAVY!
IT'S SO INTRICATE...
IT'S MY ANNUAL CHANCE— MY CHANCE TO SEND HIM A MESSAGE RIGHT OUT IN THE OPEN!!
OF COURSE I WENT ALL IN ON IT!!
Happy New Year!!!!!!!
HERE.
Toh
ARE YOU SUPPOSED TO GIVE PEOPLE NEW YEAR'S CARDS DIRECTLY?
WELL, I DON'T KNOW YOUR ADDRESS.
GIVE ME YOURS, ARISAKA.
I DIDN'T WRITE ONE.
IT'S FINE, ISN'T IT? I SEE YOU ALL THE TIME.

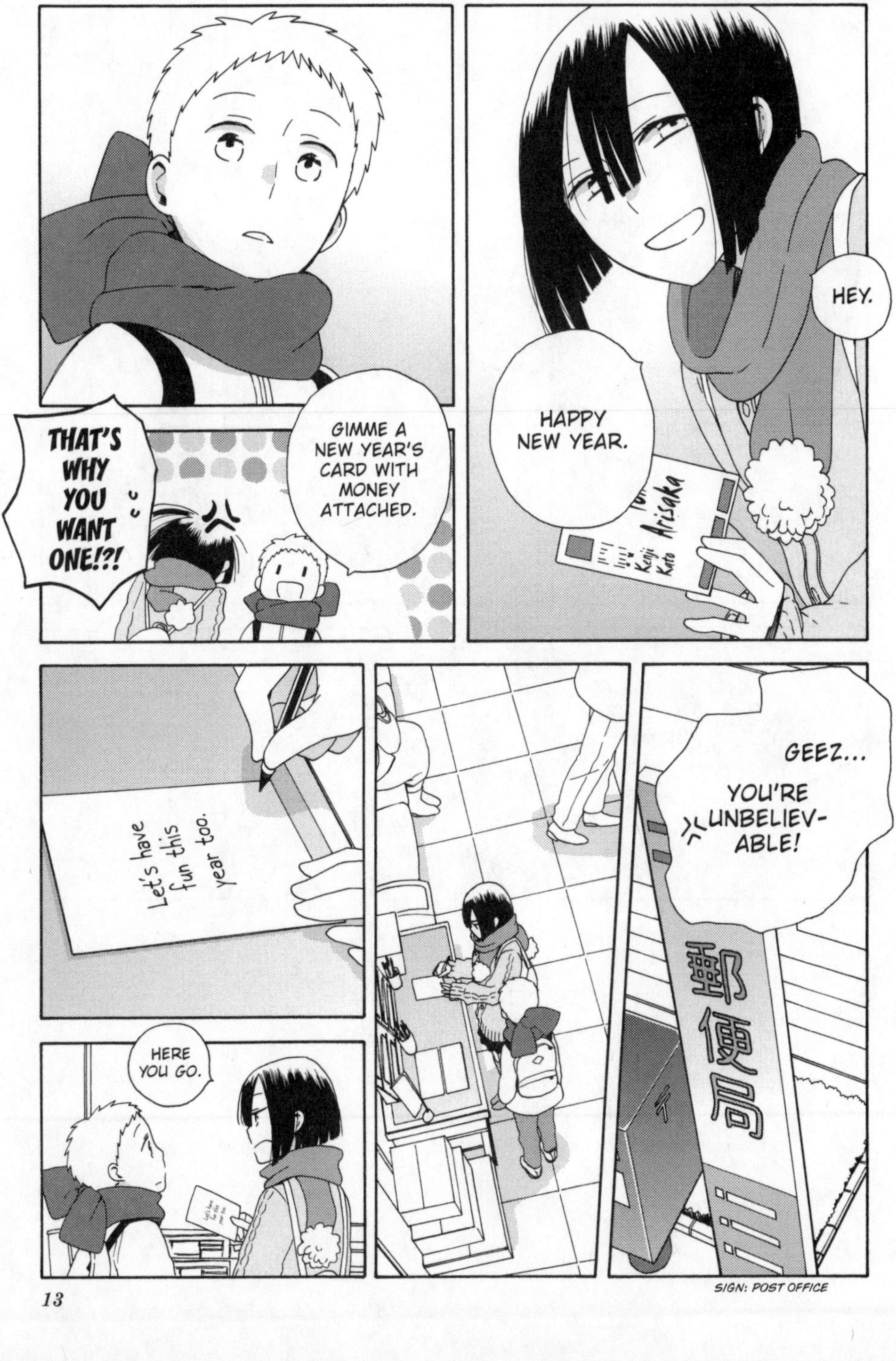
HEY.
HAPPY NEW YEAR.
Arisaka
Kenji Kato
GIMME A NEW YEAR'S CARD WITH MONEY ATTACHED.
THAT'S WHY YOU WANT ONE!?!
GEEZ...
YOU'RE UNBELIEVABLE!
郵便局
Let's have fun this year too.
HERE YOU GO.

SIGN: POST OFFICE

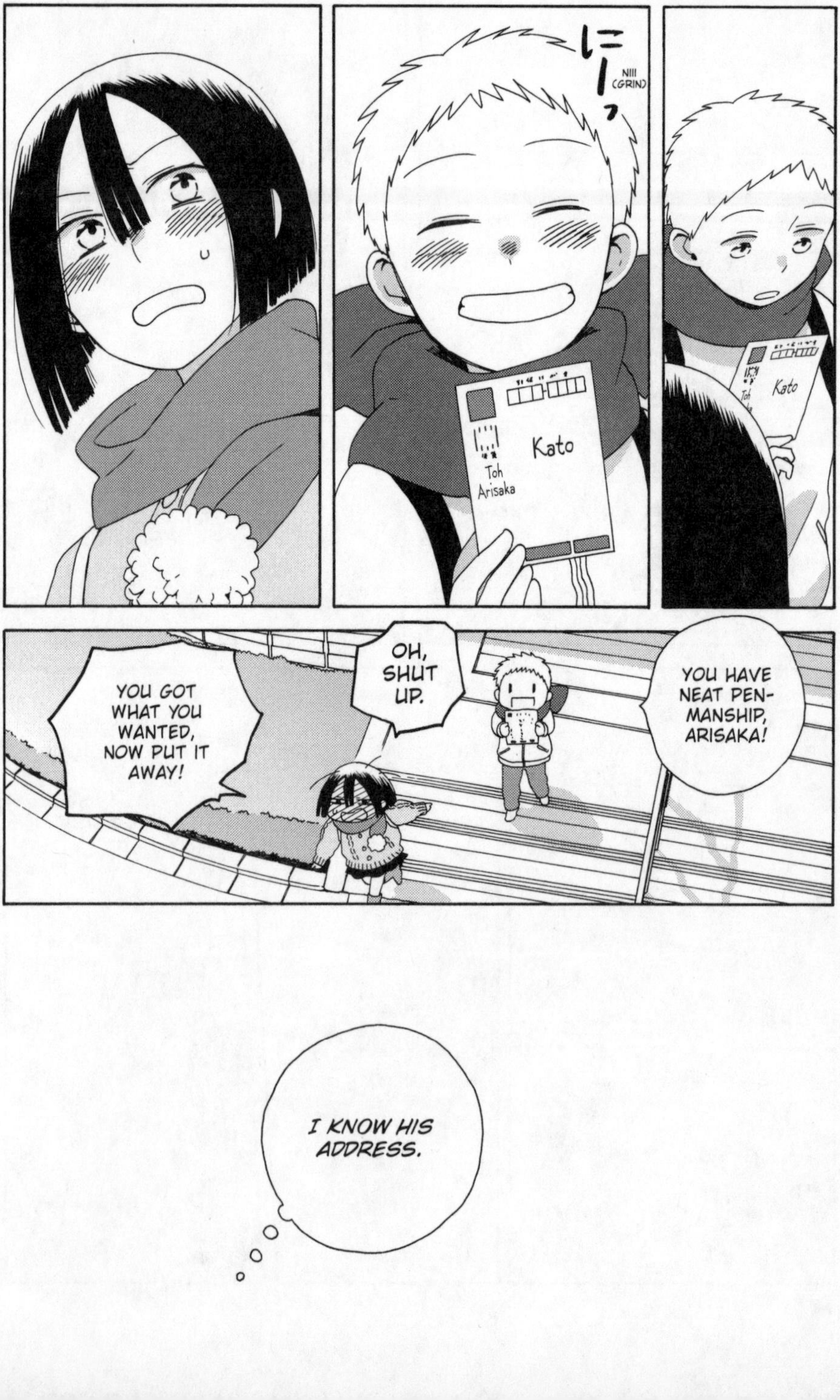
Kato
Toh Arisaka
にーっ
NIII (GRIN)
Kato
Toh Arisaka
YOU HAVE NEAT PEN-MANSHIP, ARISAKA!
OH, SHUT UP.
YOU GOT WHAT YOU WANTED, NOW PUT IT AWAY!
I KNOW HIS ADDRESS.

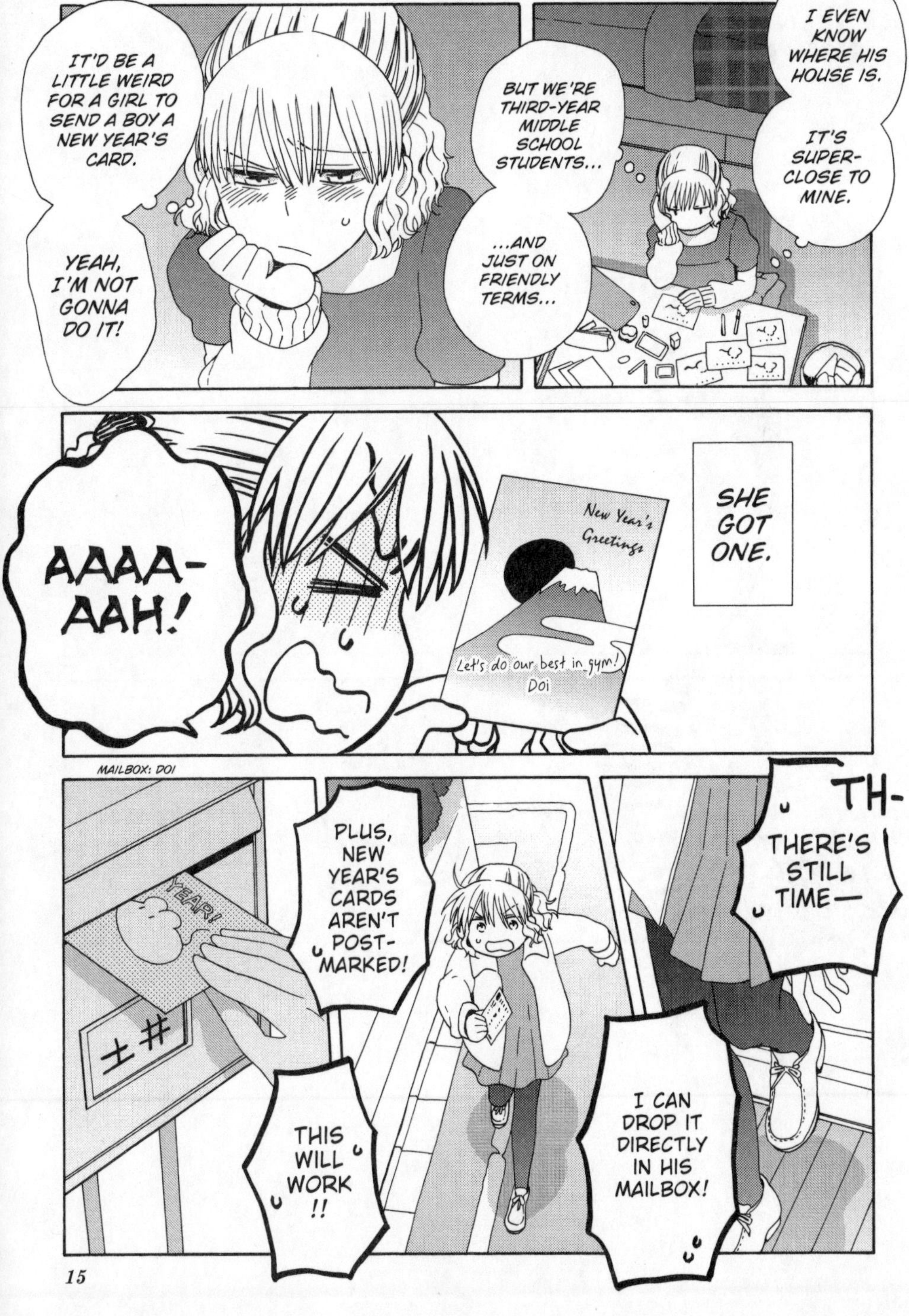
I EVEN KNOW WHERE HIS HOUSE IS.
IT'S SUPER-CLOSE TO MINE.
BUT WE'RE THIRD-YEAR MIDDLE SCHOOL STUDENTS...
...AND JUST ON FRIENDLY TERMS...
IT'D BE A LITTLE WEIRD FOR A GIRL TO SEND A BOY A NEW YEAR'S CARD.
YEAH, I'M NOT GONNA DO IT!
SHE GOT ONE.
New Year's Greetings
Let's do our best in gym!
Doi
AAAA-AAH!
TH- THERE'S STILL TIME—
I CAN DROP IT DIRECTLY IN HIS MAILBOX!
PLUS, NEW YEAR'S CARDS AREN'T POST-MARKED!
THIS WILL WORK!!
YEAR!
土井
MAILBOX: DOI

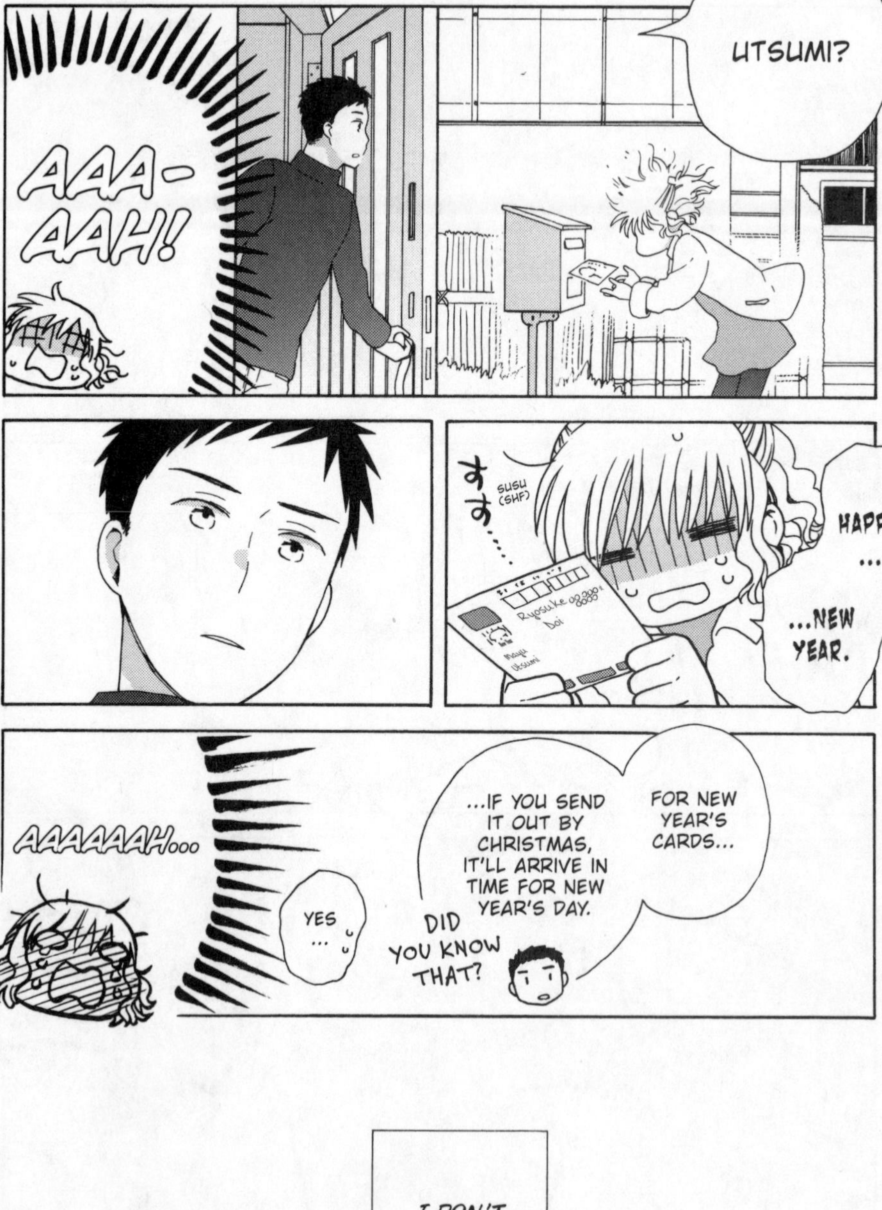
UTSUMI?
AAA-AAH!
すす
SUSU (SHF)
HAPPY ...
...NEW YEAR.
FOR NEW YEAR'S CARDS...
...IF YOU SEND IT OUT BY CHRISTMAS, IT'LL ARRIVE IN TIME FOR NEW YEAR'S DAY.
DID YOU KNOW THAT?
YES ...
AAAAAAH...
I DON'T KNOW HER ADDRESS...

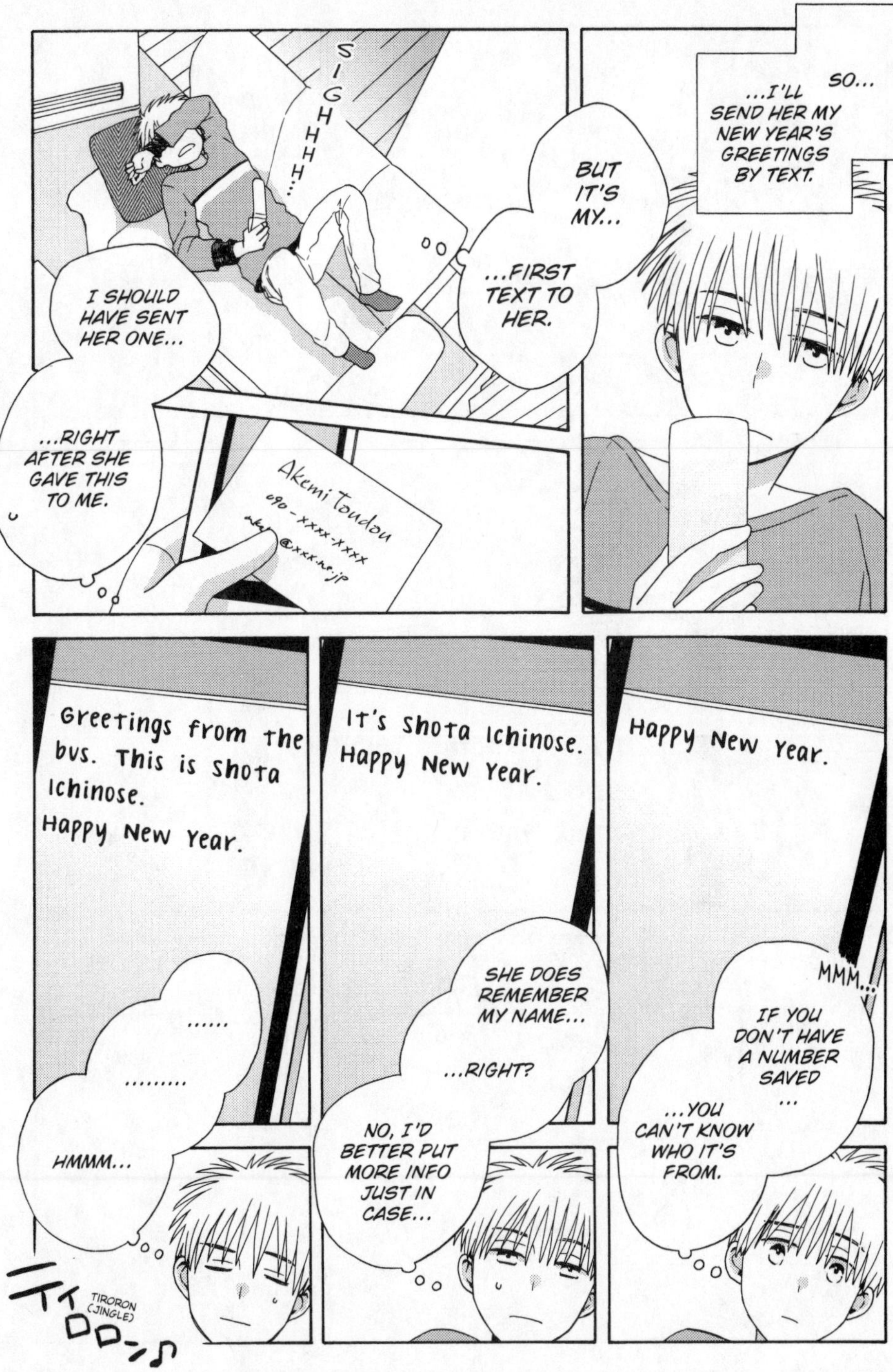
SO...
...I'LL SEND HER MY NEW YEAR'S GREETINGS BY TEXT.
SIGHHHH...
BUT IT'S MY...
...FIRST TEXT TO HER.
I SHOULD HAVE SENT HER ONE...
...RIGHT AFTER SHE GAVE THIS TO ME.
Akemi Toudou
090-xxxx-xxxx
@xxx.ne.jp
Happy New Year.
MMM...
IF YOU DON'T HAVE A NUMBER SAVED ...
...YOU CAN'T KNOW WHO IT'S FROM.
It's Shota Ichinose. Happy New Year.
SHE DOES REMEMBER MY NAME...
...RIGHT?
NO, I'D BETTER PUT MORE INFO JUST IN CASE...
Greetings from the bus. This is Shota Ichinose. Happy New Year.
......
....
HMMM...
TIRORON (JINGLE)

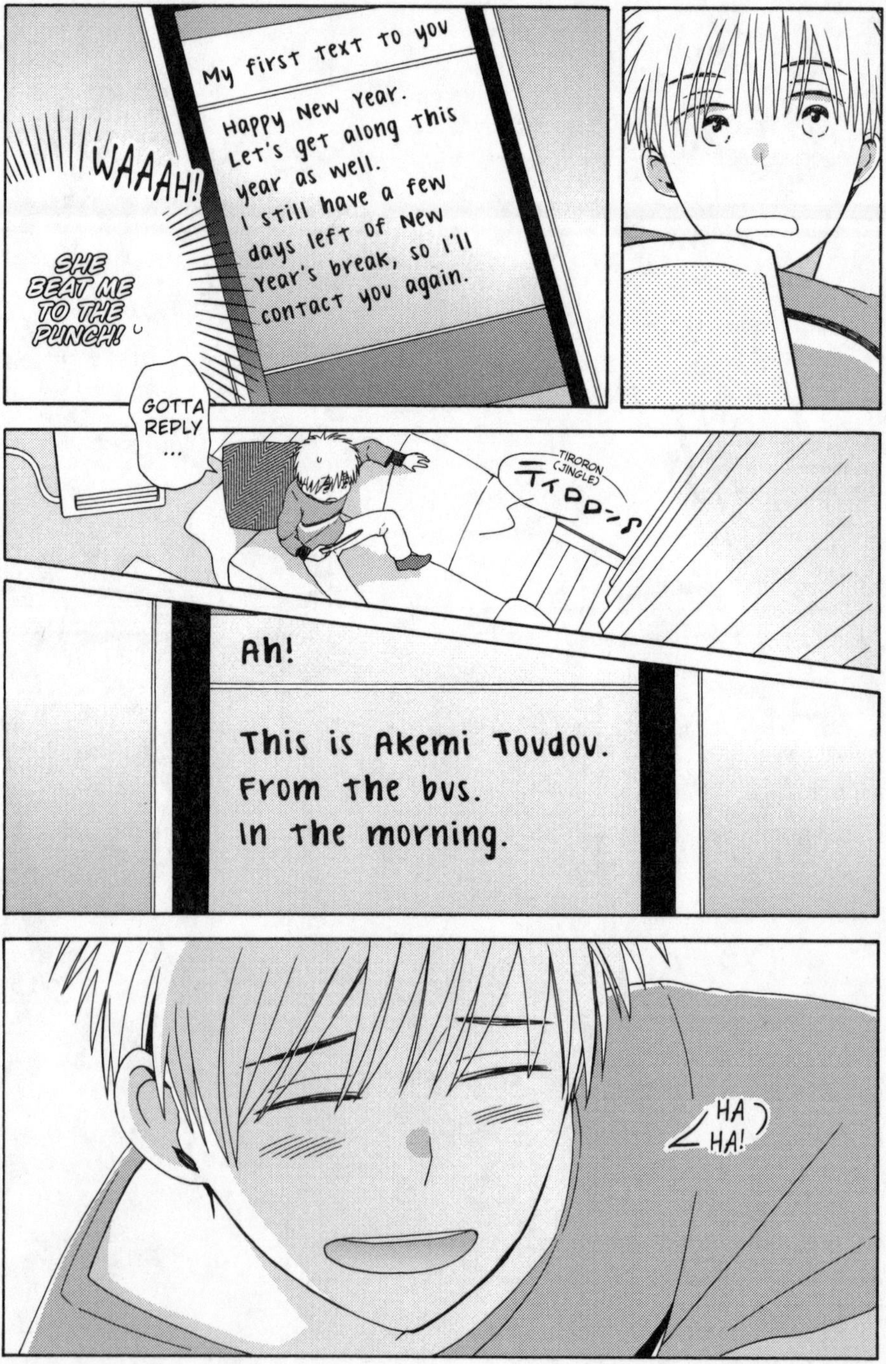

My first text to you
Happy New Year. Let's get along this year as well. I still have a few days left of New Year's break, so I'll contact you again.
WAAAH!
SHE BEAT ME TO THE PUNCH!
GOTTA REPLY ...
TIRORON (JINGLE)
Ah!
This is Akemi Toudou. From the bus. In the morning.
HA HA!

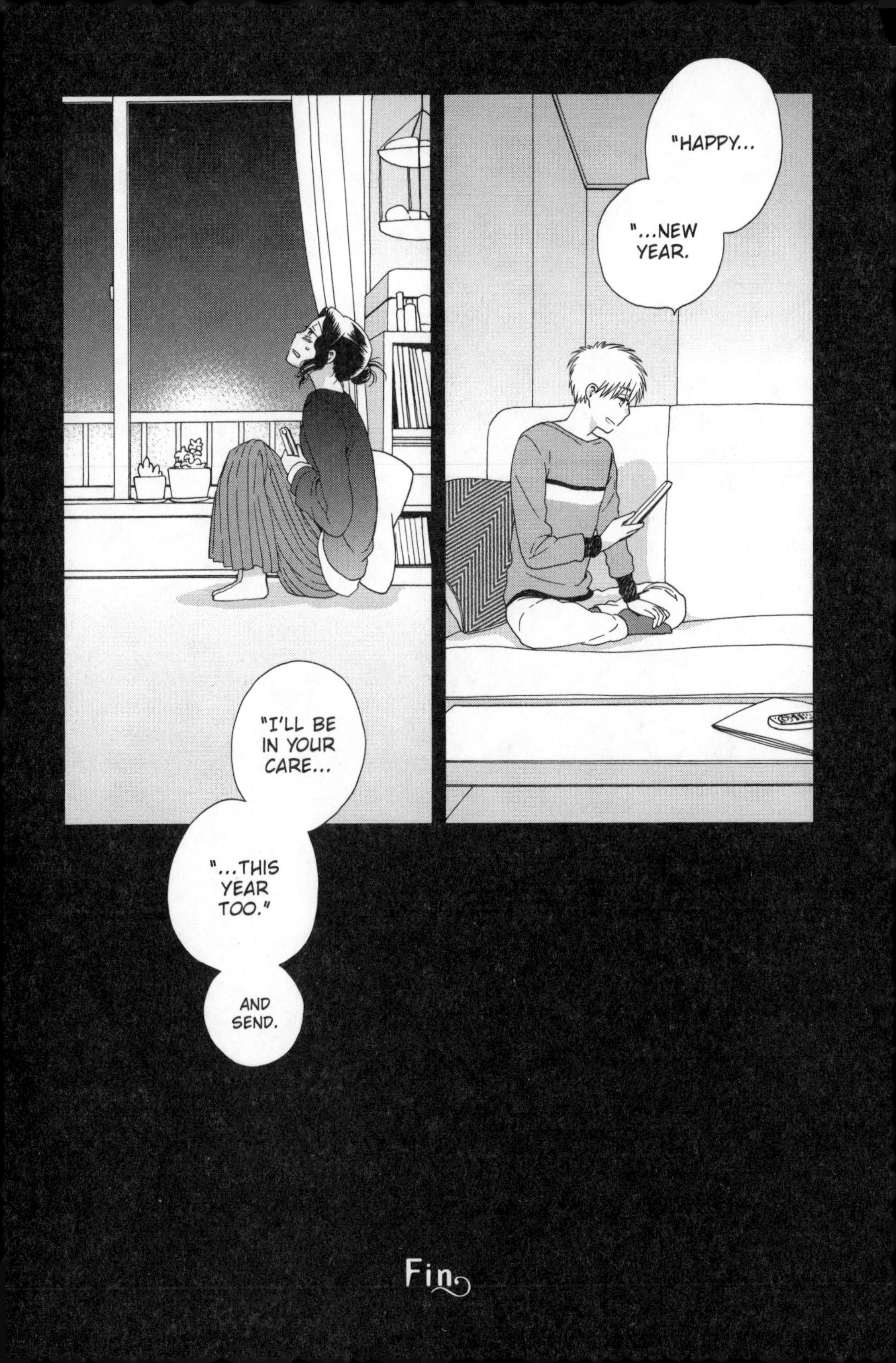
"HAPPY...
"...NEW YEAR.
"I'LL BE IN YOUR CARE...
"...THIS YEAR TOO."
AND SEND.

Fin

Love at Fourteen

Fuka Mizutani

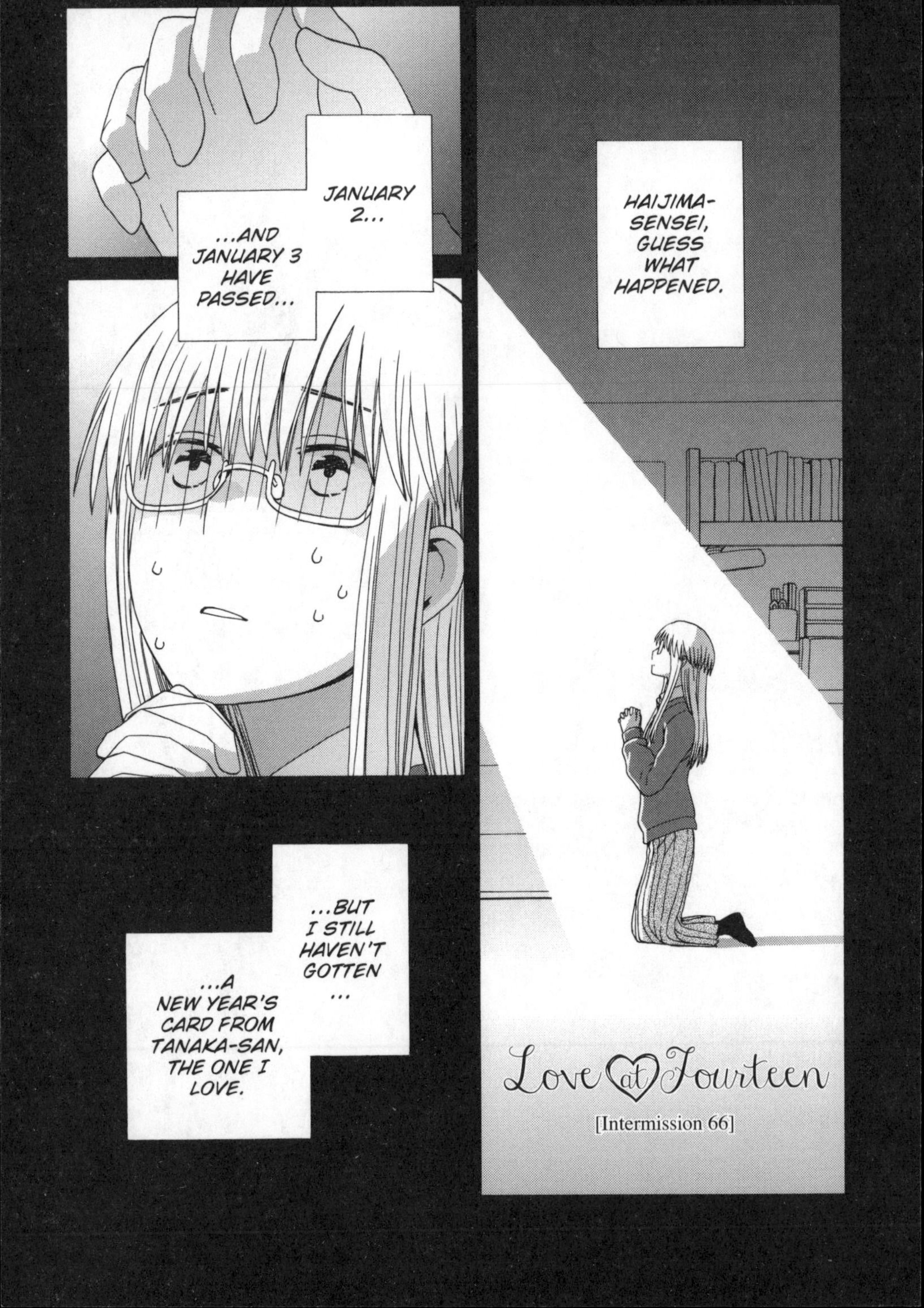
HAIJIMA-SENSEI, GUESS WHAT HAPPENED.
Love at Fourteen
[Intermission 66]
JANUARY 2...
...AND JANUARY 3 HAVE PASSED...
...BUT I STILL HAVEN'T GOTTEN ...
...A NEW YEAR'S CARD FROM TANAKA-SAN, THE ONE I LOVE.

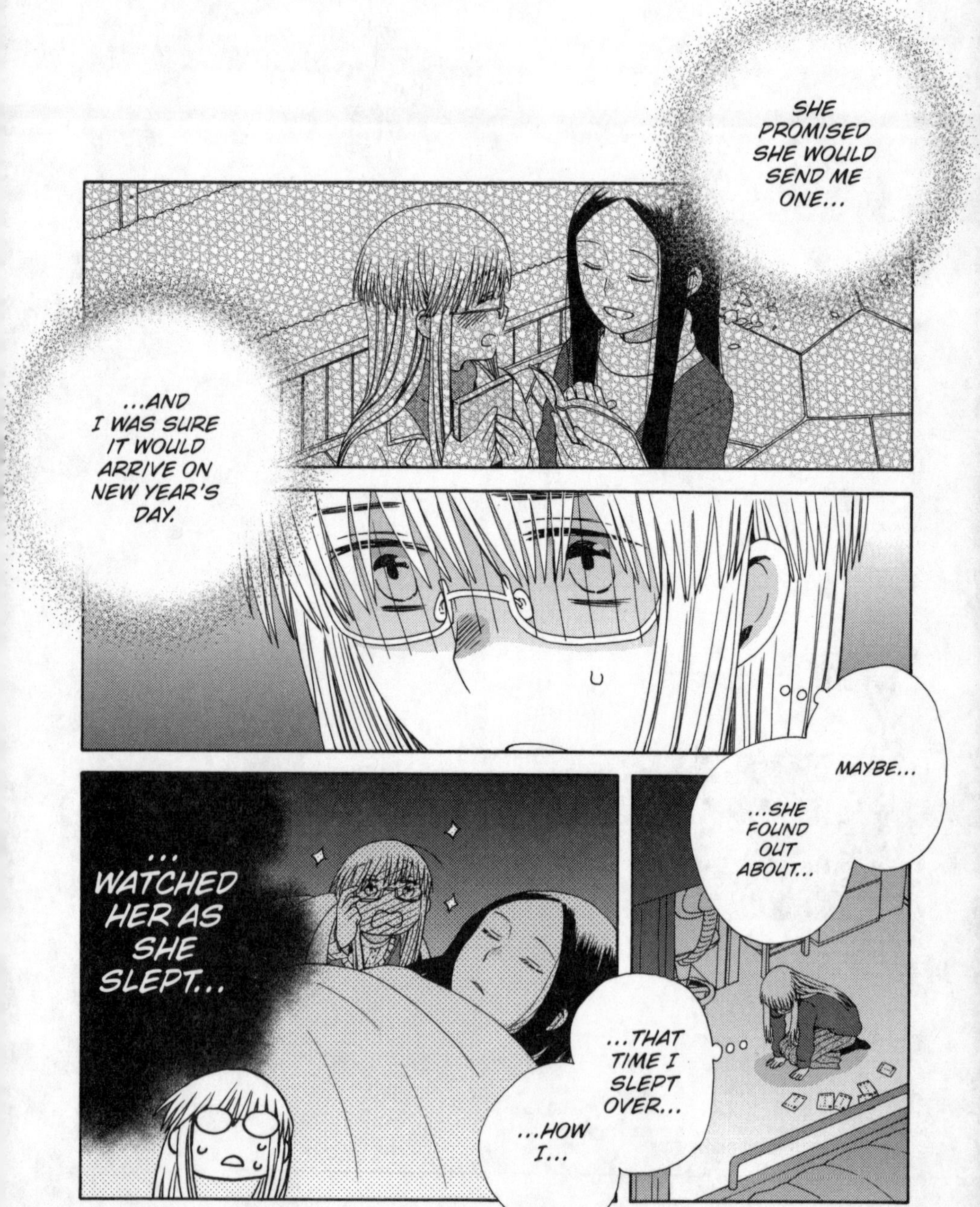
SHE PROMISED SHE WOULD SEND ME ONE...
...AND I WAS SURE IT WOULD ARRIVE ON NEW YEAR'S DAY.
MAYBE...
...SHE FOUND OUT ABOUT...
...THAT TIME I SLEPT OVER...
...HOW I...
...WATCHED HER AS SHE SLEPT...

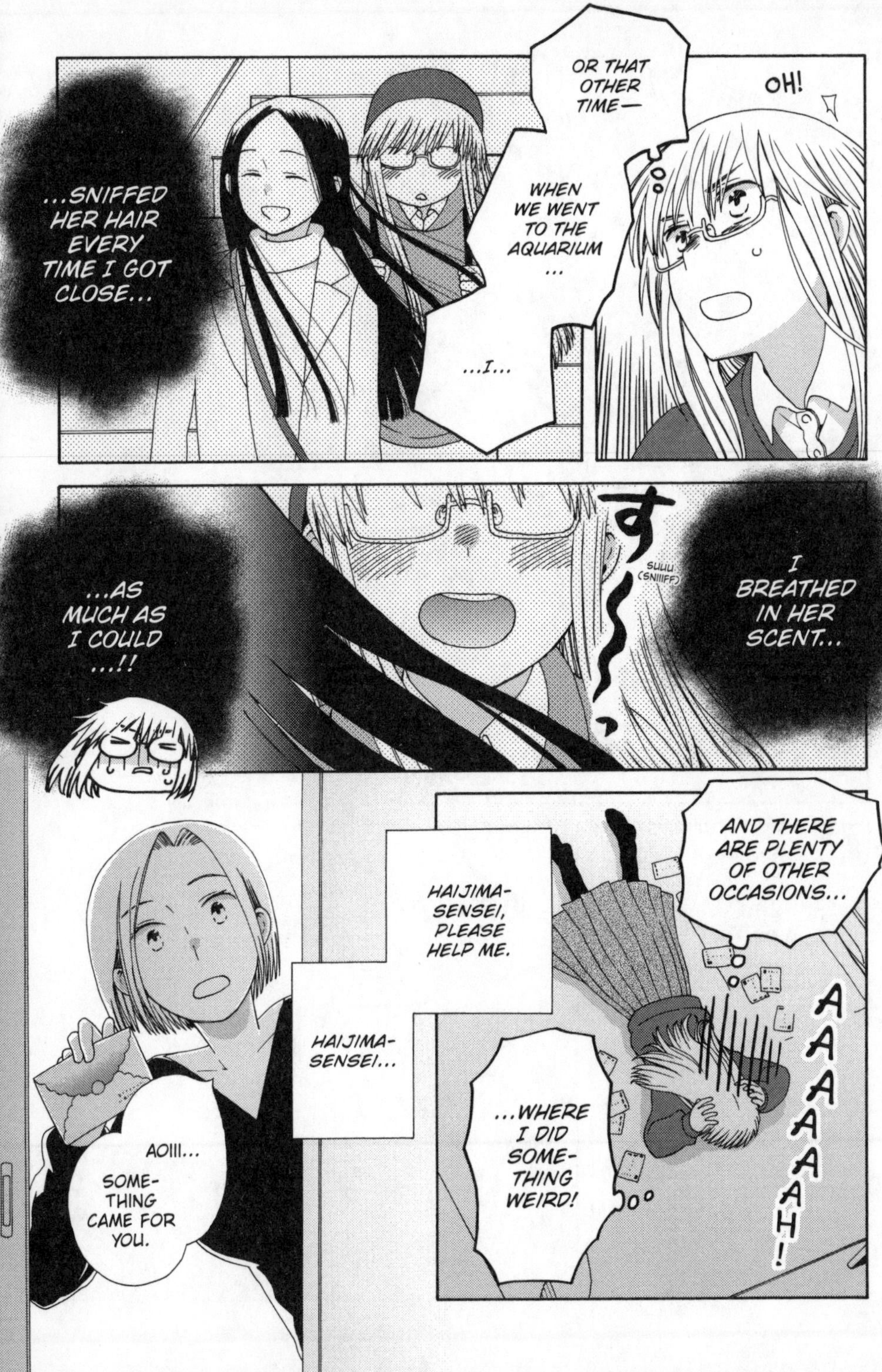
OR THAT OTHER TIME—
OH!
WHEN WE WENT TO THE AQUARIUM …
…I…
…SNIFFED HER HAIR EVERY TIME I GOT CLOSE…
I BREATHED IN HER SCENT…
すーっ
SUUU (SNIIIFF)
…AS MUCH AS I COULD …!!
AND THERE ARE PLENTY OF OTHER OCCASIONS…
AAAAAAAH!
…WHERE I DID SOME-THING WEIRD!
HAIJIMA-SENSEI, PLEASE HELP ME.
HAIJIMA-SENSEI…
AOIII…
SOME-THING CAME FOR YOU.

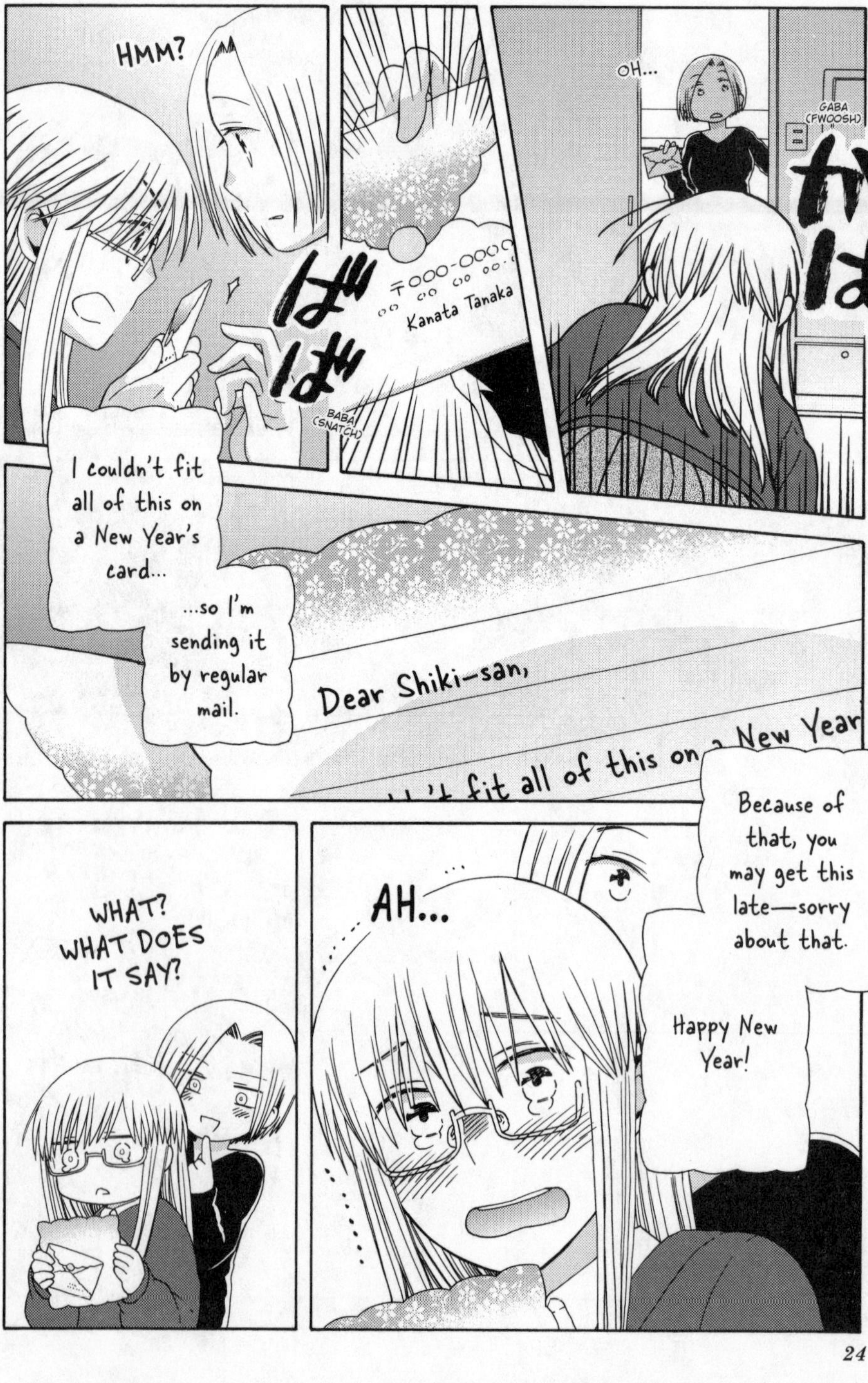
OH...
GABA (FWOOSH)
がば
ばば
Kanata Tanaka
BABA (SNATCH)
HMM?
I couldn't fit all of this on a New Year's card...
...so I'm sending it by regular mail.
Dear Shiki-san,
fit all of this on a New Year
Because of that, you may get this late—sorry about that.
Happy New Year!
AH...
WHAT? WHAT DOES IT SAY?

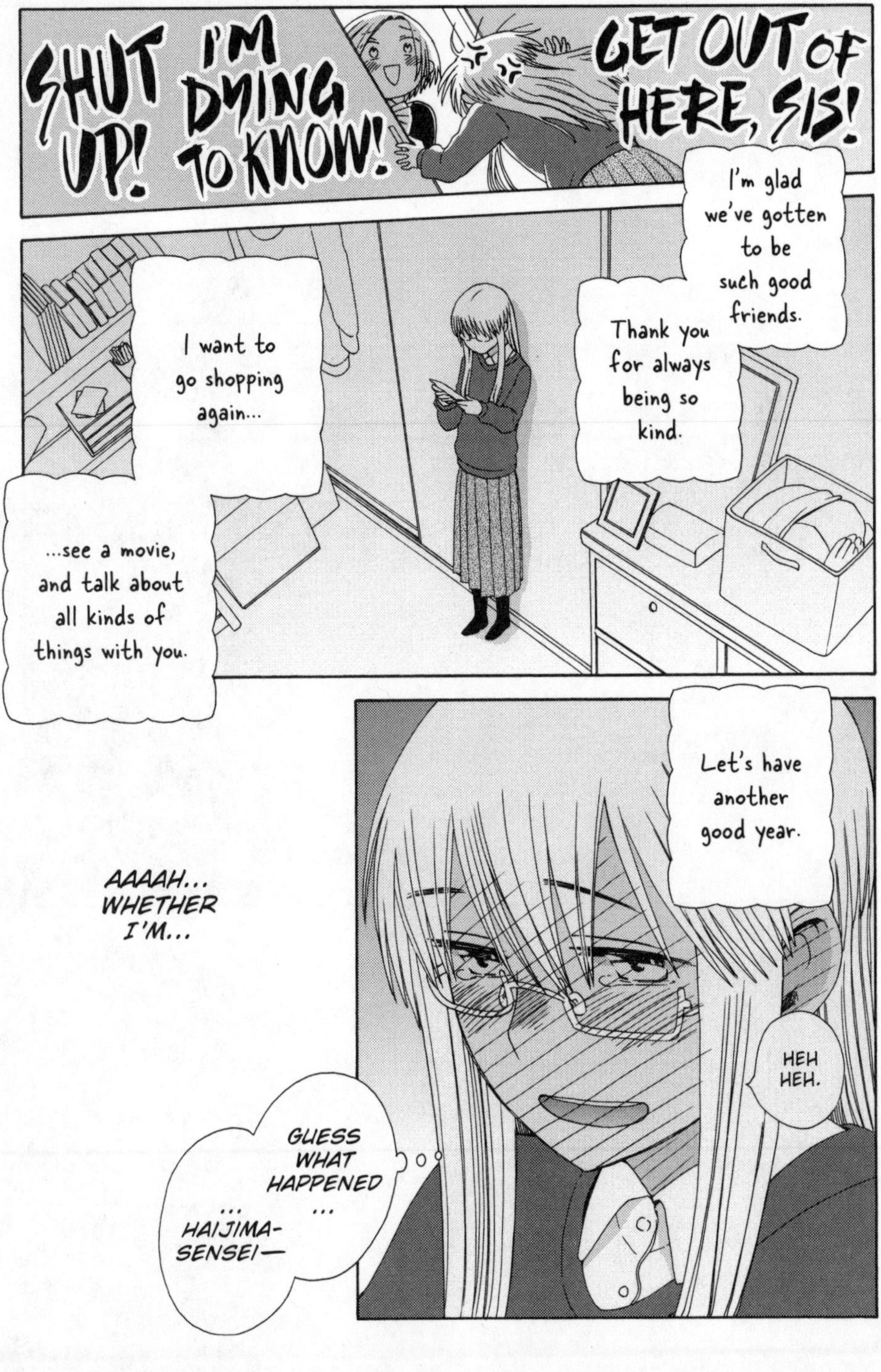
GET OUT OF HERE, SIS!
I'M DYING TO KNOW!
SHUT UP!
I'm glad we've gotten to be such good friends.
Thank you for always being so kind.
I want to go shopping again...
...see a movie, and talk about all kinds of things with you.
Let's have another good year.
HEH HEH.
AAAAH... WHETHER I'M...
GUESS WHAT HAPPENED ... ... HAIJIMA-SENSEI—

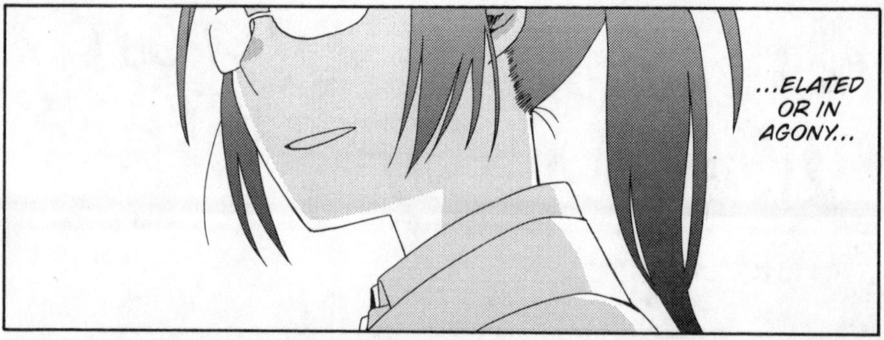
...ELATED OR IN AGONY...

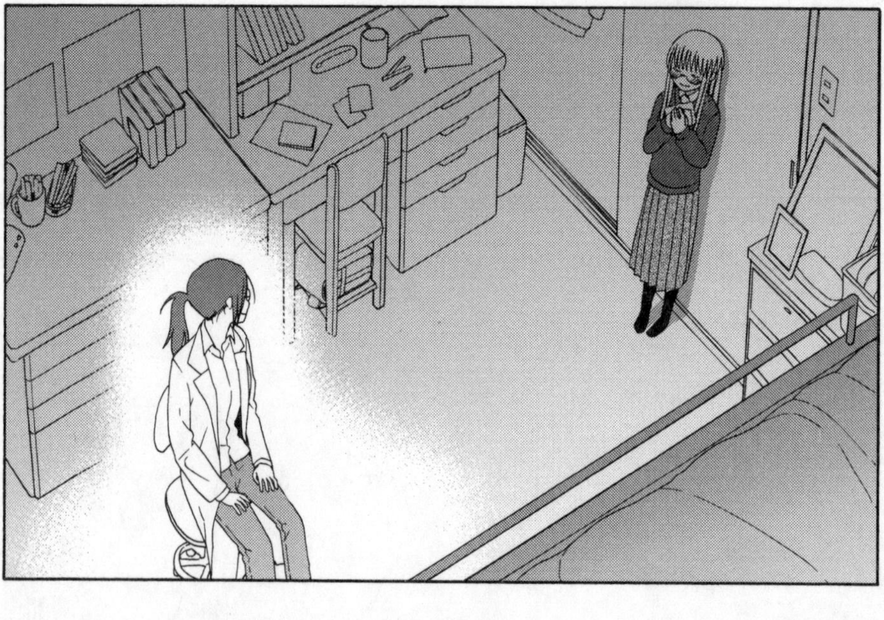

...I ALWAYS WANT TO TELL SENSEI.

Fin

Love ♡ at Fourteen

[Chapter 45]

CLASS 2-B'S...

...AOI SHIKI IS A QUIET STUDENT.

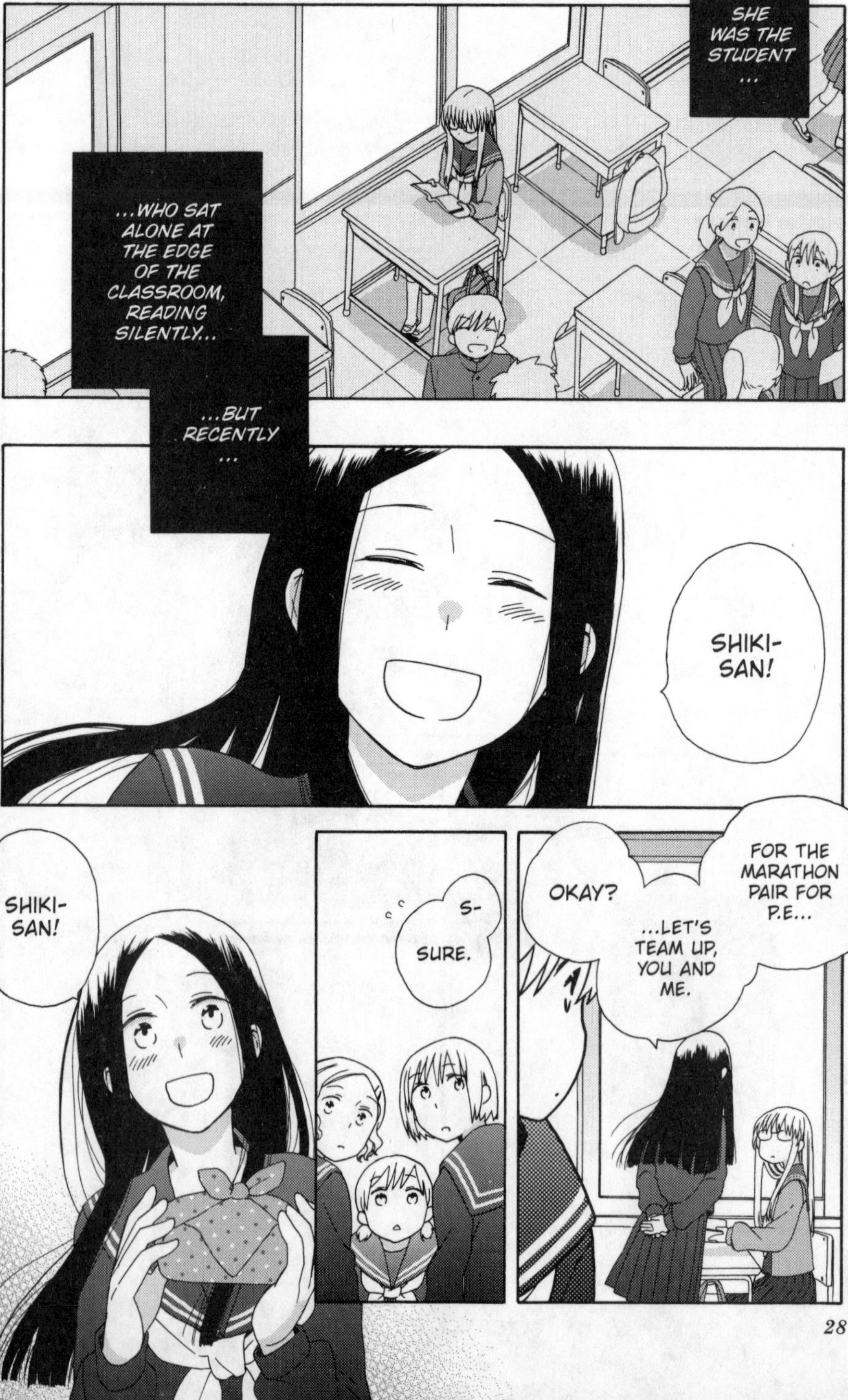
SHE WAS THE STUDENT ...
...WHO SAT ALONE AT THE EDGE OF THE CLASSROOM, READING SILENTLY...
...BUT RECENTLY ...
SHIKI-SAN!
FOR THE MARATHON PAIR FOR P.E...
...LET'S TEAM UP, YOU AND ME.
OKAY?
S- SURE.
SHIKI-SAN!

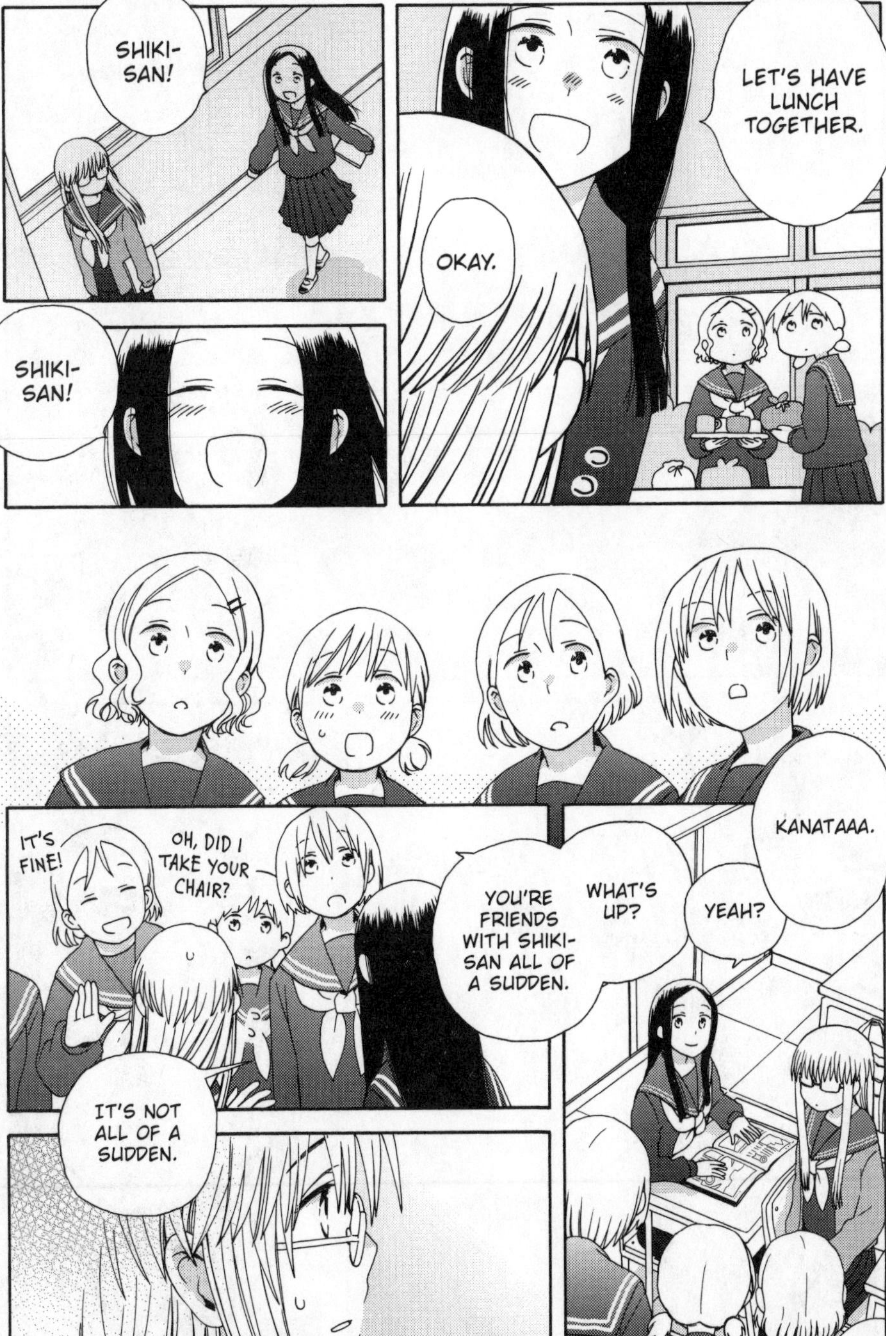
LET'S HAVE LUNCH TOGETHER.
OKAY.
SHIKI-SAN!
SHIKI-SAN!
KANATAAA.
YEAH?
WHAT'S UP?
YOU'RE FRIENDS WITH SHIKI-SAN ALL OF A SUDDEN.
OH, DID I TAKE YOUR CHAIR?
IT'S FINE!
IT'S NOT ALL OF A SUDDEN.

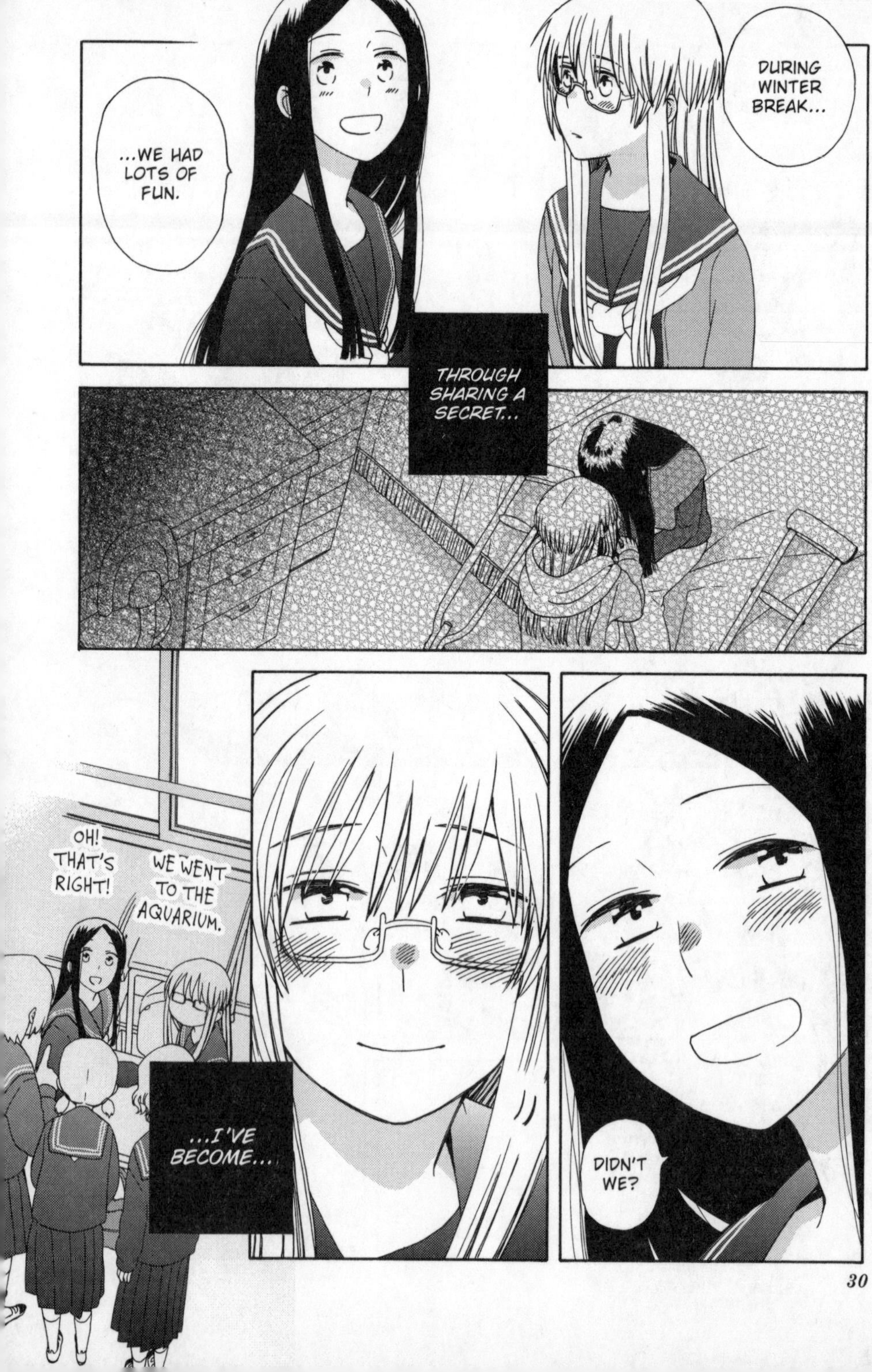
DURING WINTER BREAK...
...WE HAD LOTS OF FUN.
THROUGH SHARING A SECRET...
DIDN'T WE?
...I'VE BECOME...
WE WENT TO THE AQUARIUM.
OH! THAT'S RIGHT!

...TANAKA-SAN'S BEST FRIEND.

KIIN (DING)
キーン

KOON (DONG)
コーン

KAAN (DANG)
カーン

KOON
コーン

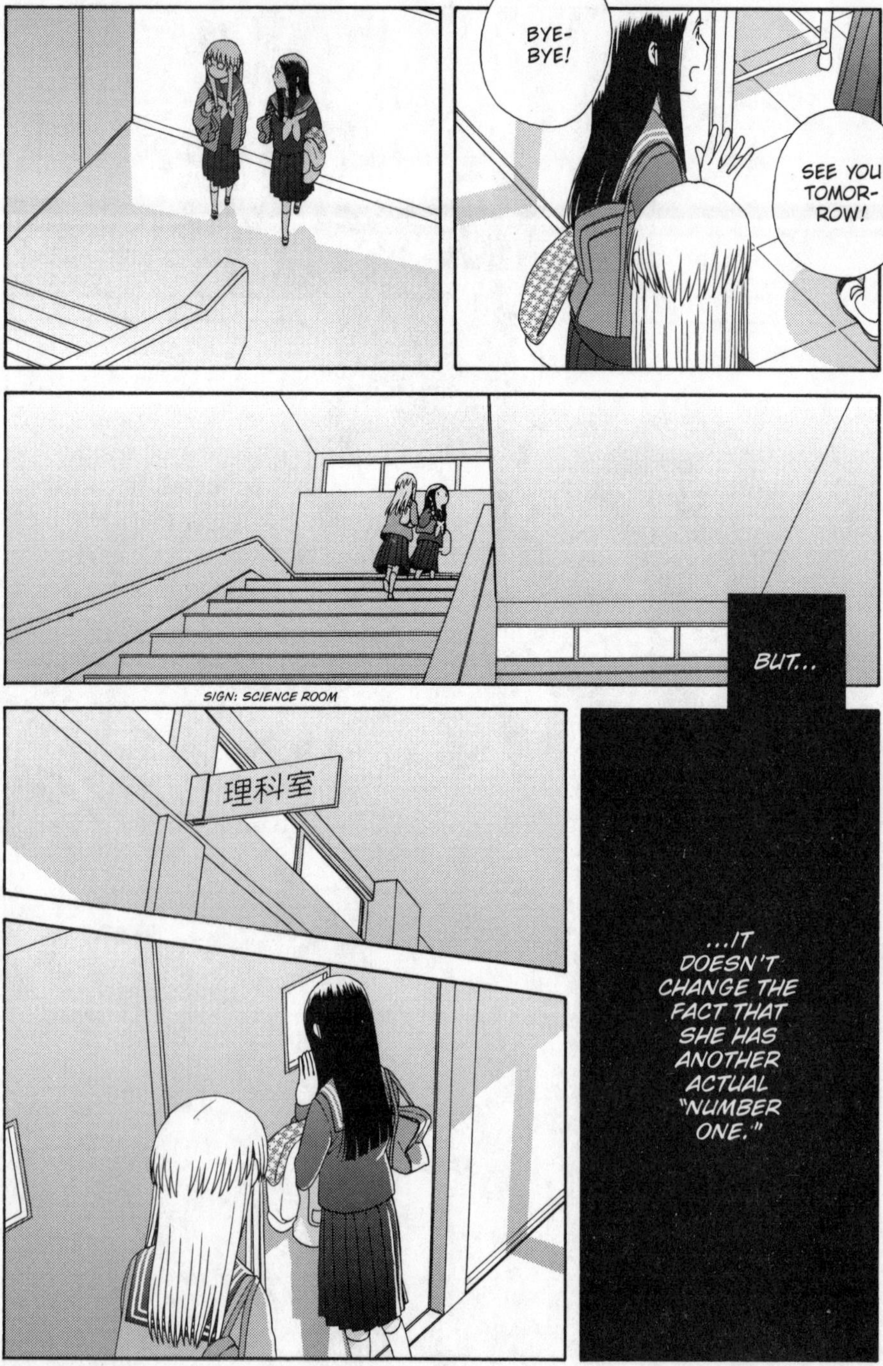
BYE-BYE!
SEE YOU TOMOR-ROW!
BUT...
...IT DOESN'T CHANGE THE FACT THAT SHE HAS ANOTHER ACTUAL "NUMBER ONE."
SIGN: SCIENCE ROOM
理科室

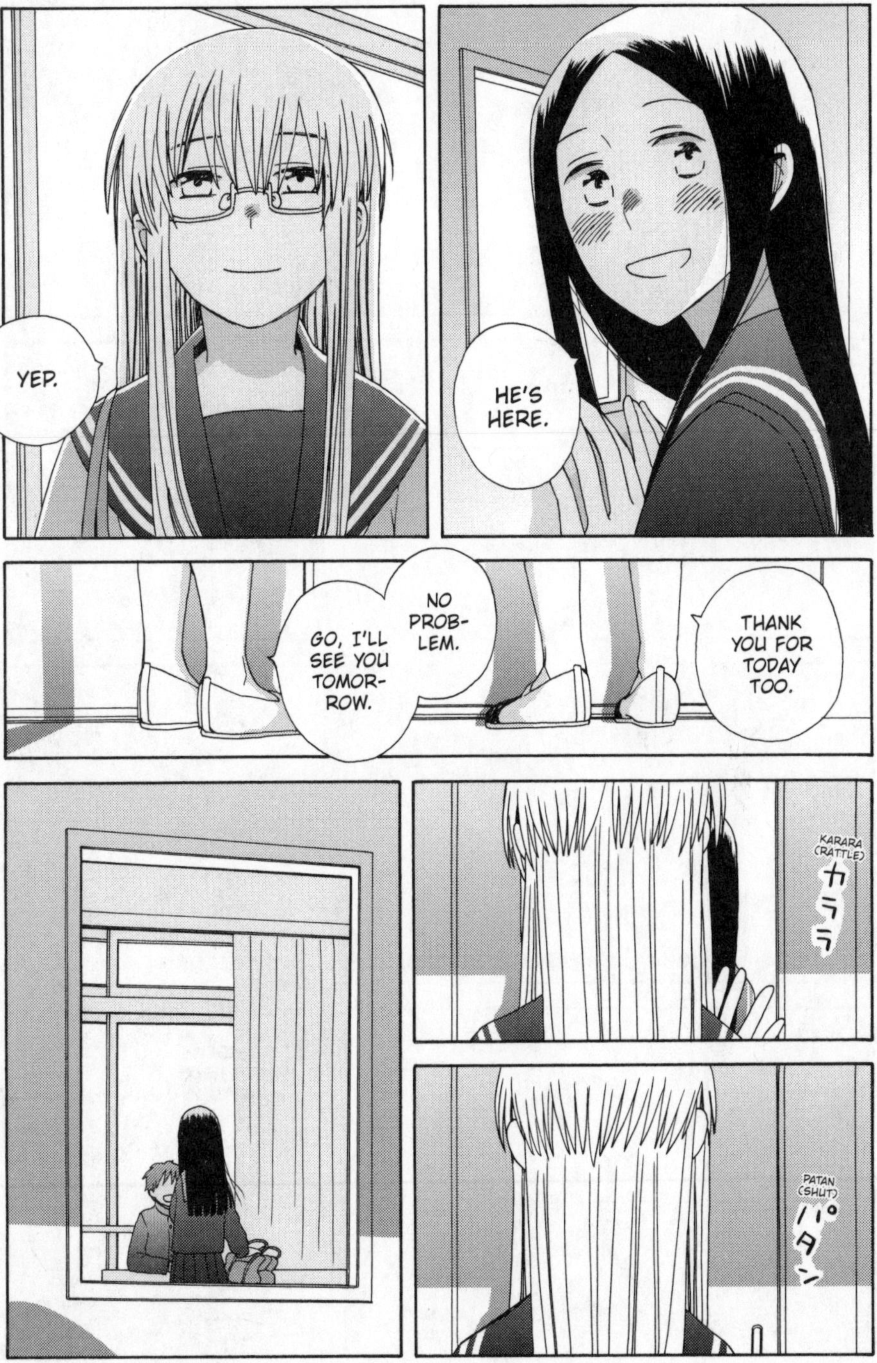
HE'S HERE.
YEP.
THANK YOU FOR TODAY TOO.
NO PROB-LEM.
GO, I'LL SEE YOU TOMOR-ROW.
KARARA (RATTLE)
カララ
PATAN (SHUT)
パタン

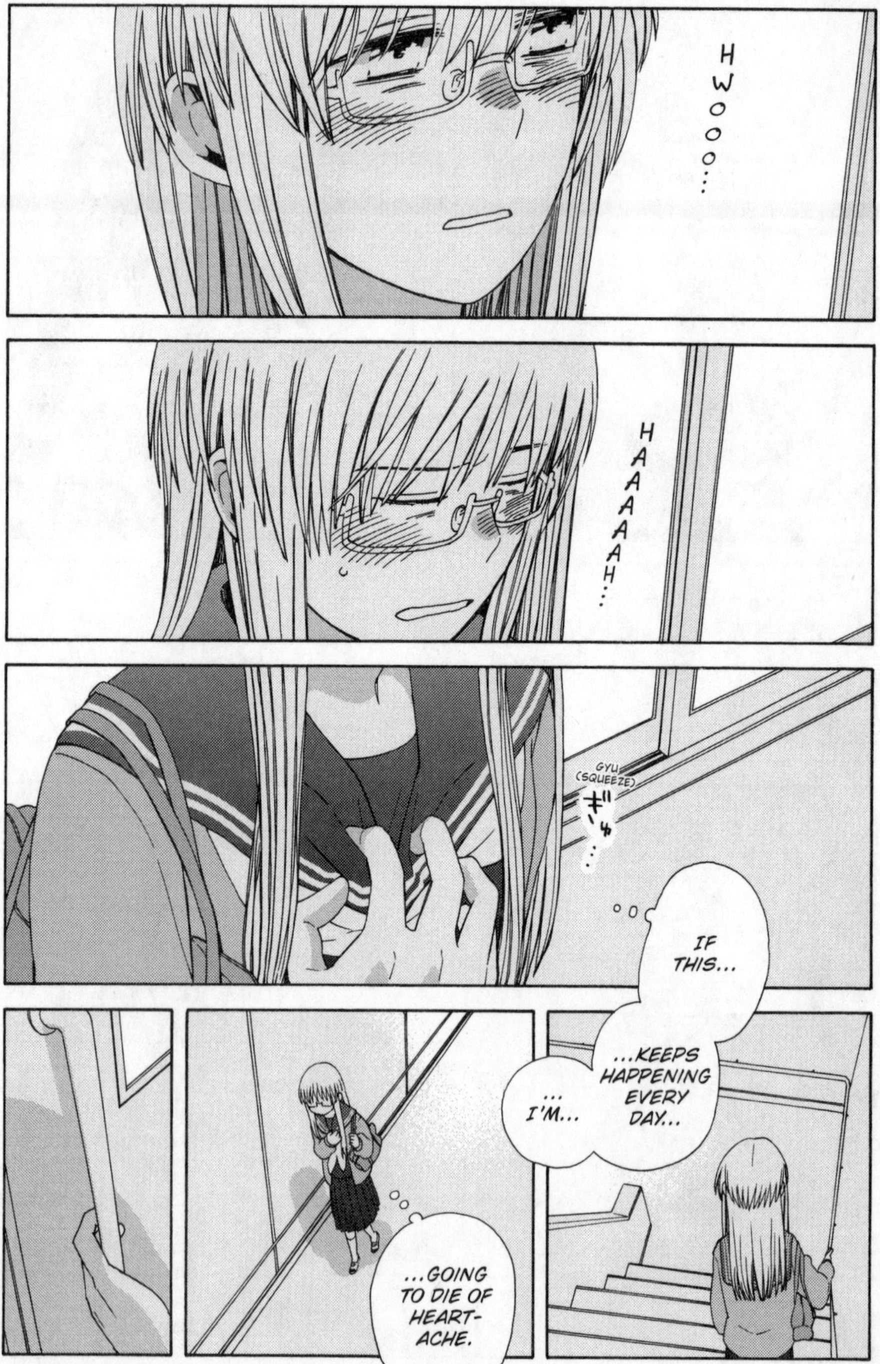
HWOOO...
HAAAAAAH...
GYU (SQUEEZE)
ぎゅ…
IF THIS...
...KEEPS HAPPENING EVERY DAY...
... I'M...
...GOING TO DIE OF HEART-ACHE.

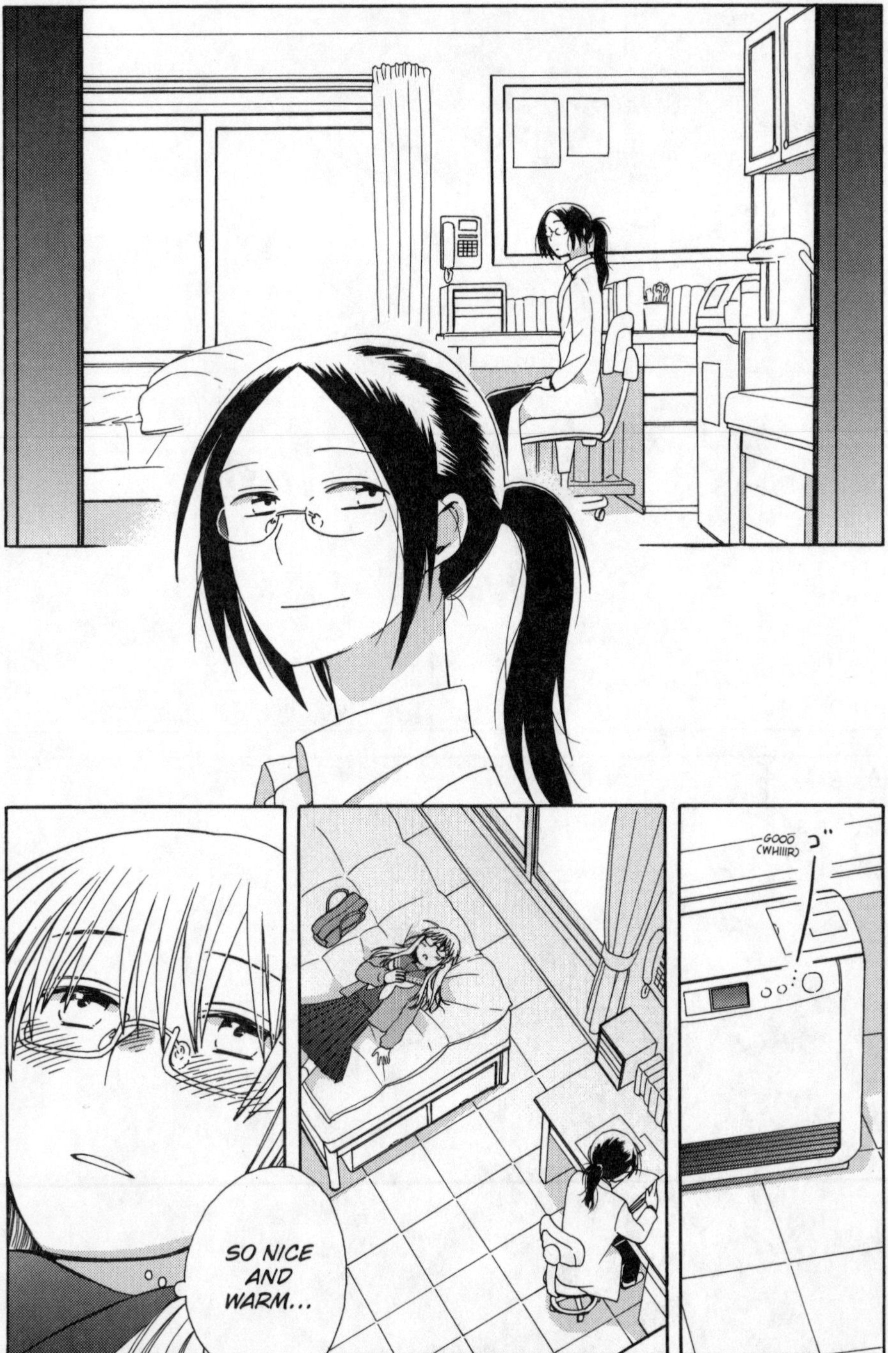
GOOO (WHIIIR)
SO NICE AND WARM...

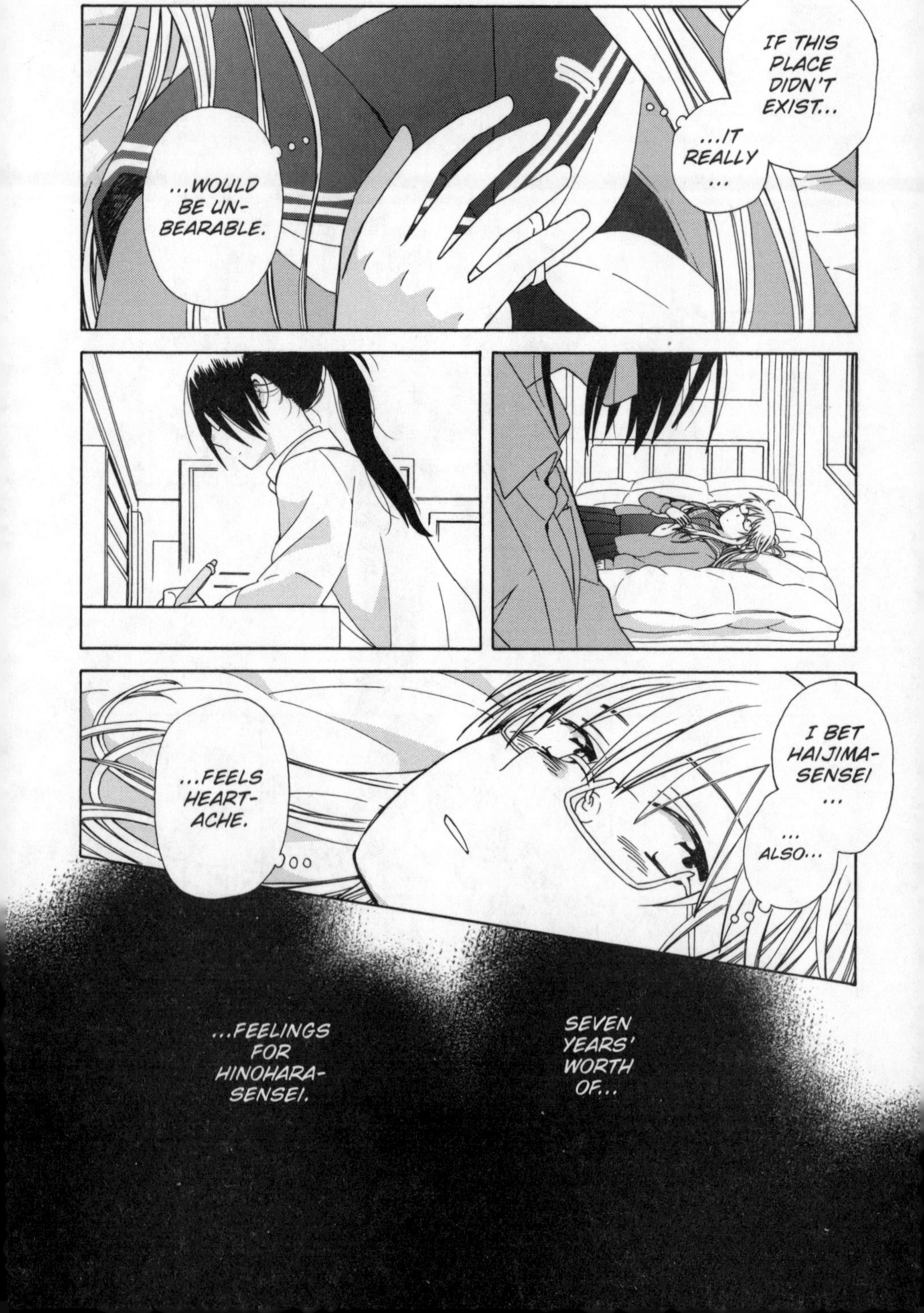
IF THIS PLACE DIDN'T EXIST...
...IT REALLY ...
...WOULD BE UN-BEARABLE.
I BET HAIJIMA-SENSEI ...
... ALSO...
...FEELS HEART-ACHE.
SEVEN YEARS' WORTH OF...
...FEELINGS FOR HINOHARA-SENSEI.

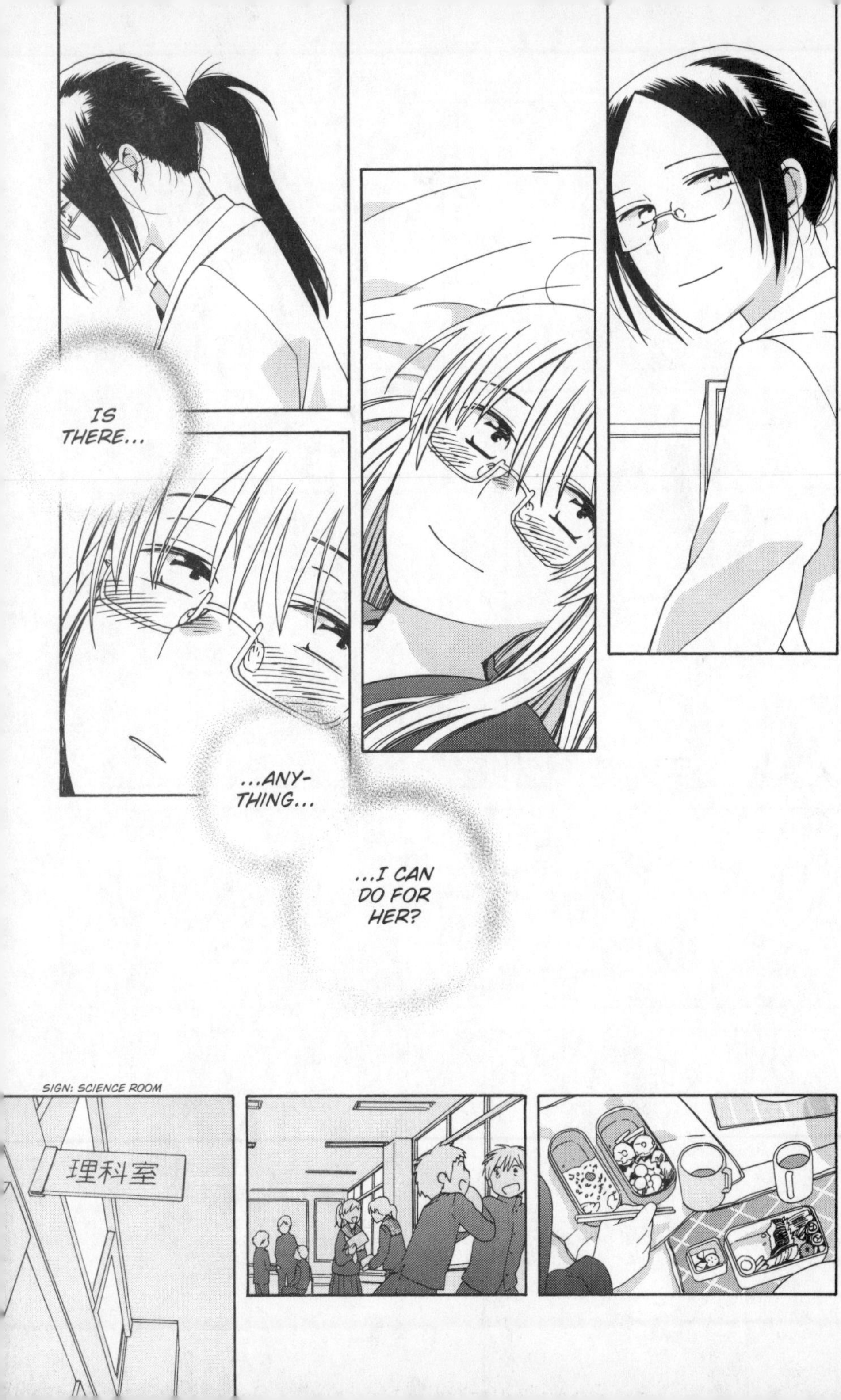
IS THERE...
...ANY-THING...
...I CAN DO FOR HER?
SIGN: SCIENCE ROOM
理科室

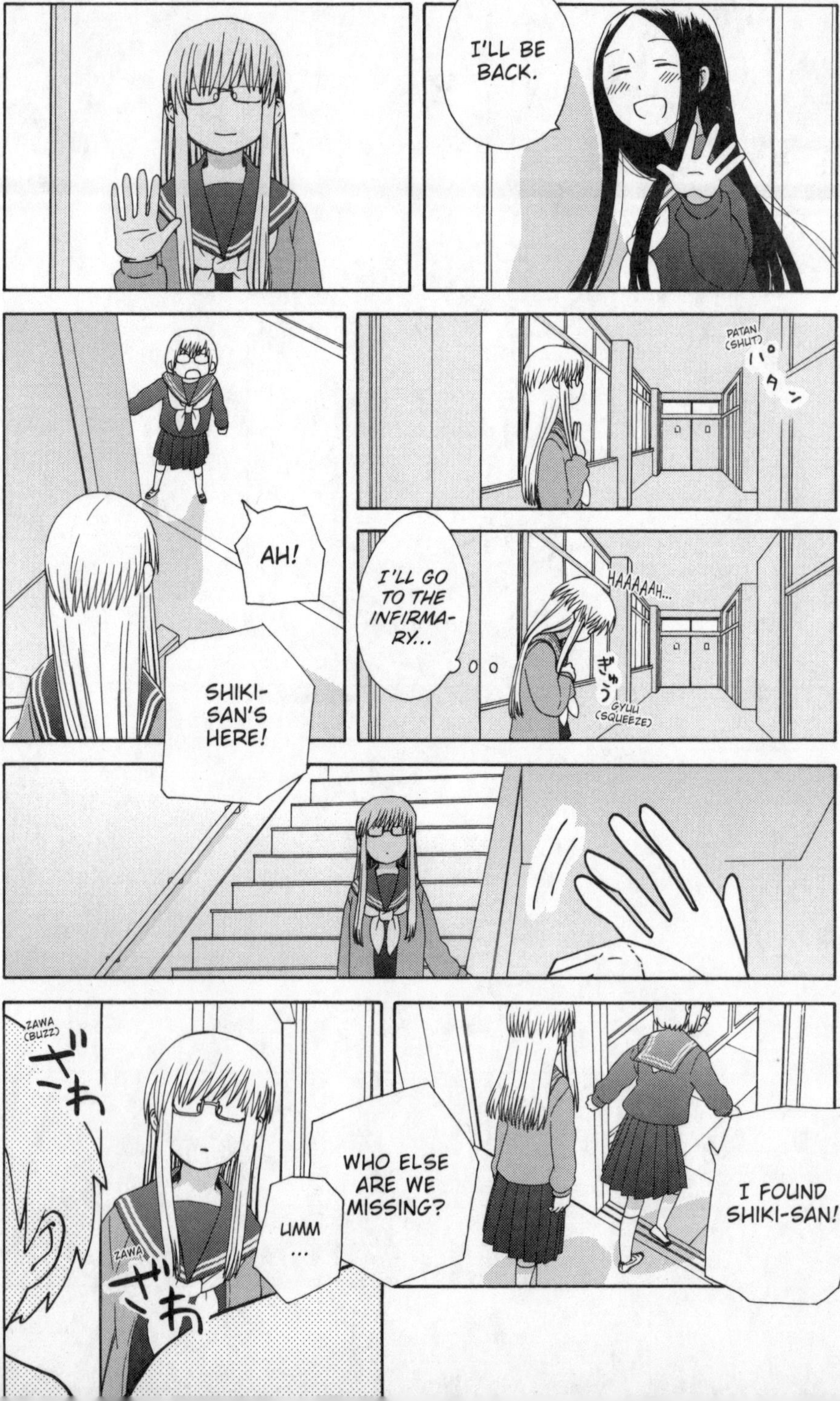
I'LL BE BACK.
PATAN (SHUT)
パタン
I'LL GO TO THE INFIRMARY...
HAAAAAH...
ぎゅう
GYUU (SQUEEZE)
AH!
SHIKI-SAN'S HERE!
I FOUND SHIKI-SAN!
WHO ELSE ARE WE MISSING?
ZAWA (BUZZ)
ざわ
UMM ...
ZAWA
ざわ

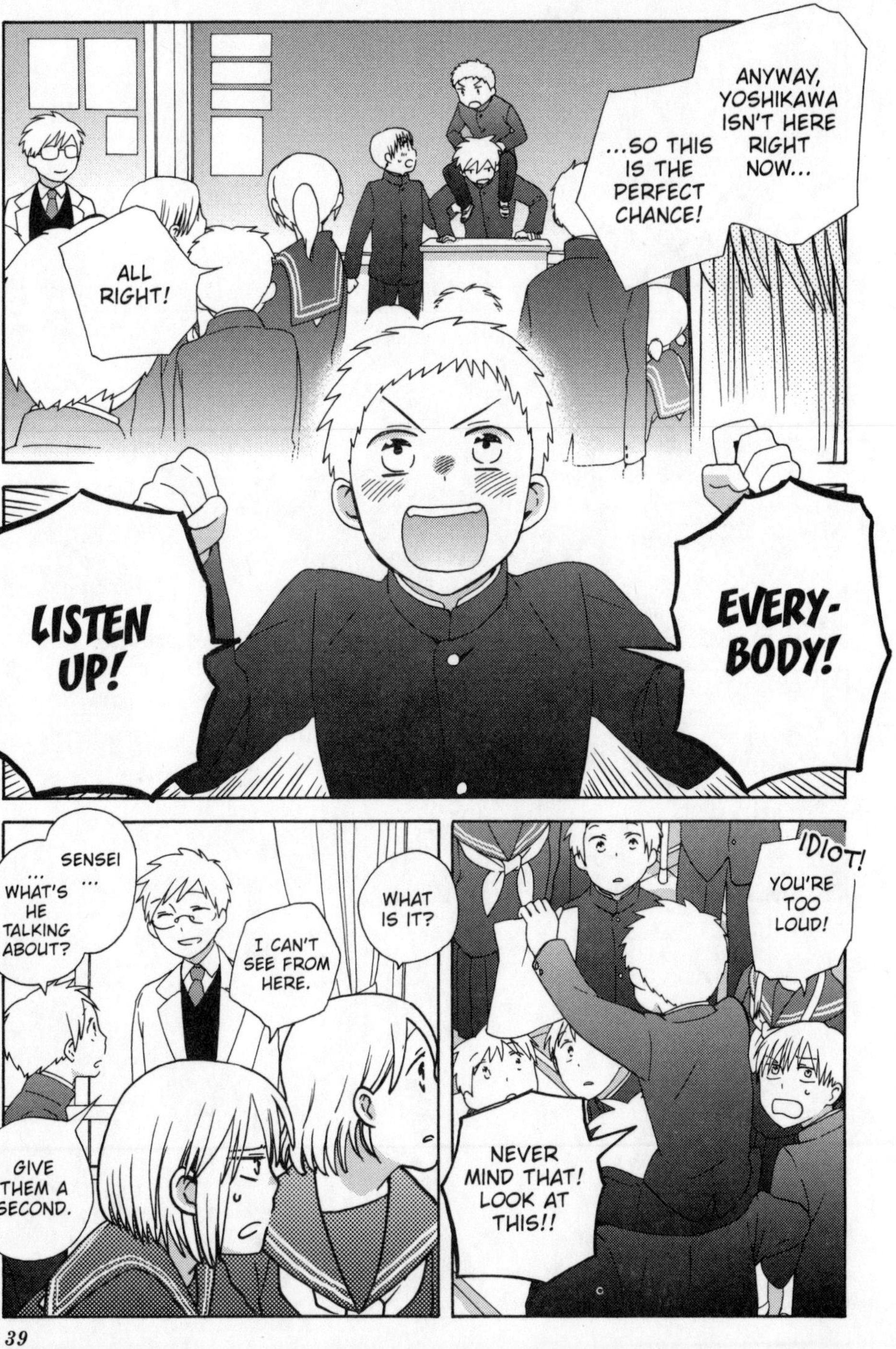
ANYWAY, YOSHIKAWA ISN'T HERE RIGHT NOW...
...SO THIS IS THE PERFECT CHANCE!
ALL RIGHT!
EVERY-BODY!
LISTEN UP!
IDIOT!
YOU'RE TOO LOUD!
NEVER MIND THAT! LOOK AT THIS!!
WHAT IS IT?
I CAN'T SEE FROM HERE.
SENSEI... ...WHAT'S HE TALKING ABOUT?
GIVE THEM A SECOND.

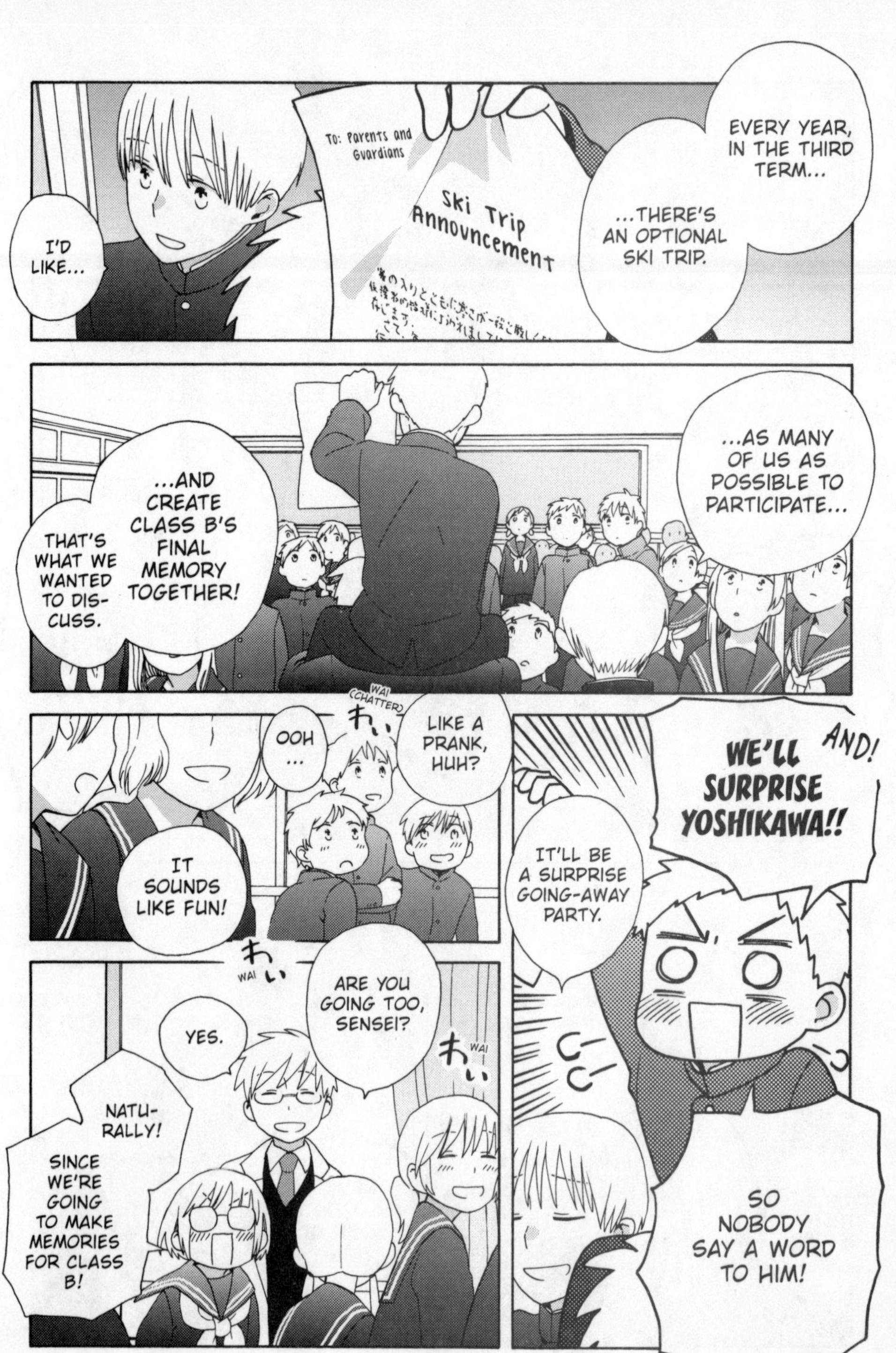
EVERY YEAR, IN THE THIRD TERM...
...THERE'S AN OPTIONAL SKI TRIP.
To: Parents and Guardians
Ski Trip Announcement
I'D LIKE...
...AS MANY OF US AS POSSIBLE TO PARTICIPATE...
...AND CREATE CLASS B'S FINAL MEMORY TOGETHER!
THAT'S WHAT WE WANTED TO DISCUSS.
AND!
WE'LL SURPRISE YOSHIKAWA!!
IT'LL BE A SURPRISE GOING-AWAY PARTY.
SO NOBODY SAY A WORD TO HIM!
WAI (CHATTER)
LIKE A PRANK, HUH?
OOH...
IT SOUNDS LIKE FUN!
WAI
ARE YOU GOING TOO, SENSEI?
WAI
YES.
NATURALLY!
SINCE WE'RE GOING TO MAKE MEMORIES FOR CLASS B!

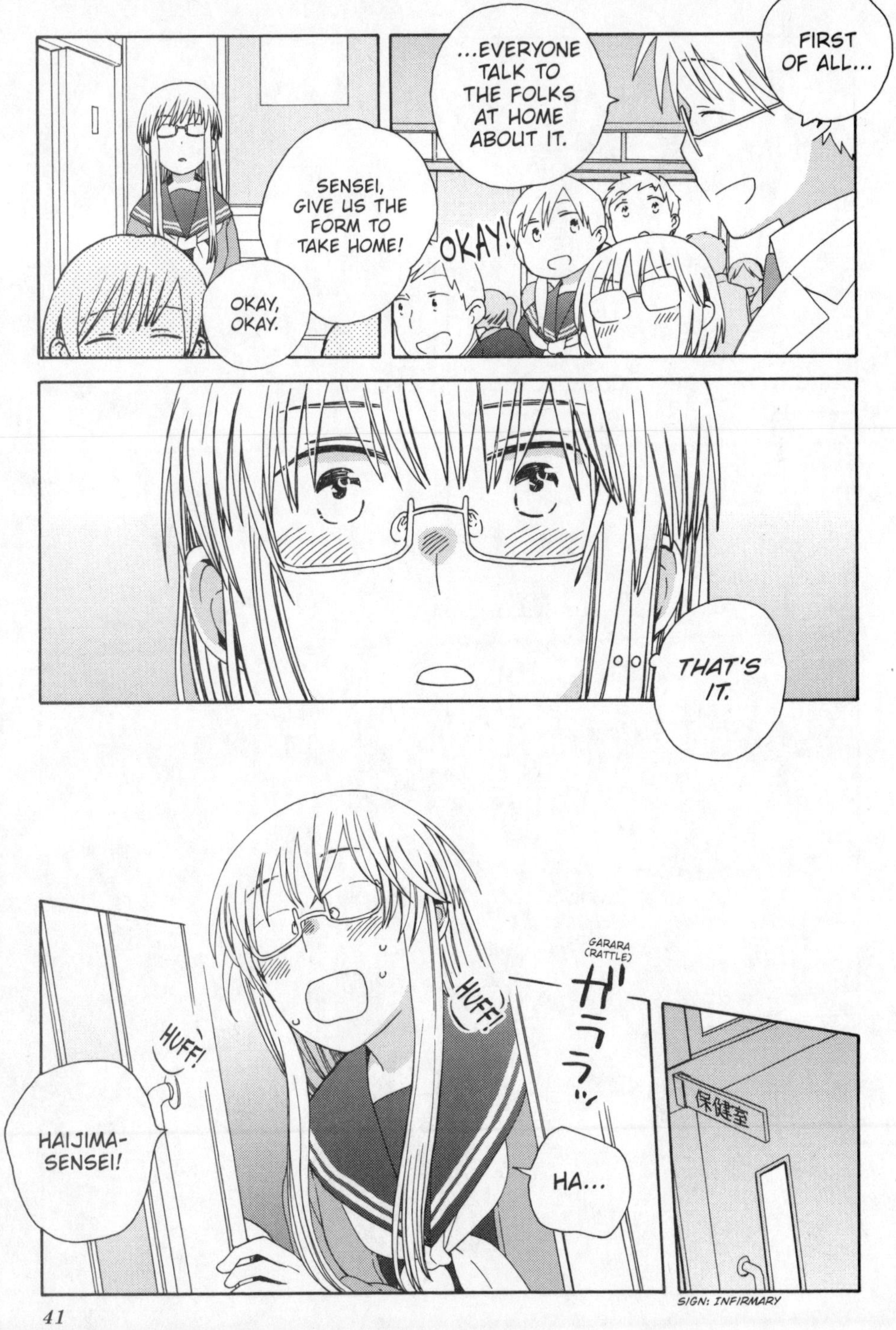
FIRST OF ALL...
...EVERYONE TALK TO THE FOLKS AT HOME ABOUT IT.
OKAY!
SENSEI, GIVE US THE FORM TO TAKE HOME!
OKAY, OKAY.
THAT'S IT.
保健室
GARARA (RATTLE)
ガラッ
HUFF!
HUFF!
HA...
HAIJIMA-SENSEI!

SIGN: INFIRMARY

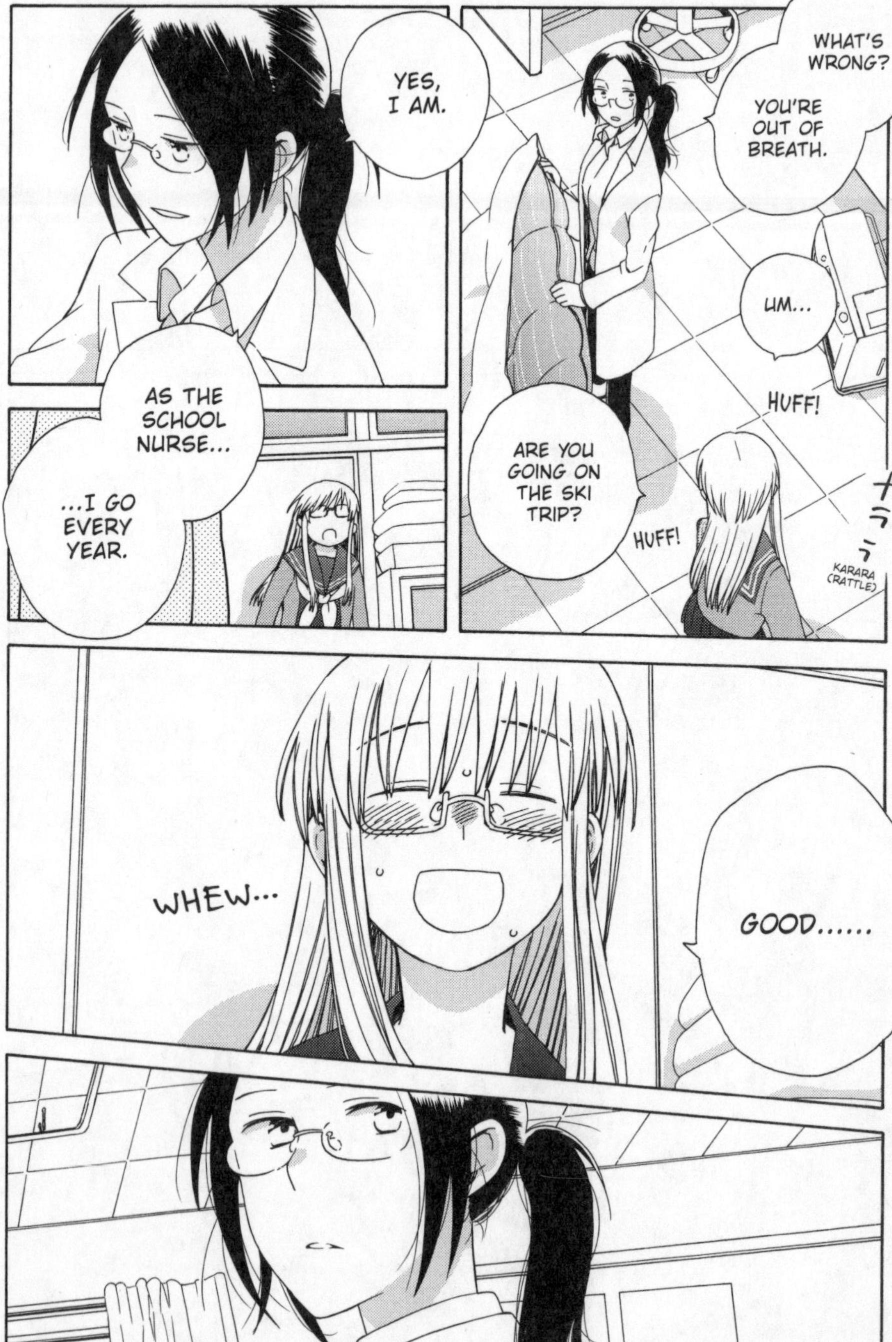

WHAT'S WRONG?
YOU'RE OUT OF BREATH.
UM...
HUFF!
カララ
KARARA (RATTLE)
ARE YOU GOING ON THE SKI TRIP?
HUFF!
YES, I AM.
AS THE SCHOOL NURSE...
...I GO EVERY YEAR.
GOOD......
WHEW...

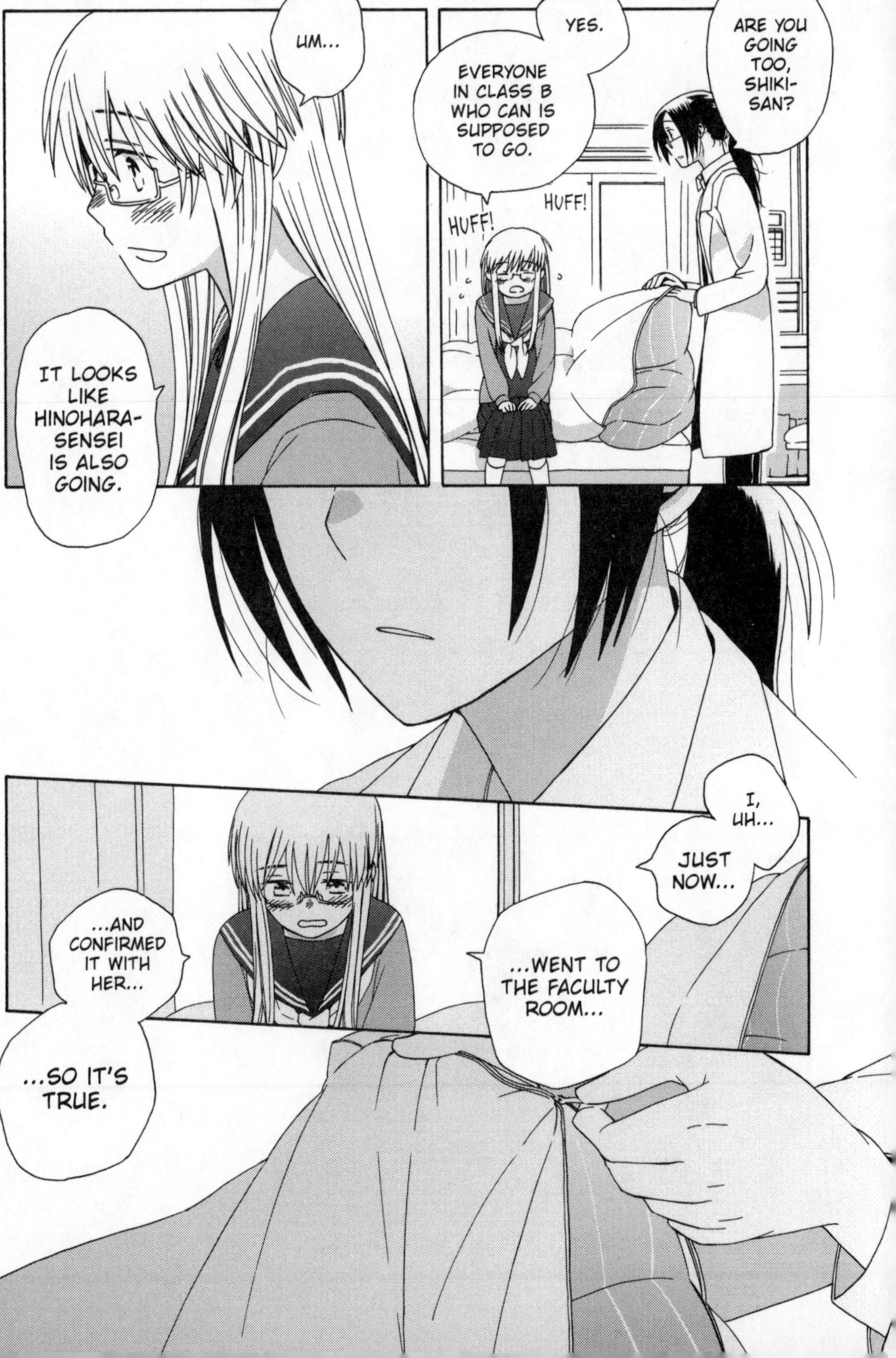
ARE YOU GOING TOO, SHIKI-SAN?
YES.
EVERYONE IN CLASS B WHO CAN IS SUPPOSED TO GO.
HUFF!
HUFF!
UM...
IT LOOKS LIKE HINOHARA-SENSEI IS ALSO GOING.
I, UH...
JUST NOW...
...WENT TO THE FACULTY ROOM...
...AND CONFIRMED IT WITH HER...
...SO IT'S TRUE.

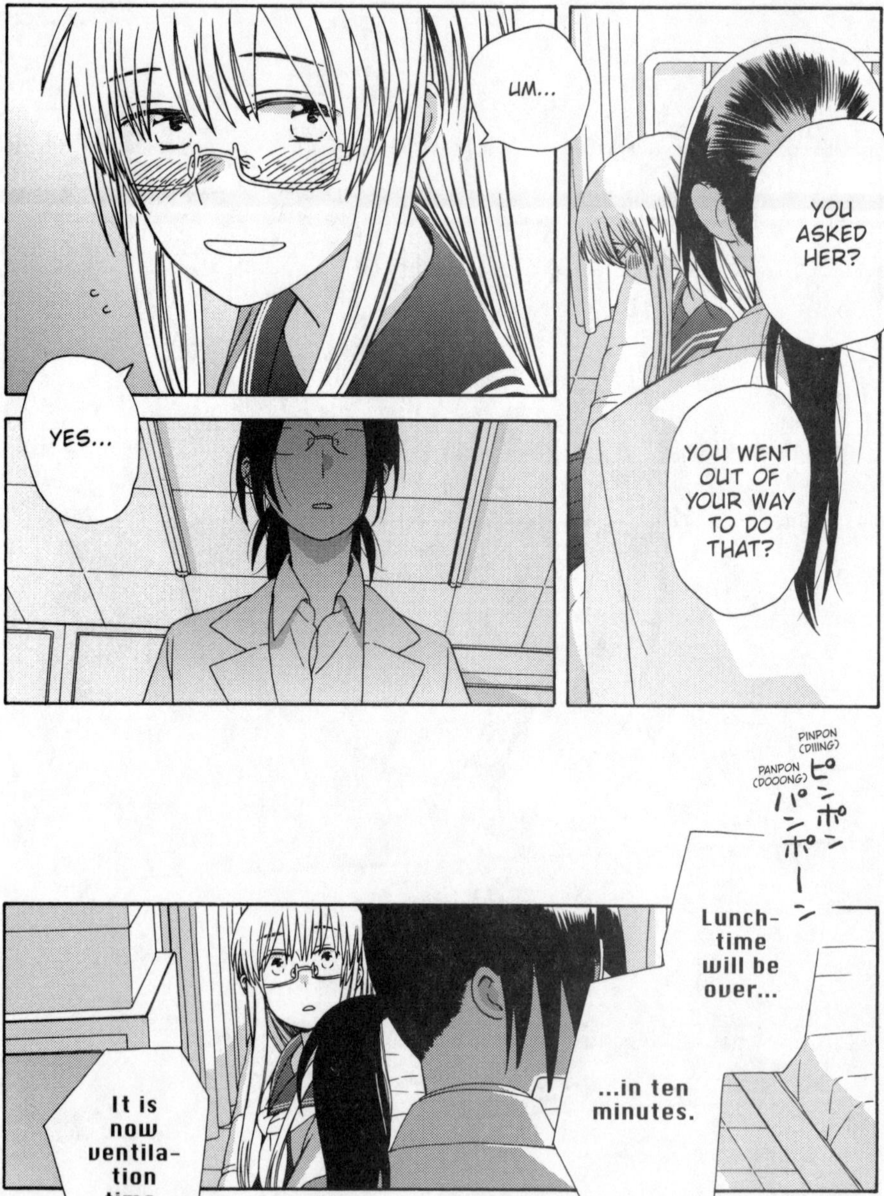
YOU ASKED HER?
YOU WENT OUT OF YOUR WAY TO DO THAT?
UM...
YES...
ピンポン
PINPON (DIIING)
パンポーン
PANPON (DOOONG)
Lunch-time will be over...
...in ten minutes.
It is now ventilation time.

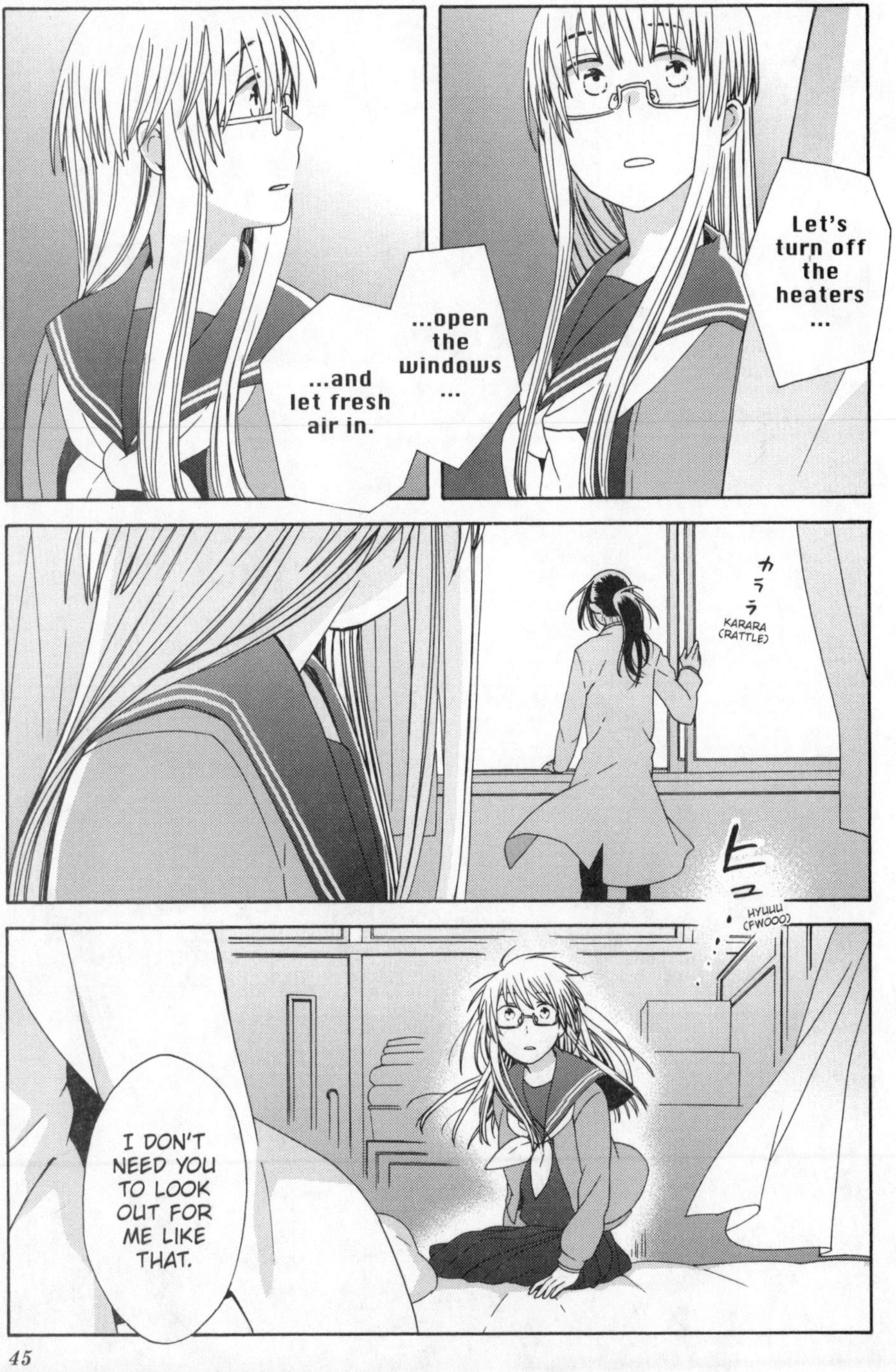
Let's turn off the heaters ...
...open the windows ...
...and let fresh air in.
カララ
KARARA (RATTLE)
ヒュ
HYUUU (FWOOO)
I DON'T NEED YOU TO LOOK OUT FOR ME LIKE THAT.

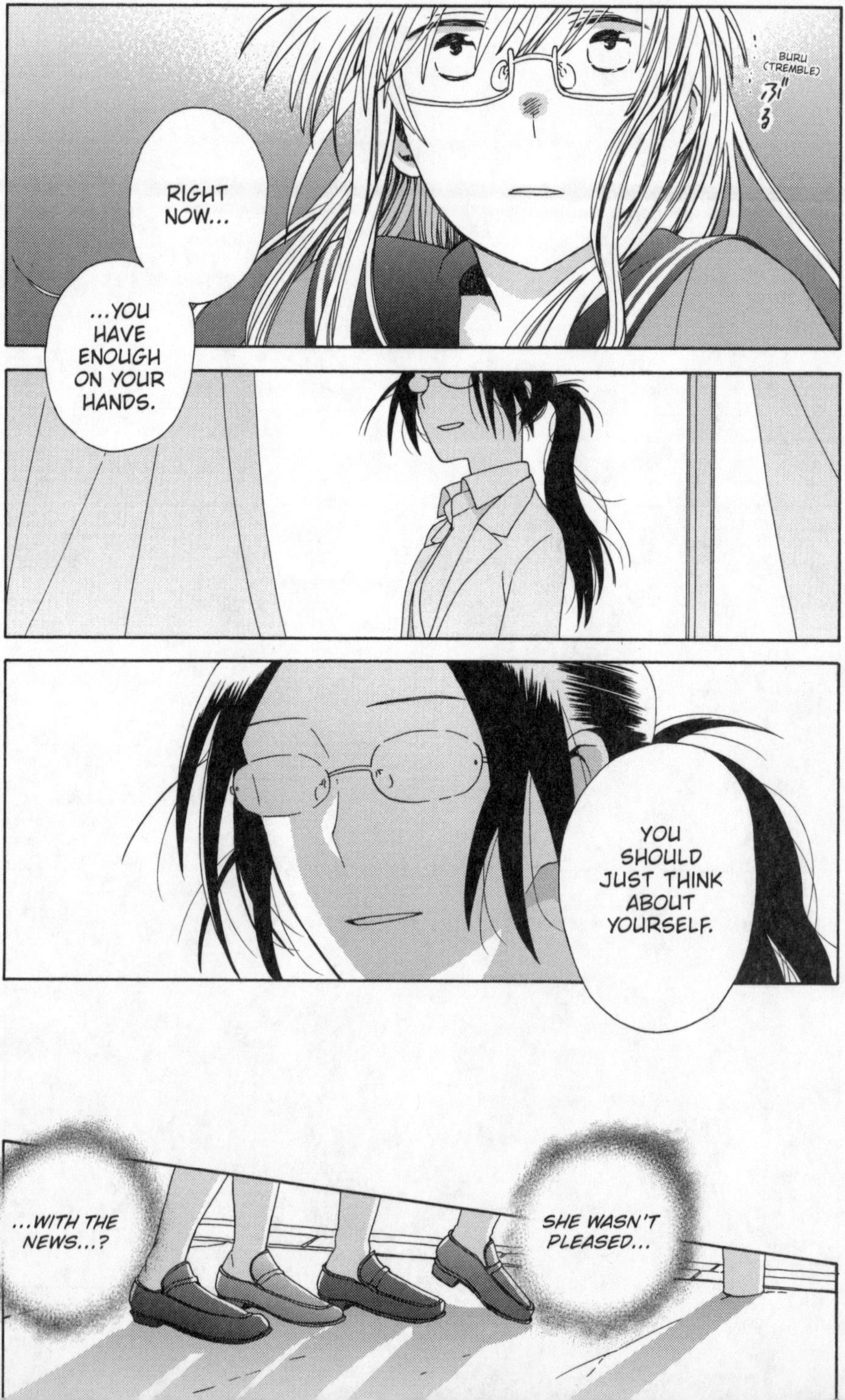
BURU (TREMBLE)
ぶる
RIGHT NOW...
...YOU HAVE ENOUGH ON YOUR HANDS.
YOU SHOULD JUST THINK ABOUT YOURSELF.
SHE WASN'T PLEASED...
...WITH THE NEWS...?

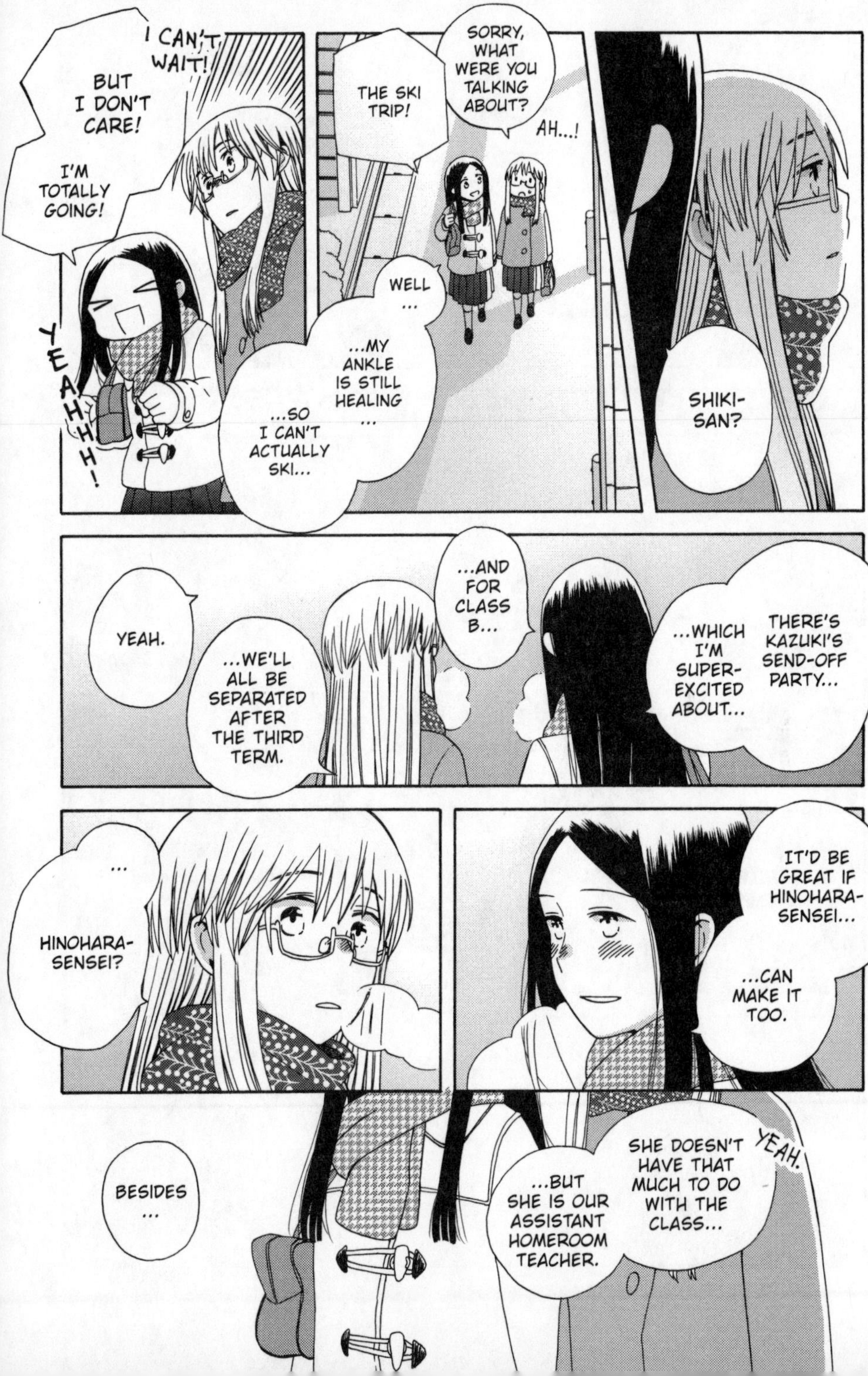
SHIKI-SAN?
SORRY, WHAT WERE YOU TALKING ABOUT?
AH...!
THE SKI TRIP!
WELL ...
...MY ANKLE IS STILL HEALING ...
...SO I CAN'T ACTUALLY SKI...
I CAN'T WAIT!
BUT I DON'T CARE!
I'M TOTALLY GOING!
YEAHHHH!
THERE'S KAZUKI'S SEND-OFF PARTY...
...WHICH I'M SUPER-EXCITED ABOUT...
...AND FOR CLASS B...
...WE'LL ALL BE SEPARATED AFTER THE THIRD TERM.
YEAH.
IT'D BE GREAT IF HINOHARA-SENSEI...
...CAN MAKE IT TOO.
...
HINOHARA-SENSEI?
YEAH.
SHE DOESN'T HAVE THAT MUCH TO DO WITH THE CLASS...
...BUT SHE IS OUR ASSISTANT HOMEROOM TEACHER.
BESIDES ...

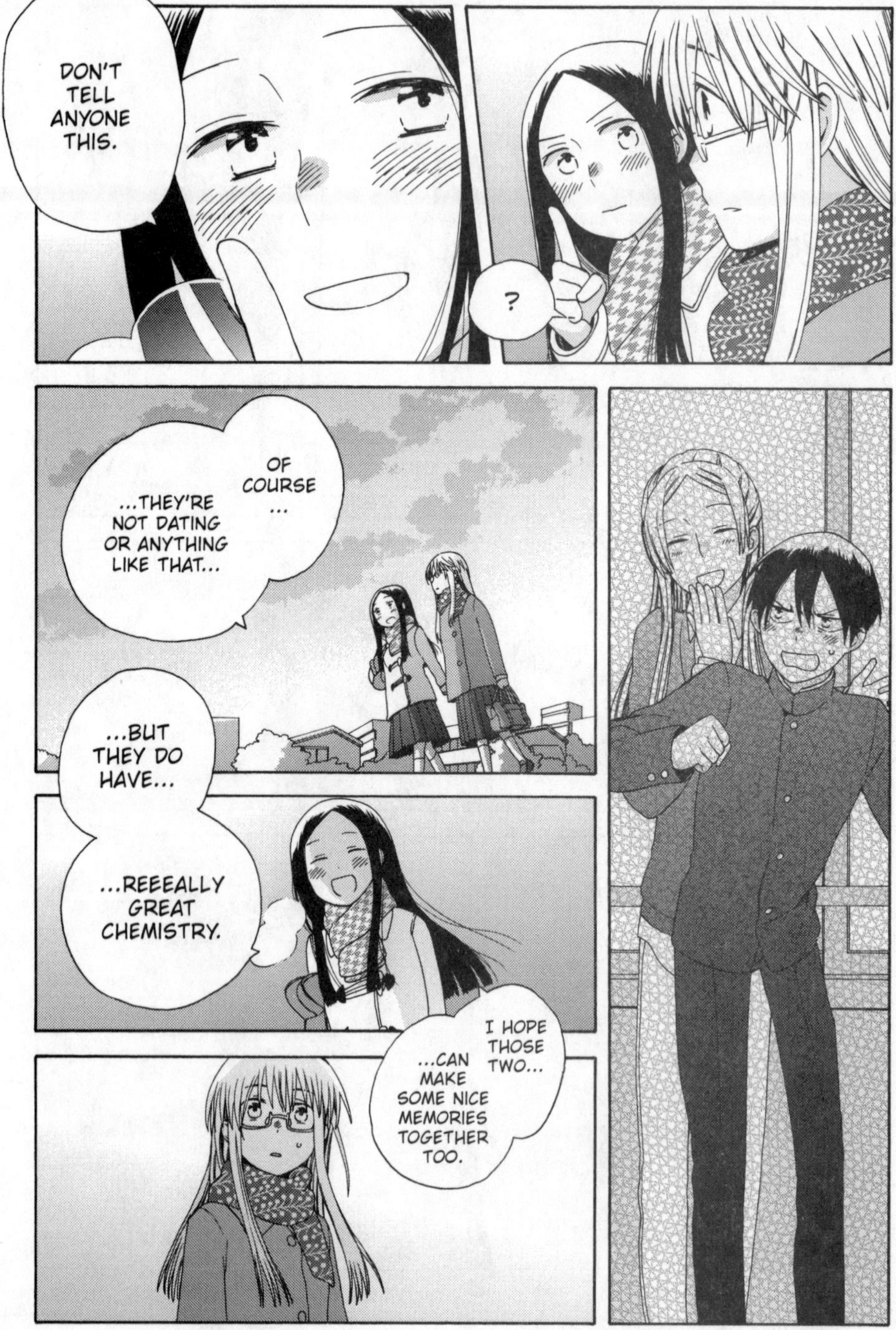
?
DON'T TELL ANYONE THIS.
OF COURSE...
...THEY'RE NOT DATING OR ANYTHING LIKE THAT...
...BUT THEY DO HAVE...
...REEEALLY GREAT CHEMISTRY.
I HOPE THOSE TWO...
...CAN MAKE SOME NICE MEMORIES TOGETHER TOO.

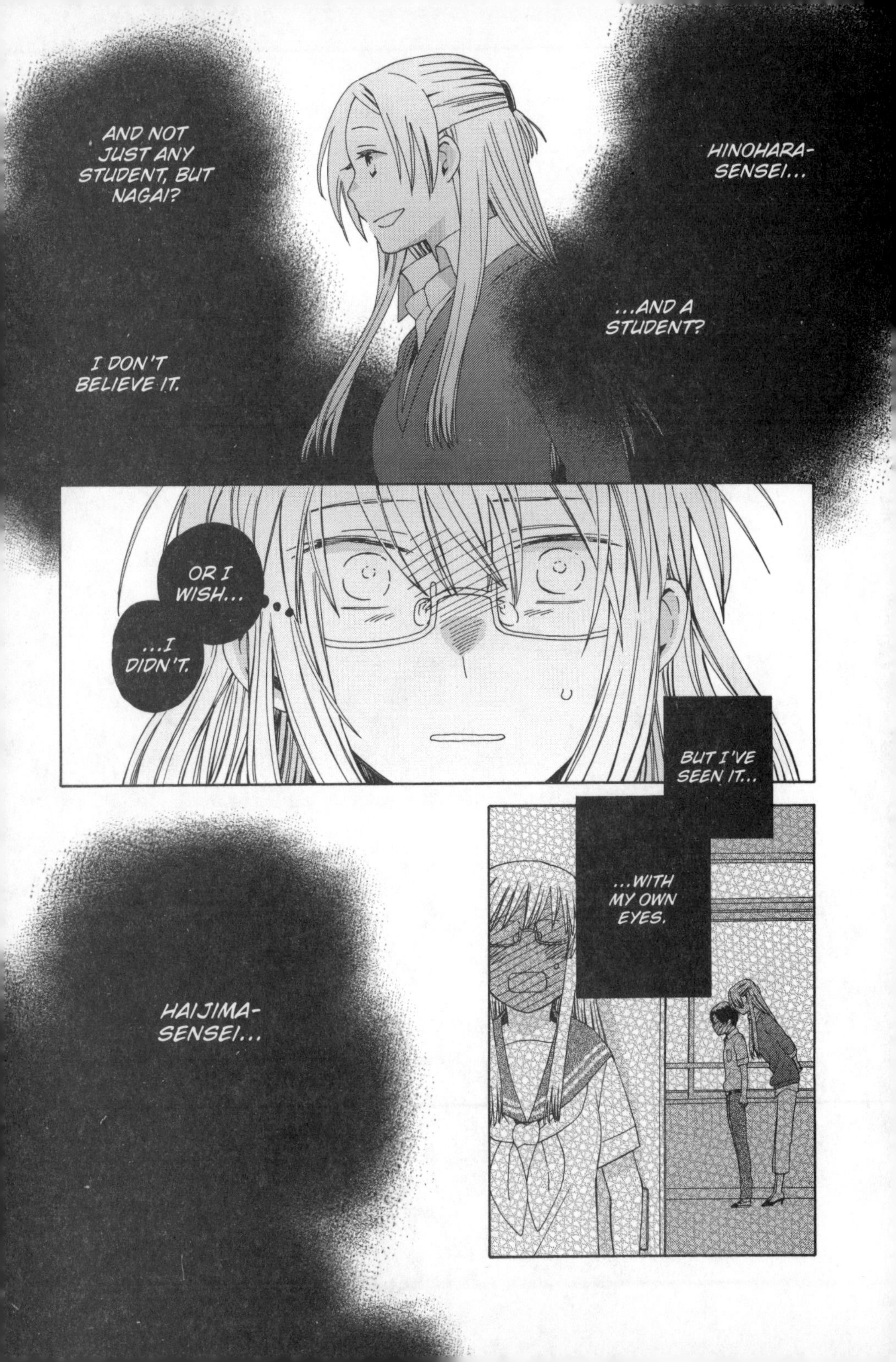
HINOHARA-SENSEI...
...AND A STUDENT?
AND NOT JUST ANY STUDENT, BUT NAGAI?
I DON'T BELIEVE IT.
OR I WISH...
...I DIDN'T.
BUT I'VE SEEN IT...
...WITH MY OWN EYES.
HAIJIMA-SENSEI...

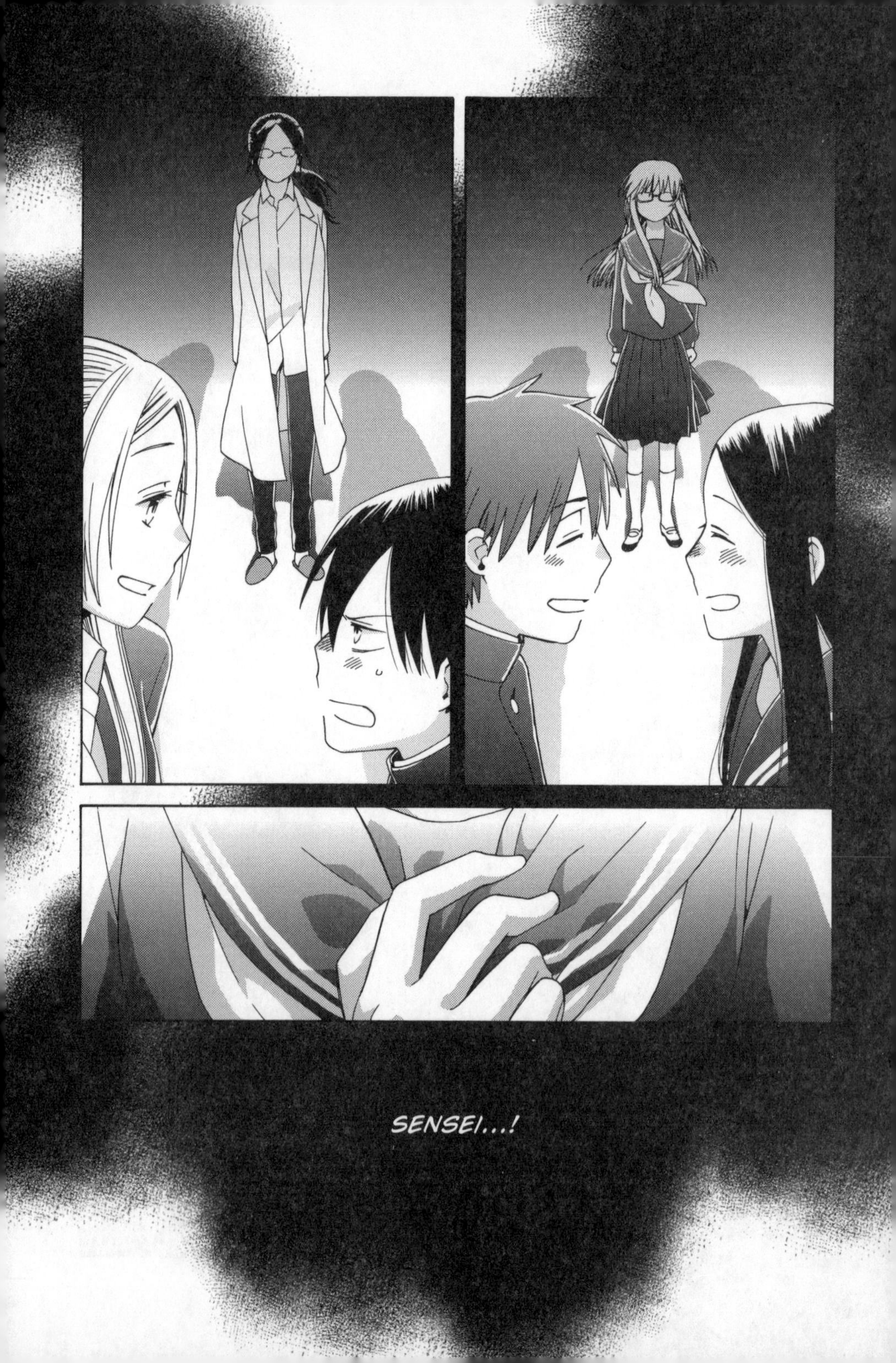
SENSEI...!

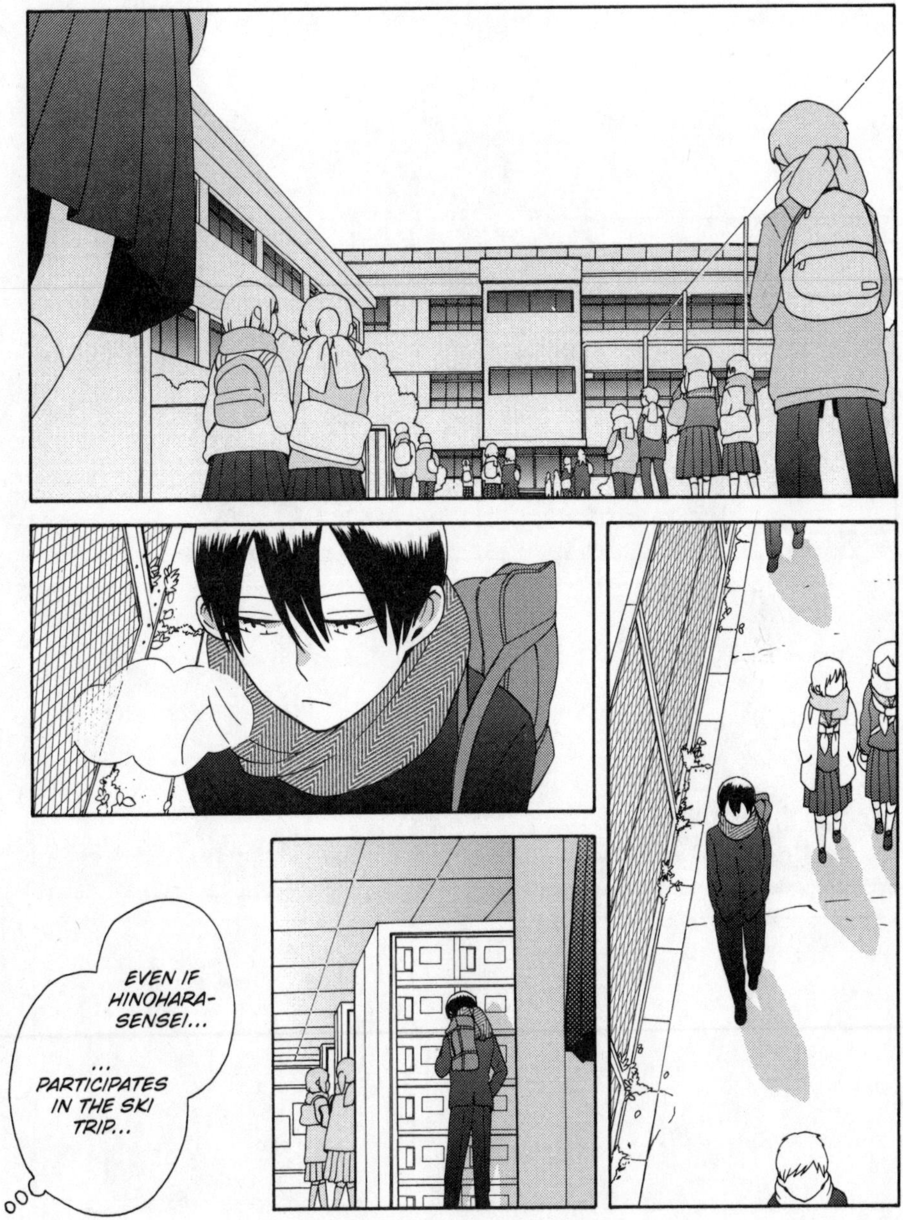
EVEN IF HINOHARA-SENSEI...
... PARTICIPATES IN THE SKI TRIP...

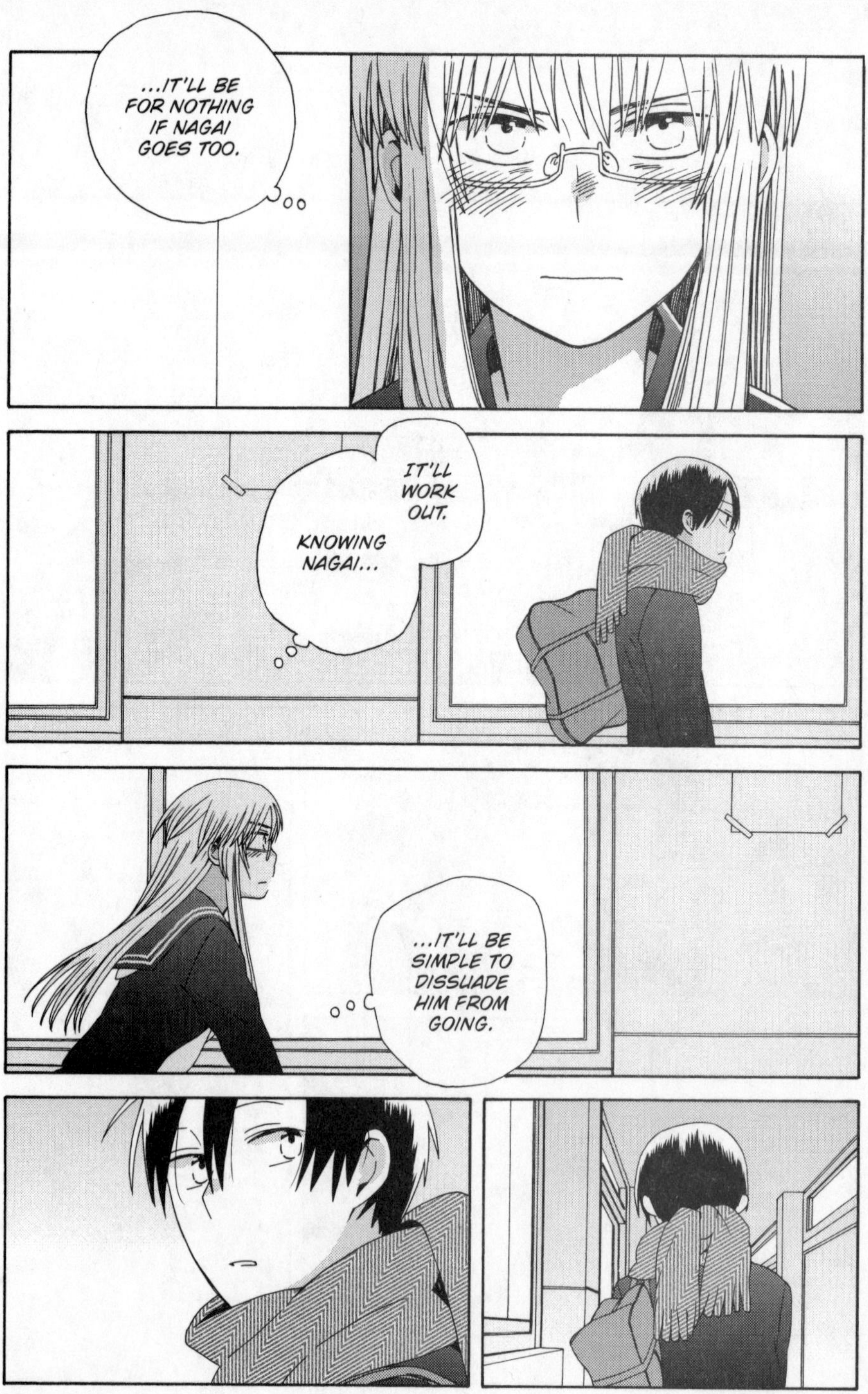
...IT'LL BE FOR NOTHING IF NAGAI GOES TOO.
IT'LL WORK OUT.
KNOWING NAGAI...
...IT'LL BE SIMPLE TO DISSUADE HIM FROM GOING.

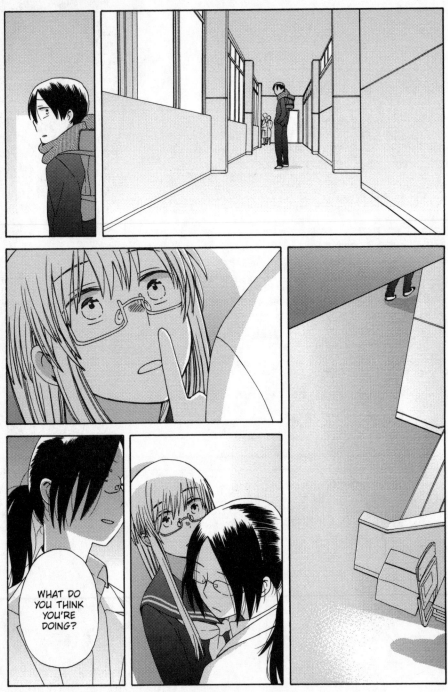

WHAT DO YOU THINK YOU'RE DOING?

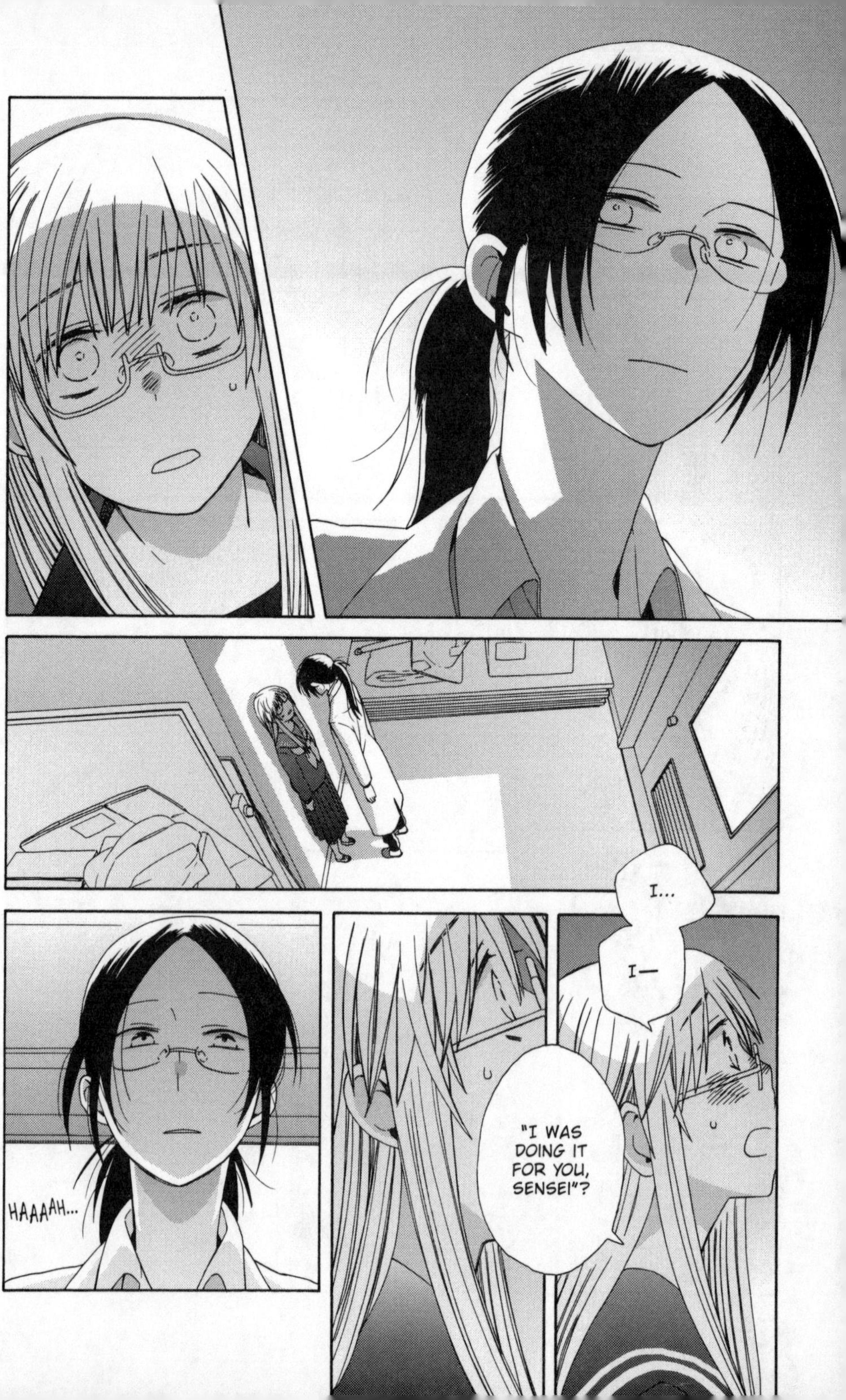
I...
I—
"I WAS DOING IT FOR YOU, SENSEI"?
HAAAAH...

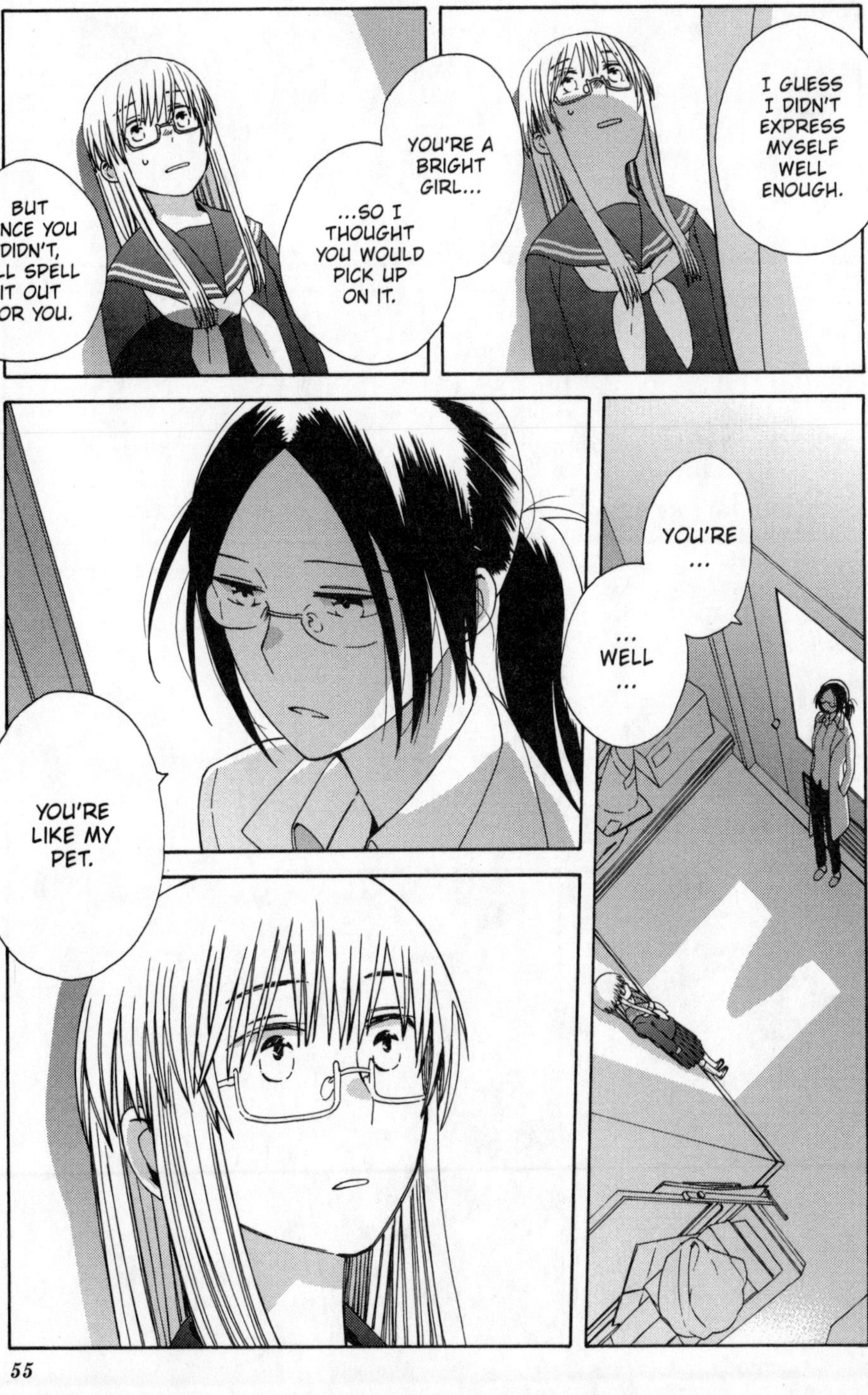
I GUESS I DIDN'T EXPRESS MYSELF WELL ENOUGH.
YOU'RE A BRIGHT GIRL...
...SO I THOUGHT YOU WOULD PICK UP ON IT.
BUT SINCE YOU DIDN'T, I'LL SPELL IT OUT FOR YOU.
YOU'RE ...
... WELL ...
YOU'RE LIKE MY PET.

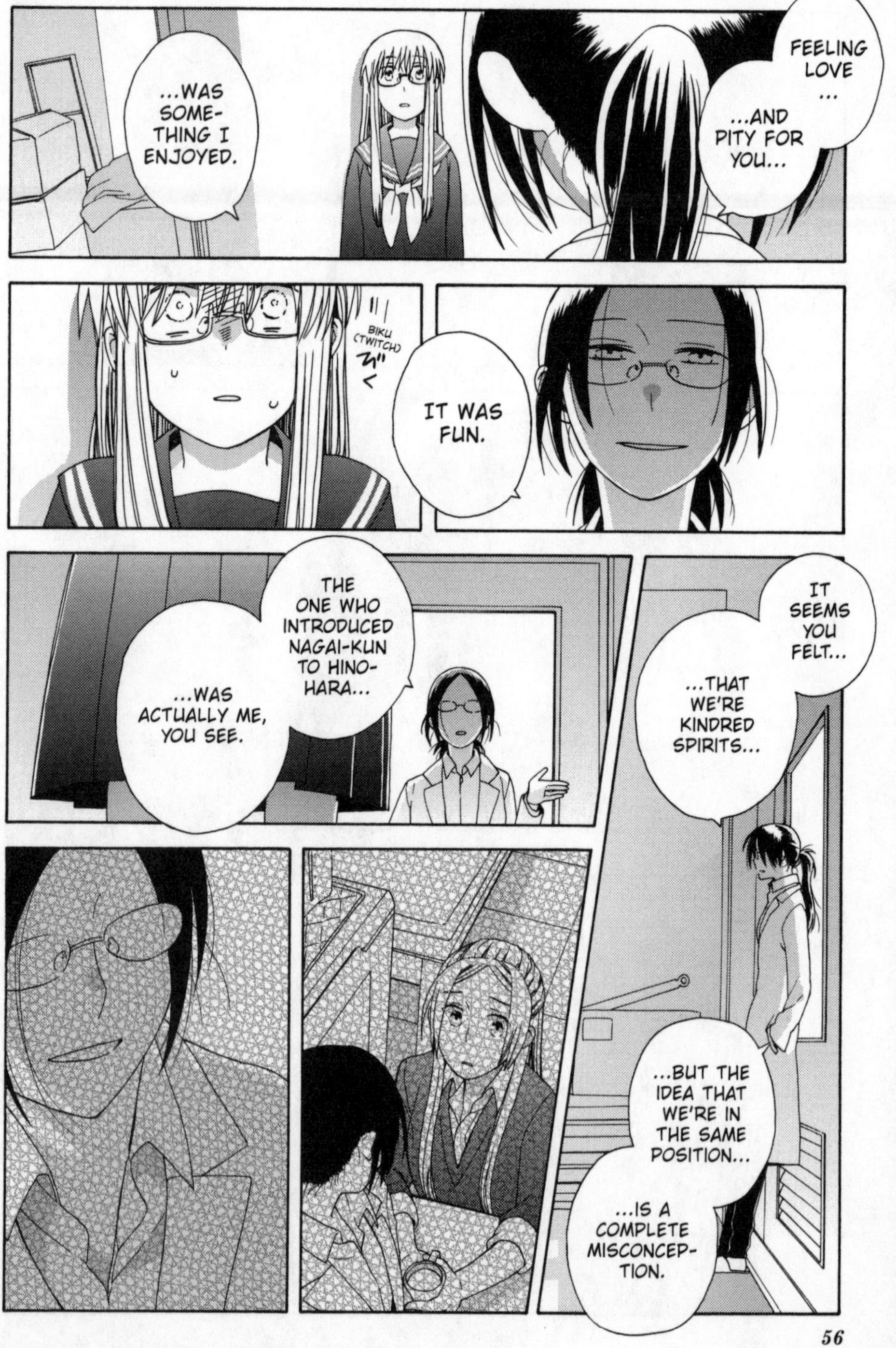
FEELING LOVE ...
...AND PITY FOR YOU...
...WAS SOME-THING I ENJOYED.
IT WAS FUN.
BIKU (TWITCH)
IT SEEMS YOU FELT...
...THAT WE'RE KINDRED SPIRITS...
...BUT THE IDEA THAT WE'RE IN THE SAME POSITION...
...IS A COMPLETE MISCONCEP-TION.
THE ONE WHO INTRODUCED NAGAI-KUN TO HINO-HARA...
...WAS ACTUALLY ME, YOU SEE.

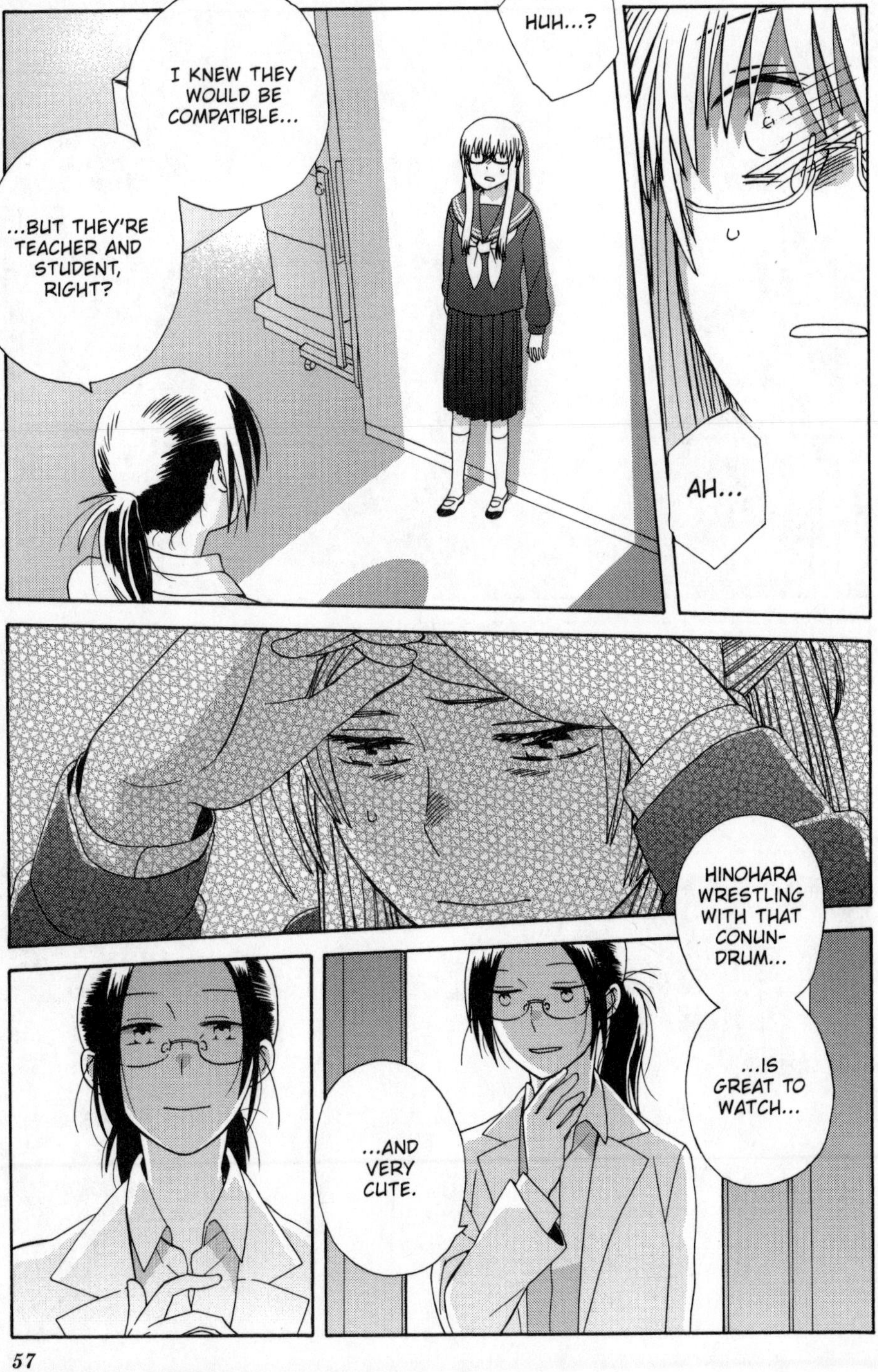
AH...
HUH...?
I KNEW THEY WOULD BE COMPATIBLE...
...BUT THEY'RE TEACHER AND STUDENT, RIGHT?
HINOHARA WRESTLING WITH THAT CONUN-DRUM...
...IS GREAT TO WATCH...
...AND VERY CUTE.

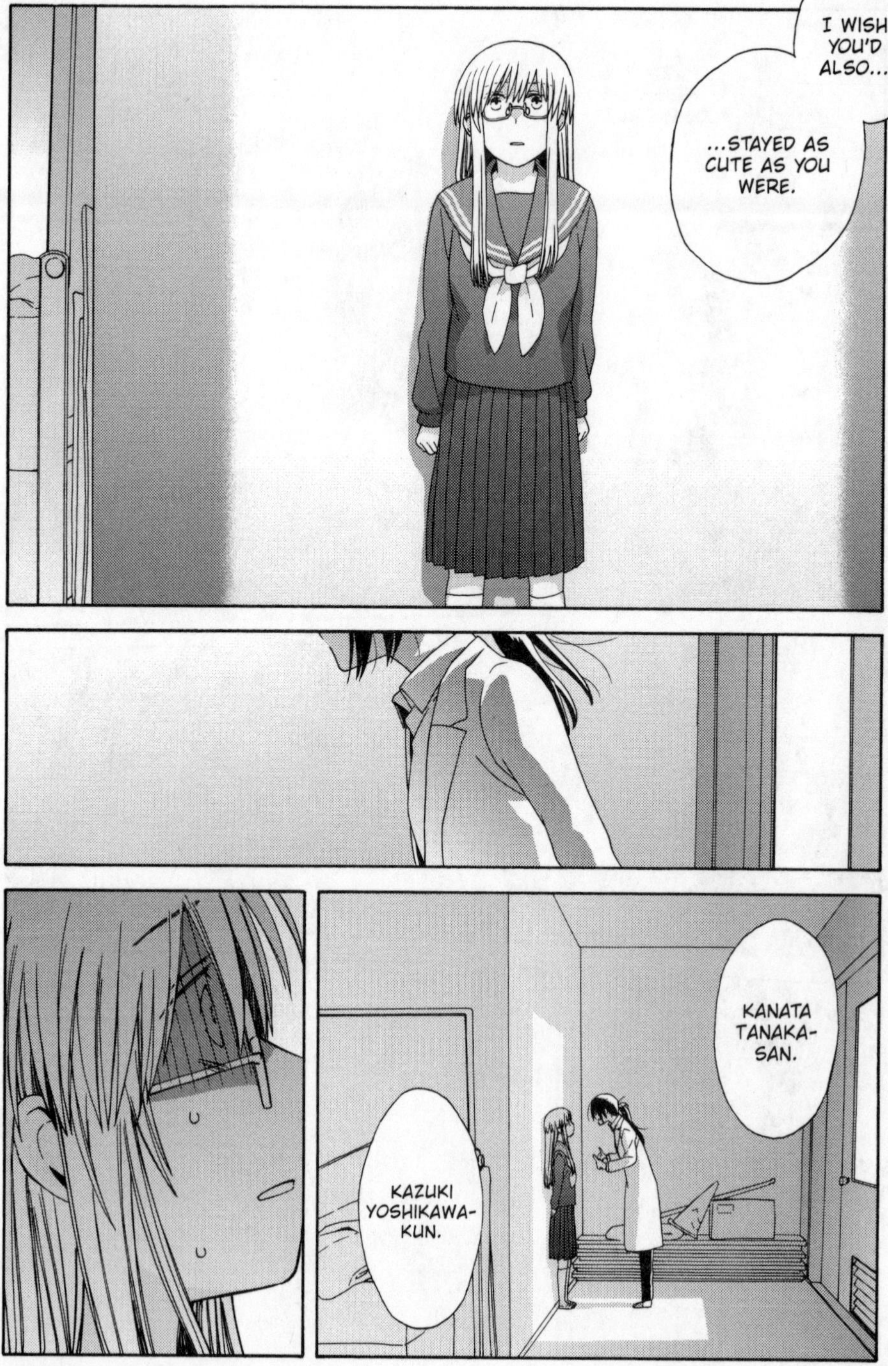
I WISH YOU'D ALSO...
...STAYED AS CUTE AS YOU WERE.
KANATA TANAKA-SAN.
KAZUKI YOSHIKAWA-KUN.

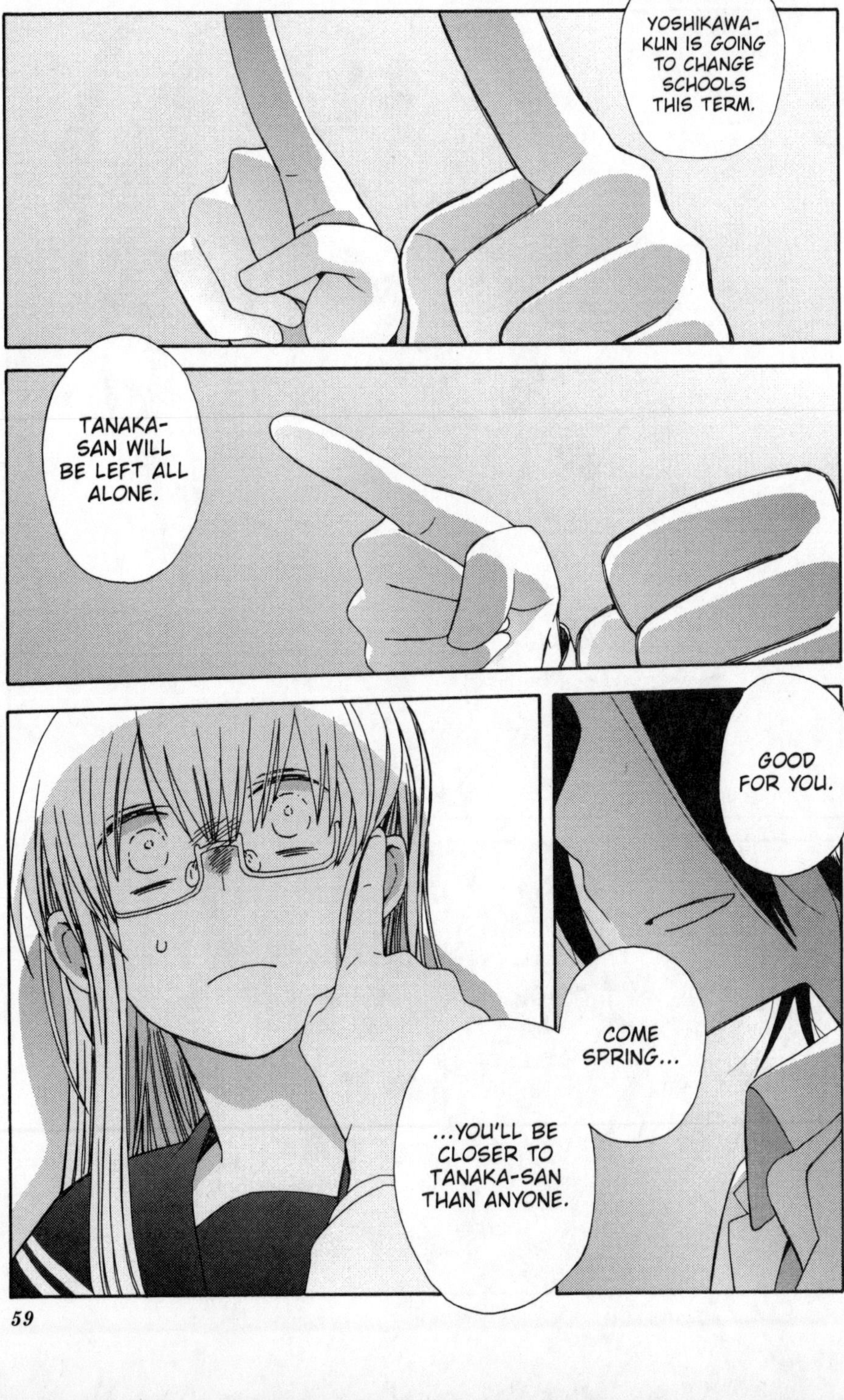
YOSHIKAWA-KUN IS GOING TO CHANGE SCHOOLS THIS TERM.
TANAKA-SAN WILL BE LEFT ALL ALONE.
GOOD FOR YOU.
COME SPRING...
...YOU'LL BE CLOSER TO TANAKA-SAN THAN ANYONE.

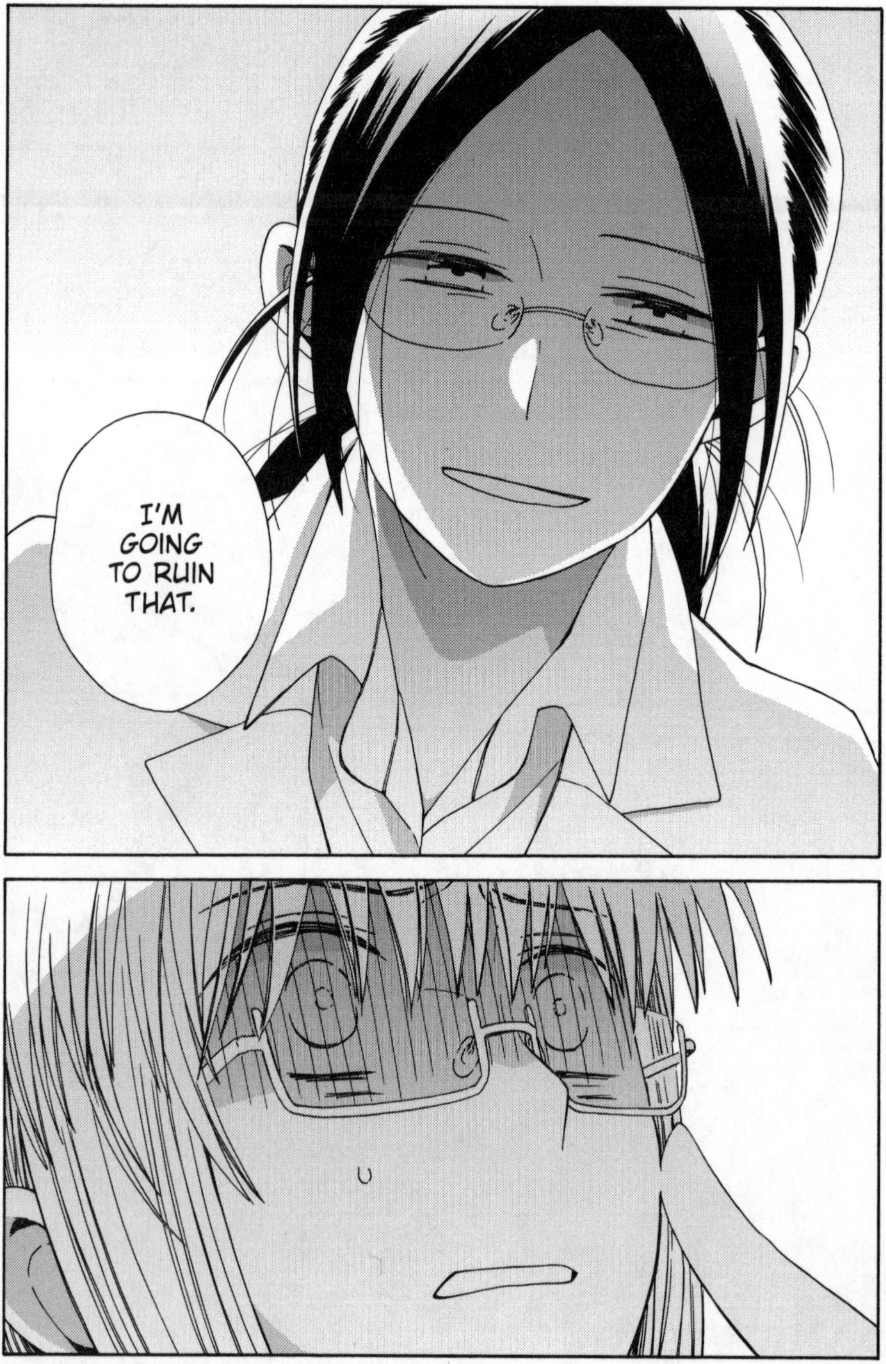
I'M GOING TO RUIN THAT.

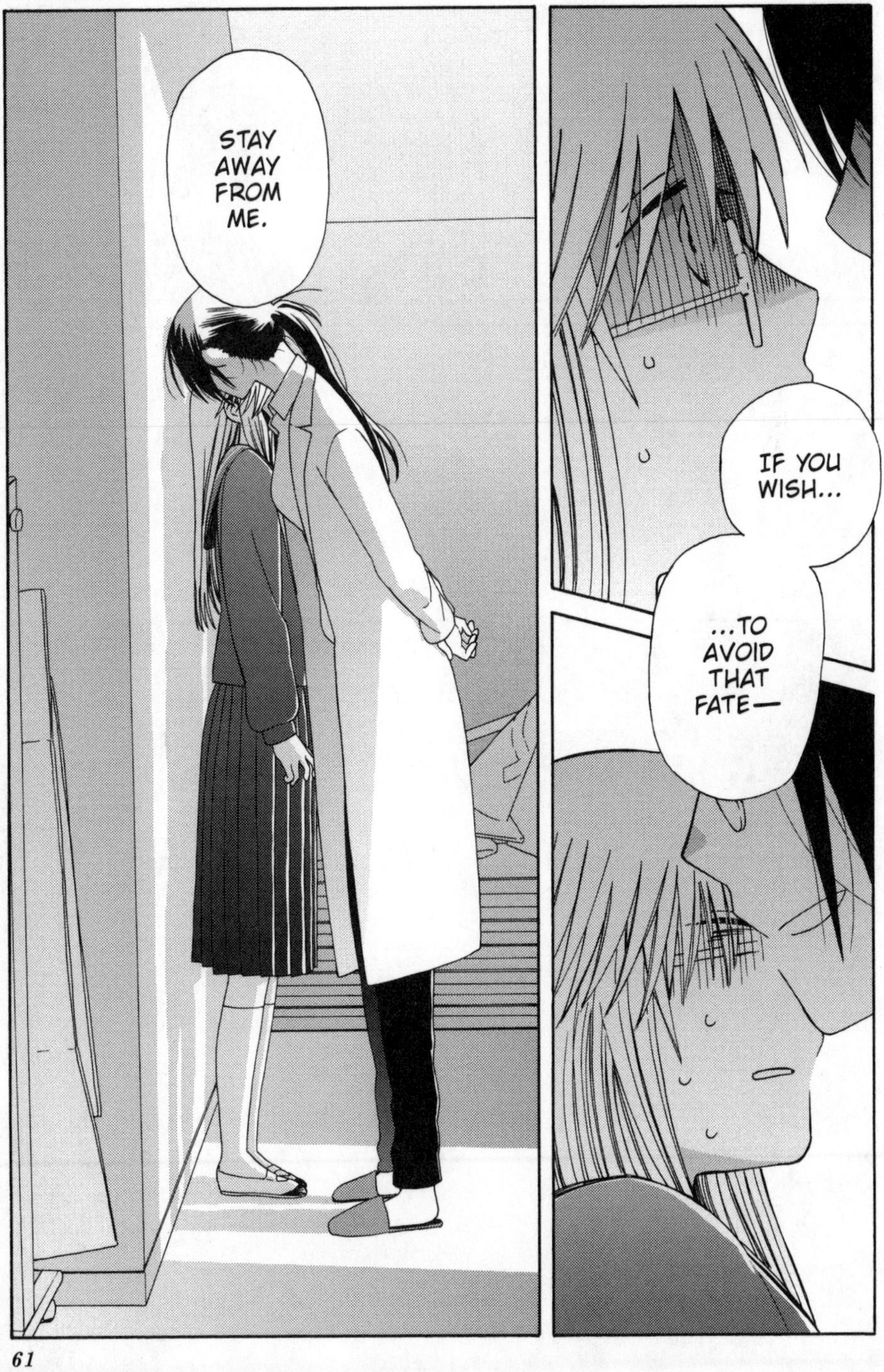
IF YOU WISH...
...TO AVOID THAT FATE—
STAY AWAY FROM ME.

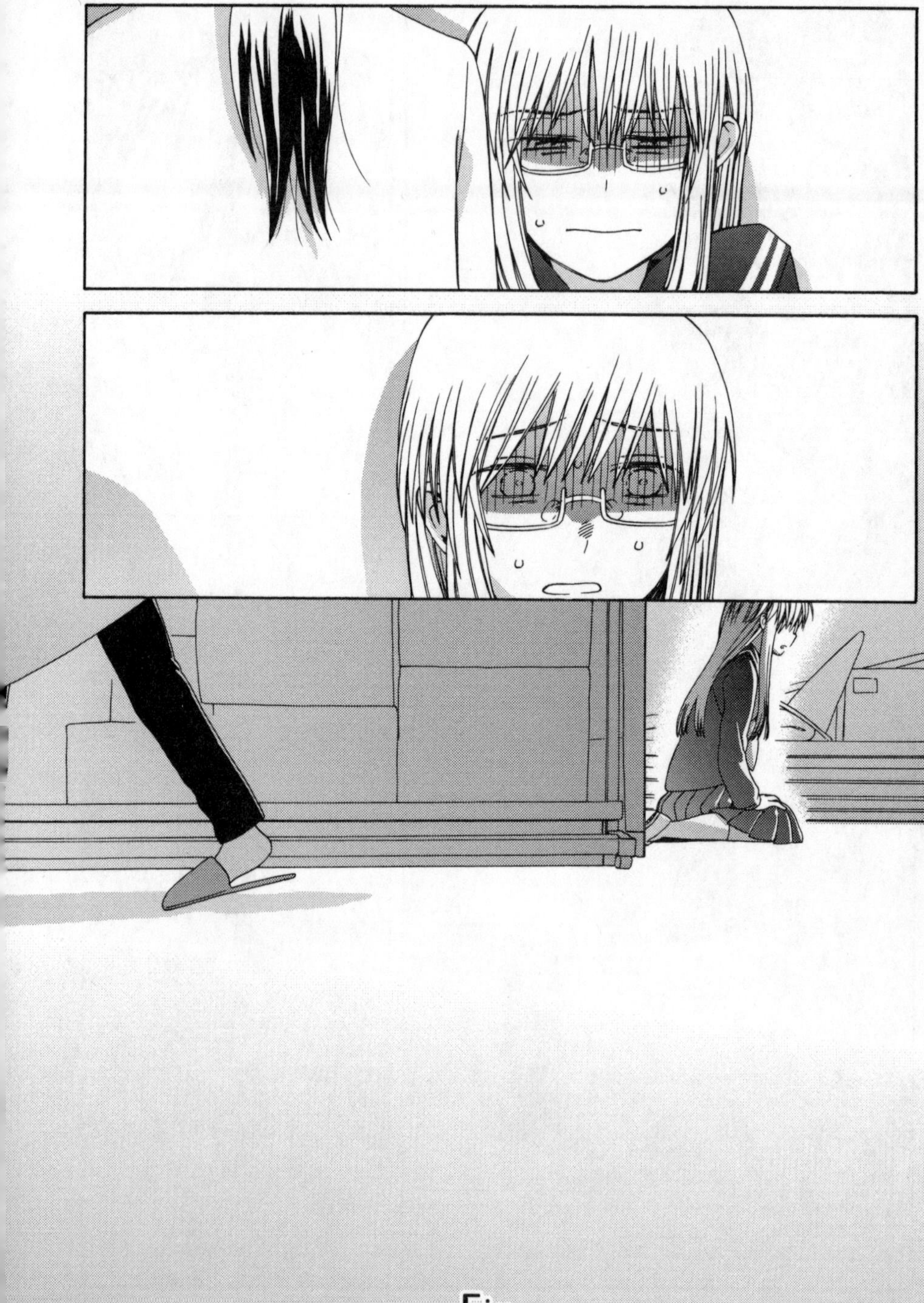
Fin

Love at Fourteen

[Intermission 67]

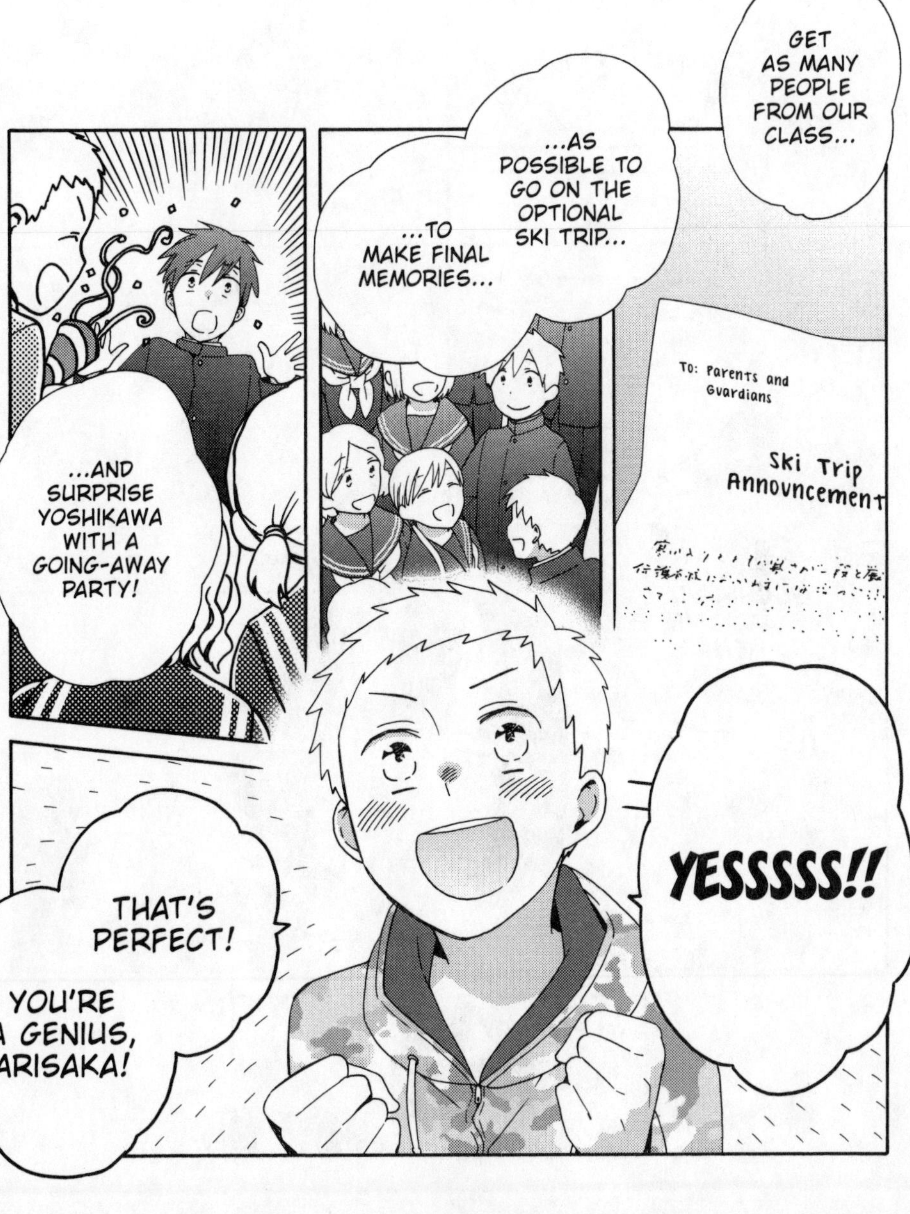
GET AS MANY PEOPLE FROM OUR CLASS...
To: Parents and Guardians
Ski Trip Announcement
...AS POSSIBLE TO GO ON THE OPTIONAL SKI TRIP...
...TO MAKE FINAL MEMORIES...
...AND SURPRISE YOSHIKAWA WITH A GOING-AWAY PARTY!
YESSSSS!!
THAT'S PERFECT!
YOU'RE A GENIUS, ARISAKA!

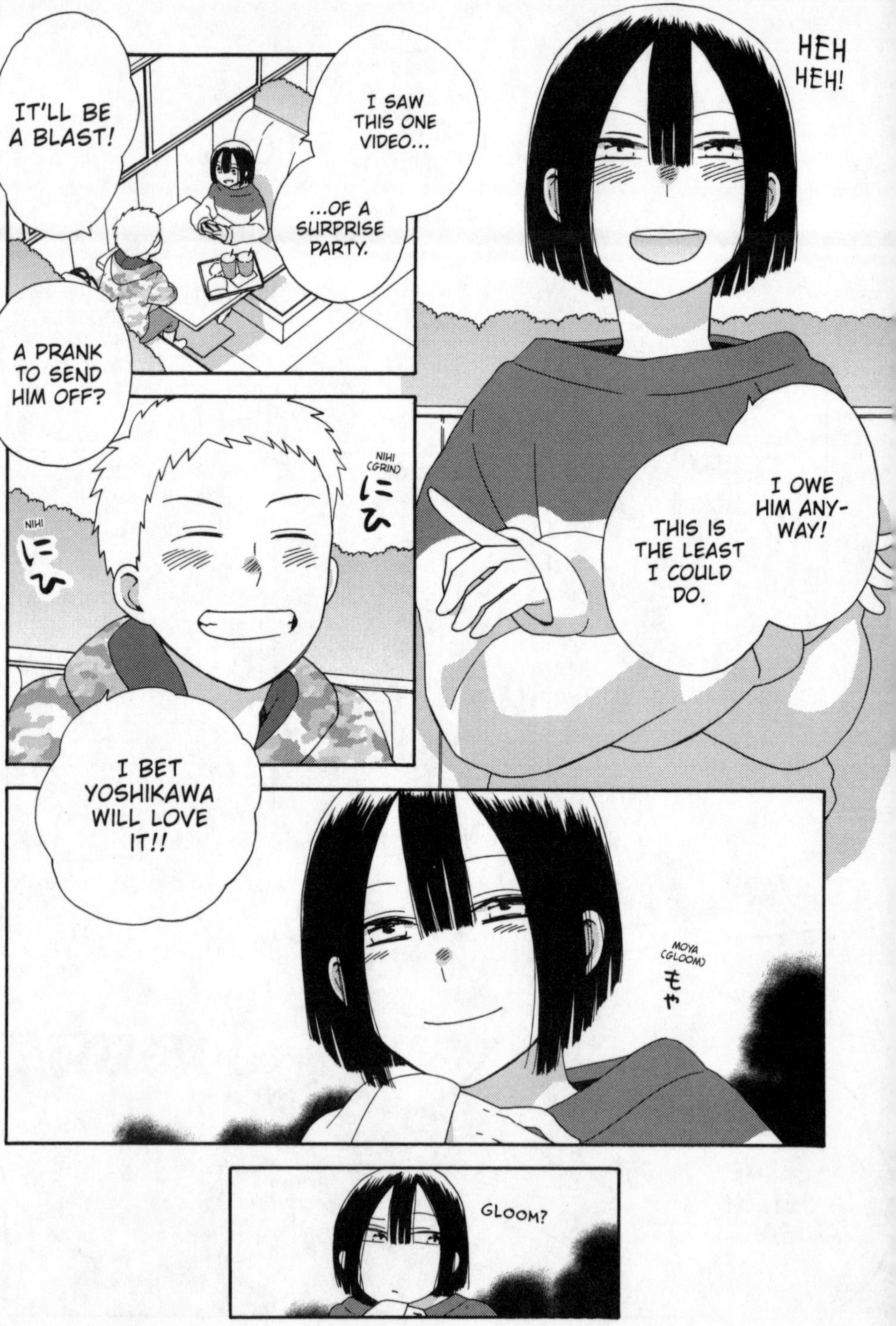
HEH HEH!
I OWE HIM ANY-WAY!
THIS IS THE LEAST I COULD DO.
I SAW THIS ONE VIDEO...
...OF A SURPRISE PARTY.
IT'LL BE A BLAST!
A PRANK TO SEND HIM OFF?
NIHI (GRIN)
にひ
NIHI
にひ
I BET YOSHIKAWA WILL LOVE IT!!
MOYA (GLOOM)
もや
GLOOM?

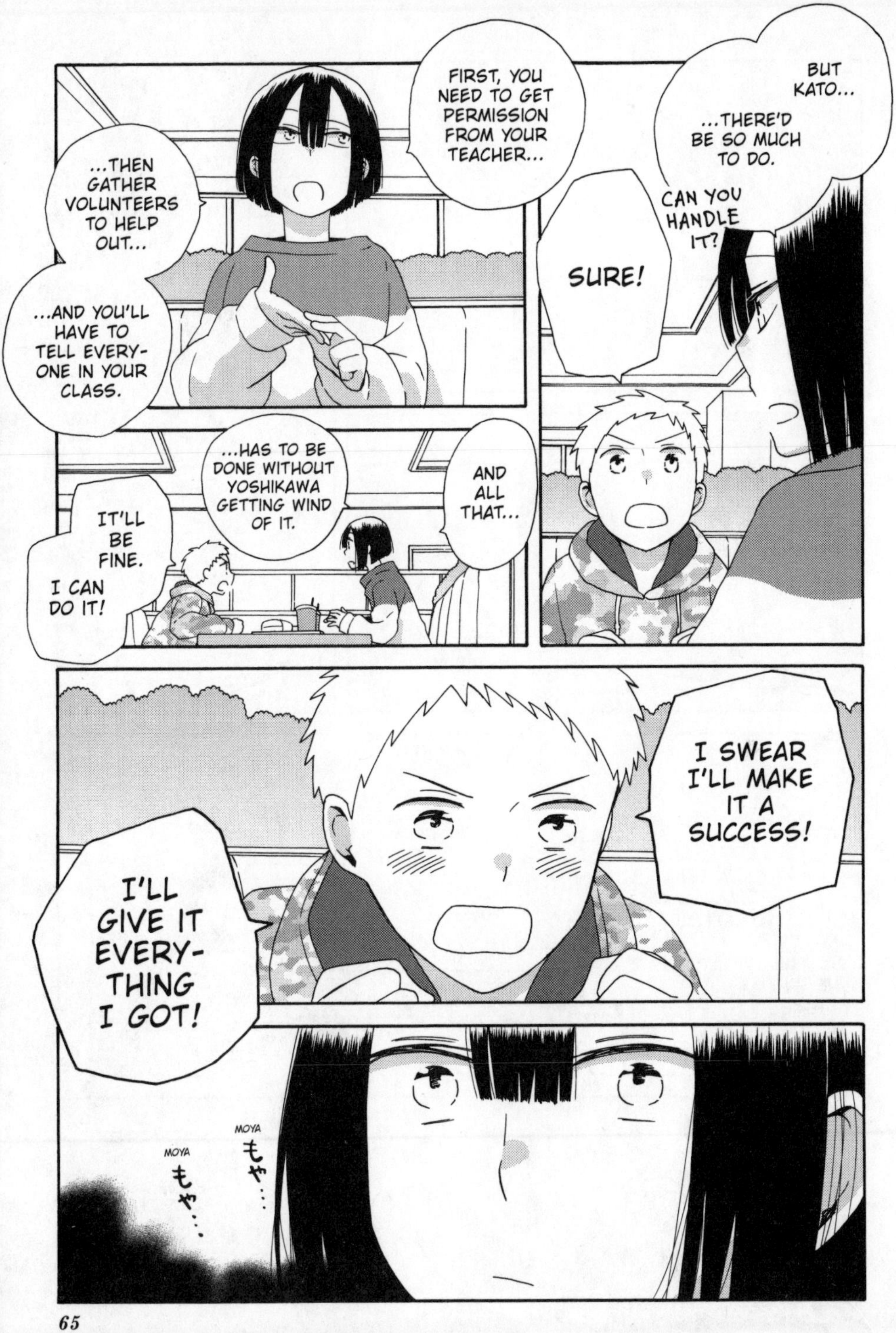
BUT KATO...
...THERE'D BE SO MUCH TO DO.
CAN YOU HANDLE IT?
SURE!
FIRST, YOU NEED TO GET PERMISSION FROM YOUR TEACHER...
...THEN GATHER VOLUNTEERS TO HELP OUT...
...AND YOU'LL HAVE TO TELL EVERY-ONE IN YOUR CLASS.
AND ALL THAT...
...HAS TO BE DONE WITHOUT YOSHIKAWA GETTING WIND OF IT.
IT'LL BE FINE.
I CAN DO IT!
I SWEAR I'LL MAKE IT A SUCCESS!
I'LL GIVE IT EVERY-THING I GOT!
MOYA
もや...
MOYA
もや...

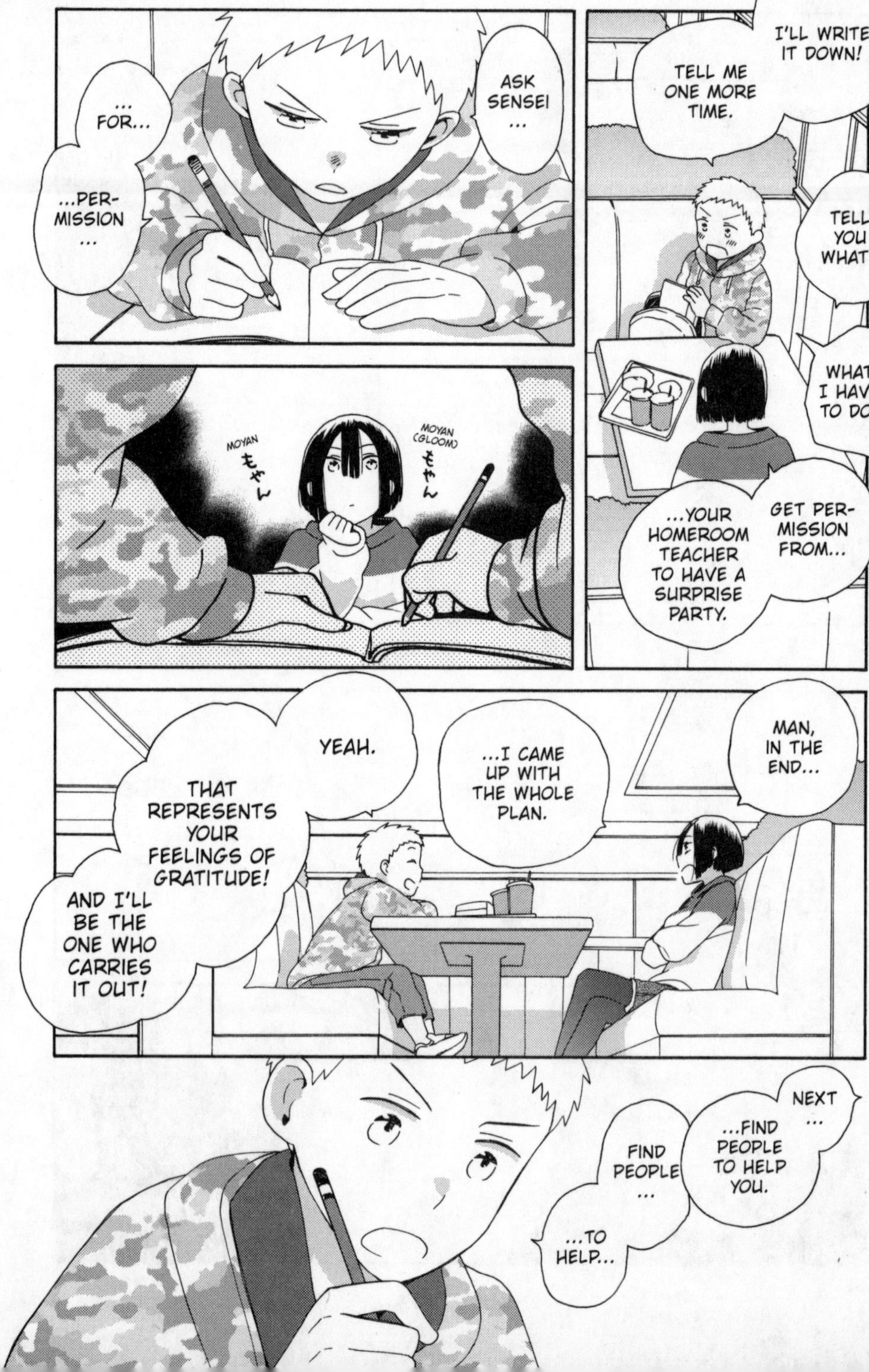
I'LL WRITE IT DOWN!
TELL ME ONE MORE TIME.
TELL YOU WHAT?
WHAT I HAVE TO DO!
GET PER-MISSION FROM...
...YOUR HOMEROOM TEACHER TO HAVE A SURPRISE PARTY.
ASK SENSEI ...
... FOR...
...PER-MISSION ...
MOYAN (GLOOM) もやん
MOYAN もやん
MAN, IN THE END...
...I CAME UP WITH THE WHOLE PLAN.
YEAH.
THAT REPRESENTS YOUR FEELINGS OF GRATITUDE!
AND I'LL BE THE ONE WHO CARRIES IT OUT!
NEXT ...
...FIND PEOPLE TO HELP YOU.
FIND PEOPLE ...
...TO HELP...

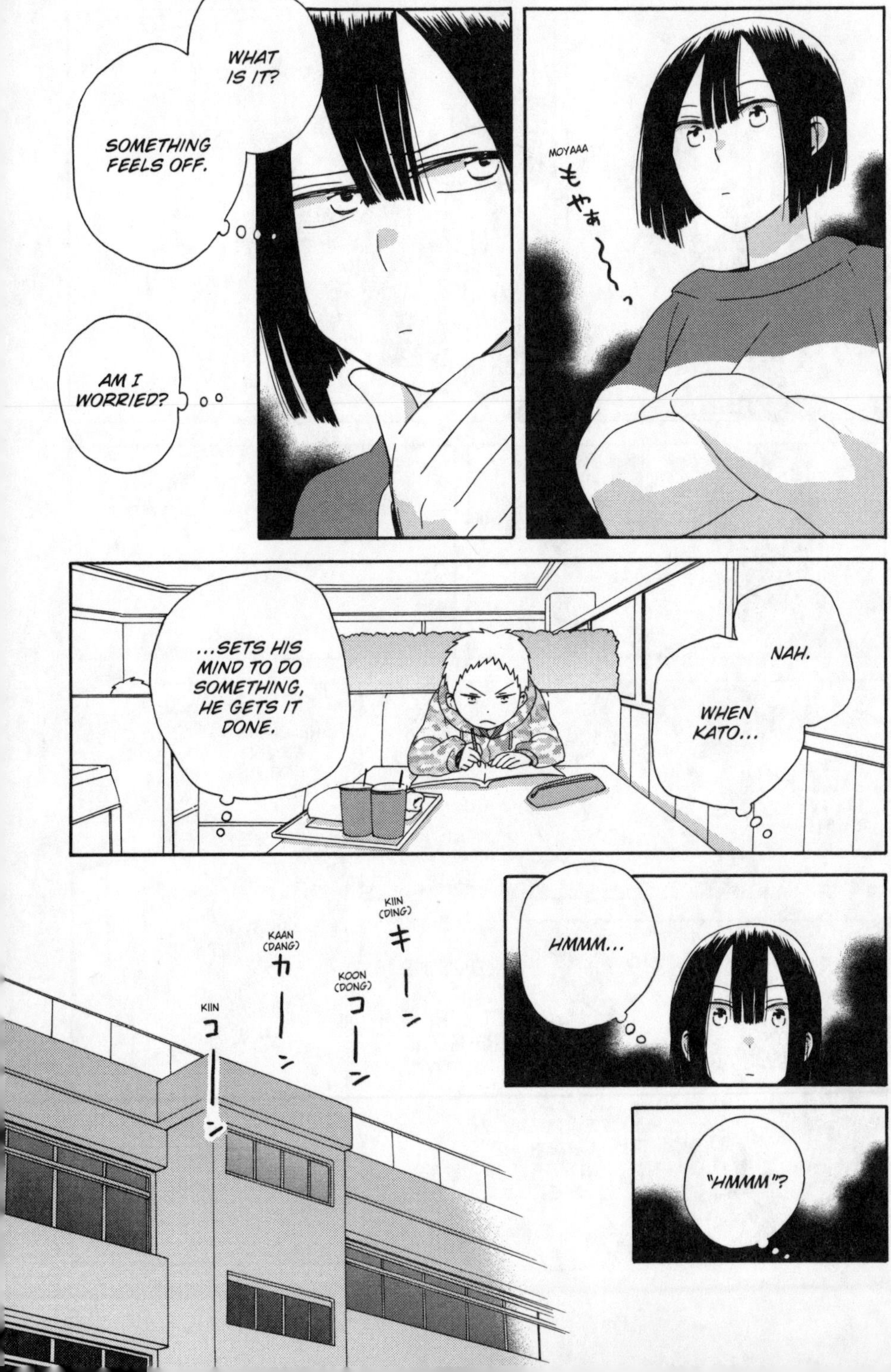
MOYAAA
もやぁ~~っ
WHAT IS IT?
SOMETHING FEELS OFF.
AM I WORRIED?
NAH.
WHEN KATO...
...SETS HIS MIND TO DO SOMETHING, HE GETS IT DONE.
HMMM...
"HMMM"?
KIIN (DING)
キーン
KOON (DONG)
コーン
KAAN (DANG)
カーン
KIIN
コーン

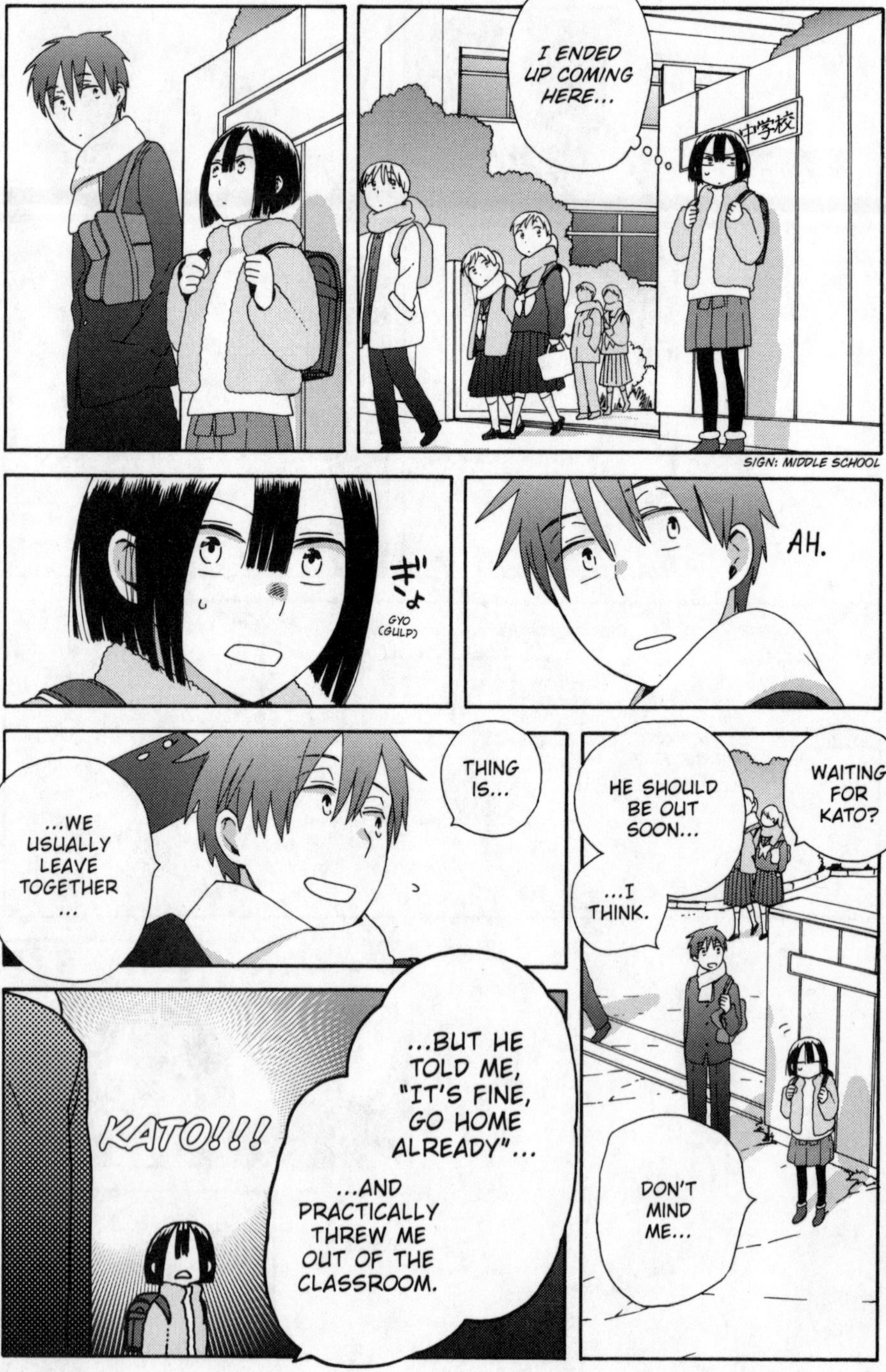
I ENDED UP COMING HERE...
中学校
SIGN: MIDDLE SCHOOL
AH.
ギョ
GYO (GULP)
WAITING FOR KATO?
HE SHOULD BE OUT SOON...
...I THINK.
DON'T MIND ME...
THING IS...
...WE USUALLY LEAVE TOGETHER...
...BUT HE TOLD ME, "IT'S FINE, GO HOME ALREADY"...
...AND PRACTICALLY THREW ME OUT OF THE CLASSROOM.
KATO!!!

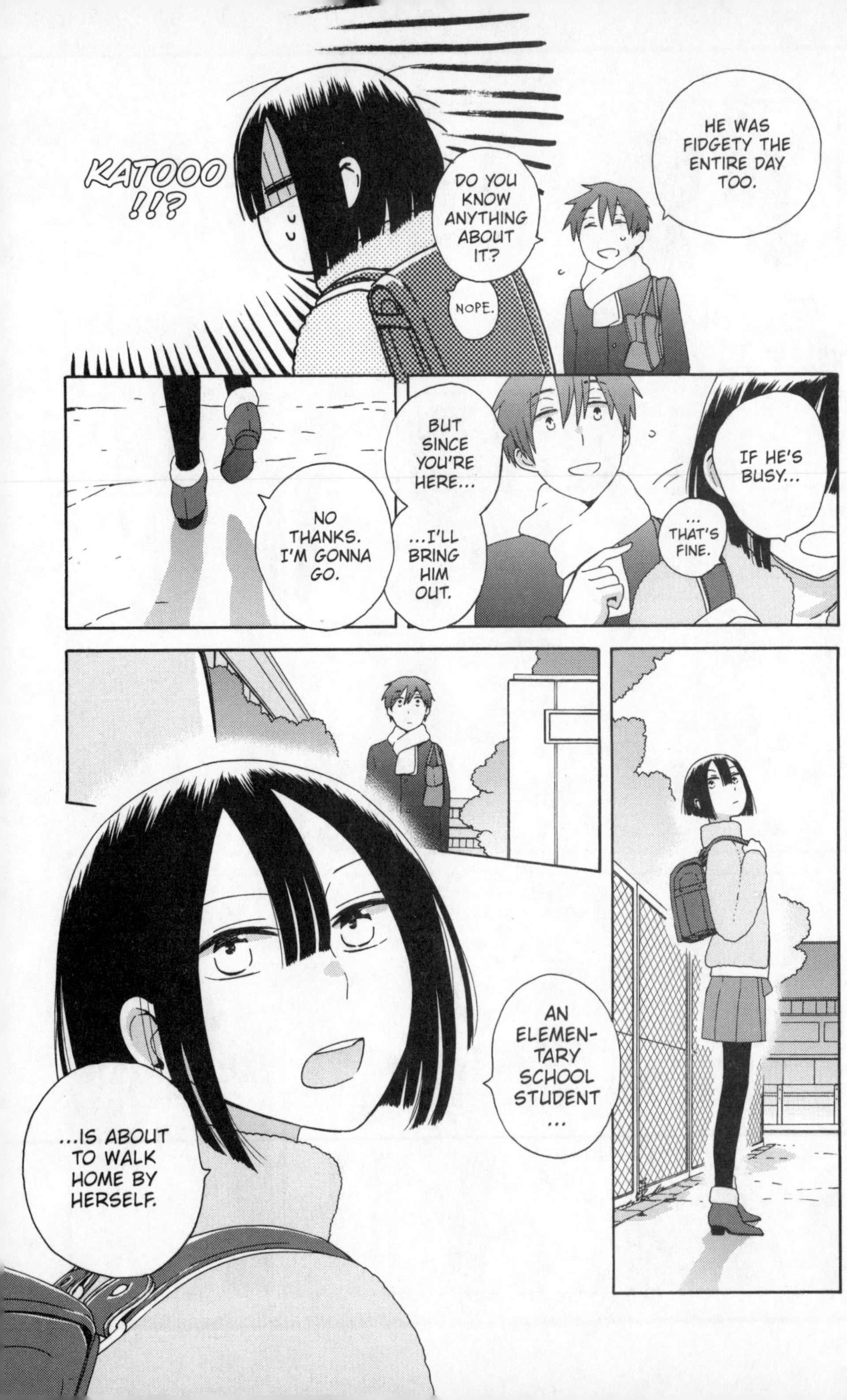
HE WAS FIDGETY THE ENTIRE DAY TOO.
DO YOU KNOW ANYTHING ABOUT IT?
NOPE.
KATOOO !!?
IF HE'S BUSY...
...THAT'S FINE.
BUT SINCE YOU'RE HERE...
...I'LL BRING HIM OUT.
NO THANKS. I'M GONNA GO.
AN ELEMENTARY SCHOOL STUDENT...
...IS ABOUT TO WALK HOME BY HERSELF.

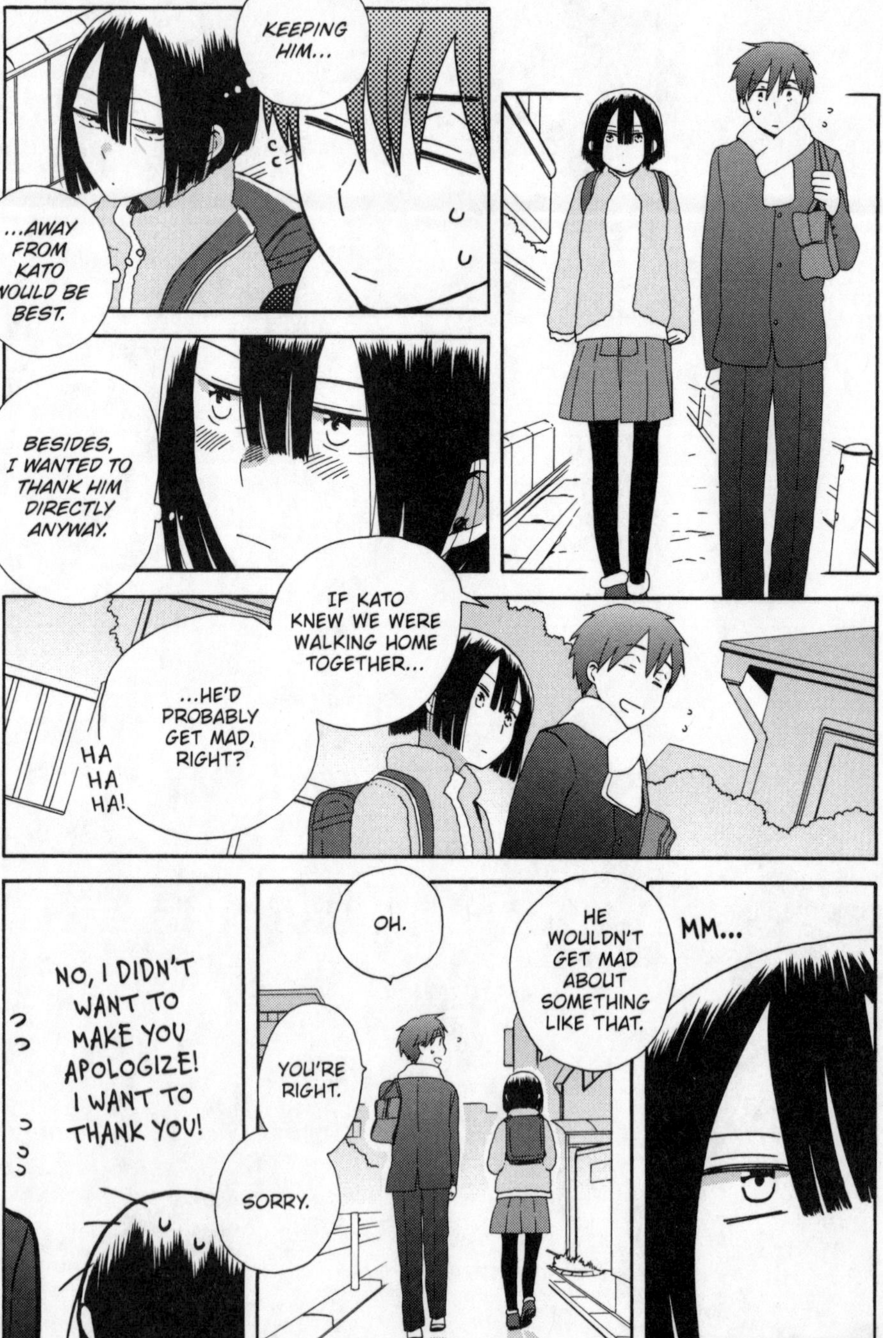
KEEPING HIM...
...AWAY FROM KATO WOULD BE BEST.
BESIDES, I WANTED TO THANK HIM DIRECTLY ANYWAY.
IF KATO KNEW WE WERE WALKING HOME TOGETHER...
...HE'D PROBABLY GET MAD, RIGHT?
HA HA HA!
MM...
HE WOULDN'T GET MAD ABOUT SOMETHING LIKE THAT.
OH.
YOU'RE RIGHT.
SORRY.
NO, I DIDN'T WANT TO MAKE YOU APOLOGIZE! I WANT TO THANK YOU!

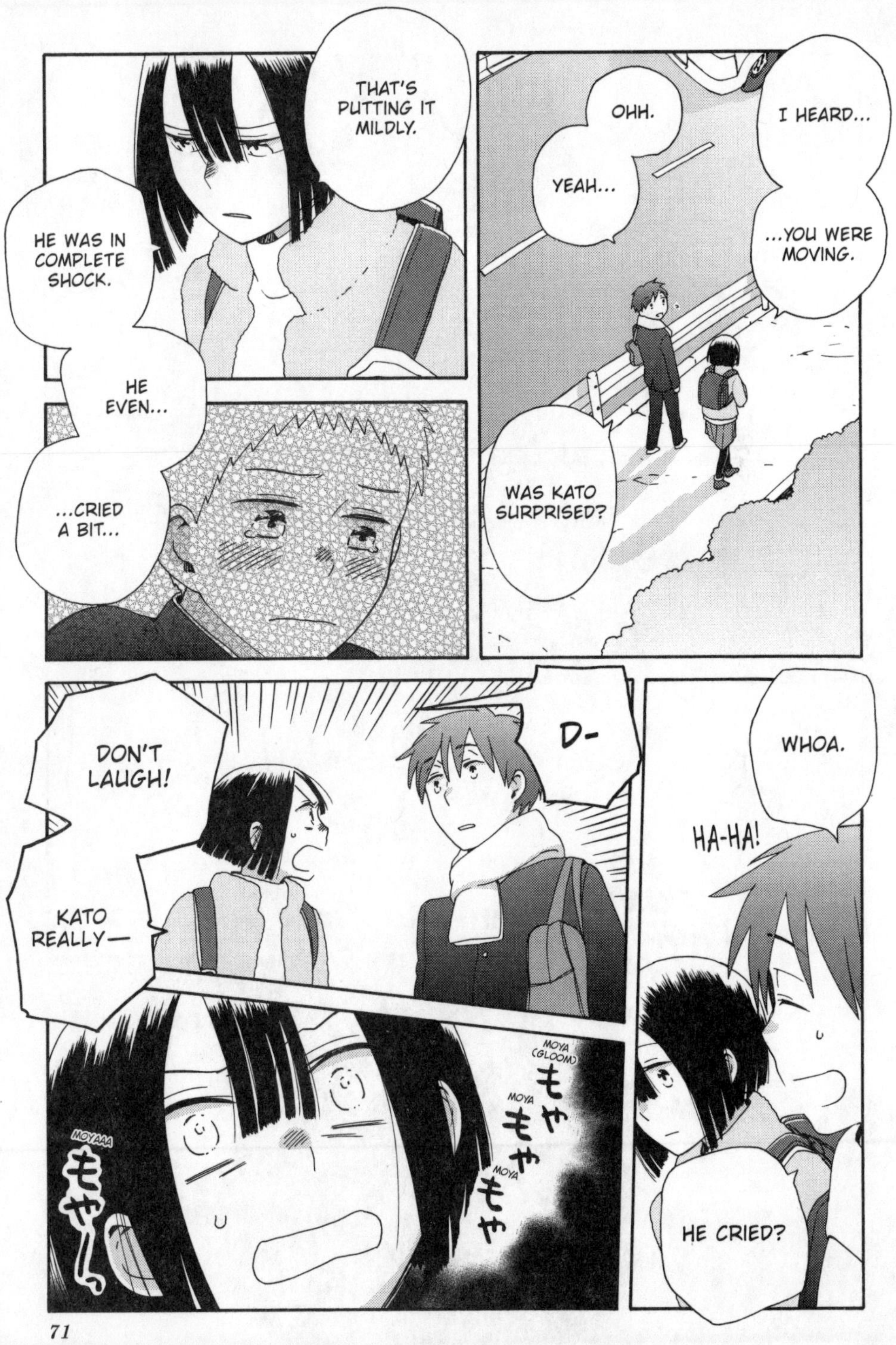
I HEARD...
...YOU WERE MOVING.
OHH.
YEAH...
WAS KATO SURPRISED?
THAT'S PUTTING IT MILDLY.
HE WAS IN COMPLETE SHOCK.
HE EVEN...
...CRIED A BIT...
WHOA.
HA-HA!
HE CRIED?
D-
DON'T LAUGH!
KATO REALLY—
MOYA (GLOOM)
もや
MOYA
もや
MOYA
もや
MOYAAA
もやん

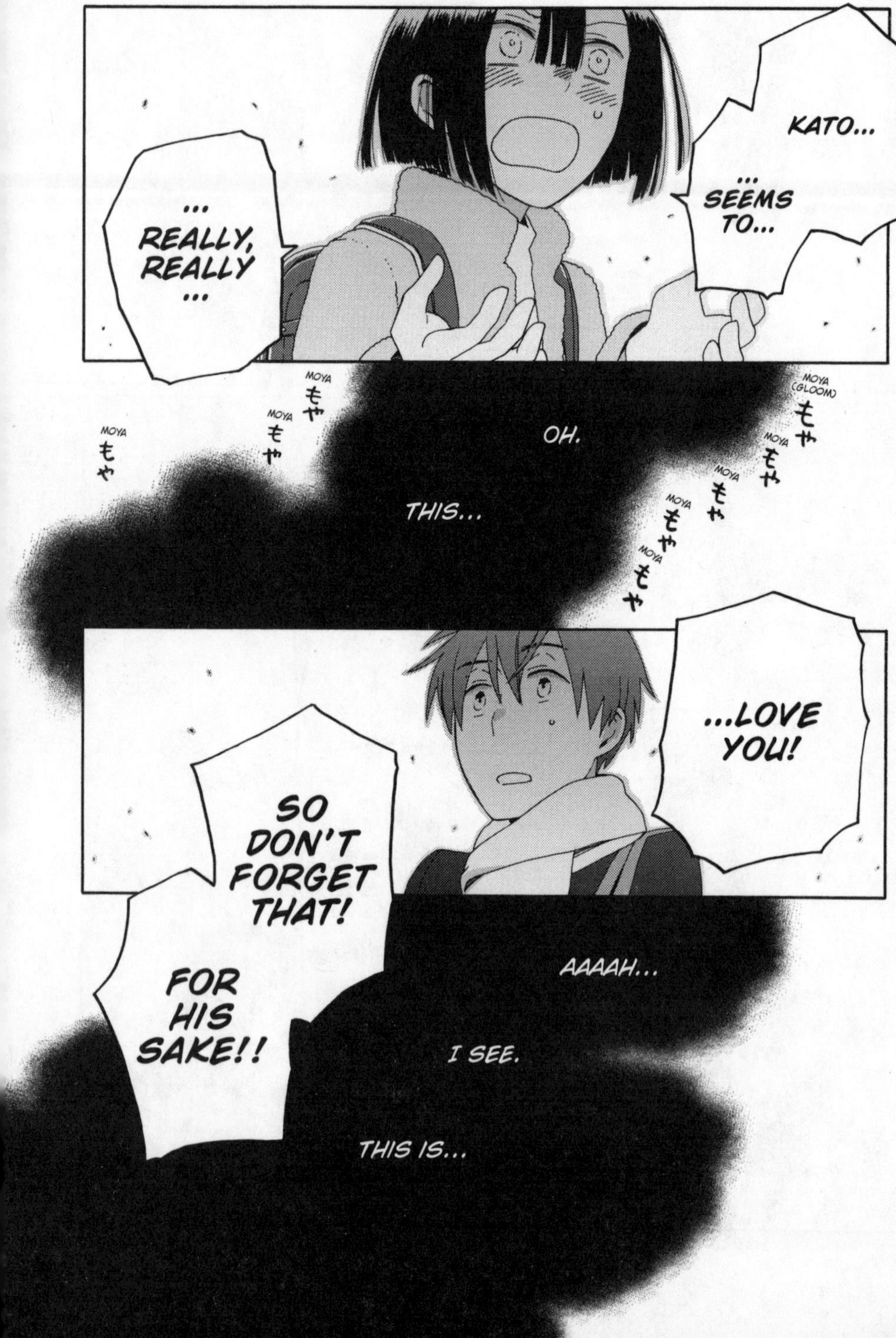
KATO... ...SEEMS TO...
...REALLY, REALLY...
MOYA (GLOOM) もや
MOYA もや
MOYA もや
MOYA もや
MOYA もや
OH.
THIS...
MOYA もや
MOYA もや
MOYA もや
...LOVE YOU!
SO DON'T FORGET THAT!
FOR HIS SAKE!!
AAAAH...
I SEE.
THIS IS...

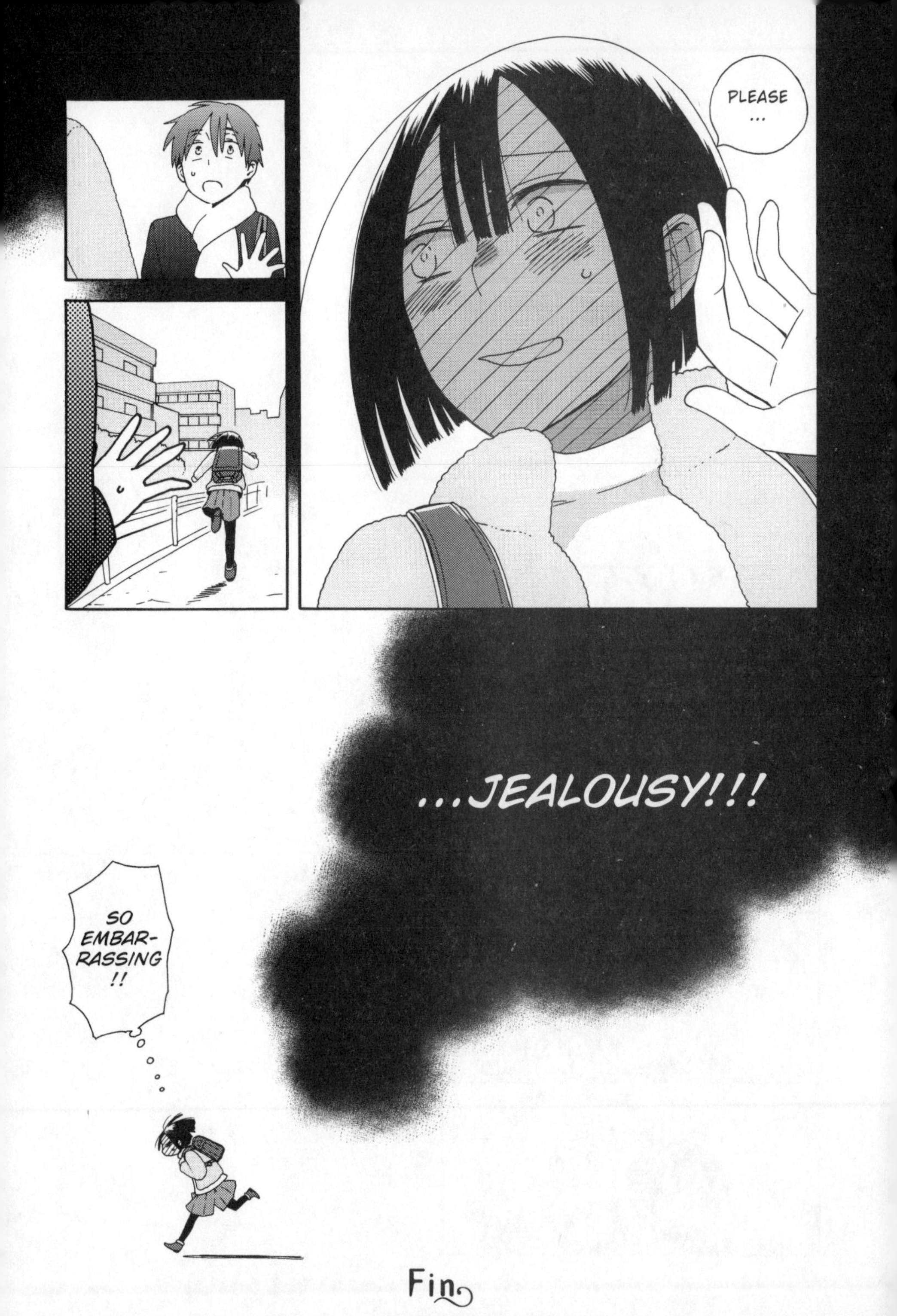
PLEASE ...
...JEALOUSY!!!
SO EMBAR-RASSING !!

Fin

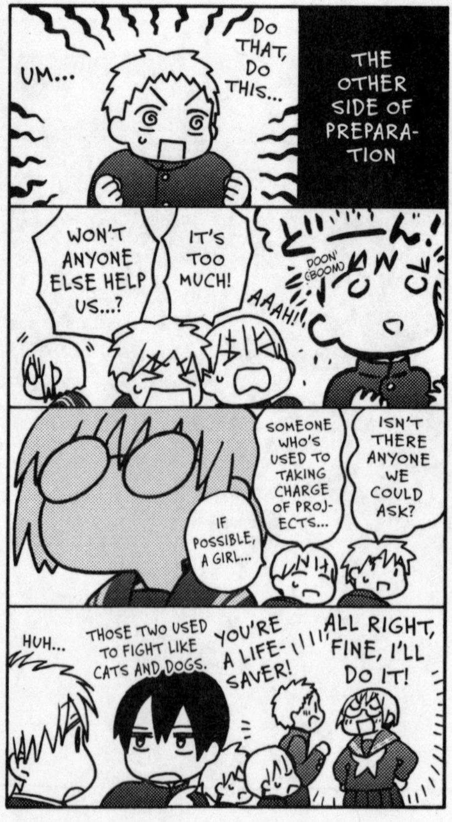
THE OTHER SIDE OF PREPARATION
DO THAT, DO THIS...
UM...
どーーん!
DOON' (BOOM)
AAAH!
IT'S TOO MUCH!
WON'T ANYONE ELSE HELP US...?
ISN'T THERE ANYONE WE COULD ASK?
SOMEONE WHO'S USED TO TAKING CHARGE OF PROJ-ECTS...
IF POSSIBLE, A GIRL...
ALL RIGHT, FINE, I'LL DO IT!
YOU'RE A LIFE-SAVER!
THOSE TWO USED TO FIGHT LIKE CATS AND DOGS.
HUH...

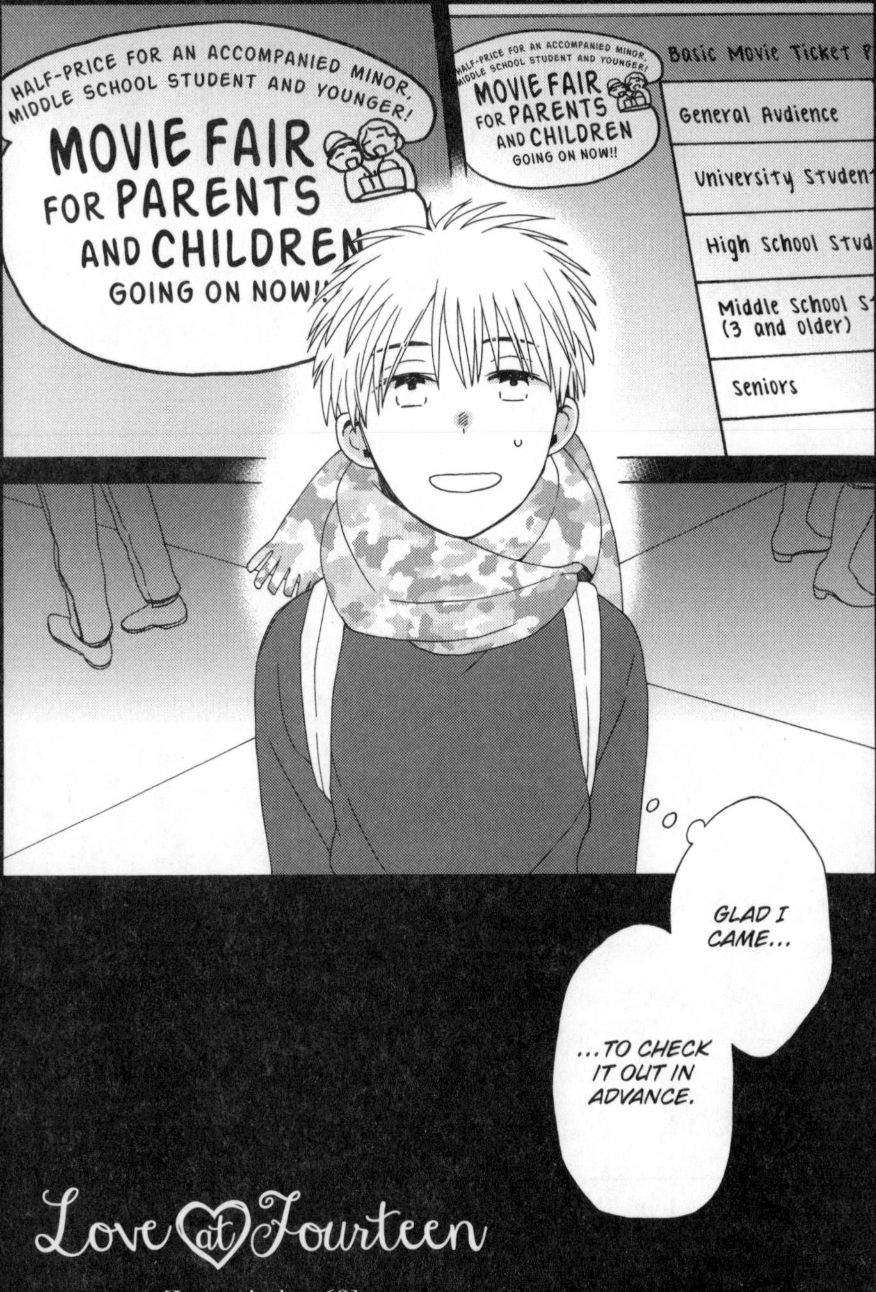
Basic Movie Ticket
General Audience
Seniors
HALF-PRICE FOR AN ACCOMPANIED MINOR, MIDDLE SCHOOL STUDENT AND YOUNGER!
MOVIE FAIR FOR PARENTS AND CHILDREN GOING ON NOW!!
HALF-PRICE FOR AN ACCOMPANIED MINOR, MIDDLE SCHOOL STUDENT AND YOUNGER!
MOVIE FAIR FOR PARENTS AND CHILDREN GOING ON NOW!!
GLAD I CAME...
...TO CHECK IT OUT IN ADVANCE.

Love at Fourteen

[Intermission 68]

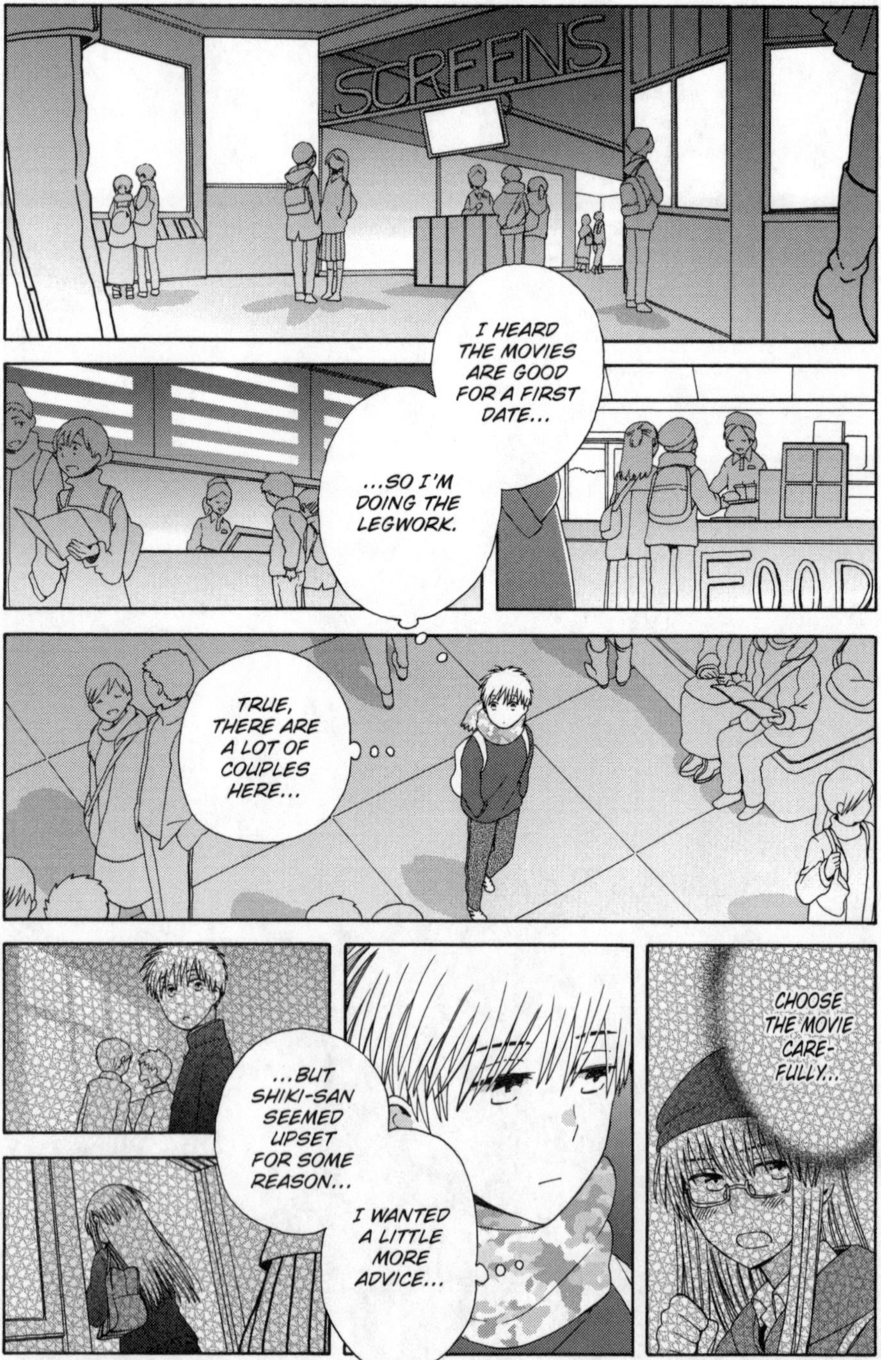

I HEARD THE MOVIES ARE GOOD FOR A FIRST DATE...
...SO I'M DOING THE LEGWORK.
TRUE, THERE ARE A LOT OF COUPLES HERE...
CHOOSE THE MOVIE CARE-FULLY...
...BUT SHIKI-SAN SEEMED UPSET FOR SOME REASON...
I WANTED A LITTLE MORE ADVICE...

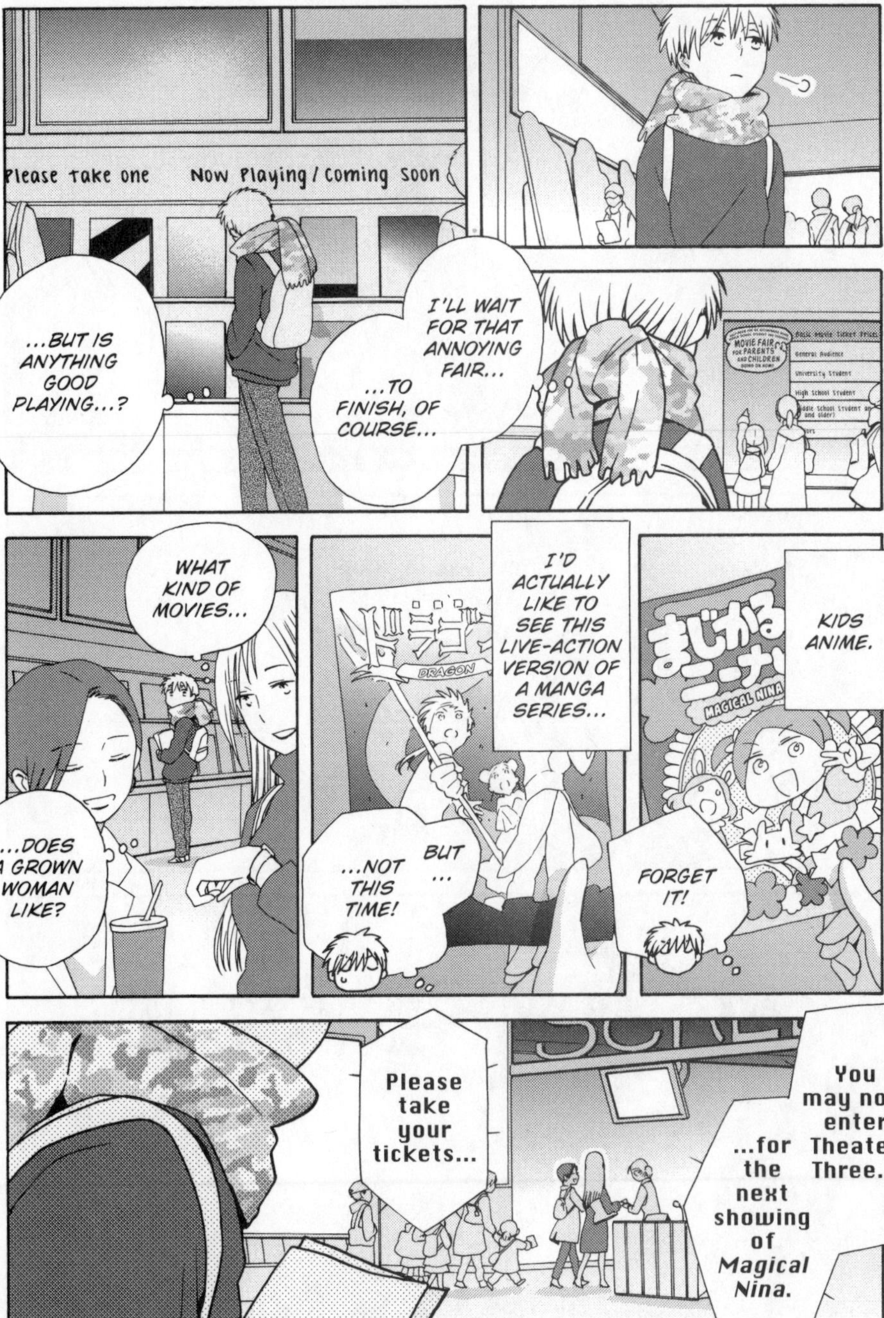
MOVIE FAIR FOR PARENTS' AND CHILDREN
I'LL WAIT FOR THAT ANNOYING FAIR...
...TO FINISH, OF COURSE...
Please Take one
Now Playing / Coming Soon
...BUT IS ANYTHING GOOD PLAYING...?
MAGICAL NINA
KIDS ANIME.
FORGET IT!
DRAGON
I'D ACTUALLY LIKE TO SEE THIS LIVE-ACTION VERSION OF A MANGA SERIES...
BUT...
...NOT THIS TIME!
WHAT KIND OF MOVIES...
...DOES A GROWN WOMAN LIKE?
You may now enter Theater Three...
...for the next showing of Magical Nina.
Please take your tickets...

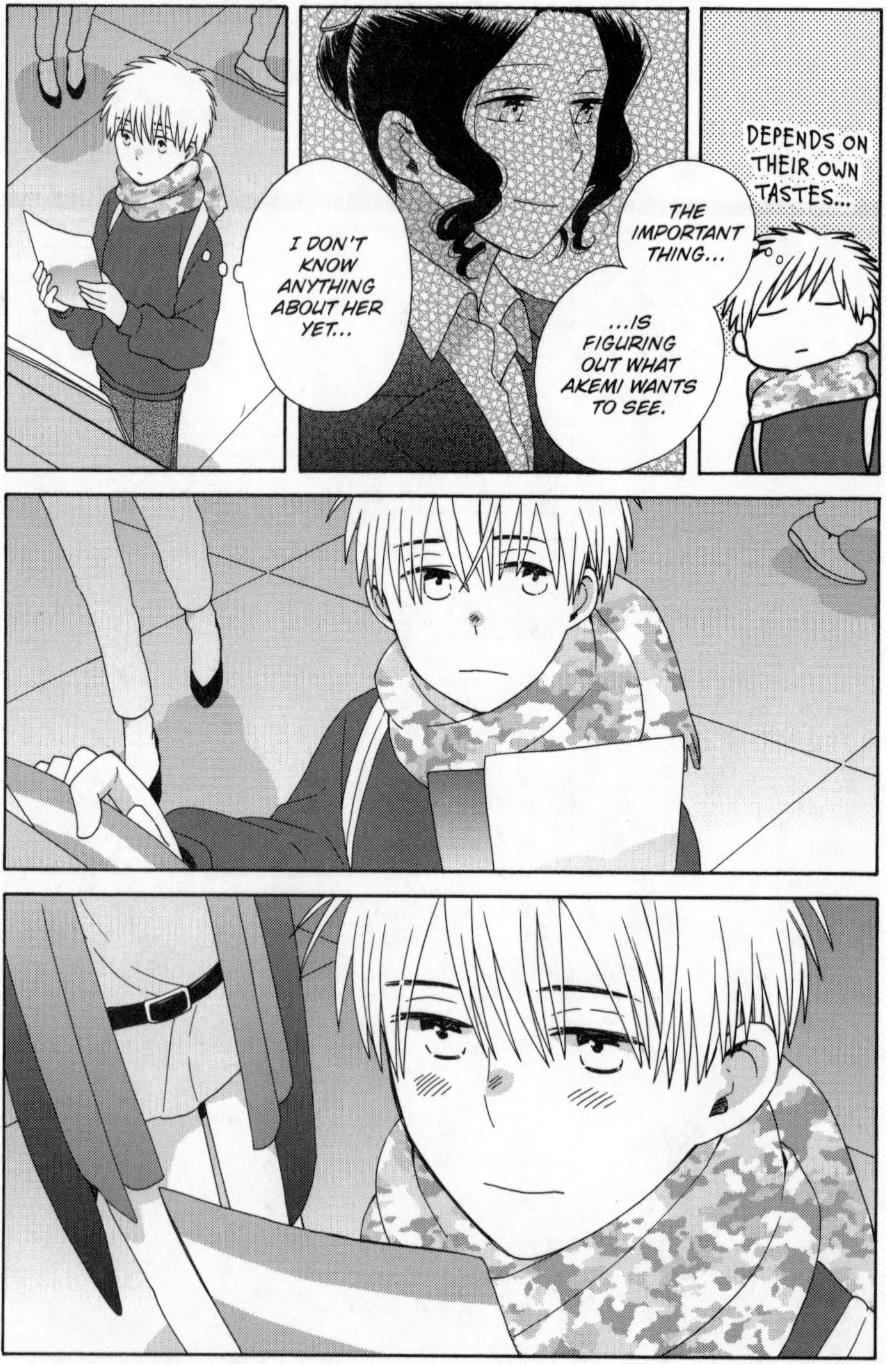
DEPENDS ON THEIR OWN TASTES...
THE IMPORTANT THING...
...IS FIGURING OUT WHAT AKEMI WANTS TO SEE.
I DON'T KNOW ANYTHING ABOUT HER YET...

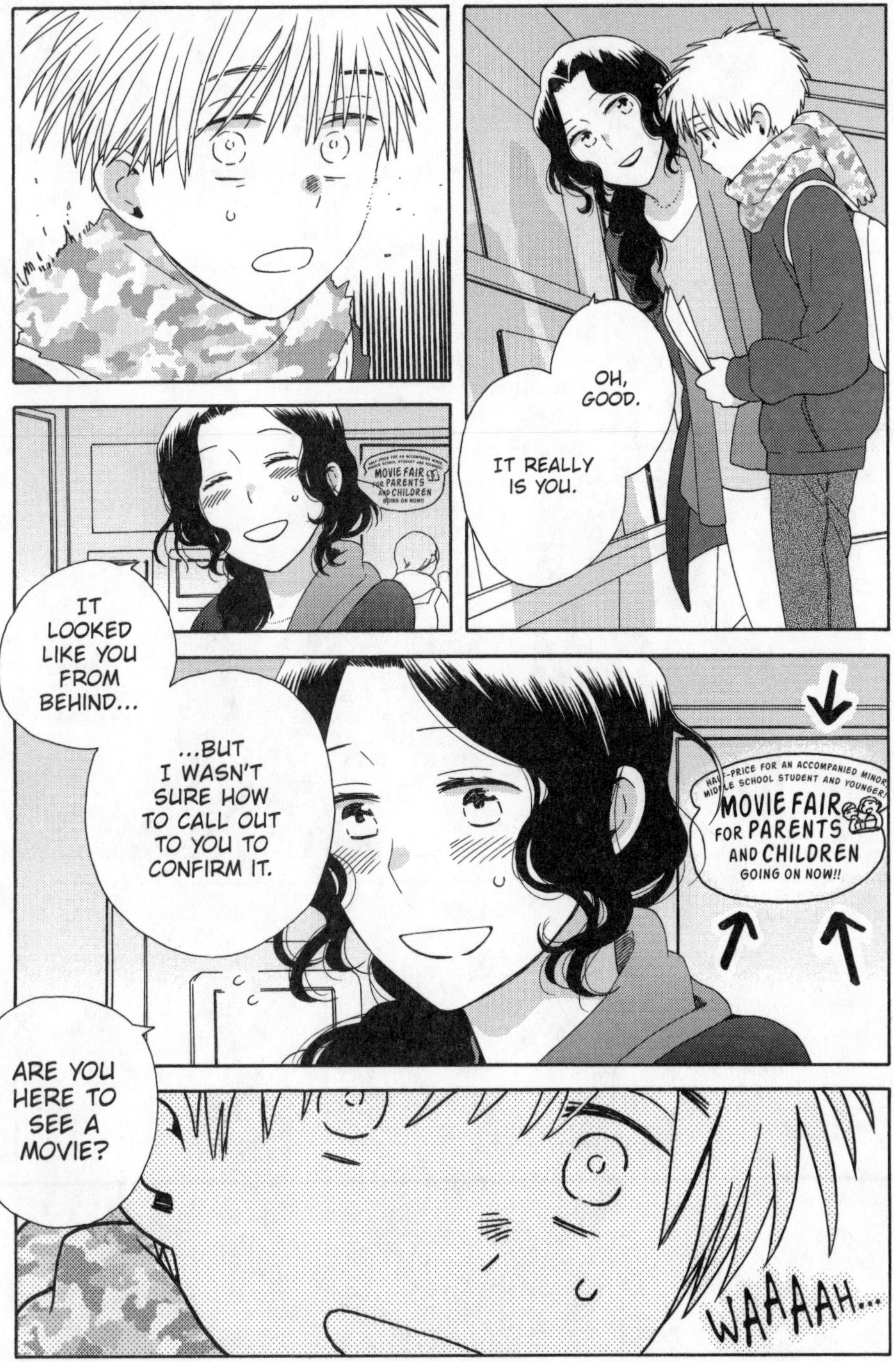
OH, GOOD.
IT REALLY IS YOU.
MOVIE FAIR FOR PARENTS AND CHILDREN GOING ON NOW!!
IT LOOKED LIKE YOU FROM BEHIND...
-PRICE FOR AN ACCOMPANIED MINOR MIDDLE SCHOOL STUDENT AND YOUNGER! MOVIE FAIR FOR PARENTS AND CHILDREN GOING ON NOW!!
...BUT I WASN'T SURE HOW TO CALL OUT TO YOU TO CONFIRM IT.
ARE YOU HERE TO SEE A MOVIE?
WAAAAH...

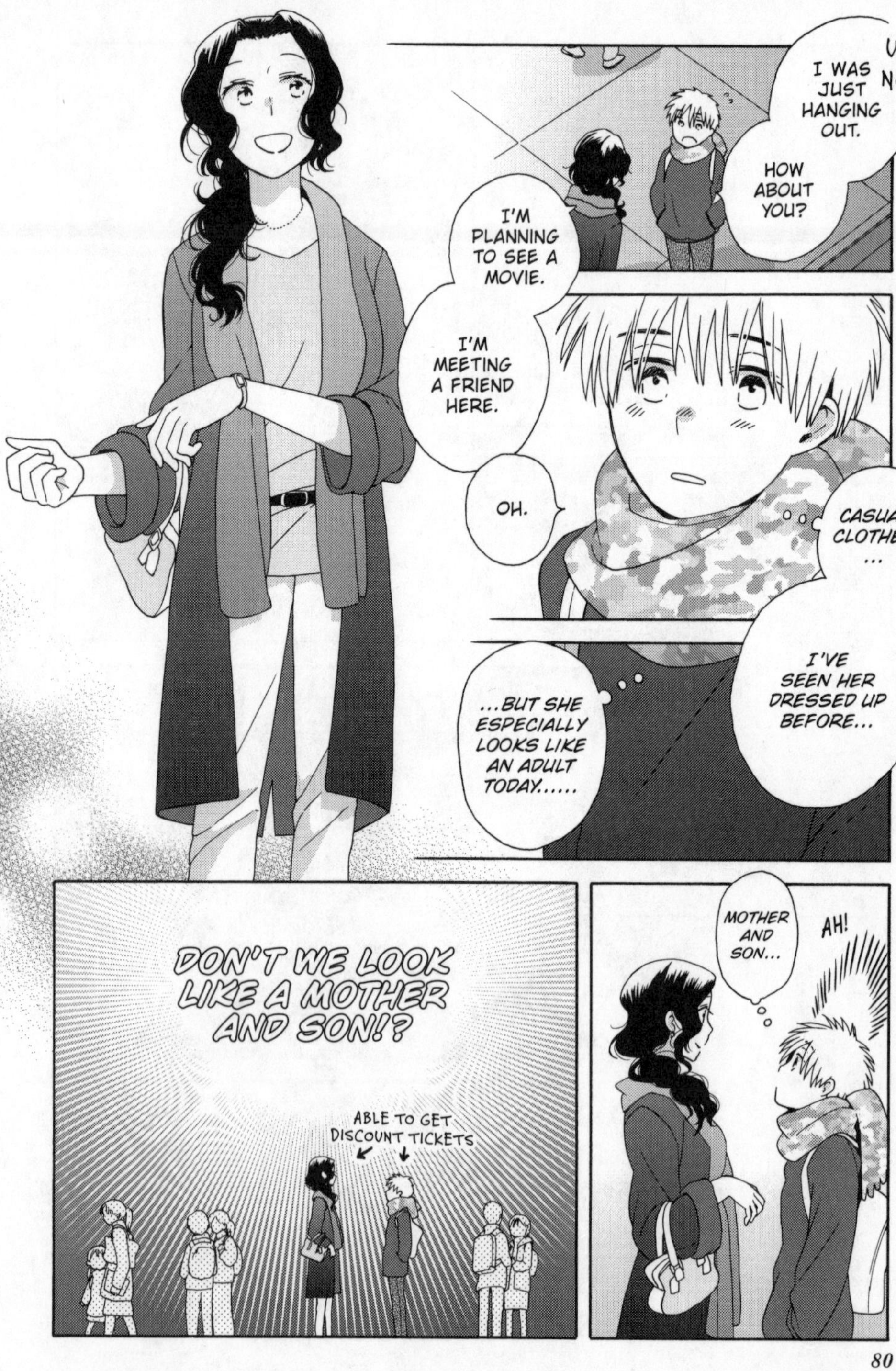
UH, NO.
I WAS JUST HANGING OUT.
HOW ABOUT YOU?
I'M PLANNING TO SEE A MOVIE.
I'M MEETING A FRIEND HERE.
OH.
CASUAL CLOTHES ...
I'VE SEEN HER DRESSED UP BEFORE...
...BUT SHE ESPECIALLY LOOKS LIKE AN ADULT TODAY......
AH!
MOTHER AND SON...
DON'T WE LOOK LIKE A MOTHER AND SON!?
ABLE TO GET DISCOUNT TICKETS

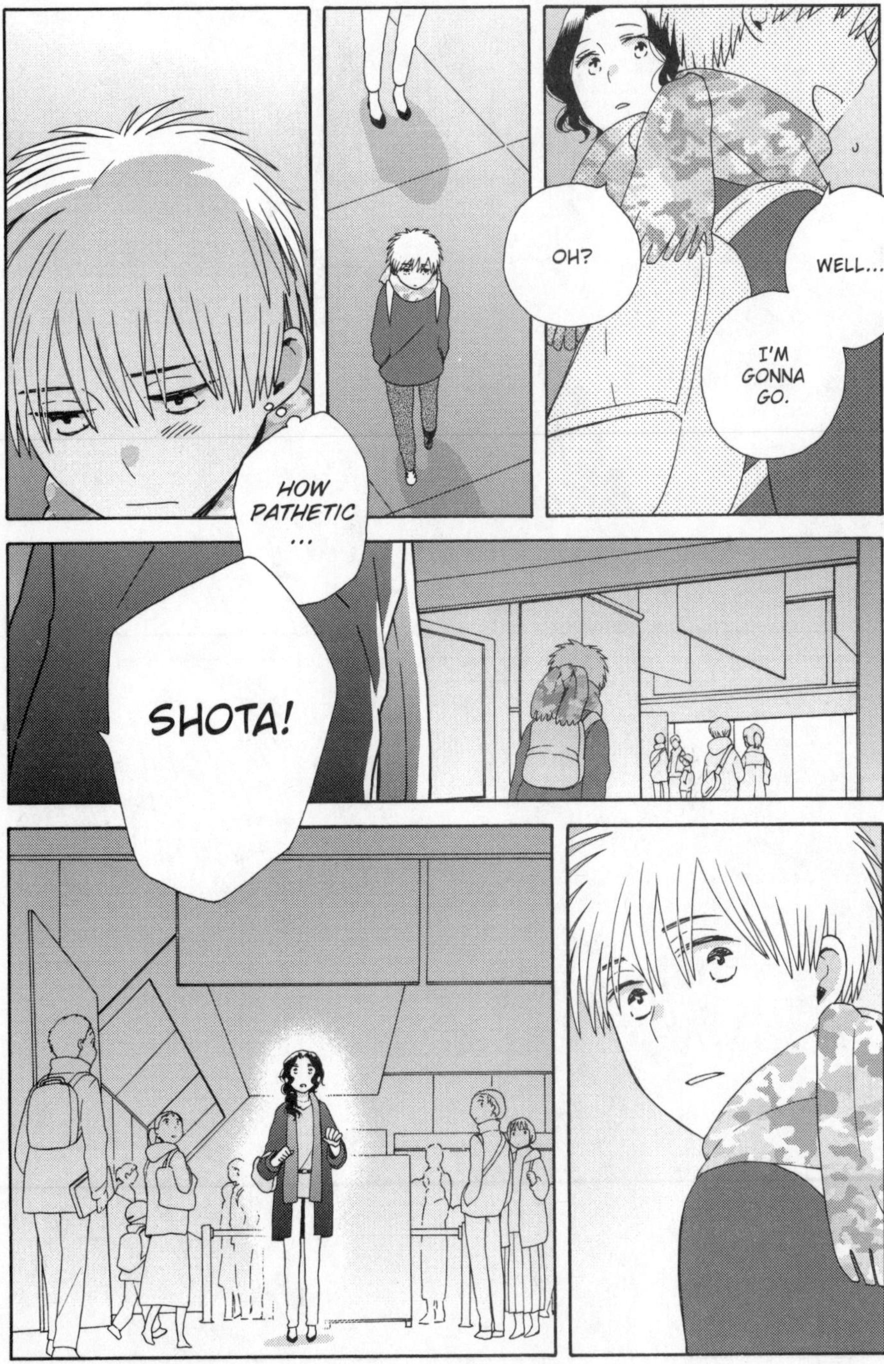
OH?
WELL...
I'M GONNA GO.
HOW PATHETIC...
SHOTA!

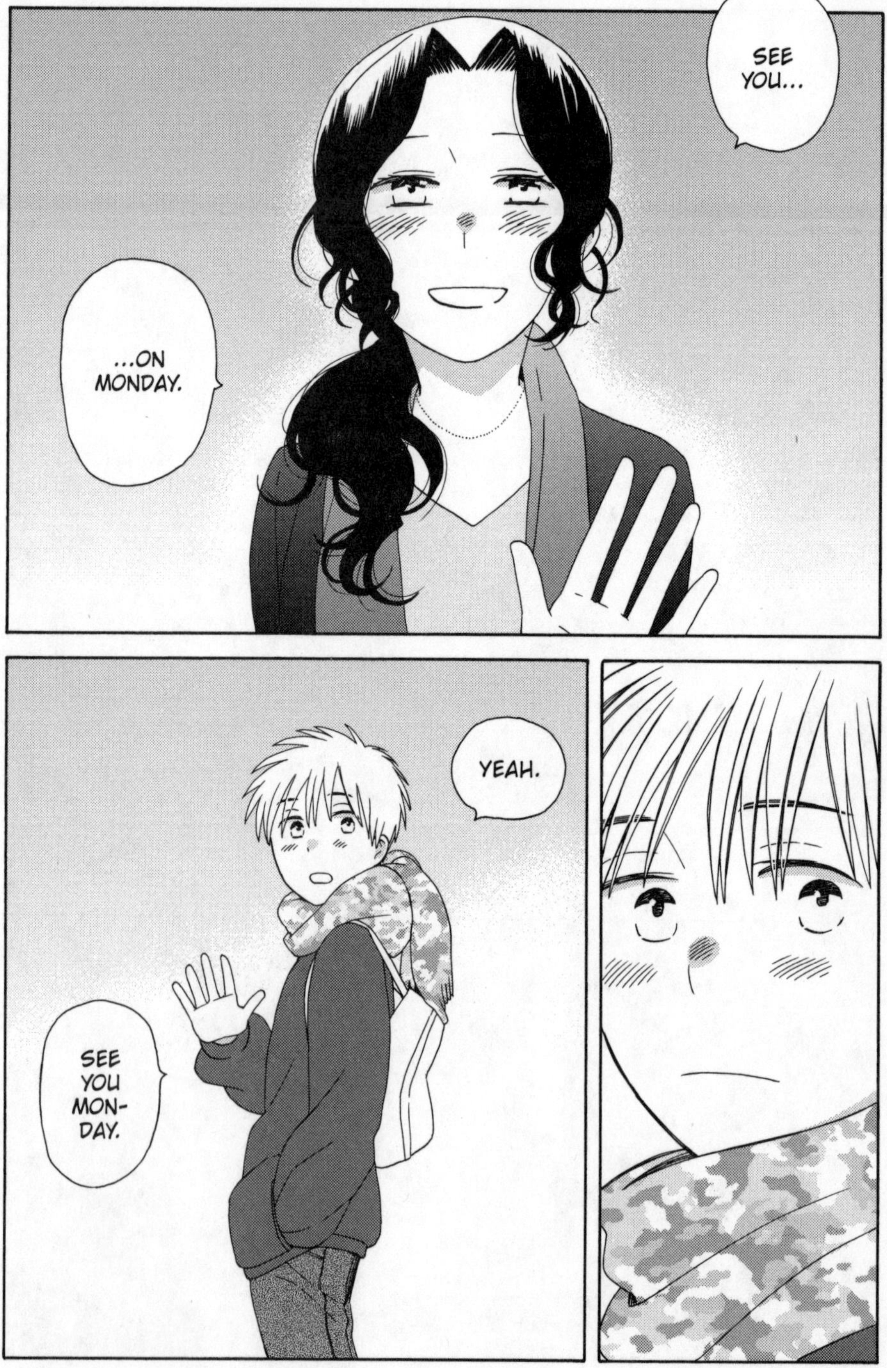
SEE YOU...
...ON MONDAY.
YEAH.
SEE YOU MON-DAY.

SHE COMES TO THE MOVIE THEATER ON SUNDAY...

...AND MAYBE LIKES MOVIES.

I LEARNED SOMETHING ABOUT HER.

"SHOTA!"

SHE CALLED OUT MY NAME.

ALMOST AS IF...

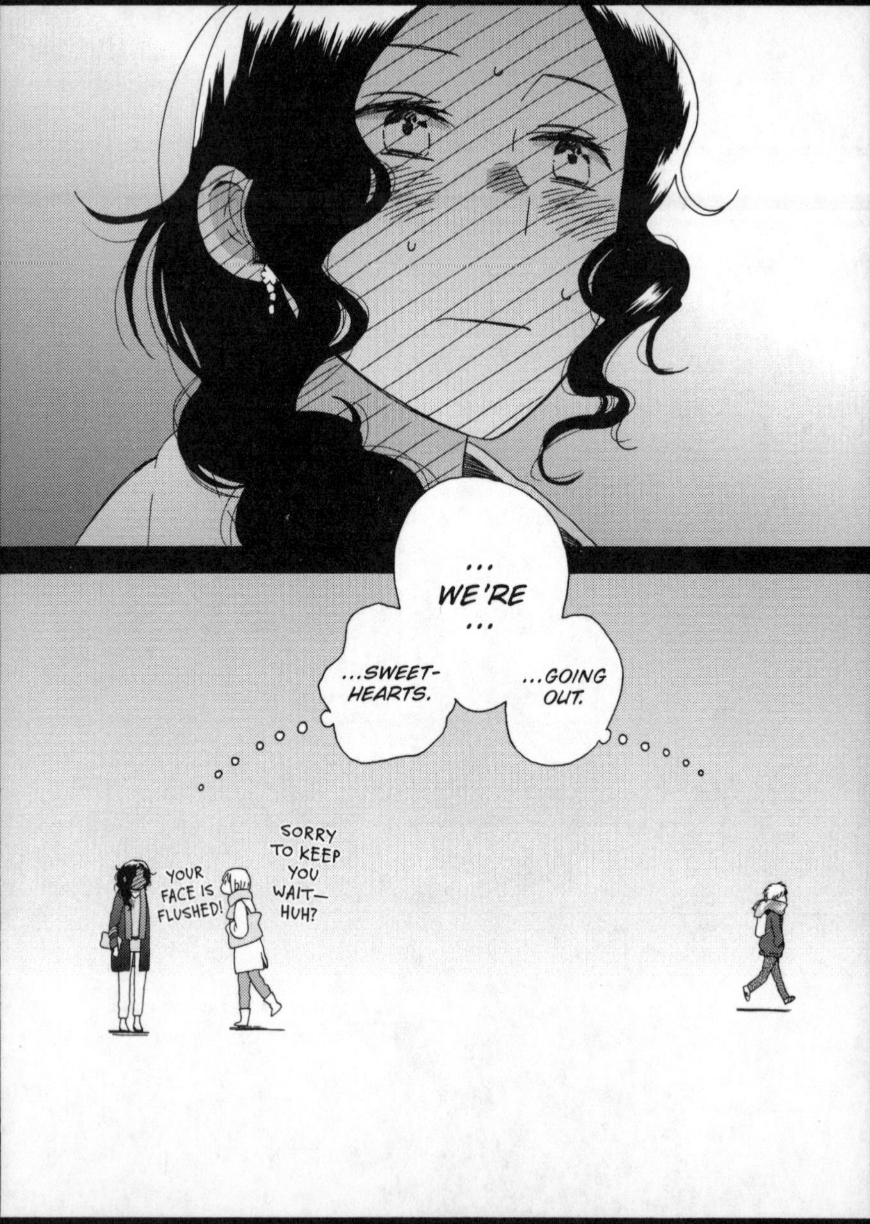
... WE'RE ...
...GOING OUT.
...SWEET-HEARTS.
SORRY TO KEEP YOU WAIT— HUH?
YOUR FACE IS FLUSHED!

Fin

Love at Fourteen

[Chapter 46]

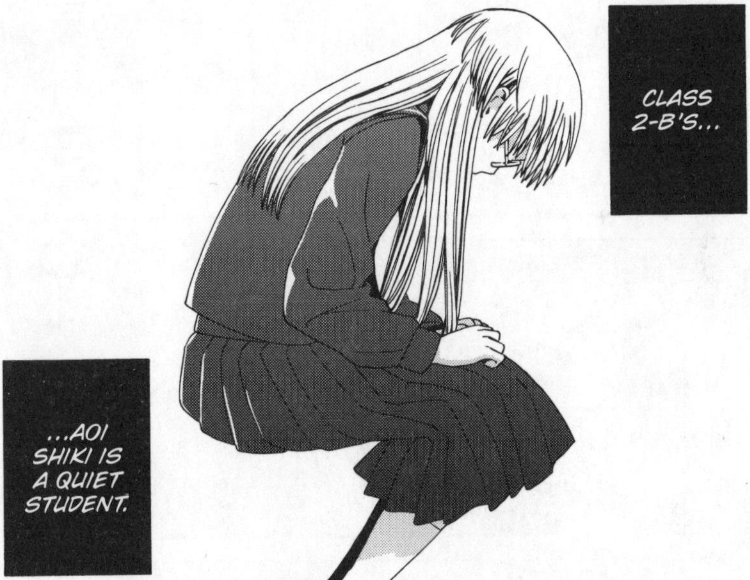
CLASS 2-B'S...
...AOI SHIKI IS A QUIET STUDENT.

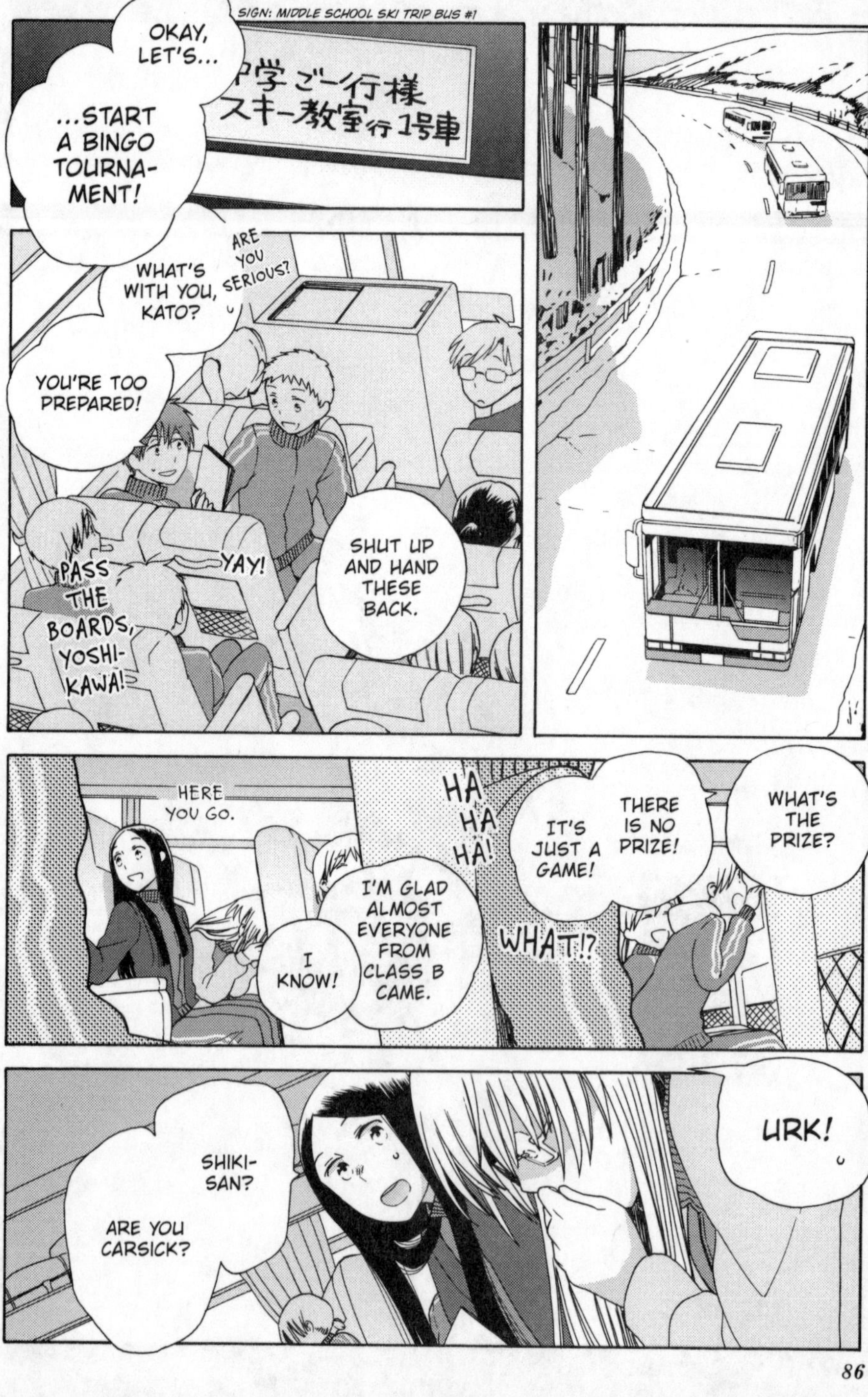
SIGN: MIDDLE SCHOOL SKI TRIP BUS #1
中学ご一行様
スキー教室行1号車
OKAY, LET'S...
...START A BINGO TOURNAMENT!
ARE YOU SERIOUS?
WHAT'S WITH YOU, KATO?
YOU'RE TOO PREPARED!
SHUT UP AND HAND THESE BACK.
YAY!
PASS THE BOARDS, YOSHIKAWA!
WHAT'S THE PRIZE?
THERE IS NO PRIZE!
IT'S JUST A GAME!
WHAT!?
HA HA HA!
I'M GLAD ALMOST EVERYONE FROM CLASS B CAME.
I KNOW!
HERE YOU GO.
URK!
SHIKI-SAN?
ARE YOU CARSICK?

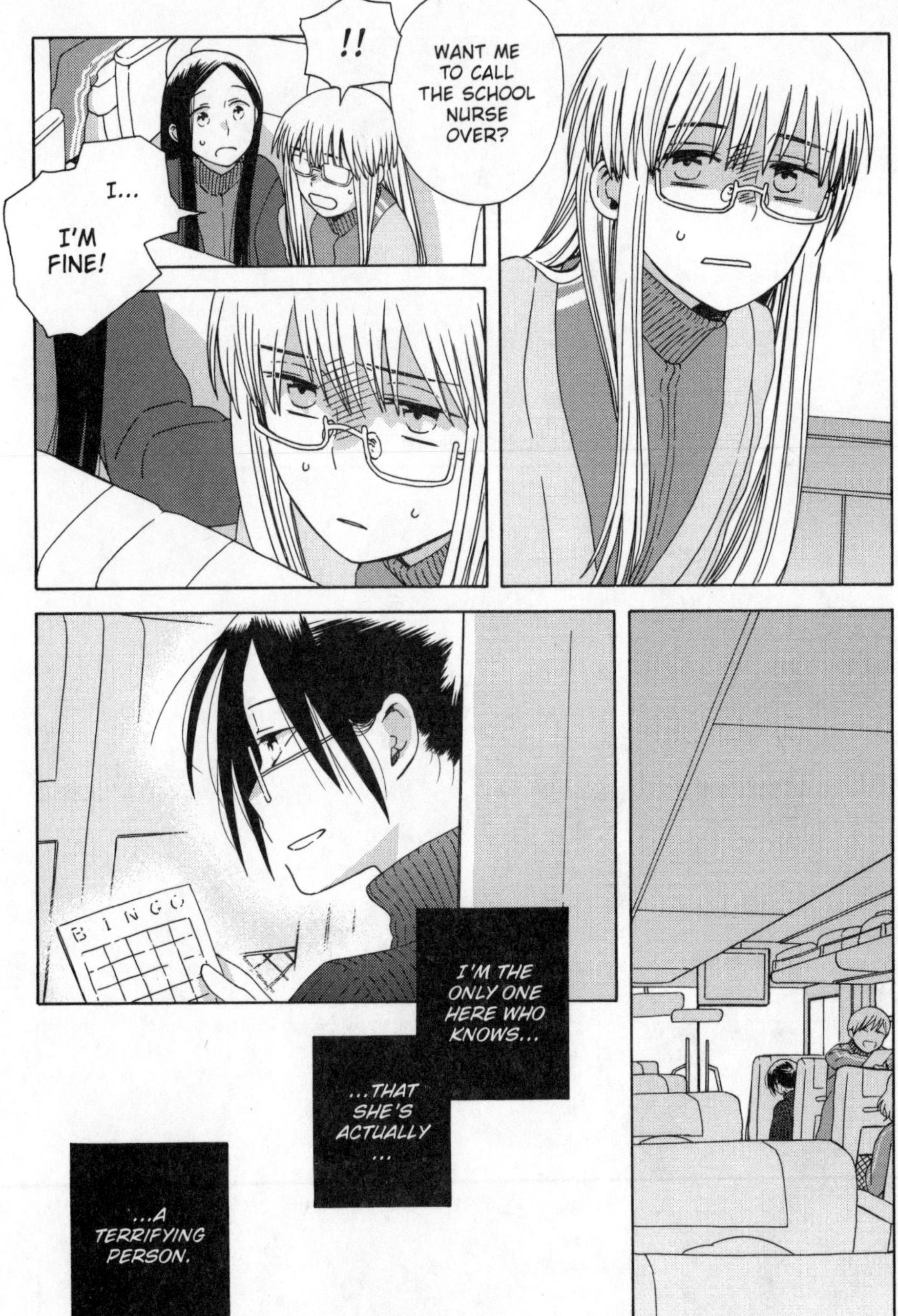
WANT ME TO CALL THE SCHOOL NURSE OVER?
!!
I... I'M FINE!
BINGO
I'M THE ONLY ONE HERE WHO KNOWS...
...THAT SHE'S ACTUALLY...
...A TERRIFYING PERSON.

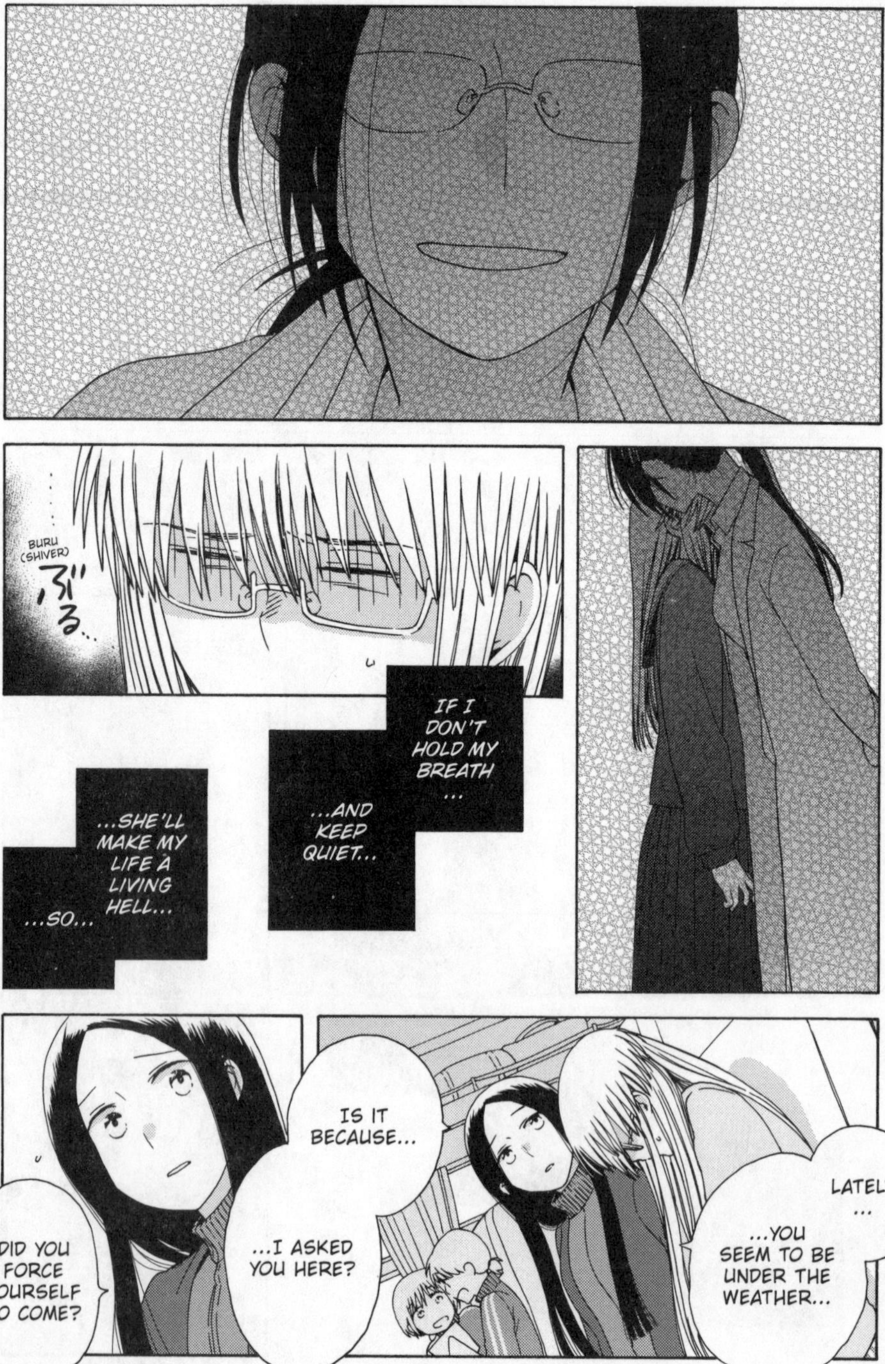
...
BURU (SHIVER)
ぶる...
IF I DON'T HOLD MY BREATH...
...AND KEEP QUIET...
...SHE'LL MAKE MY LIFE A LIVING HELL...
...SO...
LATELY...
...YOU SEEM TO BE UNDER THE WEATHER...
IS IT BECAUSE...
...I ASKED YOU HERE?
DID YOU FORCE YOURSELF TO COME?

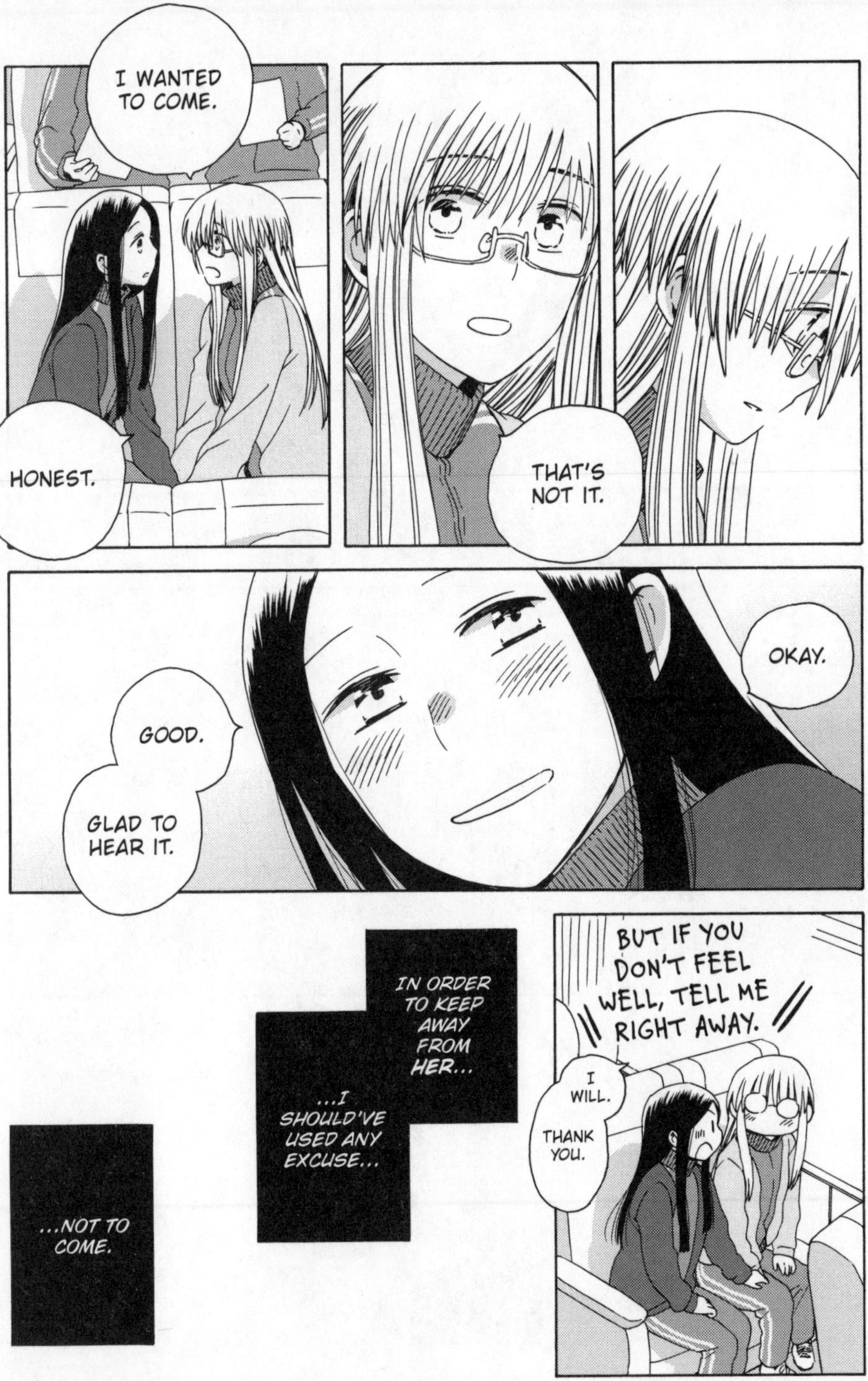
THAT'S NOT IT.
I WANTED TO COME.
HONEST.
OKAY.
GOOD.
GLAD TO HEAR IT.
BUT IF YOU DON'T FEEL WELL, TELL ME RIGHT AWAY.
I WILL.
THANK YOU.
IN ORDER TO KEEP AWAY FROM HER...
...I SHOULD'VE USED ANY EXCUSE...
...NOT TO COME.

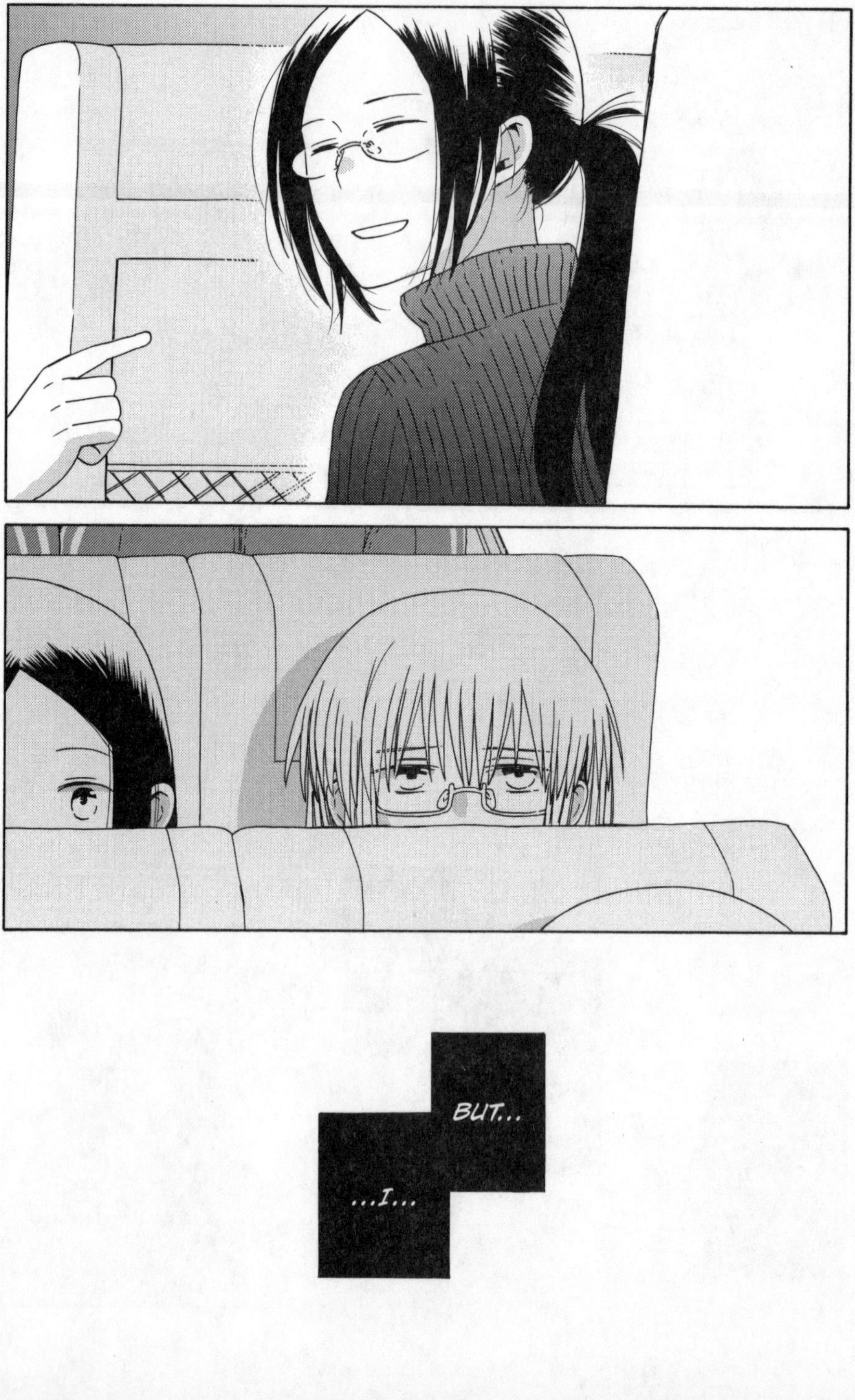
BUT...
...I...

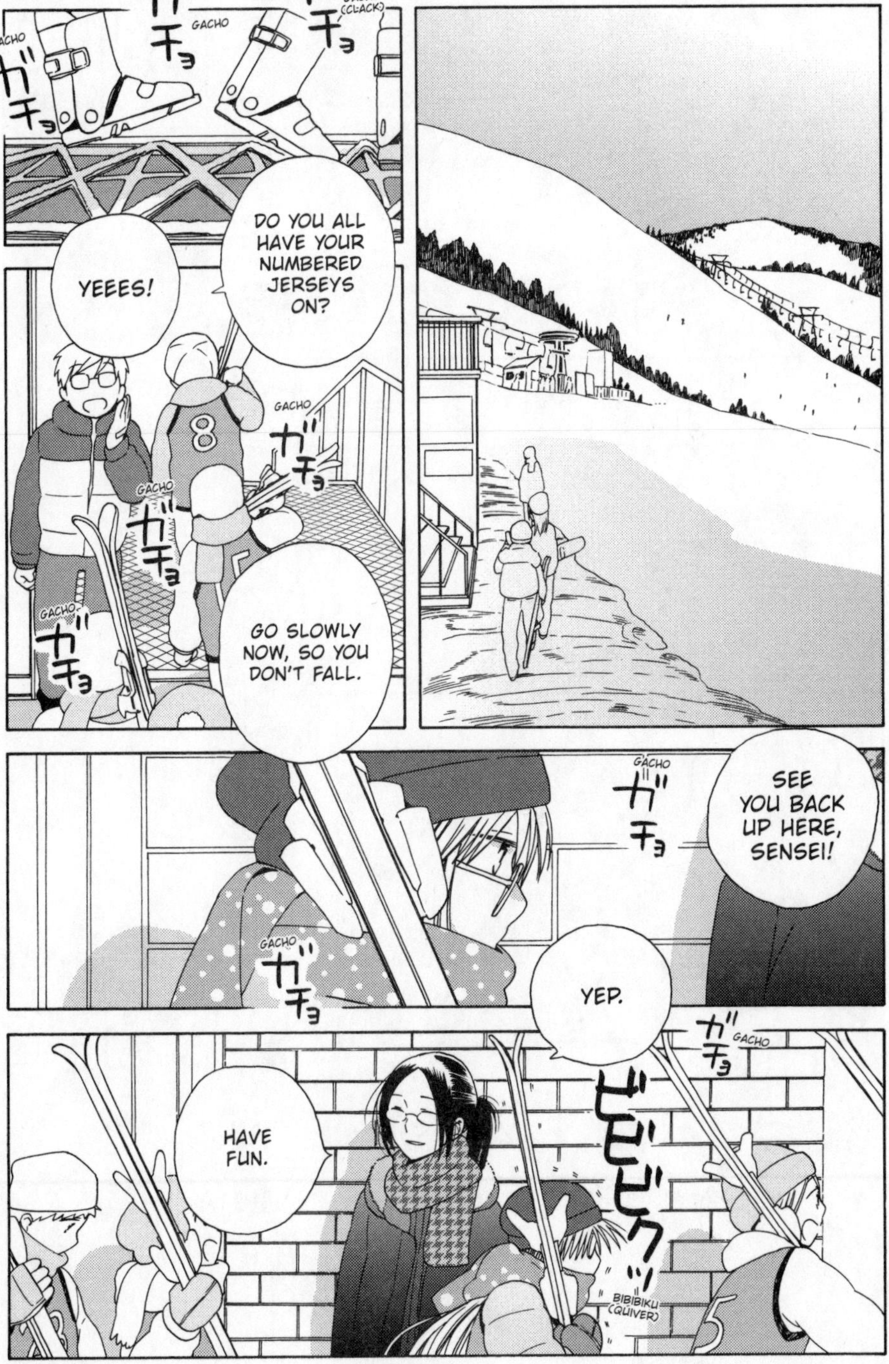
ガチョ
GACHO (CLACK)
ガチョ
GACHO
ガチョ
GACHO
DO YOU ALL HAVE YOUR NUMBERED JERSEYS ON?
YEEES!
ガチョ
GACHO
ガチョ
GACHO
ガチョ
GACHO
GO SLOWLY NOW, SO YOU DON'T FALL.
SEE YOU BACK UP HERE, SENSEI!
ガチョ
GACHO
ガチョ
GACHO
YEP.
ガチョ
GACHO
ビビビクッ
BIBIBIKU (QUIVER)
HAVE FUN.

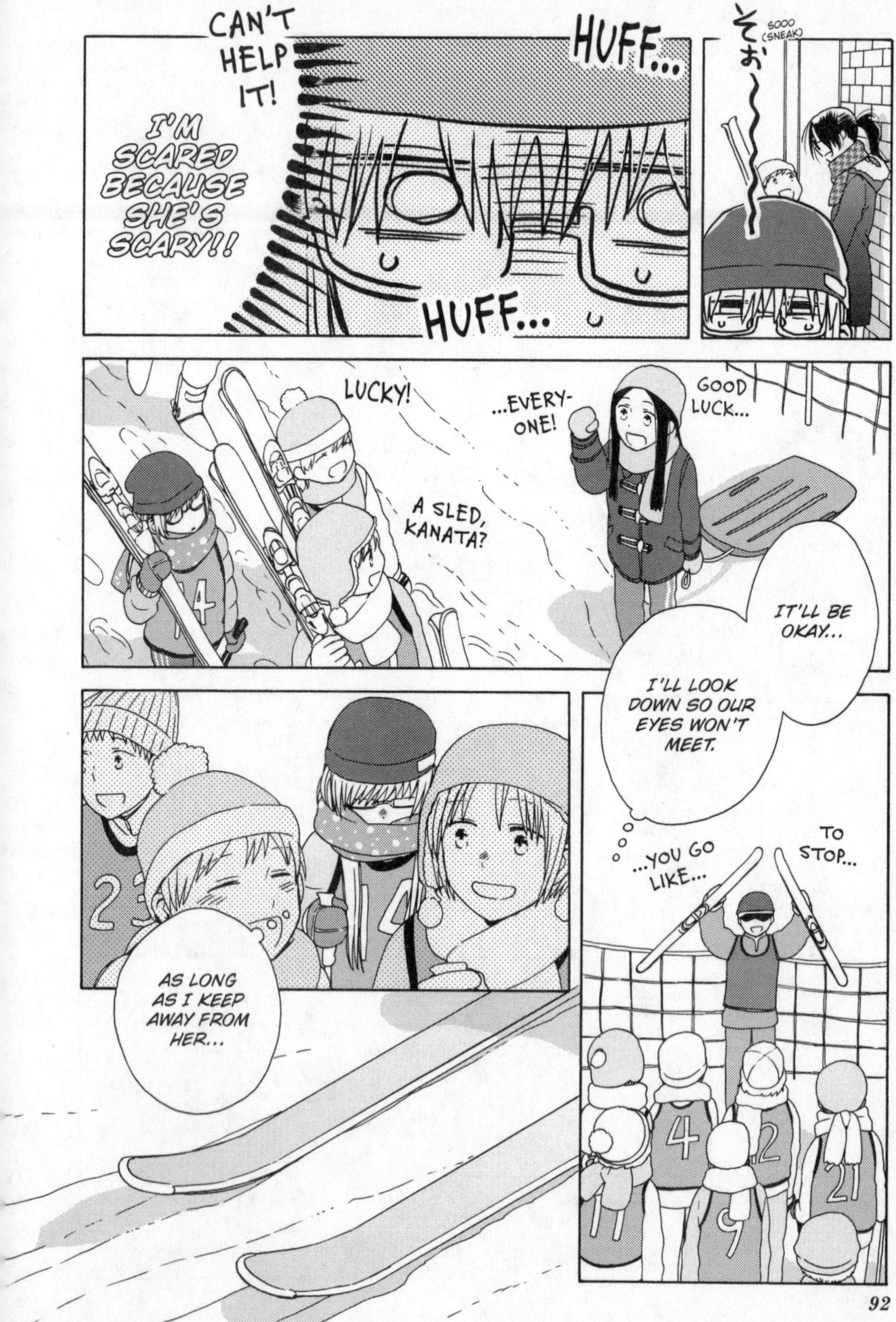
そぉ~~~
SOOO (SNEAK)
HUFF...
CAN'T HELP IT!
I'M SCARED BECAUSE SHE'S SCARY!!
HUFF...
GOOD LUCK...
...EVERY-ONE!
LUCKY!
A SLED, KANATA?
IT'LL BE OKAY...
I'LL LOOK DOWN SO OUR EYES WON'T MEET.
TO STOP...
...YOU GO LIKE...
AS LONG AS I KEEP AWAY FROM HER...

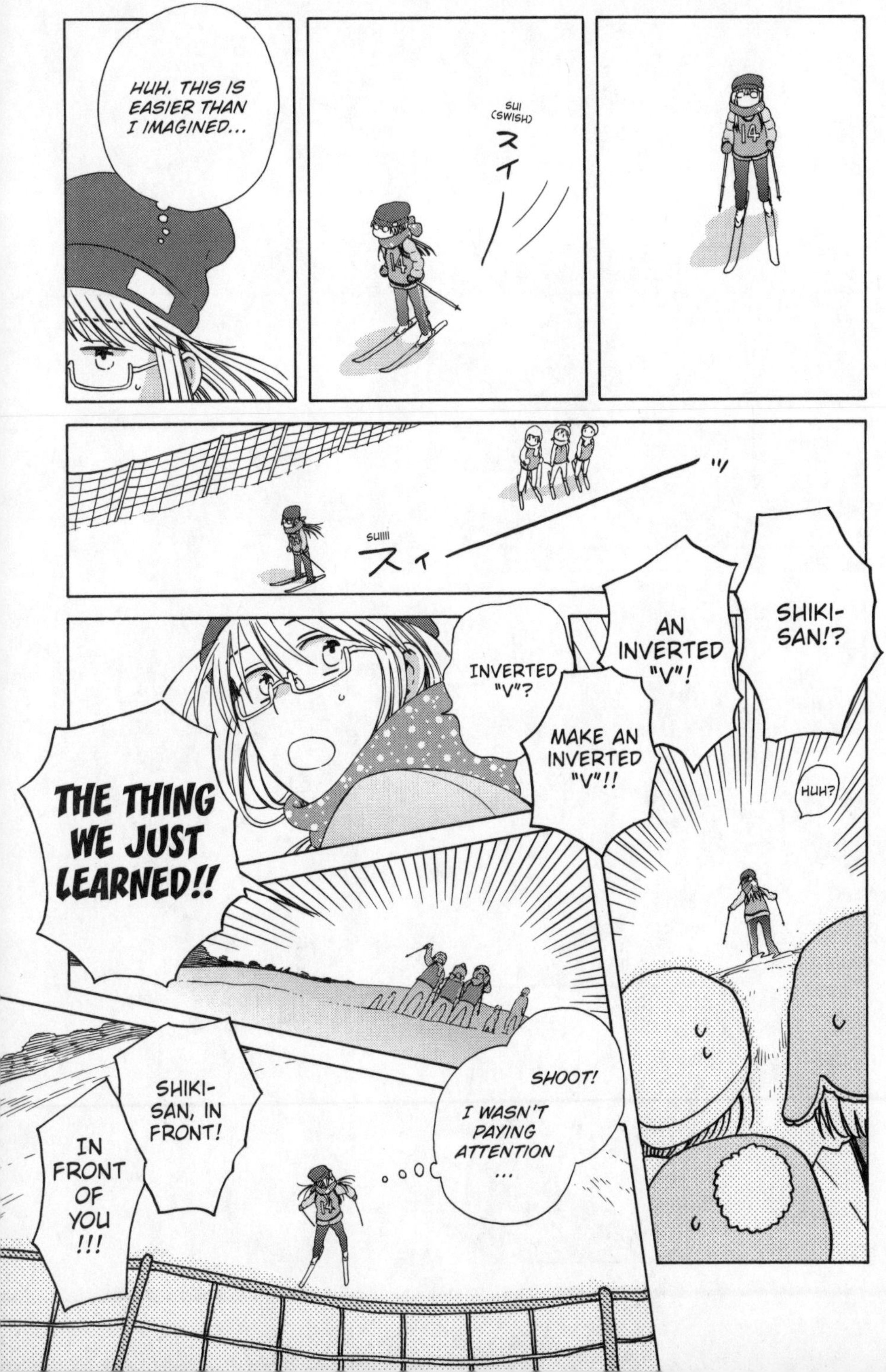
SUI (SWISH)
スイ
HUH. THIS IS EASIER THAN I IMAGINED...
ッ
SUIII
スィ
SHIKI-SAN!?
AN INVERTED "V"!
MAKE AN INVERTED "V"!!
HUH?
INVERTED "V"?
THE THING WE JUST LEARNED!!
SHOOT!
I WASN'T PAYING ATTENTION...
SHIKI-SAN, IN FRONT!
IN FRONT OF YOU!!!

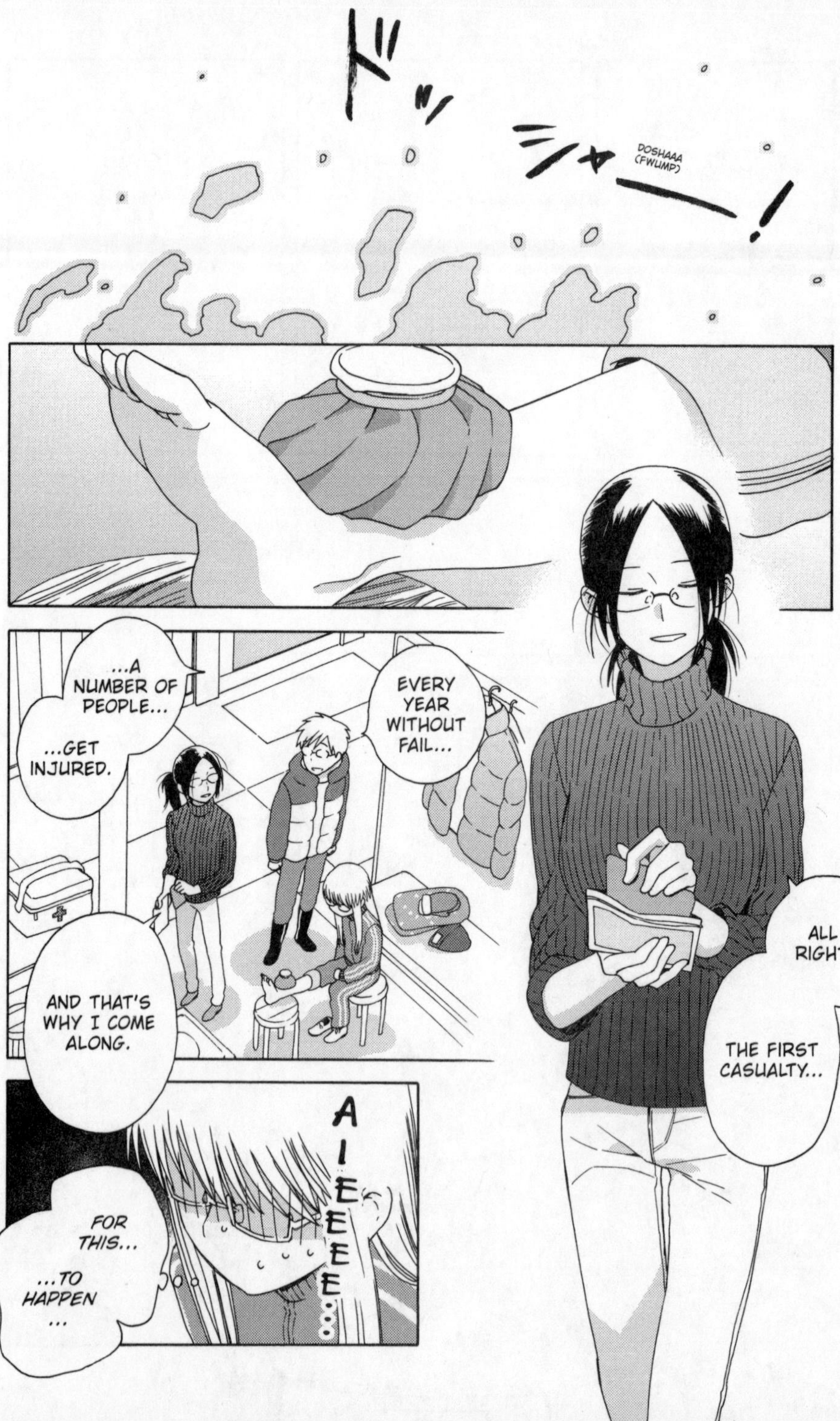
ドッシャー!
DOSHAAA (FWUMP)
ALL RIGHT.
THE FIRST CASUALTY...
EVERY YEAR WITHOUT FAIL...
...A NUMBER OF PEOPLE...
...GET INJURED.
AND THAT'S WHY I COME ALONG.
FOR THIS...
...TO HAPPEN...
AIEEEE...

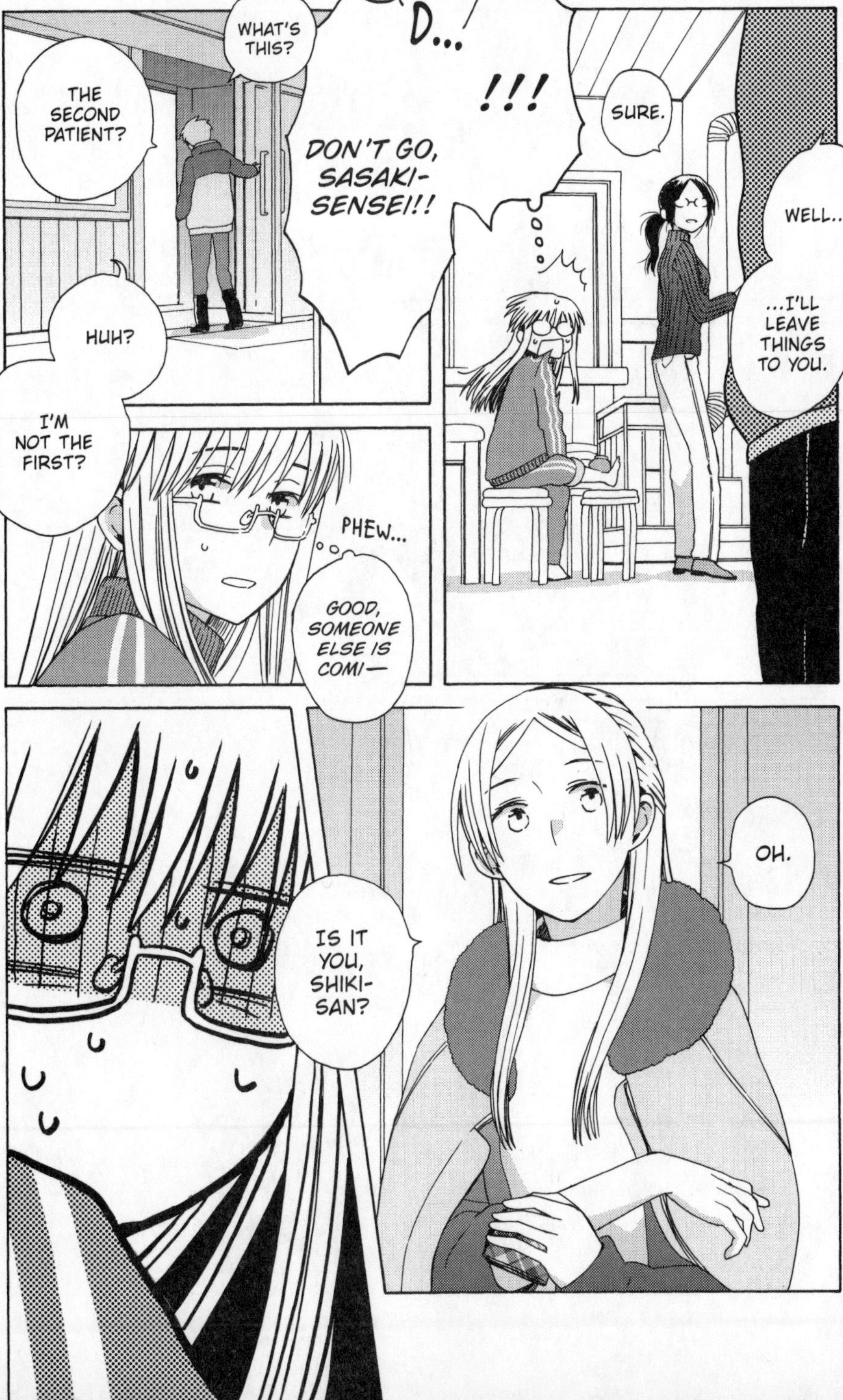
WELL...
...I'LL LEAVE THINGS TO YOU.
SURE.
D...
!!!
DON'T GO, SASAKI-SENSEI!!!
WHAT'S THIS?
THE SECOND PATIENT?
HUH?
I'M NOT THE FIRST?
PHEW...
GOOD, SOMEONE ELSE IS COMI—
OH.
IS IT YOU, SHIKI-SAN?

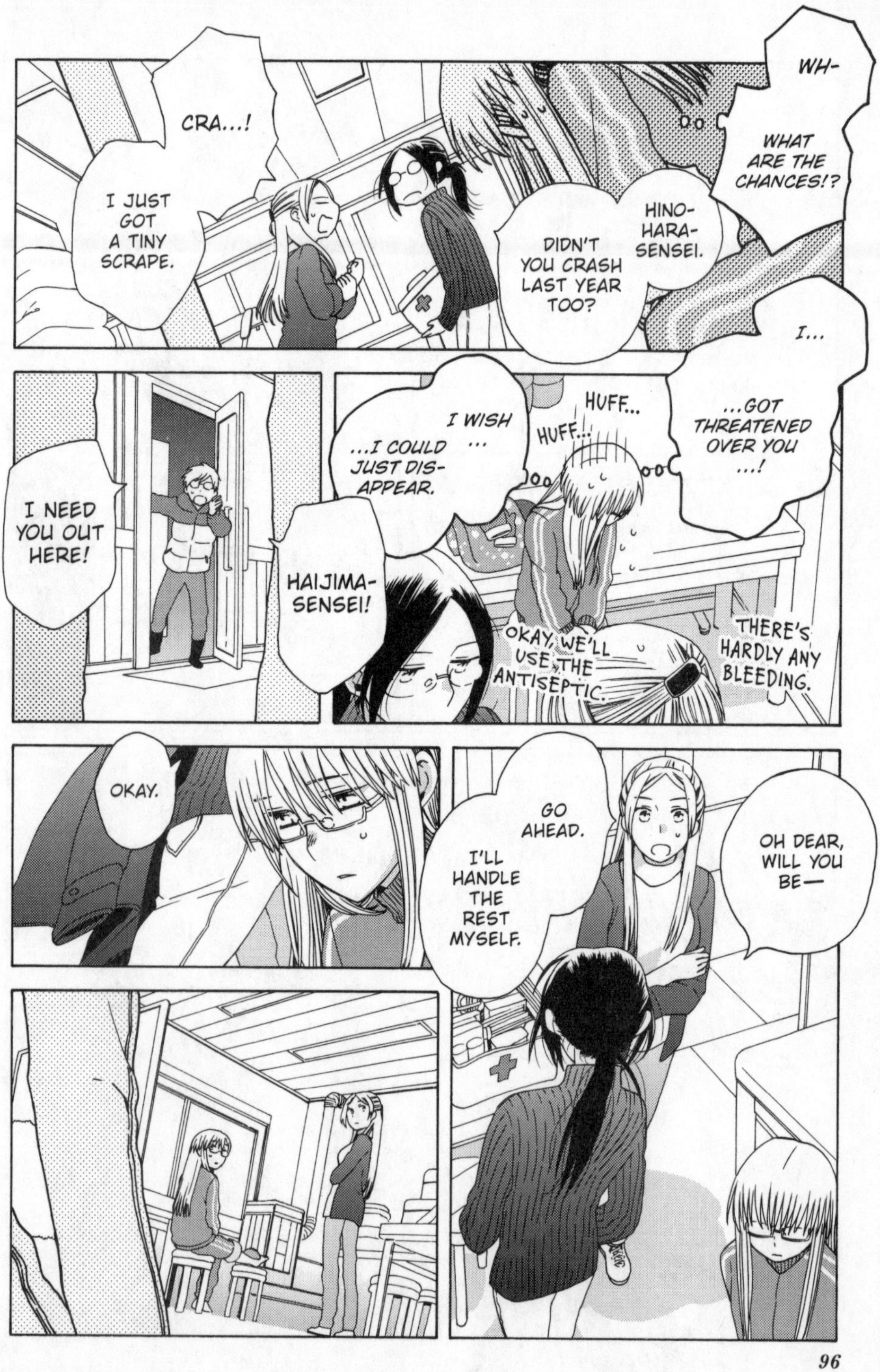
WH-
WHAT ARE THE CHANCES!?
HINO-HARA-SENSEI.
DIDN'T YOU CRASH LAST YEAR TOO?
CRA...!
I JUST GOT A TINY SCRAPE.
I...
...GOT THREATENED OVER YOU ...!
HUFF...
HUFF...
I WISH ...
...I COULD JUST DIS-APPEAR.
HAIJIMA-SENSEI!
THERE'S HARDLY ANY BLEEDING.
OKAY, WE'LL USE THE ANTISEPTIC.
I NEED YOU OUT HERE!
OH DEAR, WILL YOU BE—
GO AHEAD.
I'LL HANDLE THE REST MYSELF.
OKAY.

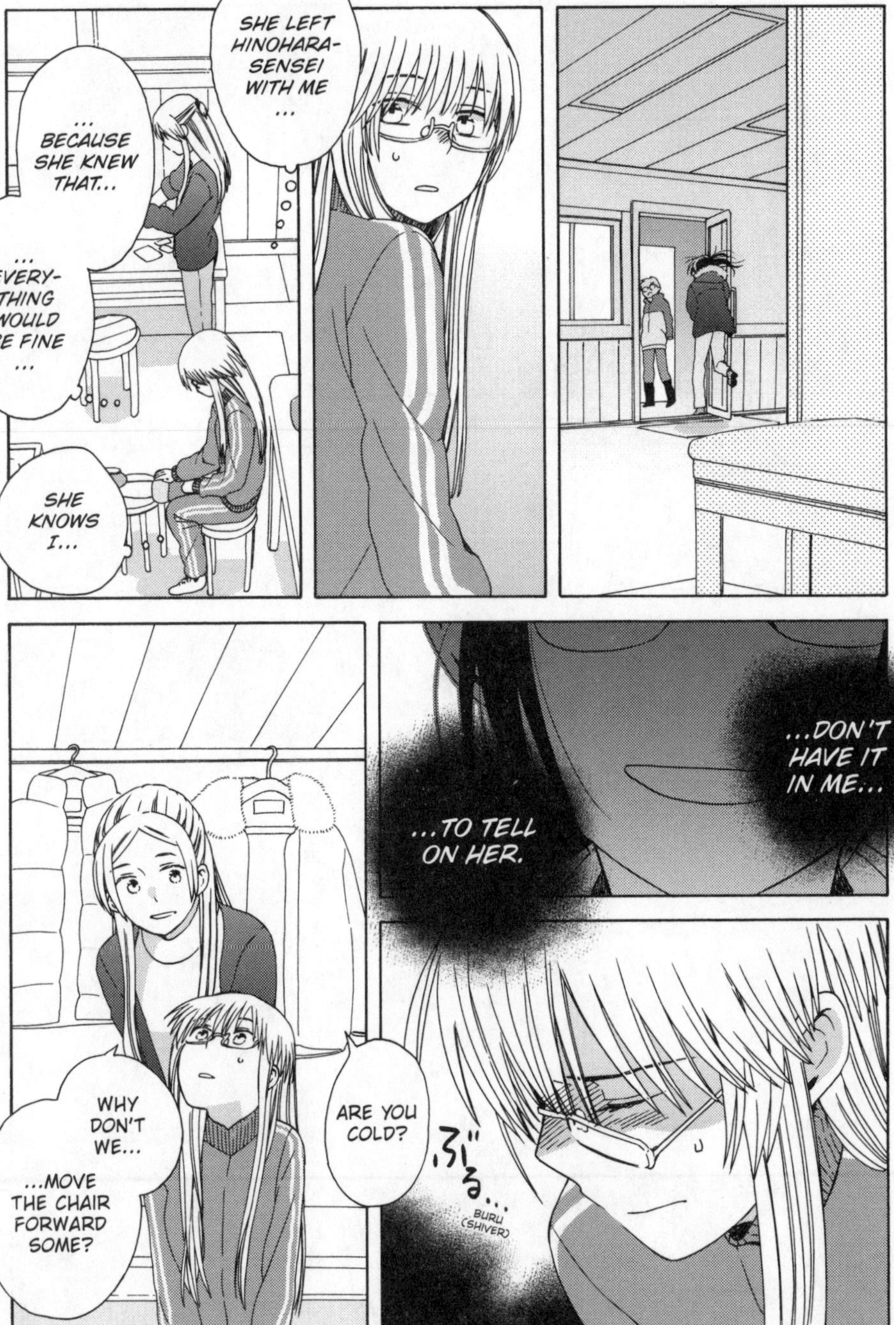
SHE LEFT HINOHARA-SENSEI WITH ME...
...BECAUSE SHE KNEW THAT...
...EVERYTHING WOULD BE FINE...
SHE KNOWS I...
...DON'T HAVE IT IN ME...
...TO TELL ON HER.
ぶる…
BURU (SHIVER)
ARE YOU COLD?
WHY DON'T WE...
...MOVE THE CHAIR FORWARD SOME?

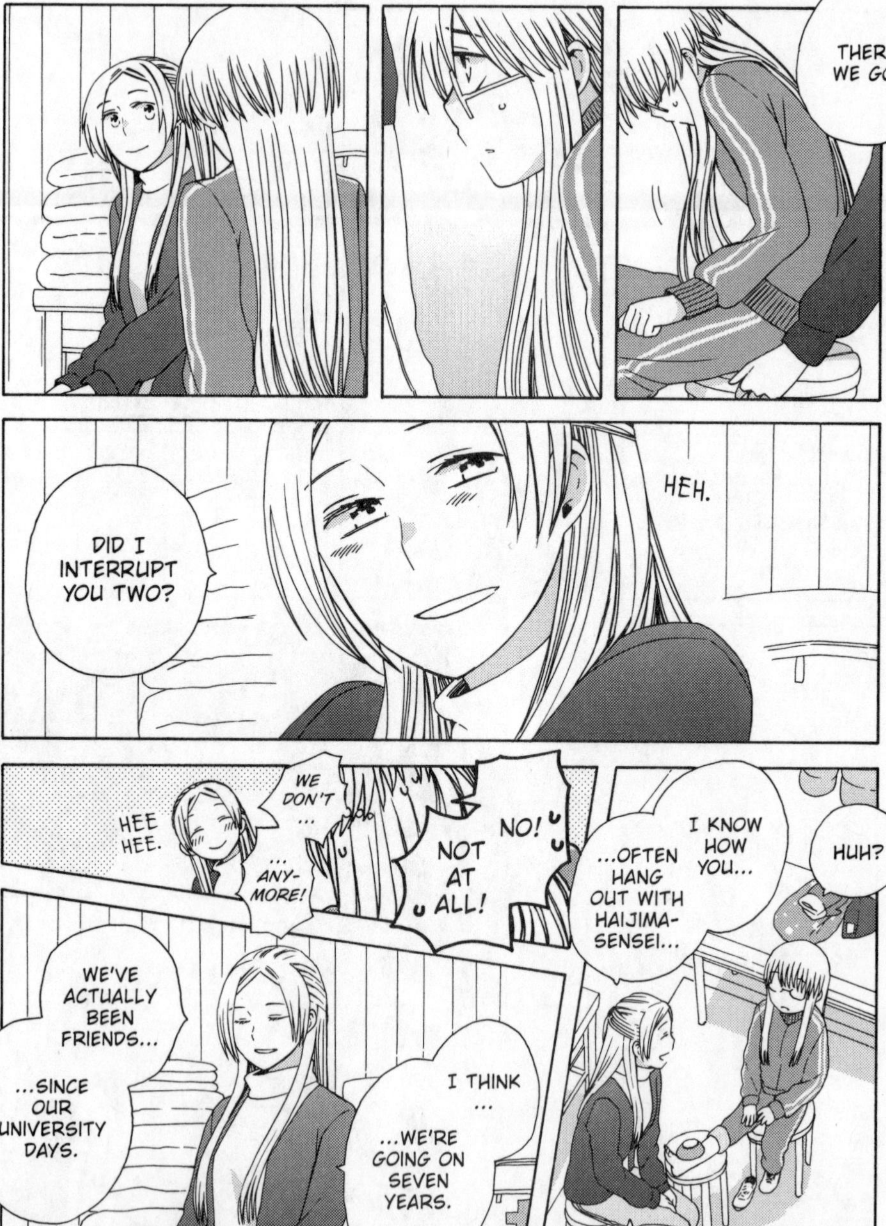
THERE WE GO.
HEH.
DID I INTERRUPT YOU TWO?
HUH?
I KNOW HOW YOU...
...OFTEN HANG OUT WITH HAIJIMA-SENSEI...
...IN THE INFIRMARY.
NO! NOT AT ALL!
WE DON'T ...
... ANYMORE!
HEE HEE.
WE'VE ACTUALLY BEEN FRIENDS...
...SINCE OUR UNIVERSITY DAYS.
I THINK ...
...WE'RE GOING ON SEVEN YEARS.

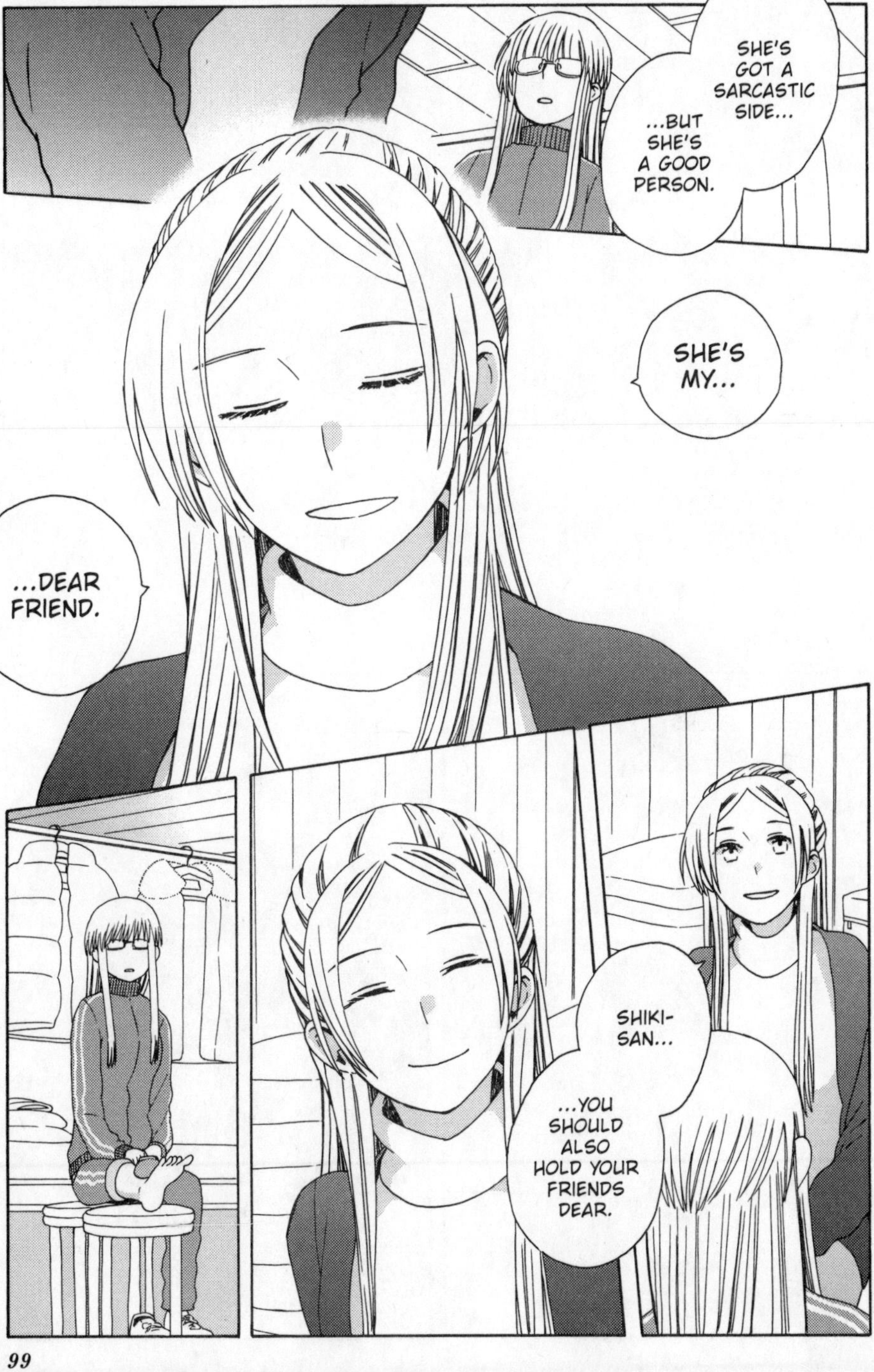
SHE'S GOT A SARCASTIC SIDE...
...BUT SHE'S A GOOD PERSON.
SHE'S MY...
...DEAR FRIEND.
SHIKI-SAN...
...YOU SHOULD ALSO HOLD YOUR FRIENDS DEAR.

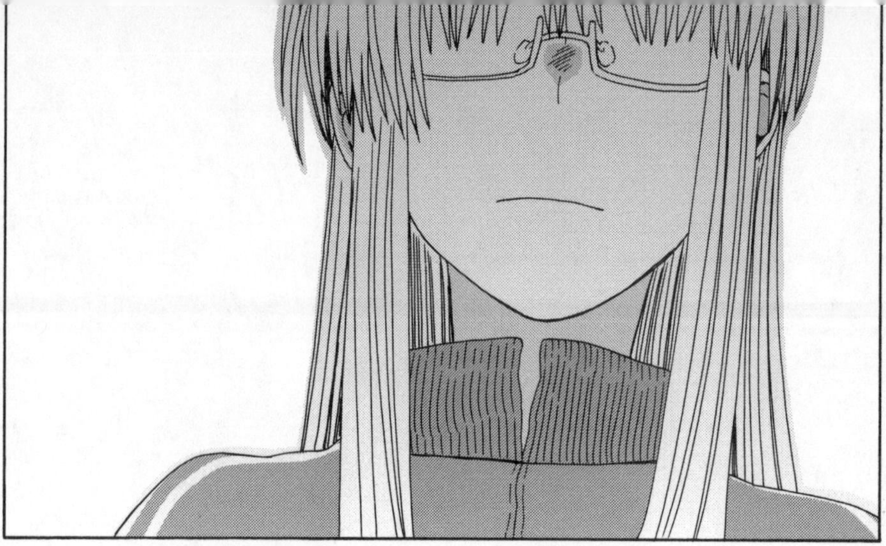
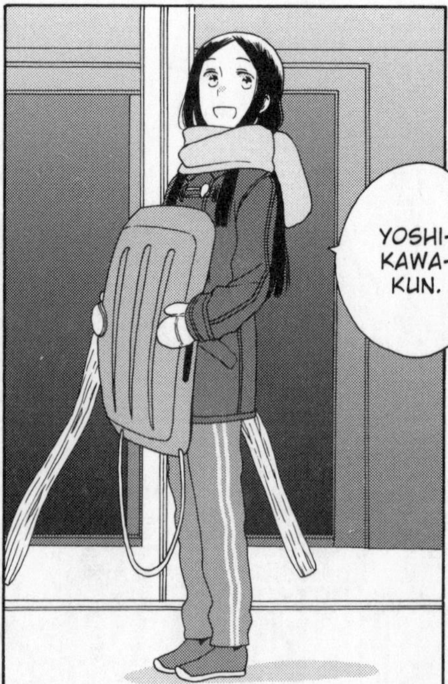
YOSHI-
KAWA-
KUN.
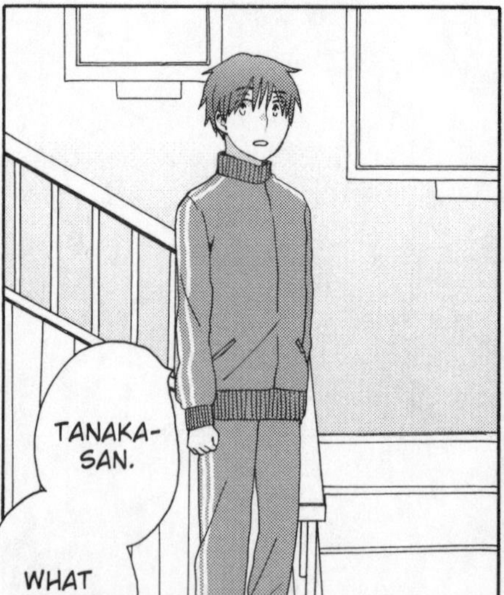
TANAKA-
SAN.
WHAT
ARE YOU
DOING?

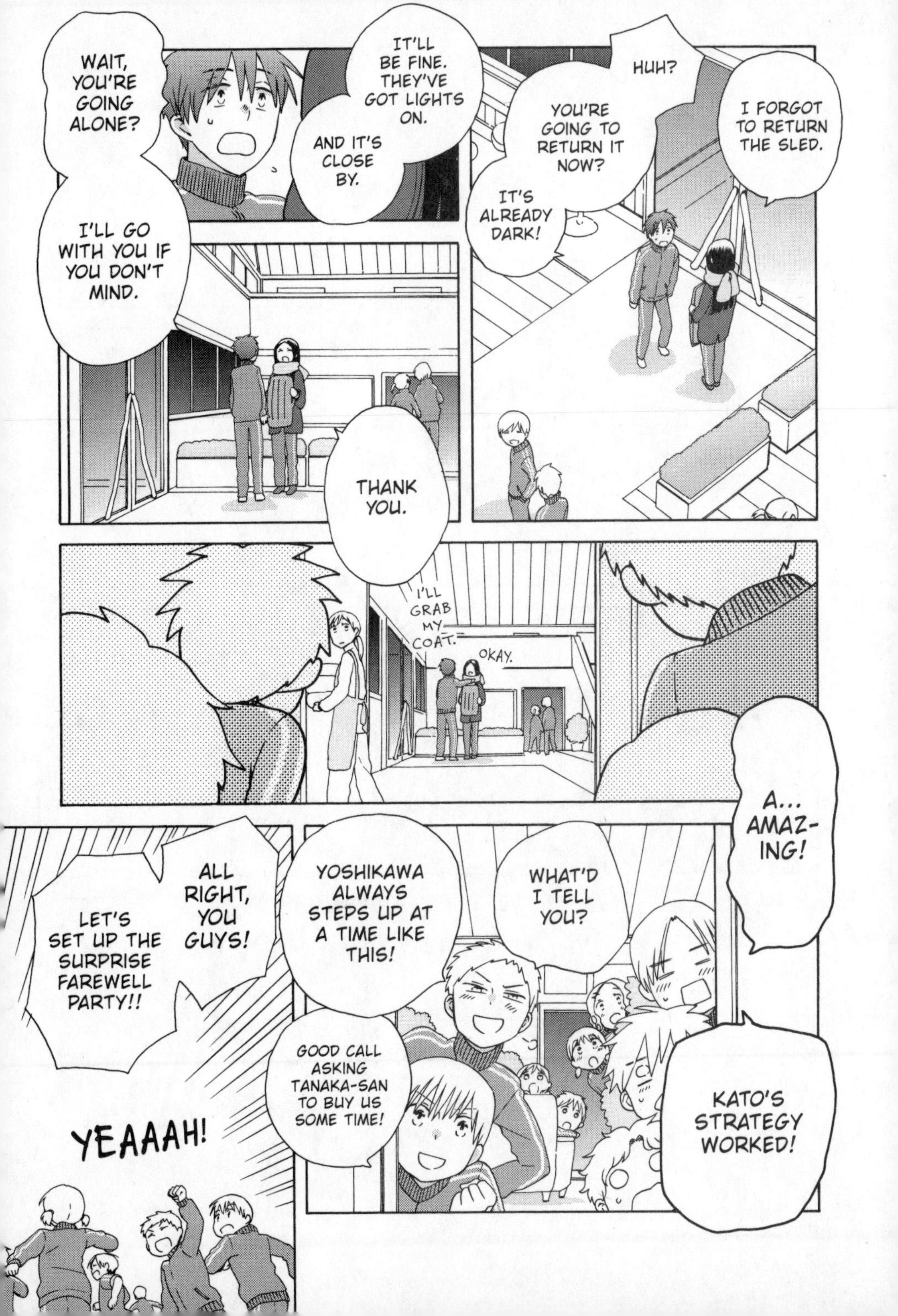
I FORGOT TO RETURN THE SLED.
HUH?
YOU'RE GOING TO RETURN IT NOW?
IT'S ALREADY DARK!
IT'LL BE FINE. THEY'VE GOT LIGHTS ON.
AND IT'S CLOSE BY.
WAIT, YOU'RE GOING ALONE?
I'LL GO WITH YOU IF YOU DON'T MIND.
THANK YOU.
I'LL GRAB MY COAT.
OKAY.
A... AMAZ-ING!
WHAT'D I TELL YOU?
YOSHIKAWA ALWAYS STEPS UP AT A TIME LIKE THIS!
KATO'S STRATEGY WORKED!
GOOD CALL ASKING TANAKA-SAN TO BUY US SOME TIME!
ALL RIGHT, YOU GUYS!
LET'S SET UP THE SURPRISE FAREWELL PARTY!!
YEAAAH!

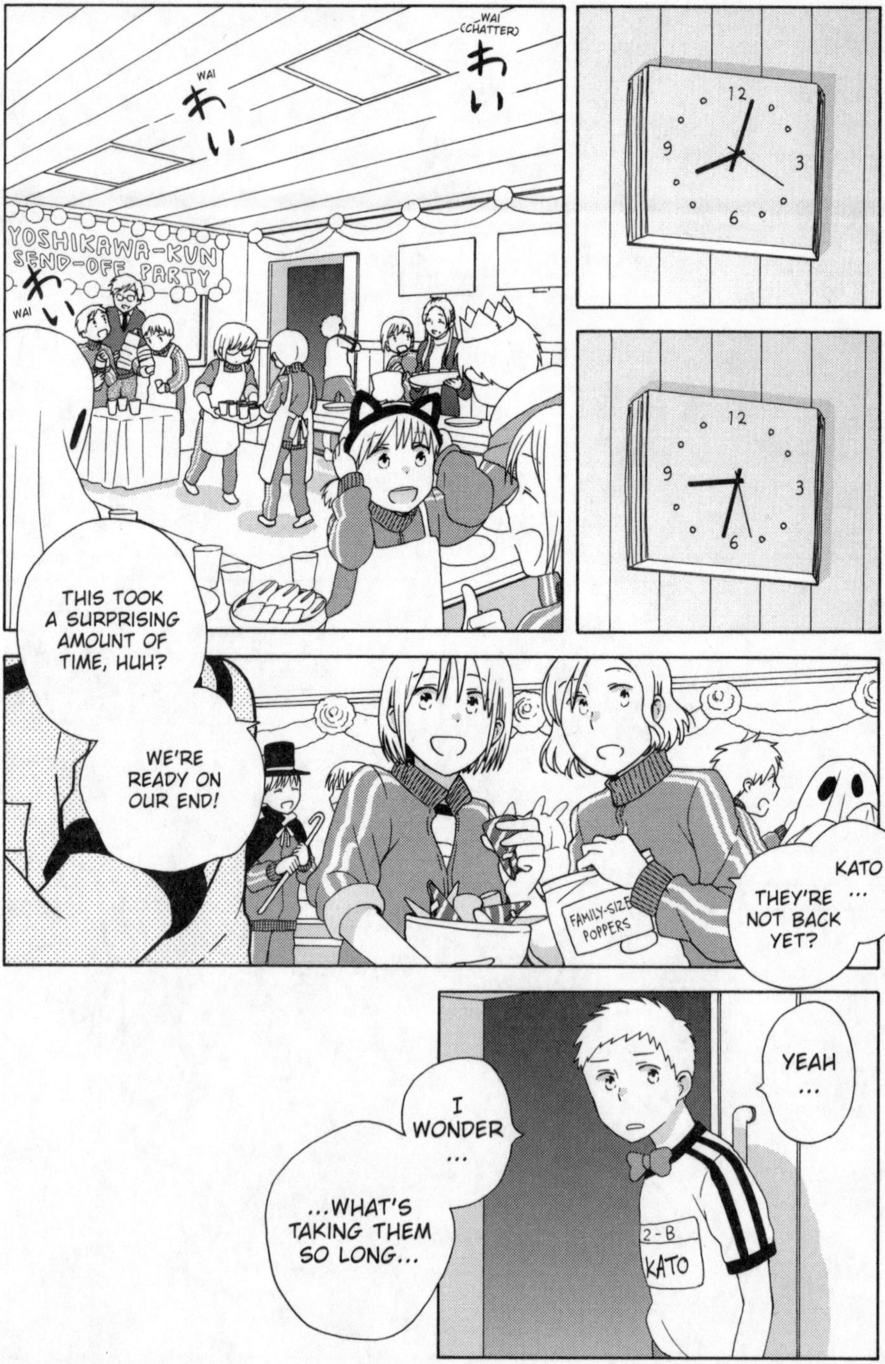
12
9
3
6
12
9
3
6
WAI (CHATTER)
わい
WAI
わい
YOSHIKAWA-KUN SEND-OFF PARTY
WAI
わい
THIS TOOK A SURPRISING AMOUNT OF TIME, HUH?
WE'RE READY ON OUR END!
FAMILY-SIZE POPPERS
KATO... THEY'RE NOT BACK YET?
YEAH...
I WONDER...
...WHAT'S TAKING THEM SO LONG...
2-B
KATO

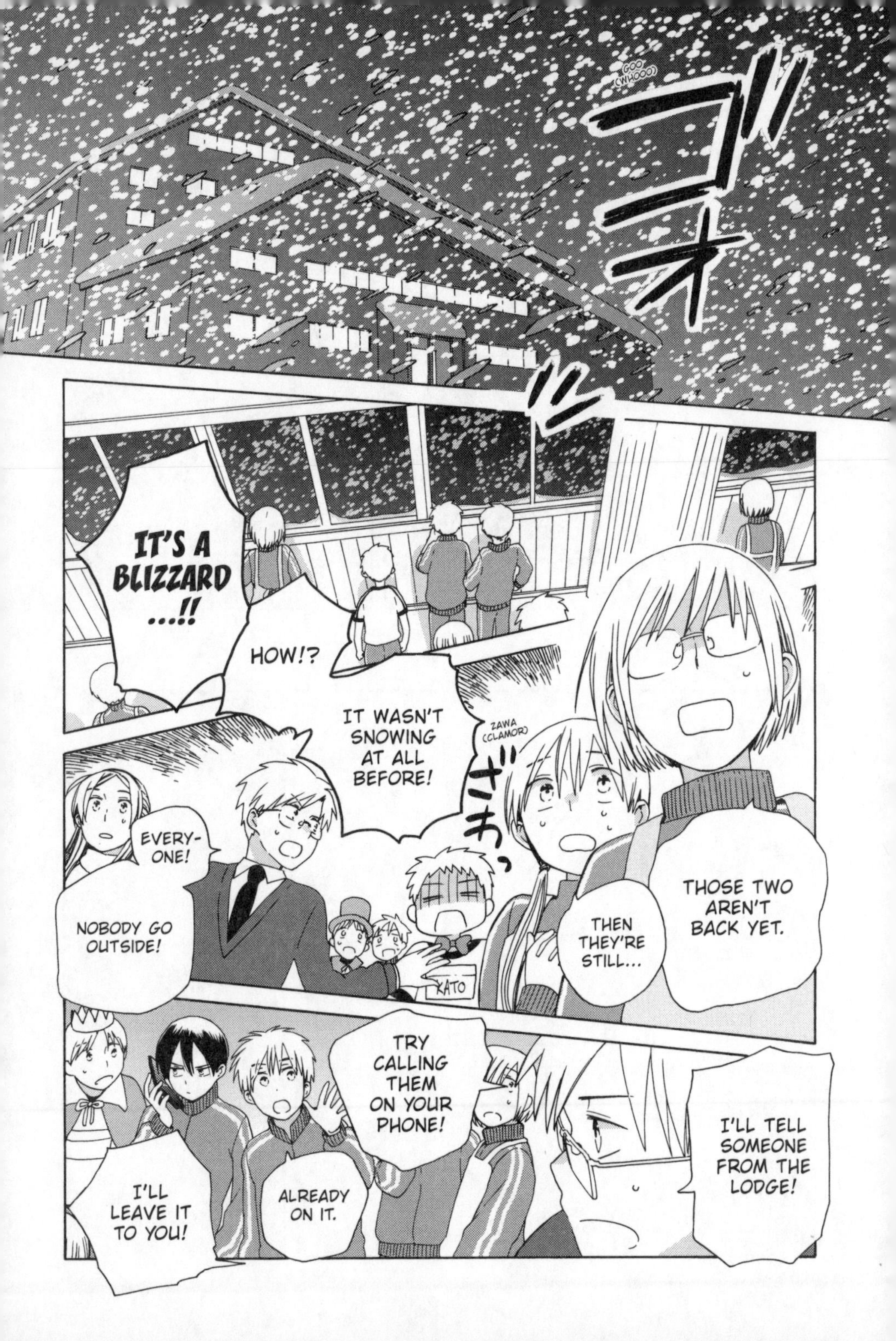
GOO (WHOOO)
IT'S A BLIZZARD ...!!
HOW!?
IT WASN'T SNOWING AT ALL BEFORE!
THOSE TWO AREN'T BACK YET.
THEN THEY'RE STILL...
ZAWA (CLAMOR)
EVERY-ONE!
NOBODY GO OUTSIDE!
KATO
I'LL TELL SOMEONE FROM THE LODGE!
TRY CALLING THEM ON YOUR PHONE!
ALREADY ON IT.
I'LL LEAVE IT TO YOU!

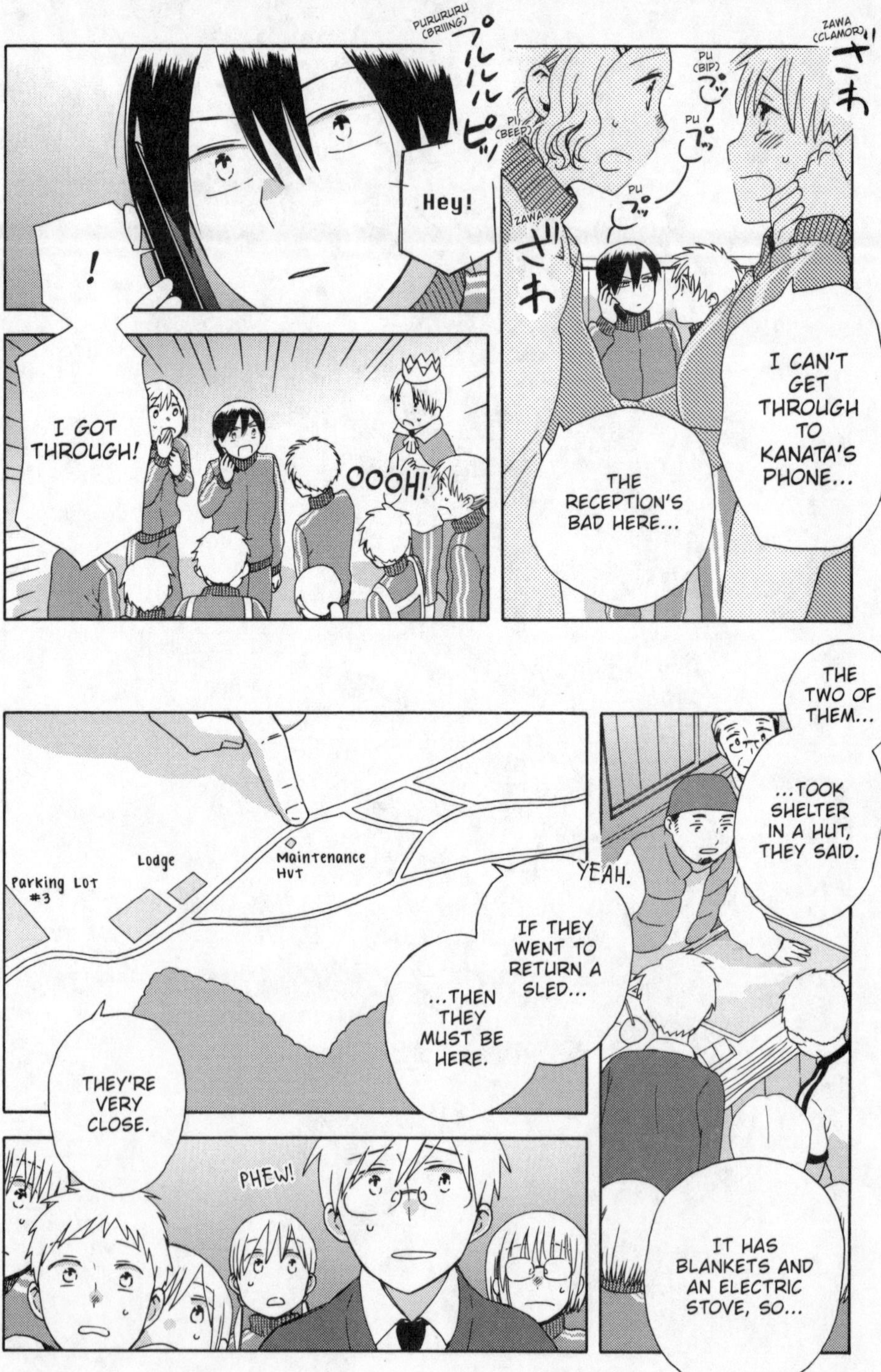
ZAWA (CLAMOR)
ざわ
PU (BIP)
プッ
PU
プッ
PU
プッ
ZAWA
ざわ
I CAN'T GET THROUGH TO KANATA'S PHONE...
THE RECEPTION'S BAD HERE...
PURURURU (BRIIING)
プルルル
PI (BEEP)
ピッ
Hey!
!
I GOT THROUGH!
OOOH!
THE TWO OF THEM...
...TOOK SHELTER IN A HUT, THEY SAID.
IT HAS BLANKETS AND AN ELECTRIC STOVE, SO...
Maintenance Hut
Lodge
Parking Lot #3
YEAH.
IF THEY WENT TO RETURN A SLED...
...THEN THEY MUST BE HERE.
THEY'RE VERY CLOSE.
PHEW!

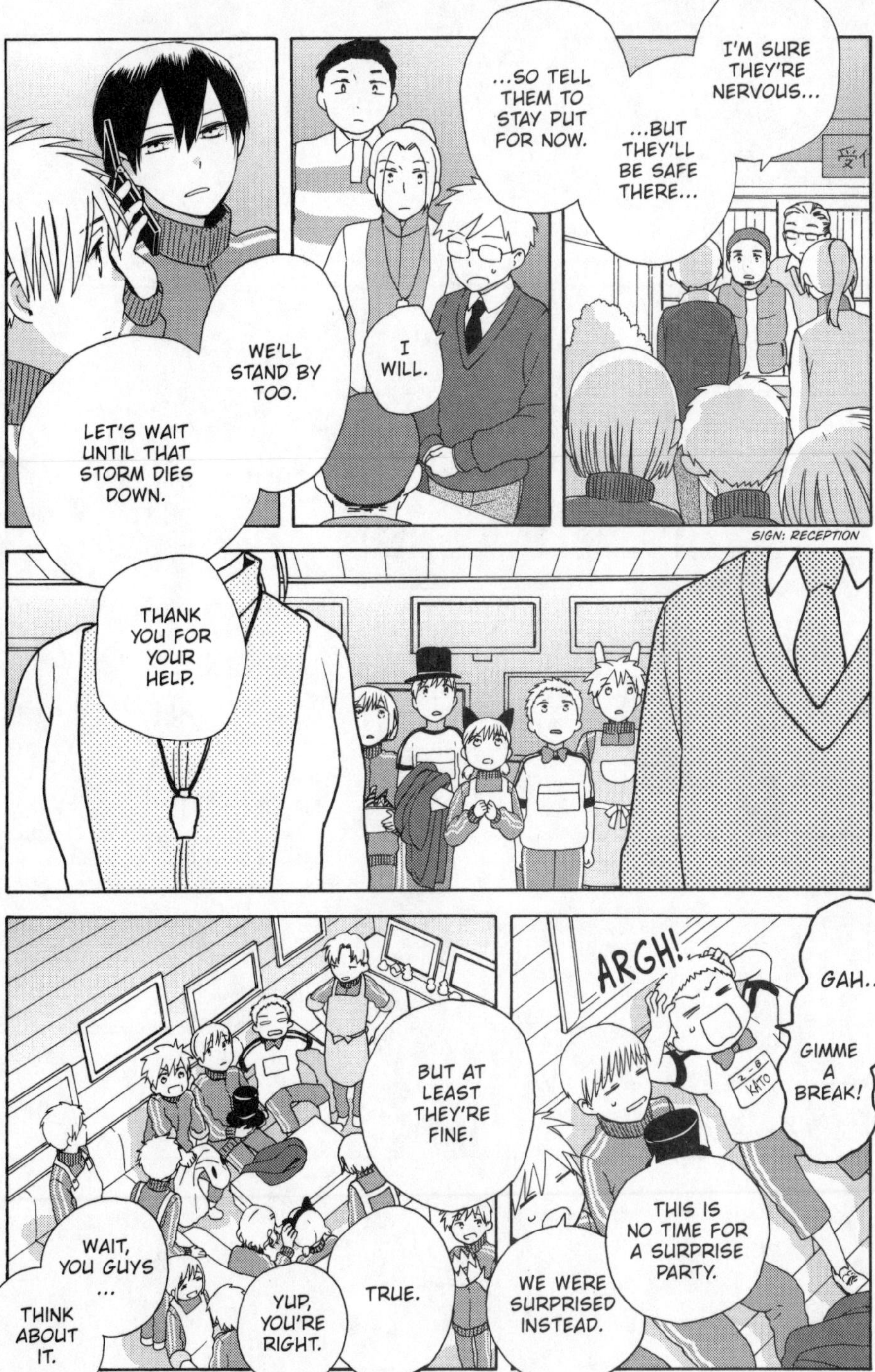
I'M SURE THEY'RE NERVOUS...
...BUT THEY'LL BE SAFE THERE...
...SO TELL THEM TO STAY PUT FOR NOW.
I WILL.
WE'LL STAND BY TOO.
LET'S WAIT UNTIL THAT STORM DIES DOWN.
THANK YOU FOR YOUR HELP.
ARGH!
GAH...
GIMME A BREAK!
THIS IS NO TIME FOR A SURPRISE PARTY.
WE WERE SURPRISED INSTEAD.
BUT AT LEAST THEY'RE FINE.
TRUE.
YUP, YOU'RE RIGHT.
WAIT, YOU GUYS...
THINK ABOUT IT.
SIGN: RECEPTION

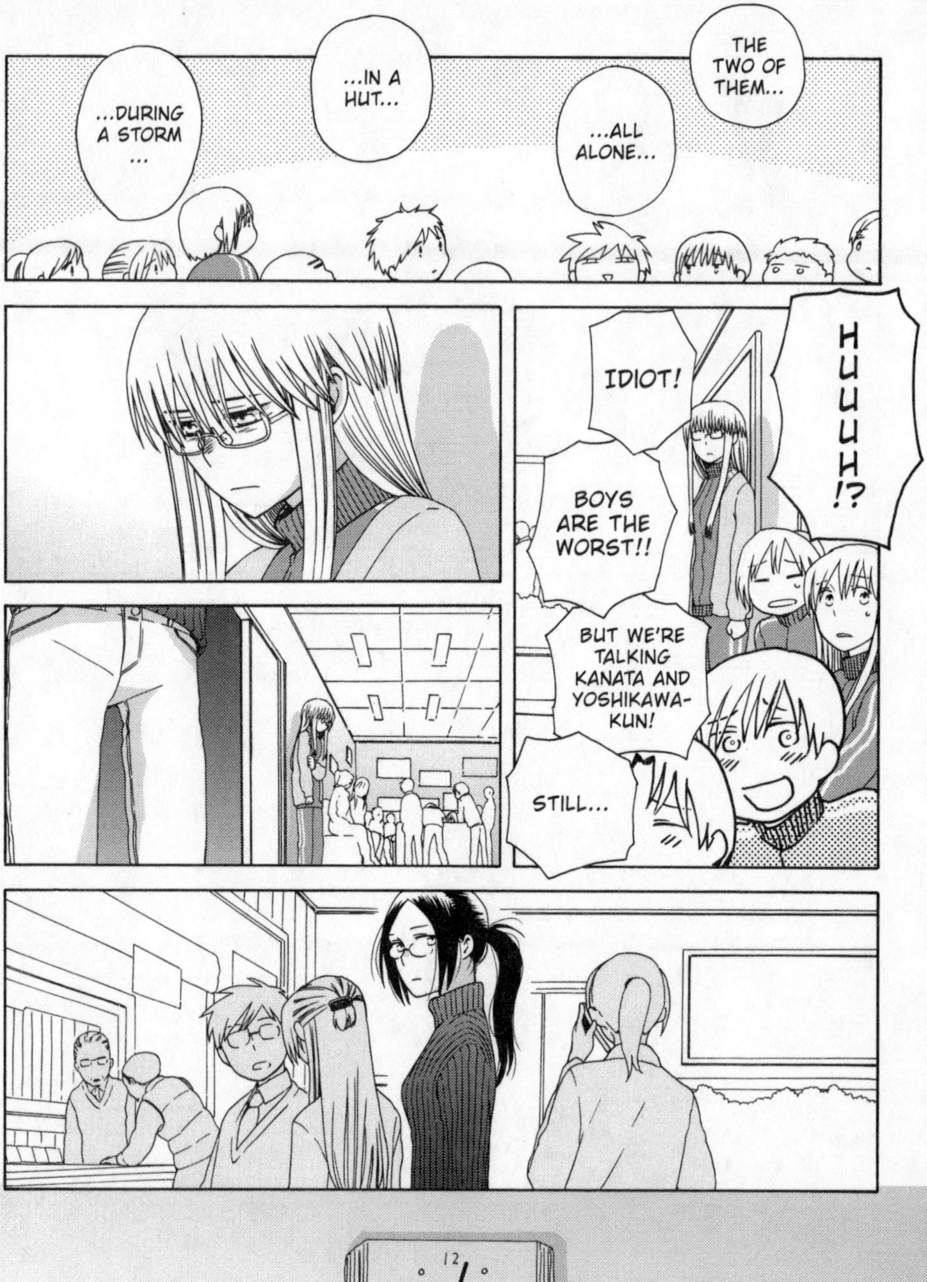
THE TWO OF THEM...
...ALL ALONE...
...IN A HUT...
...DURING A STORM ...
HUUUH!?
IDIOT!
BOYS ARE THE WORST!!
BUT WE'RE TALKING KANATA AND YOSHIKAWA-KUN!
STILL...

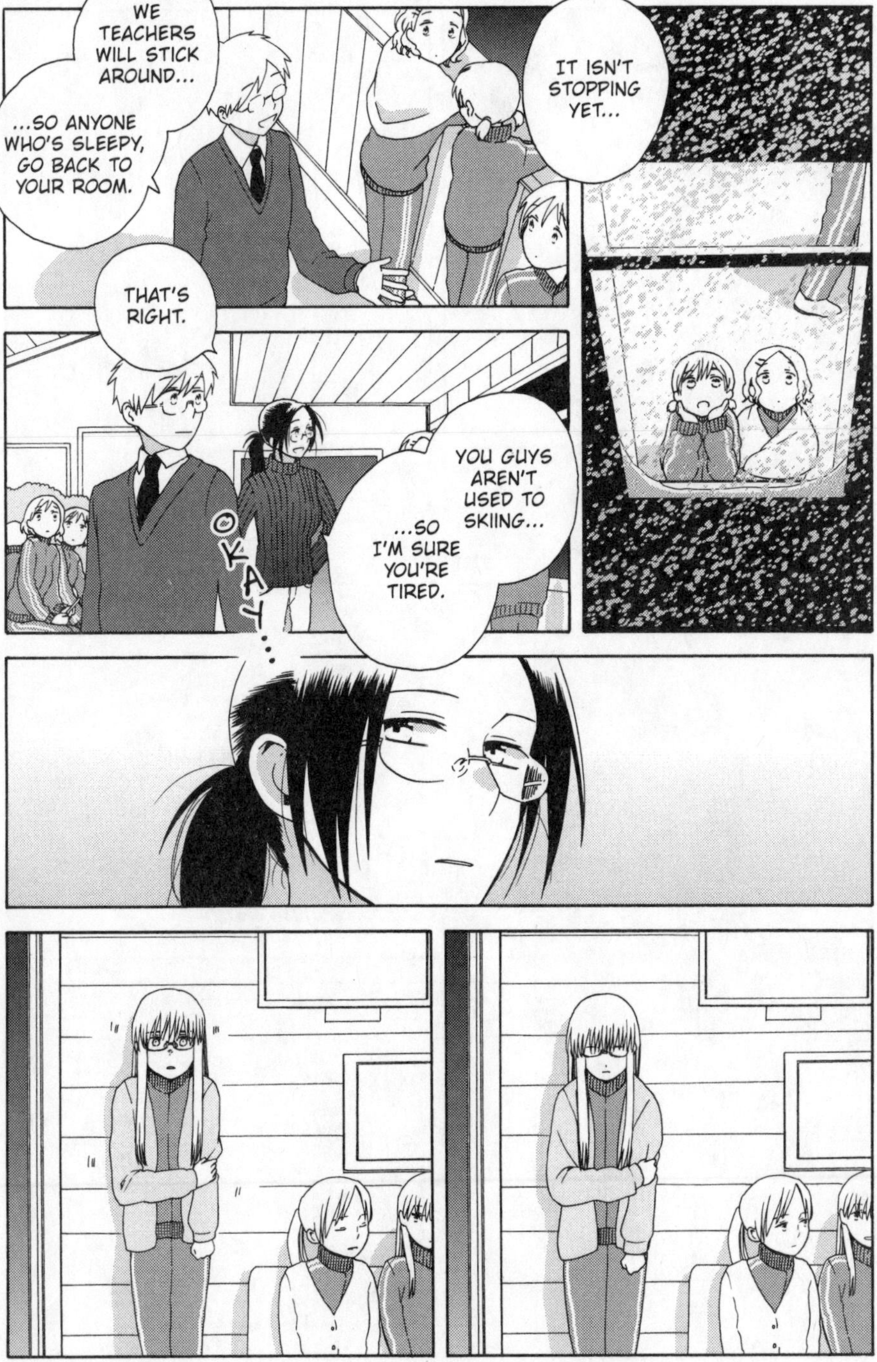
IT ISN'T STOPPING YET...
WE TEACHERS WILL STICK AROUND...
...SO ANYONE WHO'S SLEEPY, GO BACK TO YOUR ROOM.
THAT'S RIGHT.
YOU GUYS AREN'T USED TO SKIING...
...SO I'M SURE YOU'RE TIRED.
OKAY...

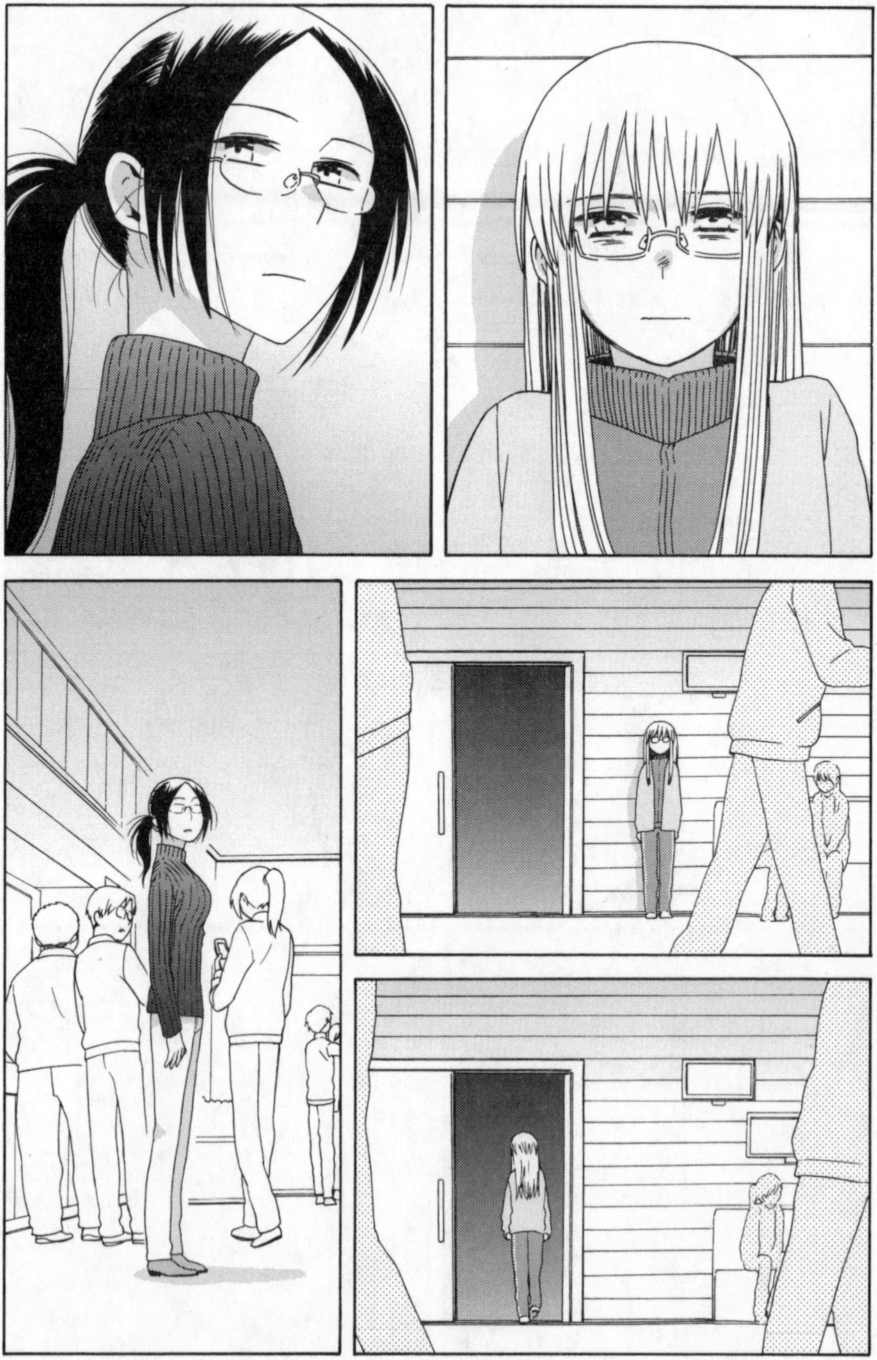

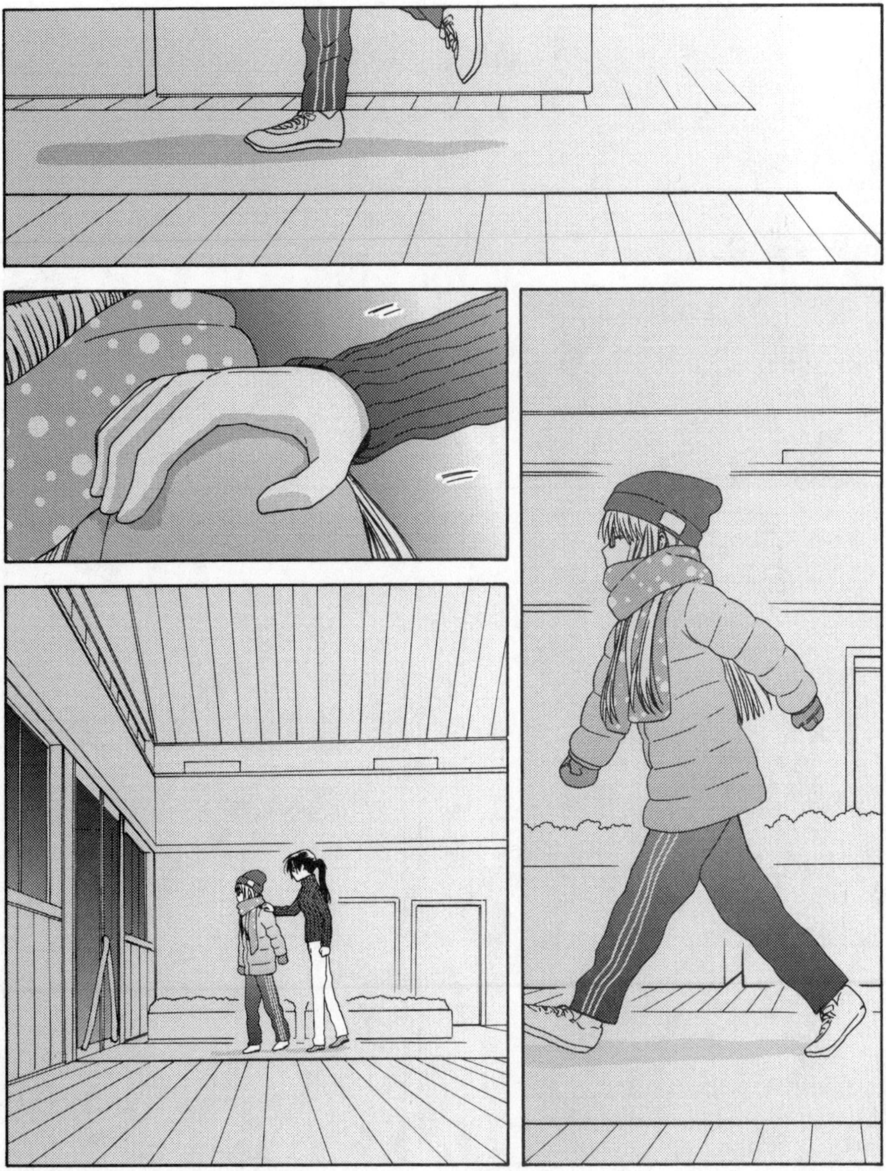

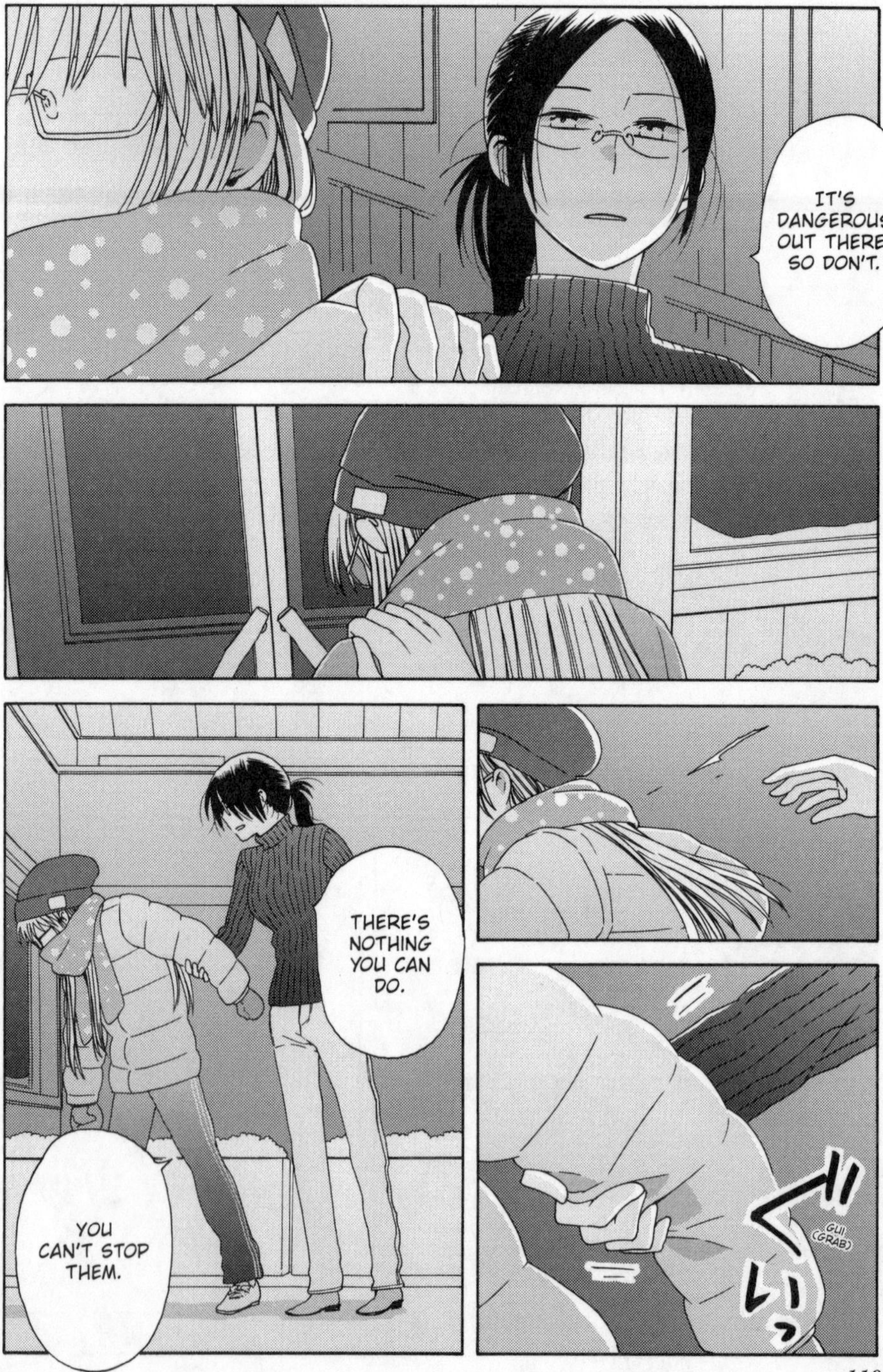
IT'S DANGEROUS OUT THERE, SO DON'T.
GUI (GRAB)
THERE'S NOTHING YOU CAN DO.
YOU CAN'T STOP THEM.

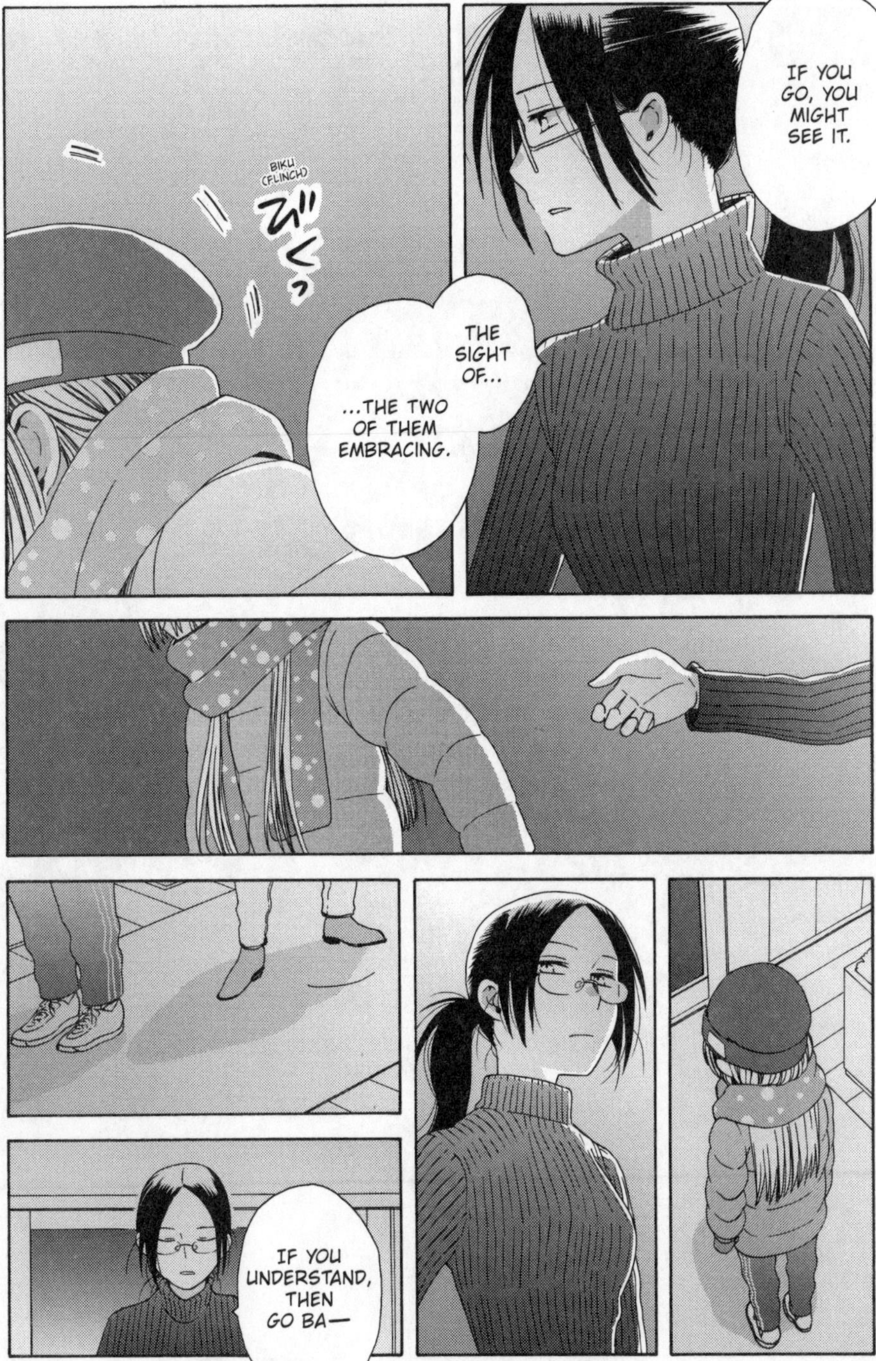
IF YOU GO, YOU MIGHT SEE IT.
THE SIGHT OF...
...THE TWO OF THEM EMBRACING.
BIKU (FLINCH)
びくっ
IF YOU UNDERSTAND, THEN GO BA—

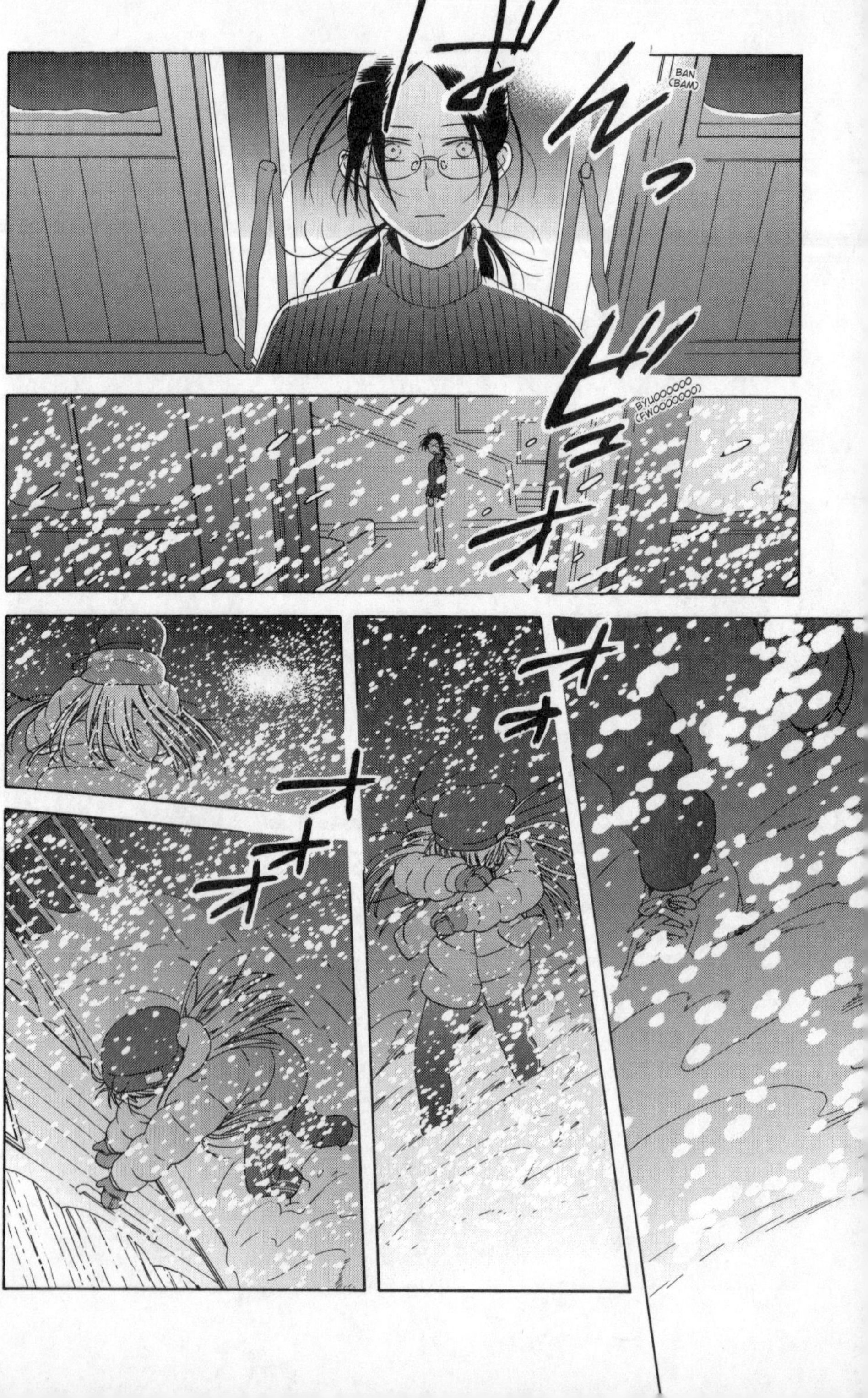
ばんっ
BAN
(BAM)
ビュオオオオオオオ
BYUOOOOOOO
(FWOOOOOOOO)

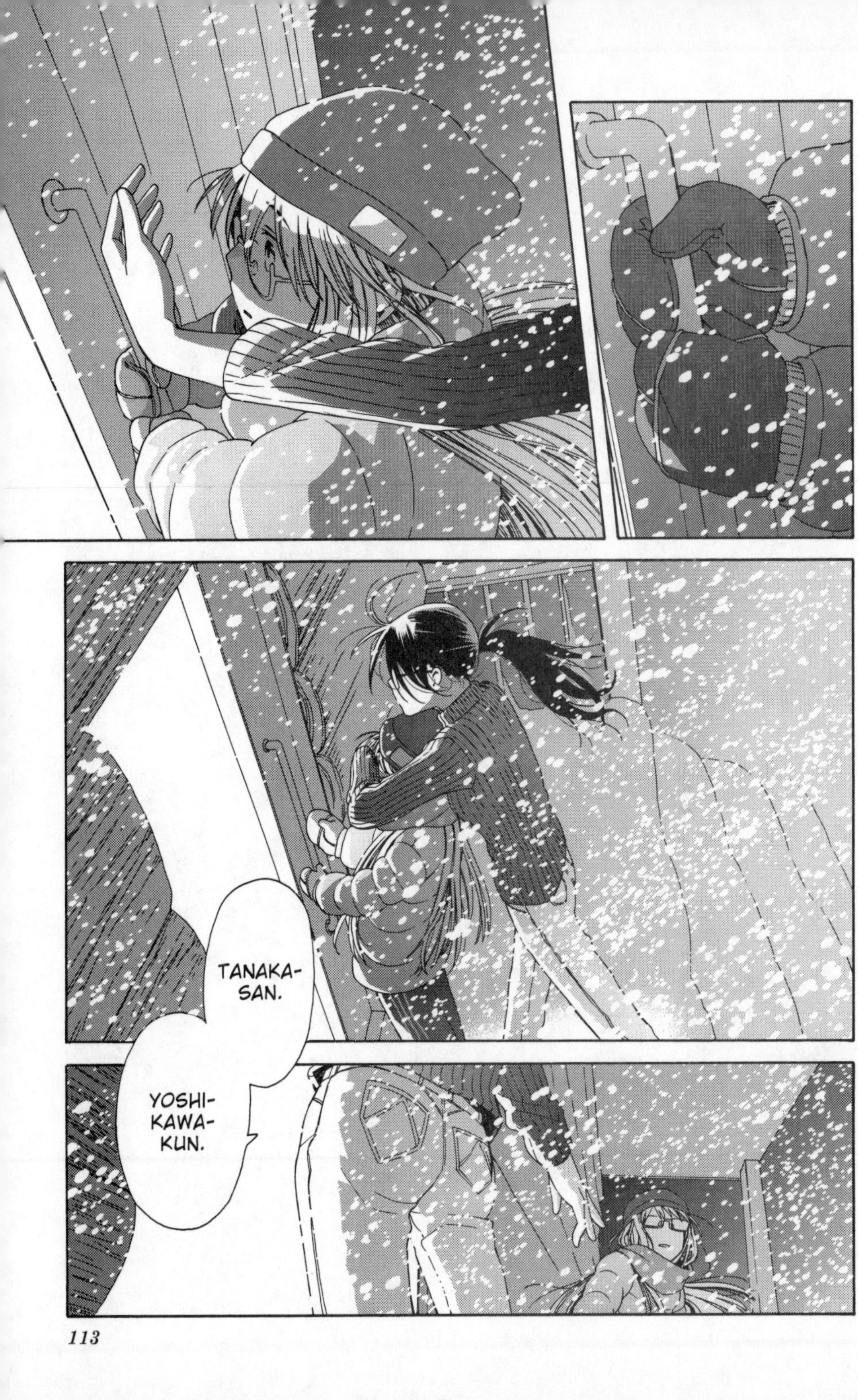
TANAKA-SAN.
YOSHI-KAWA-KUN.

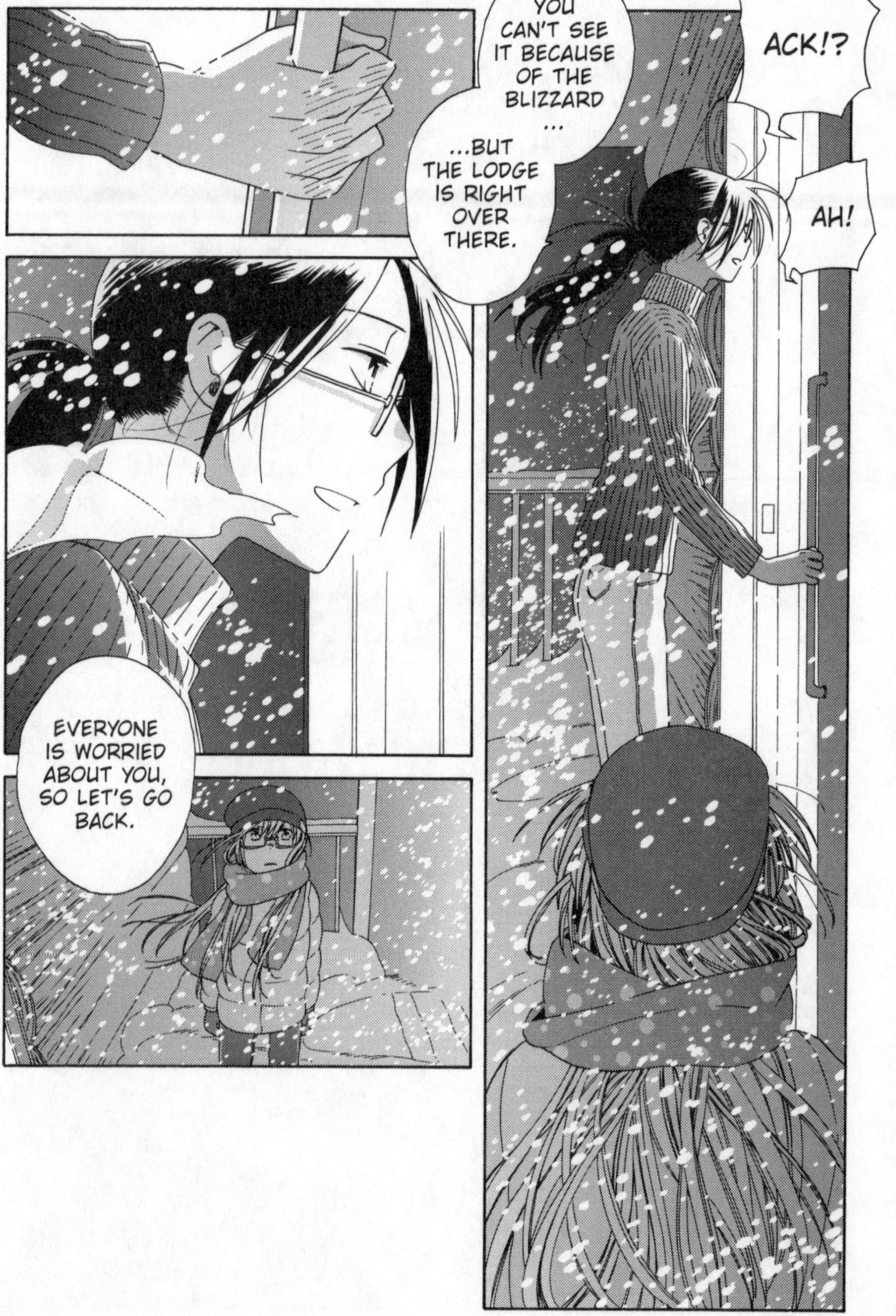
ACK!?
AH!
YOU CAN'T SEE IT BECAUSE OF THE BLIZZARD ...
...BUT THE LODGE IS RIGHT OVER THERE.
EVERYONE IS WORRIED ABOUT YOU, SO LET'S GO BACK.

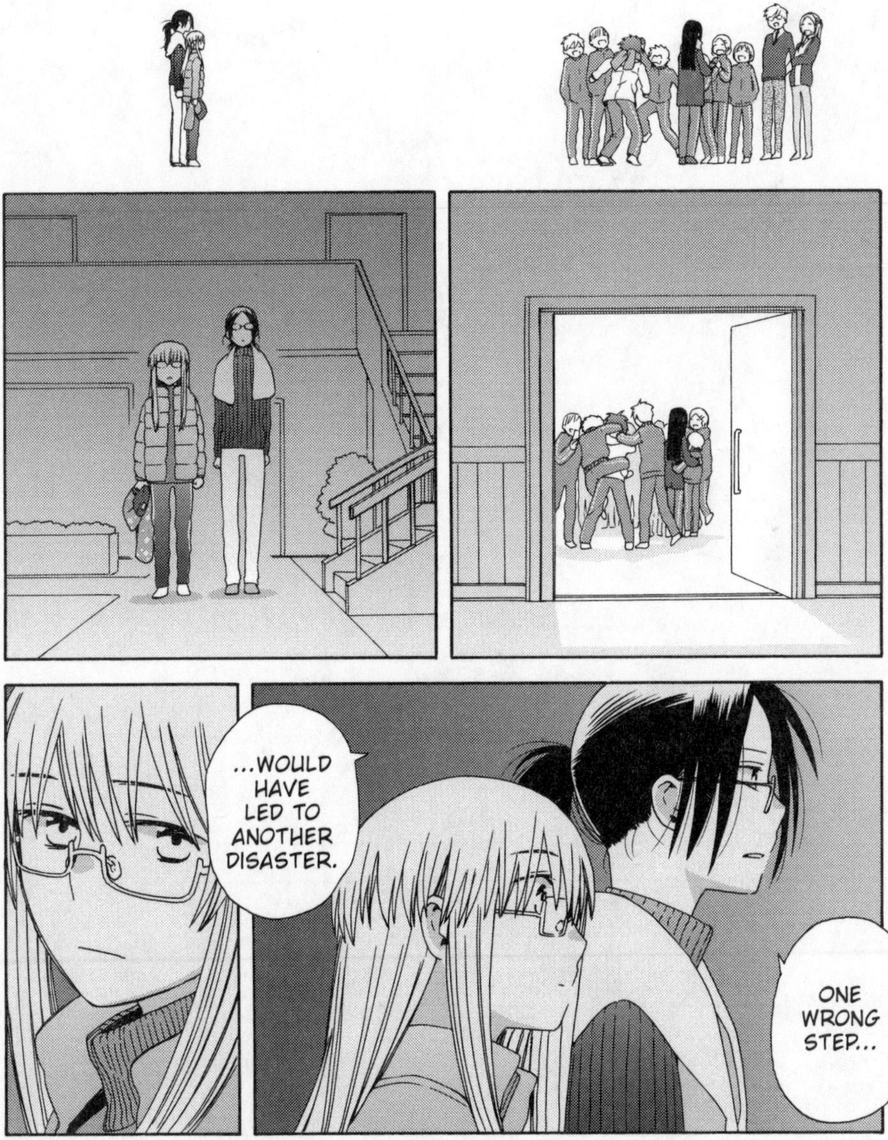
ONE WRONG STEP...
...WOULD HAVE LED TO ANOTHER DISASTER.

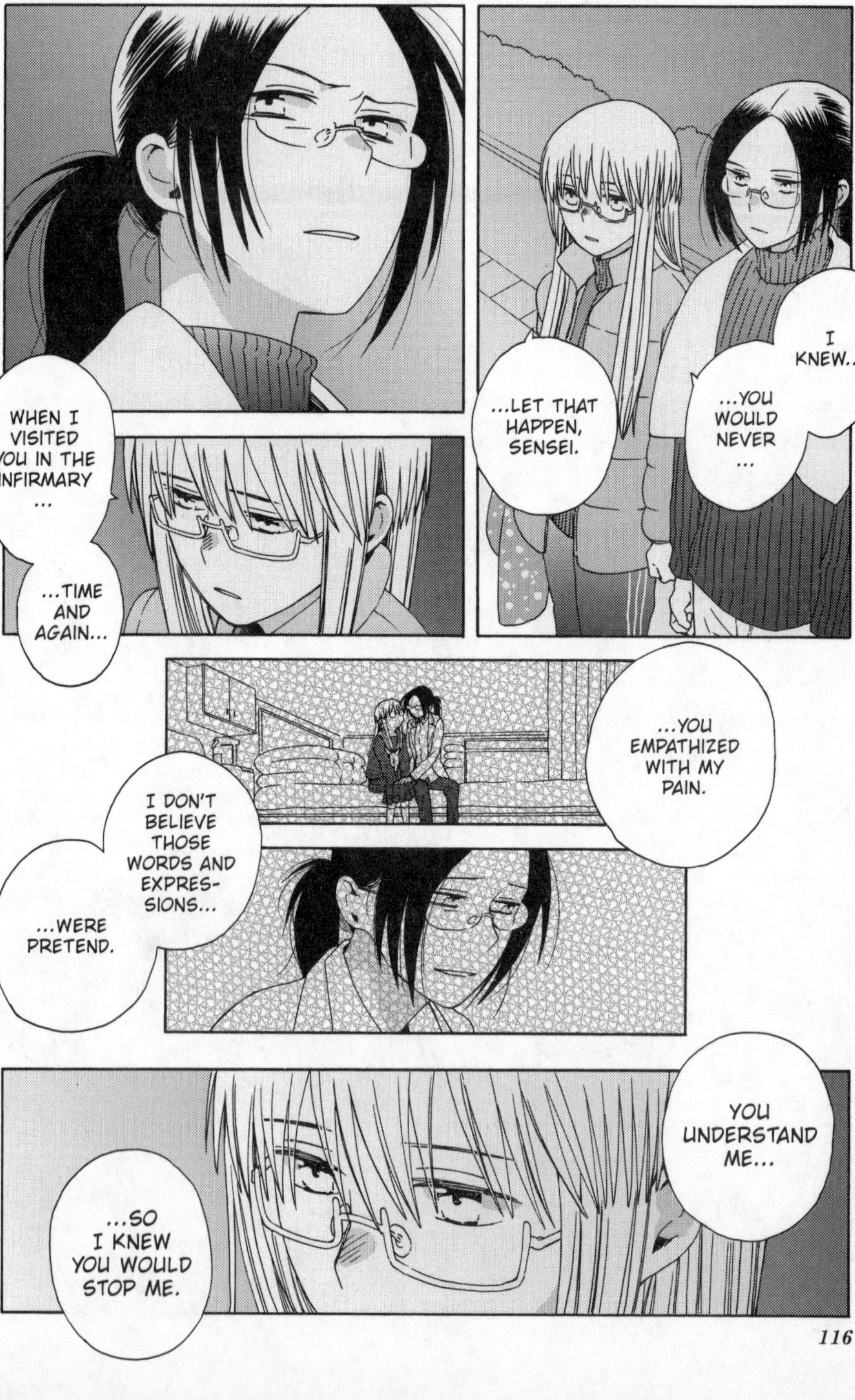
I KNEW...
...YOU WOULD NEVER...
...LET THAT HAPPEN, SENSEI.
WHEN I VISITED YOU IN THE INFIRMARY...
...TIME AND AGAIN...
...YOU EMPATHIZED WITH MY PAIN.
I DON'T BELIEVE THOSE WORDS AND EXPRES-SIONS...
...WERE PRETEND.
YOU UNDERSTAND ME...
...SO I KNEW YOU WOULD STOP ME.

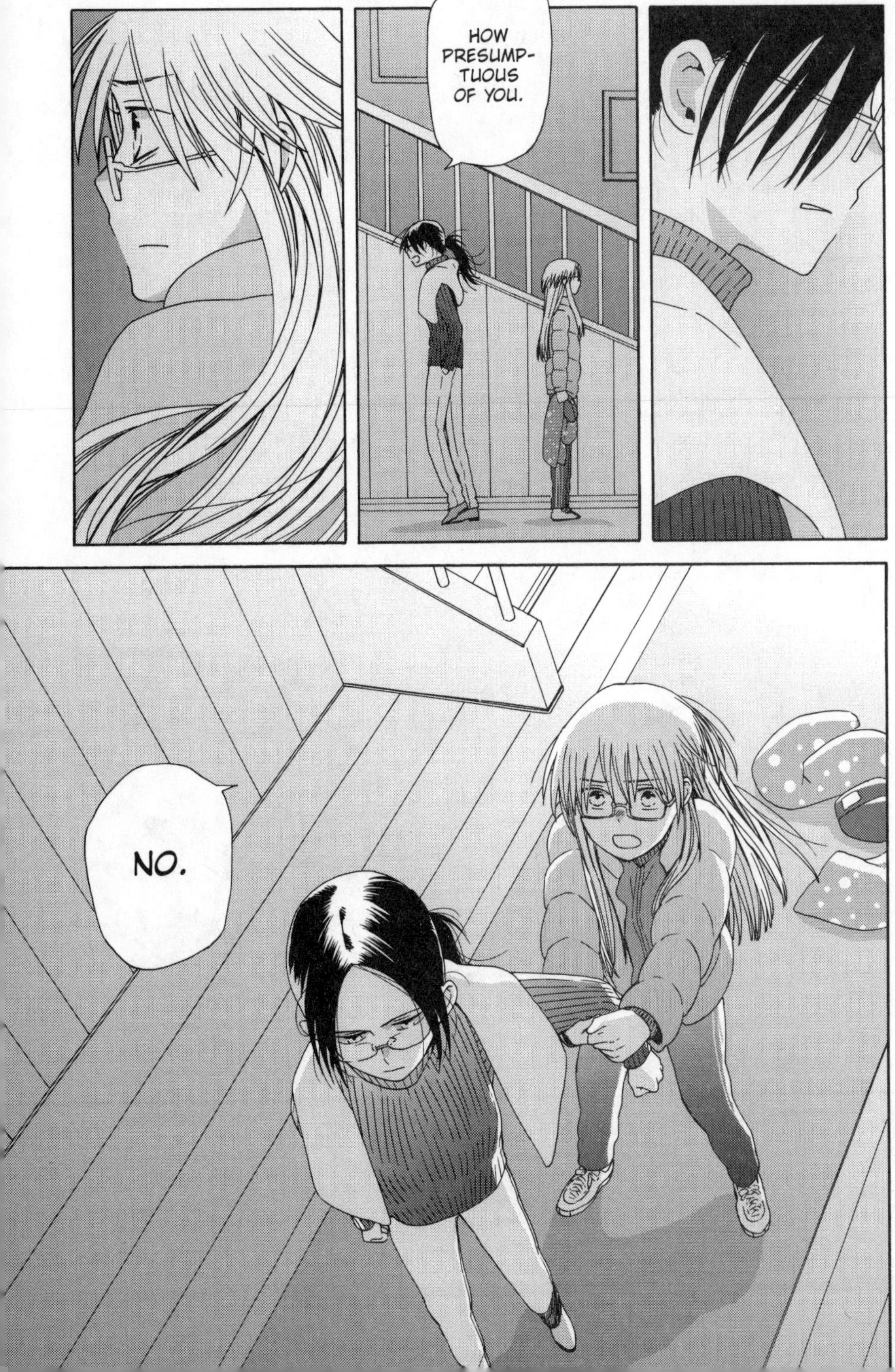
HOW PRESUMP-TUOUS OF YOU.
NO.

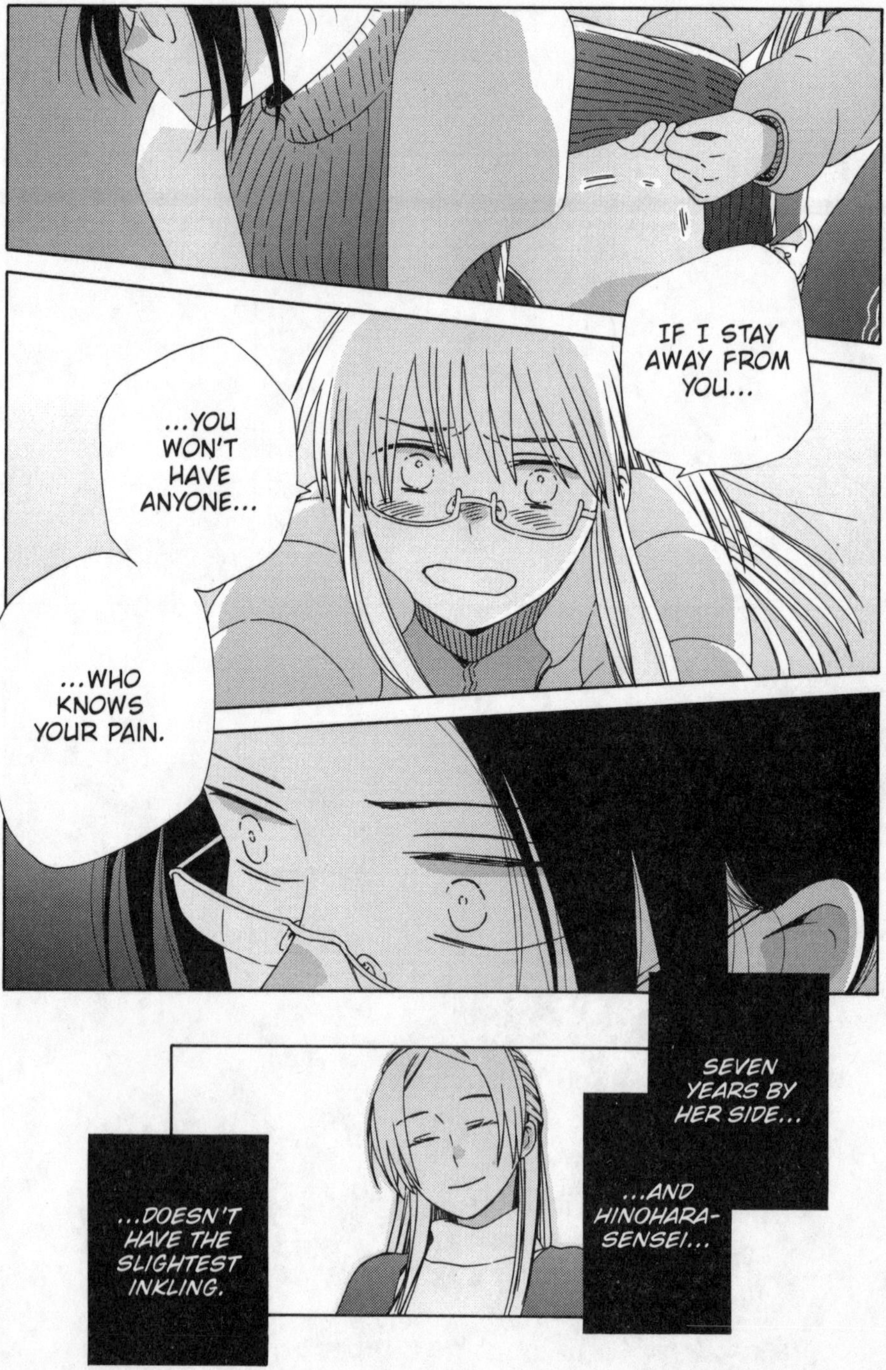
IF I STAY AWAY FROM YOU...
...YOU WON'T HAVE ANYONE...
...WHO KNOWS YOUR PAIN.
SEVEN YEARS BY HER SIDE...
...AND HINOHARA-SENSEI...
...DOESN'T HAVE THE SLIGHTEST INKLING.

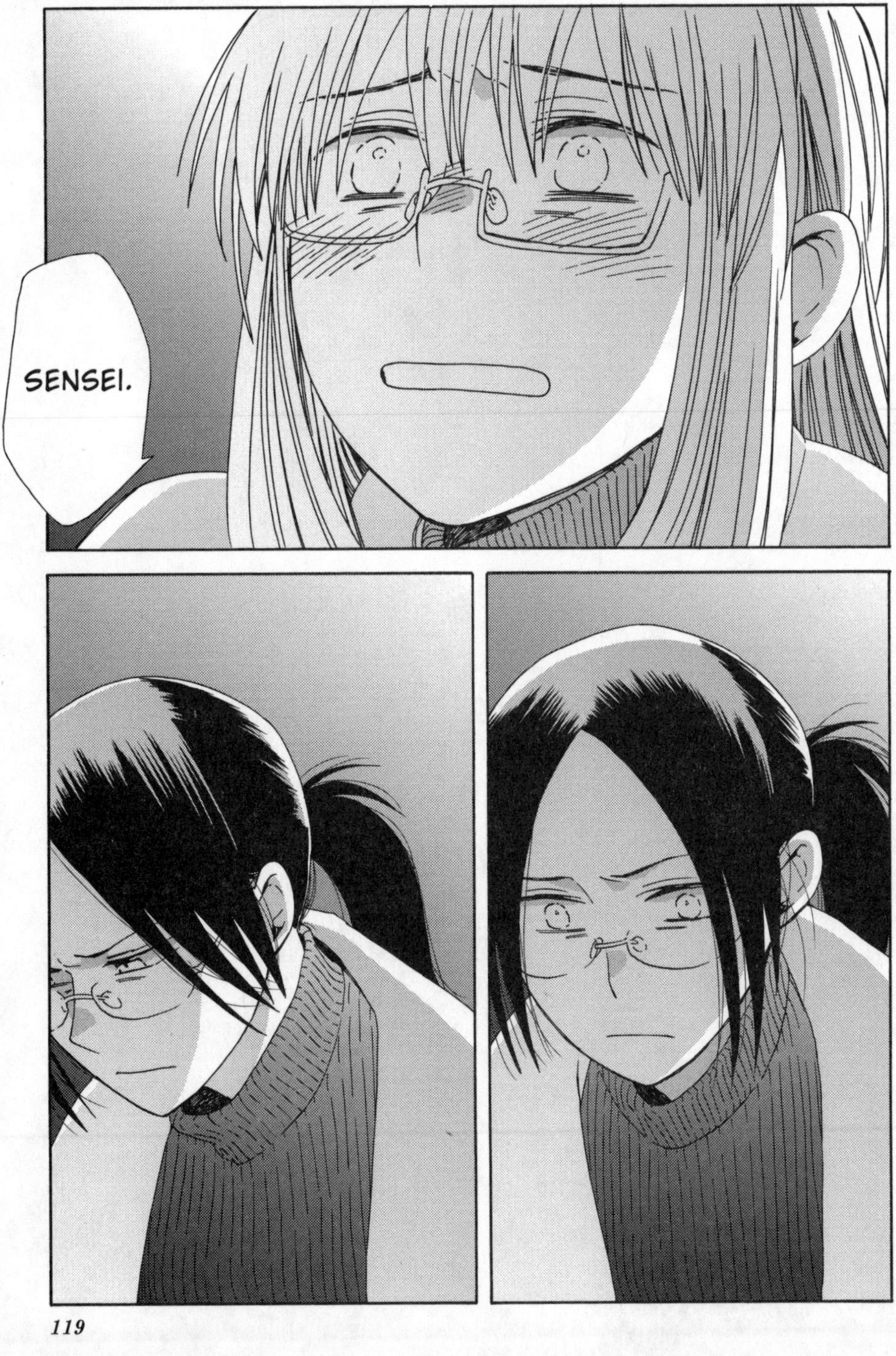
SENSEI.

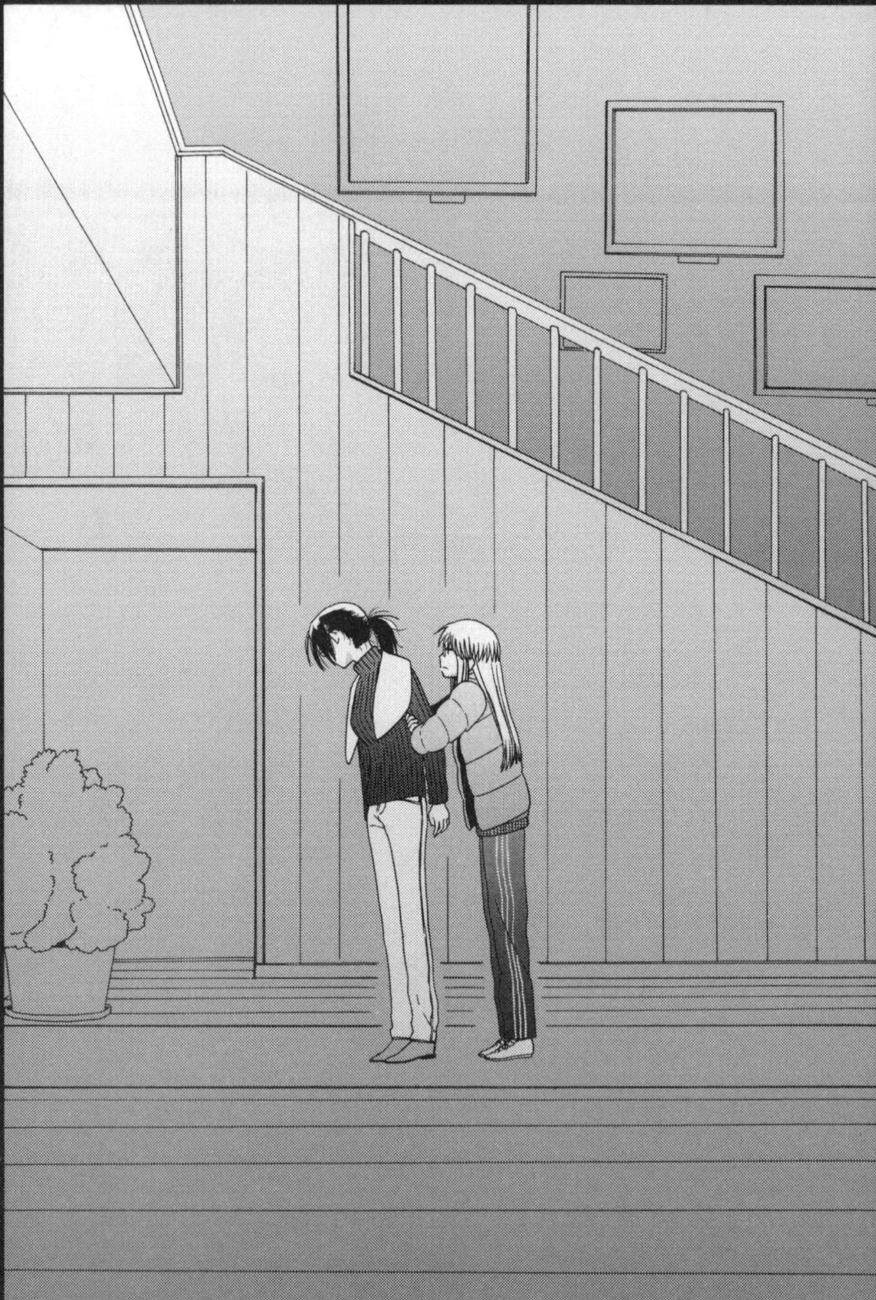

Fin

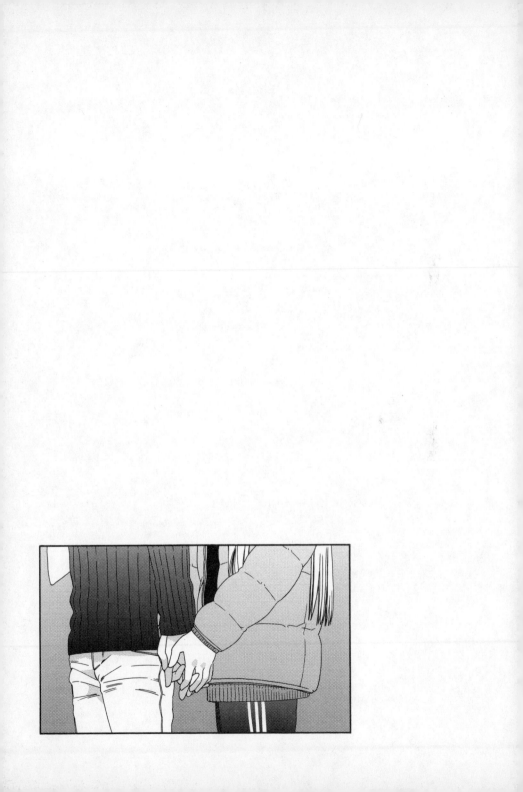

Love at Fourteen

Fuka Mizutani

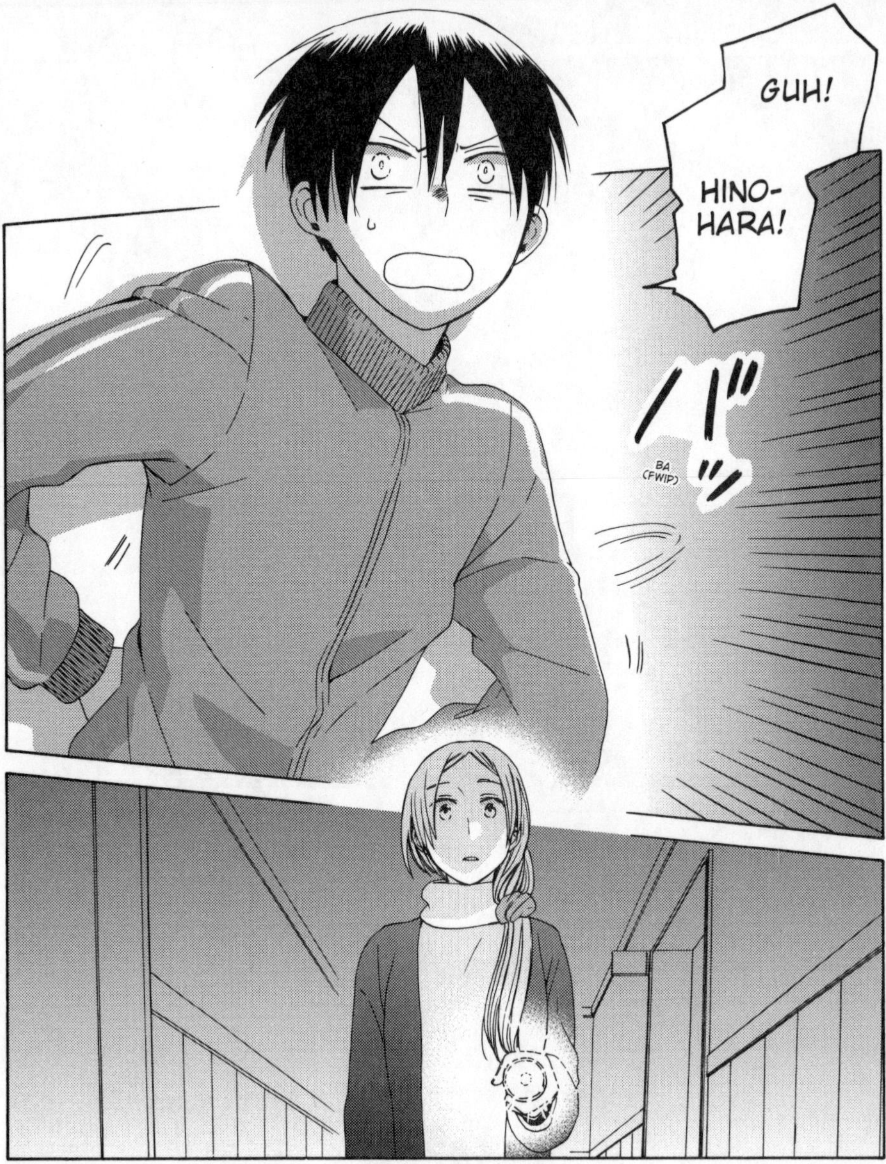
GUH!
HINO-HARA!
バッ
BA (FWIP)

Love at Fourteen

[Intermission 69]

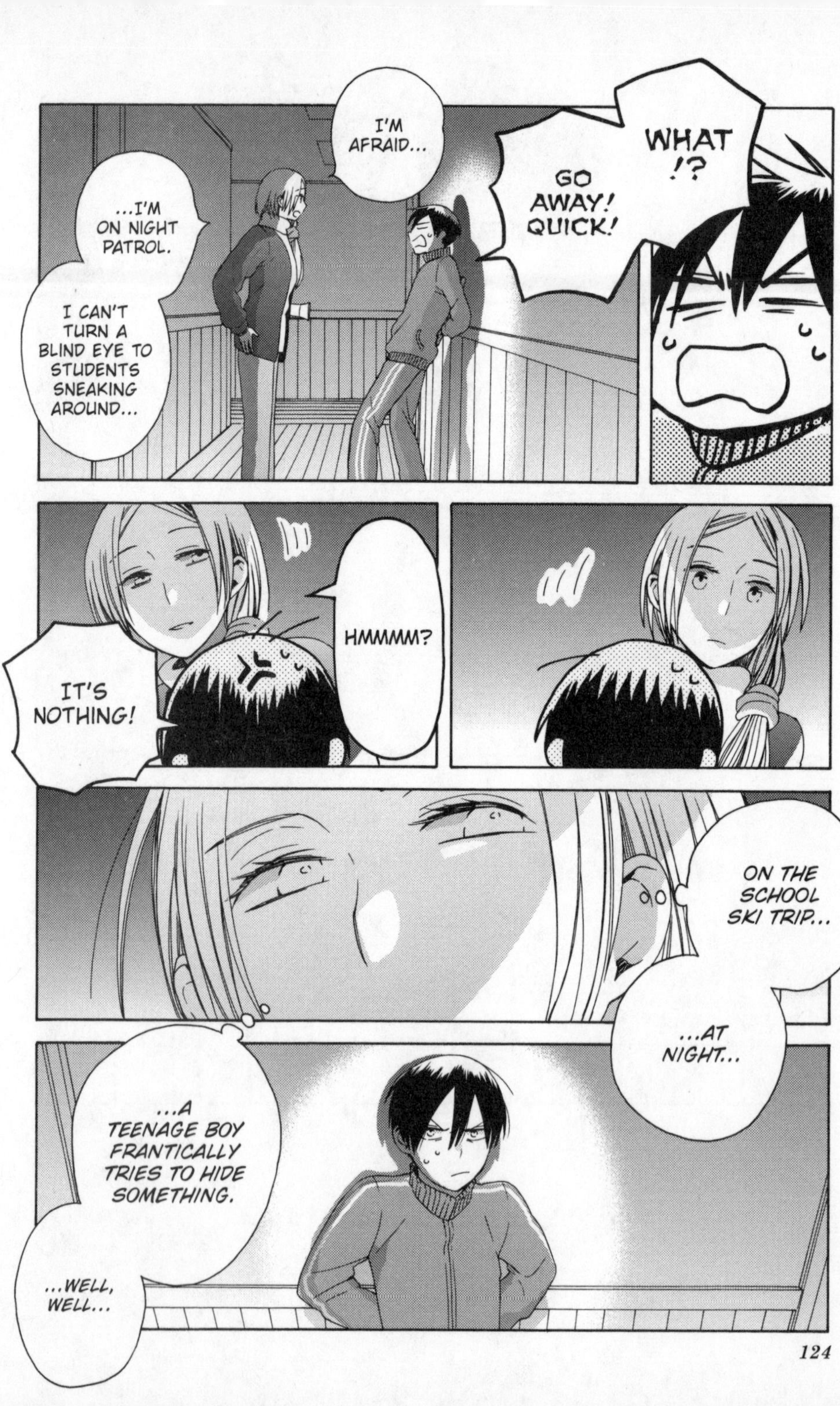
WHAT!?
GO AWAY! QUICK!
I'M AFRAID...
...I'M ON NIGHT PATROL.
I CAN'T TURN A BLIND EYE TO STUDENTS SNEAKING AROUND...
HMMMM?
IT'S NOTHING!
ON THE SCHOOL SKI TRIP...
...AT NIGHT...
...A TEENAGE BOY FRANTICALLY TRIES TO HIDE SOMETHING.
...WELL, WELL...

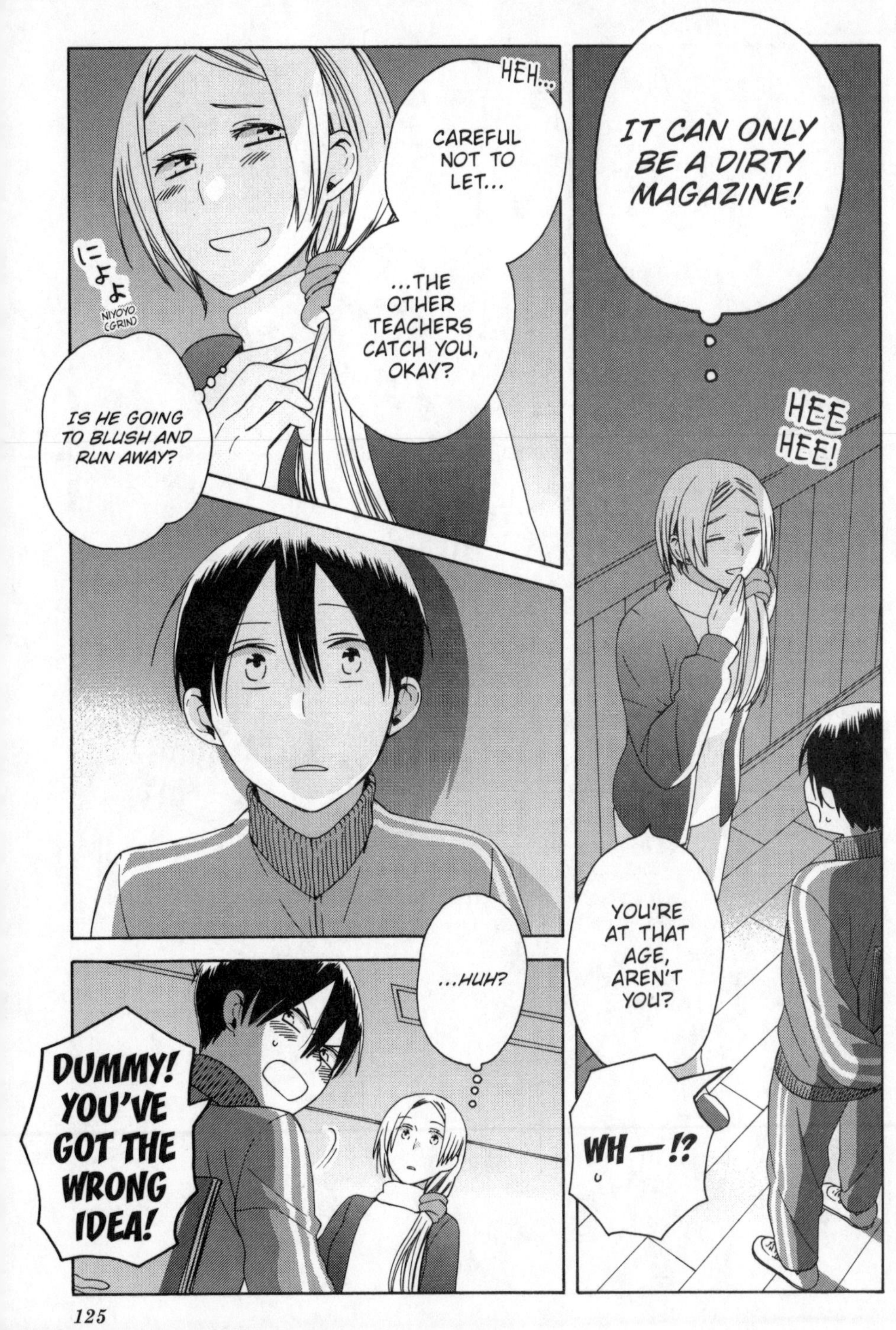
IT CAN ONLY BE A DIRTY MAGAZINE!
HEE HEE!
YOU'RE AT THAT AGE, AREN'T YOU?
WH—!?
HEH...
CAREFUL NOT TO LET...
...THE OTHER TEACHERS CATCH YOU, OKAY?
にょよ
NIYOYO (GRIN)
IS HE GOING TO BLUSH AND RUN AWAY?
...HUH?
DUMMY! YOU'VE GOT THE WRONG IDEA!

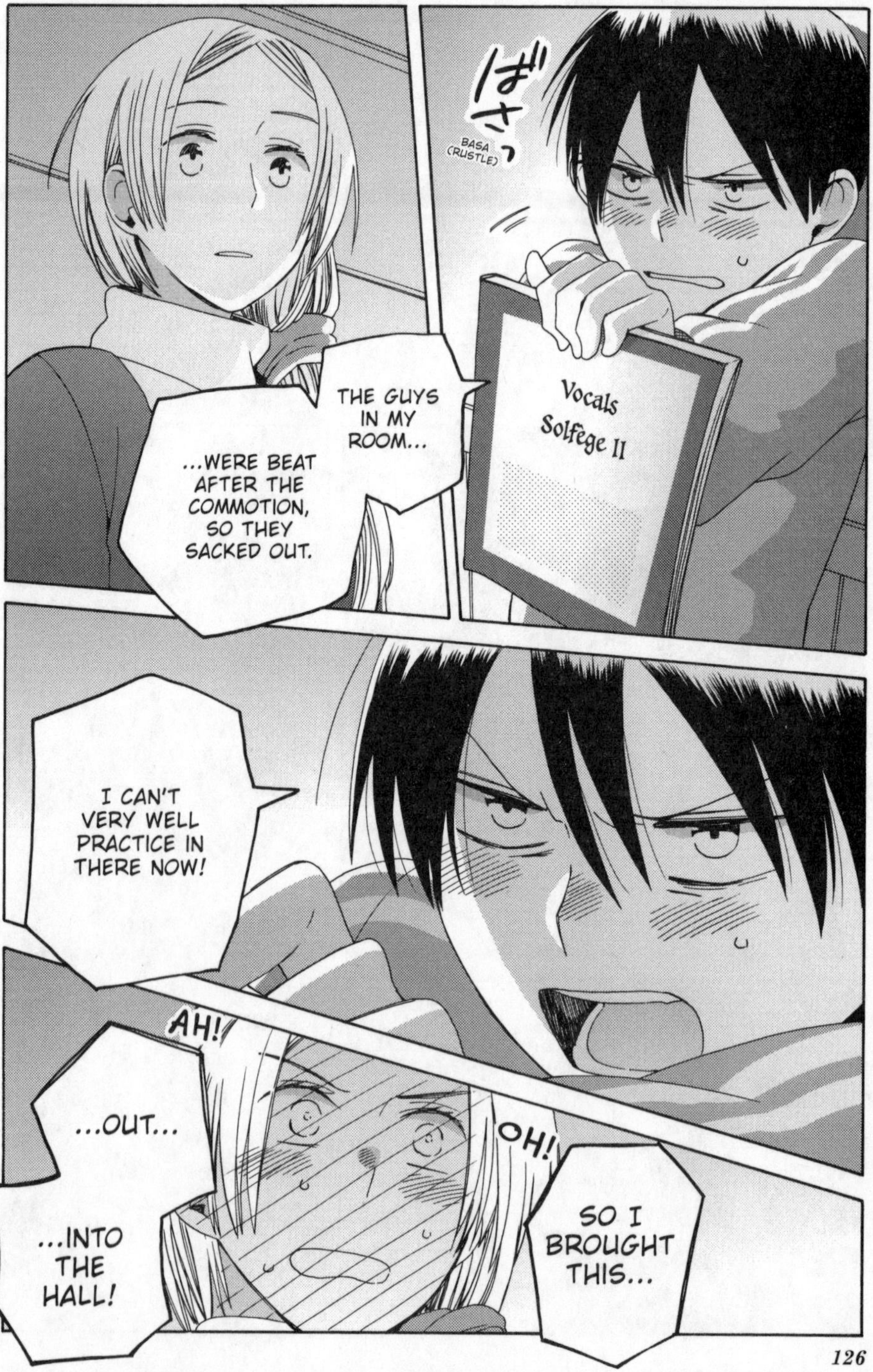
ばさっ
BASA (RUSTLE)
Vocals
Solfege II
THE GUYS IN MY ROOM...
...WERE BEAT AFTER THE COMMOTION, SO THEY SACKED OUT.
I CAN'T VERY WELL PRACTICE IN THERE NOW!
SO I BROUGHT THIS...
OH!
AH!
...OUT...
...INTO THE HALL!

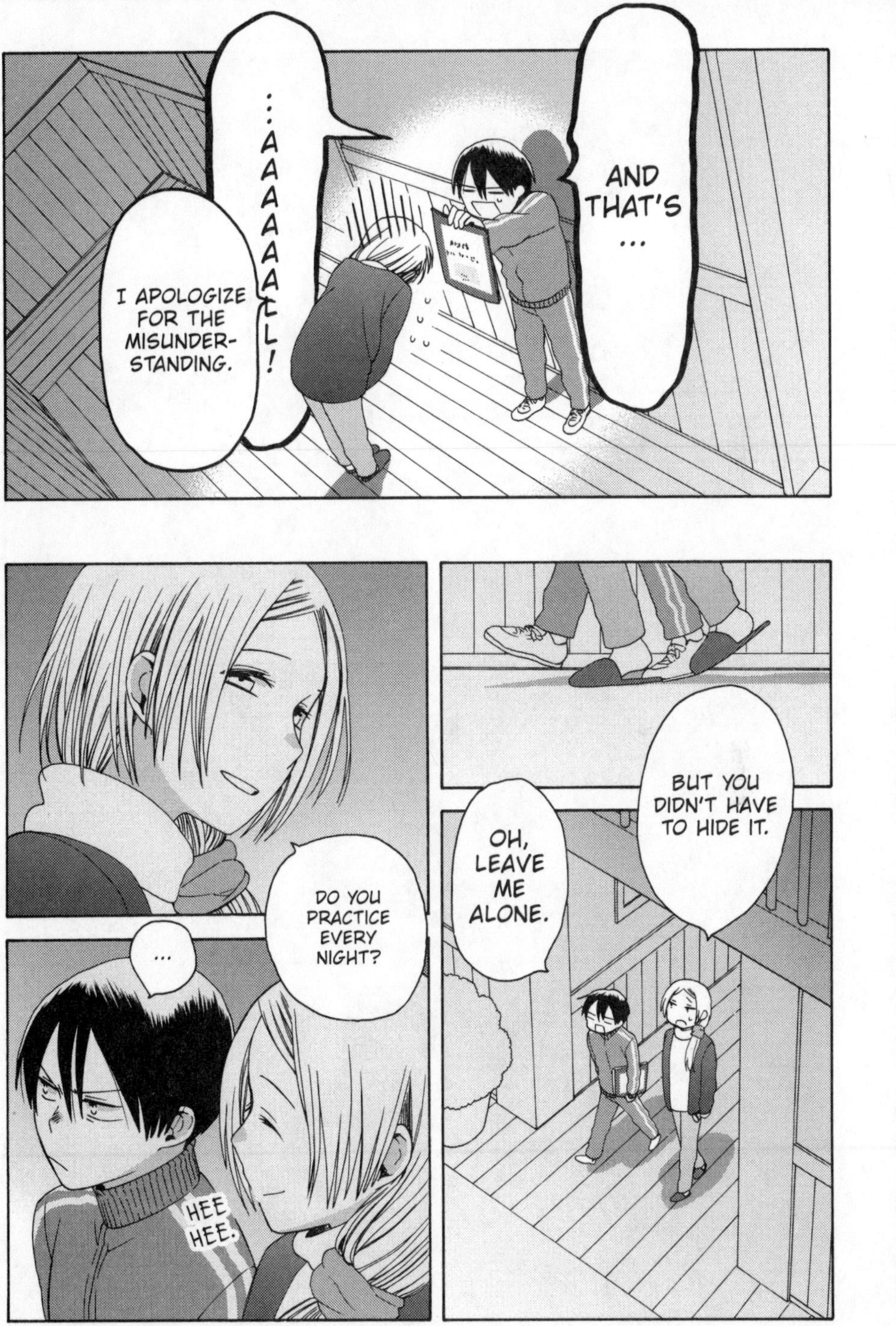
AND THAT'S ...
...AAAAAAALL!
I APOLOGIZE FOR THE MISUNDERSTANDING.
BUT YOU DIDN'T HAVE TO HIDE IT.
OH, LEAVE ME ALONE.
DO YOU PRACTICE EVERY NIGHT?
...
HEE HEE.

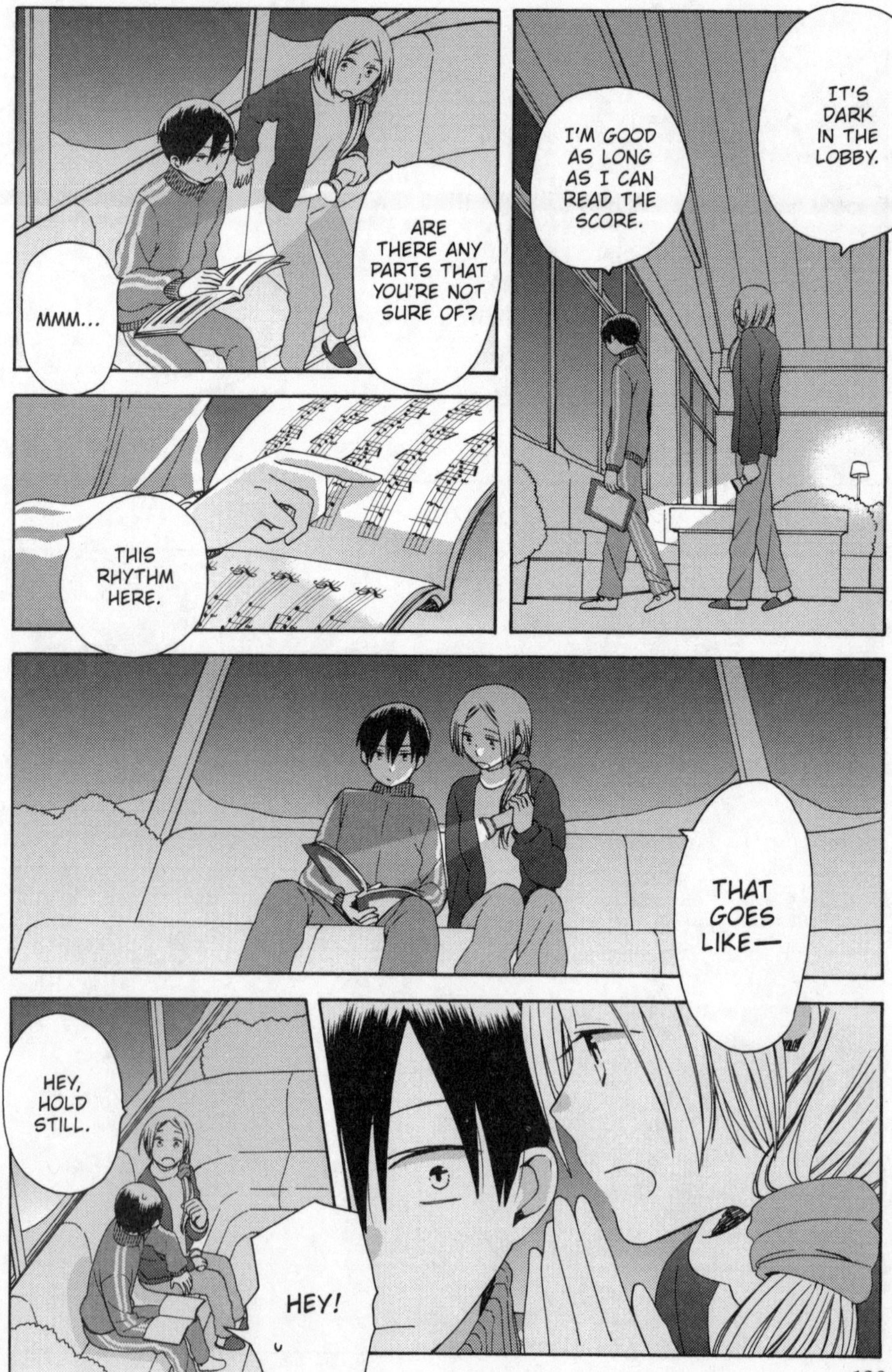
IT'S DARK IN THE LOBBY.
I'M GOOD AS LONG AS I CAN READ THE SCORE.
ARE THERE ANY PARTS THAT YOU'RE NOT SURE OF?
MMM...
THIS RHYTHM HERE.
THAT GOES LIKE—
HEY!
HEY, HOLD STILL.

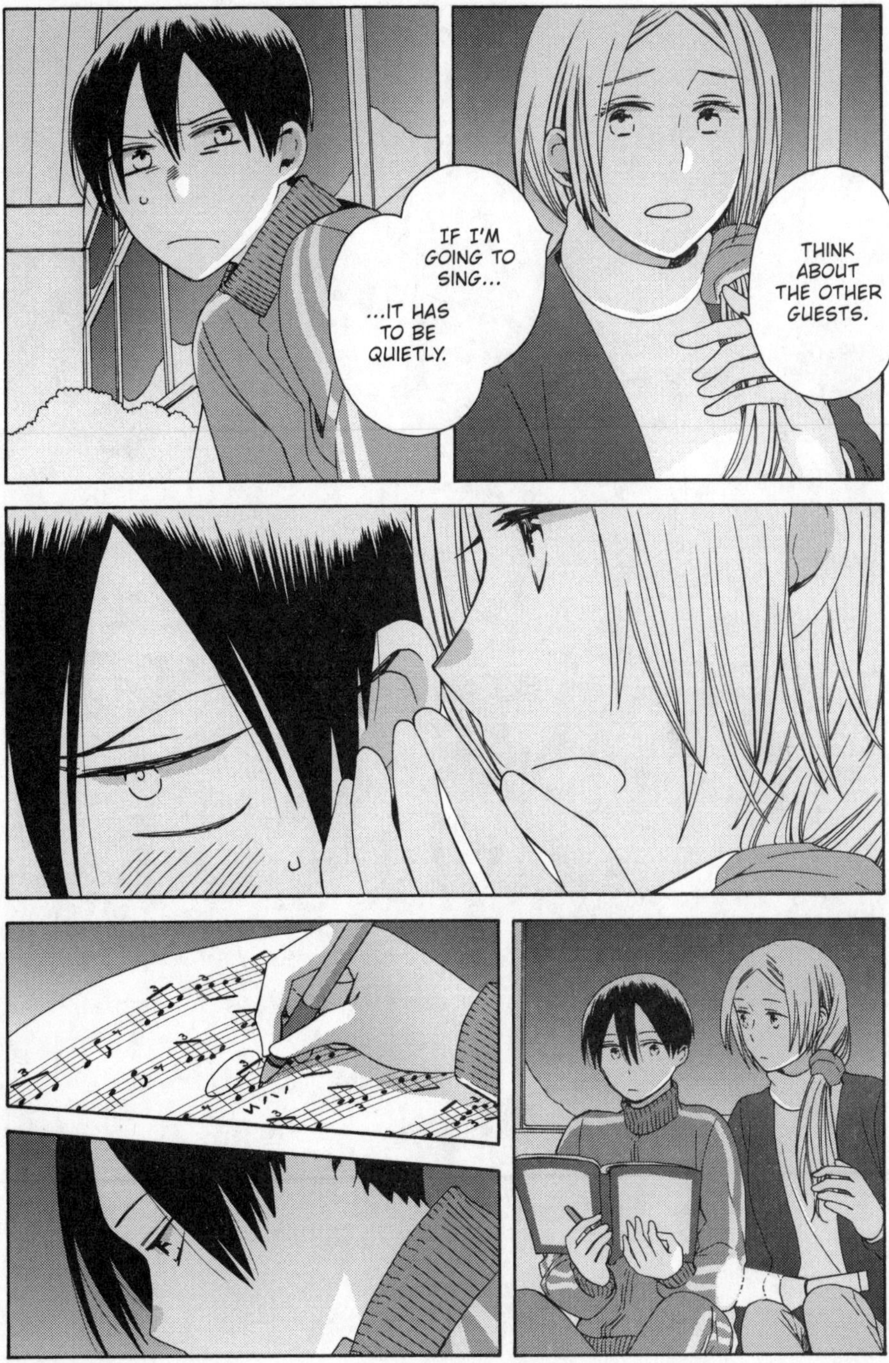
THINK ABOUT THE OTHER GUESTS.
IF I'M GOING TO SING...
...IT HAS TO BE QUIETLY.

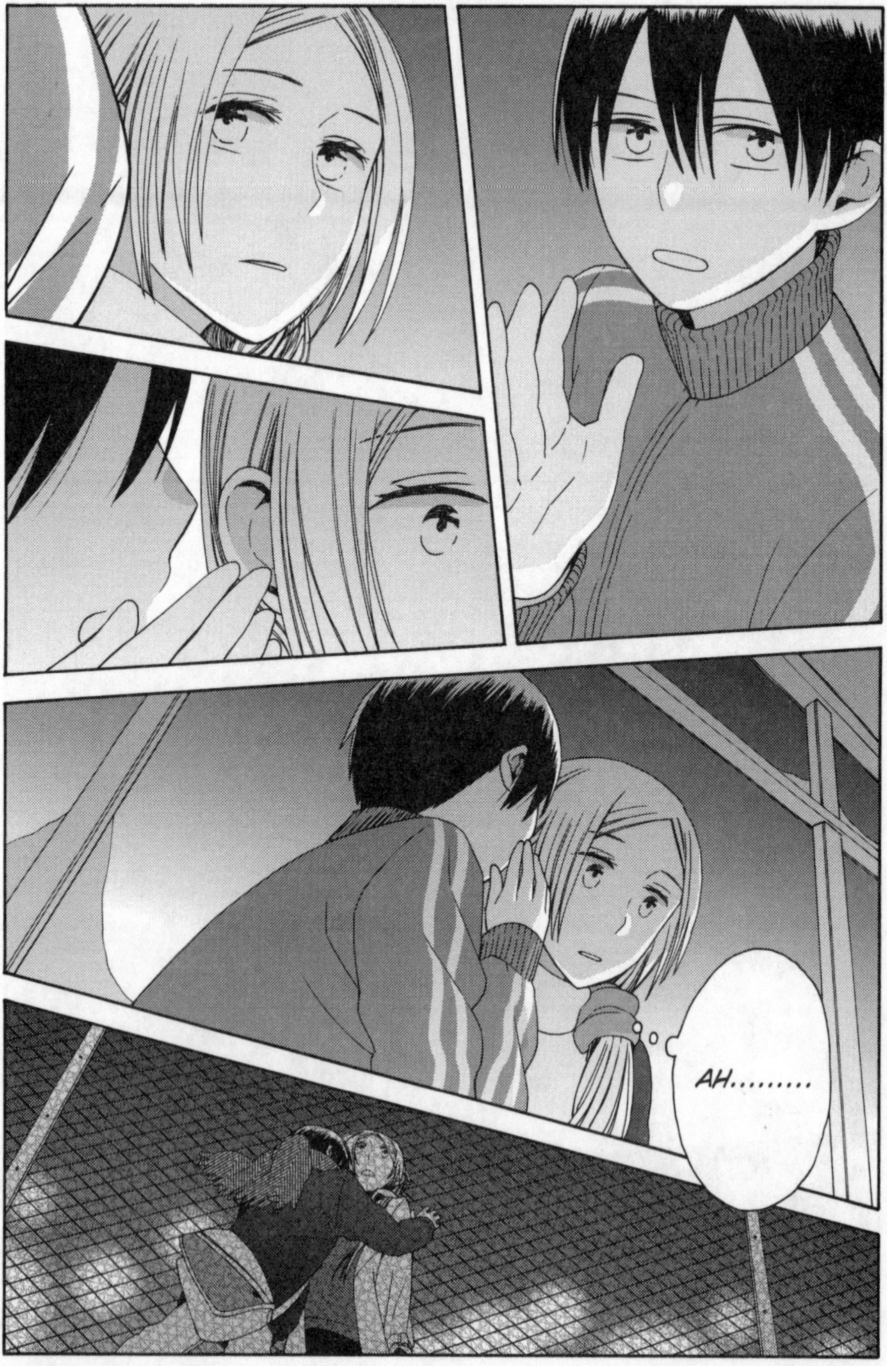
AH.........

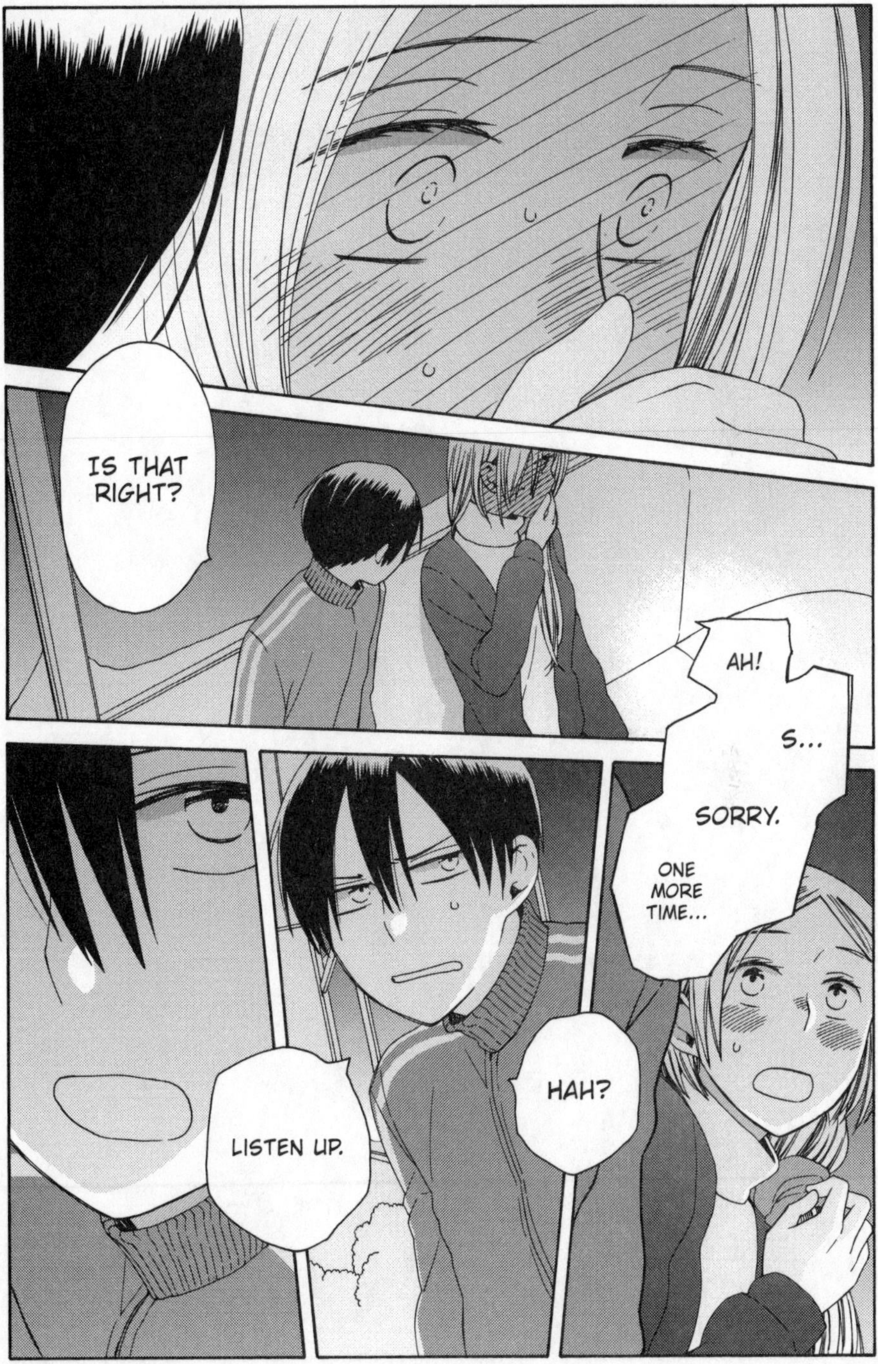

IS THAT RIGHT?
AH! S... SORRY. ONE MORE TIME...
HAH?
LISTEN UP.

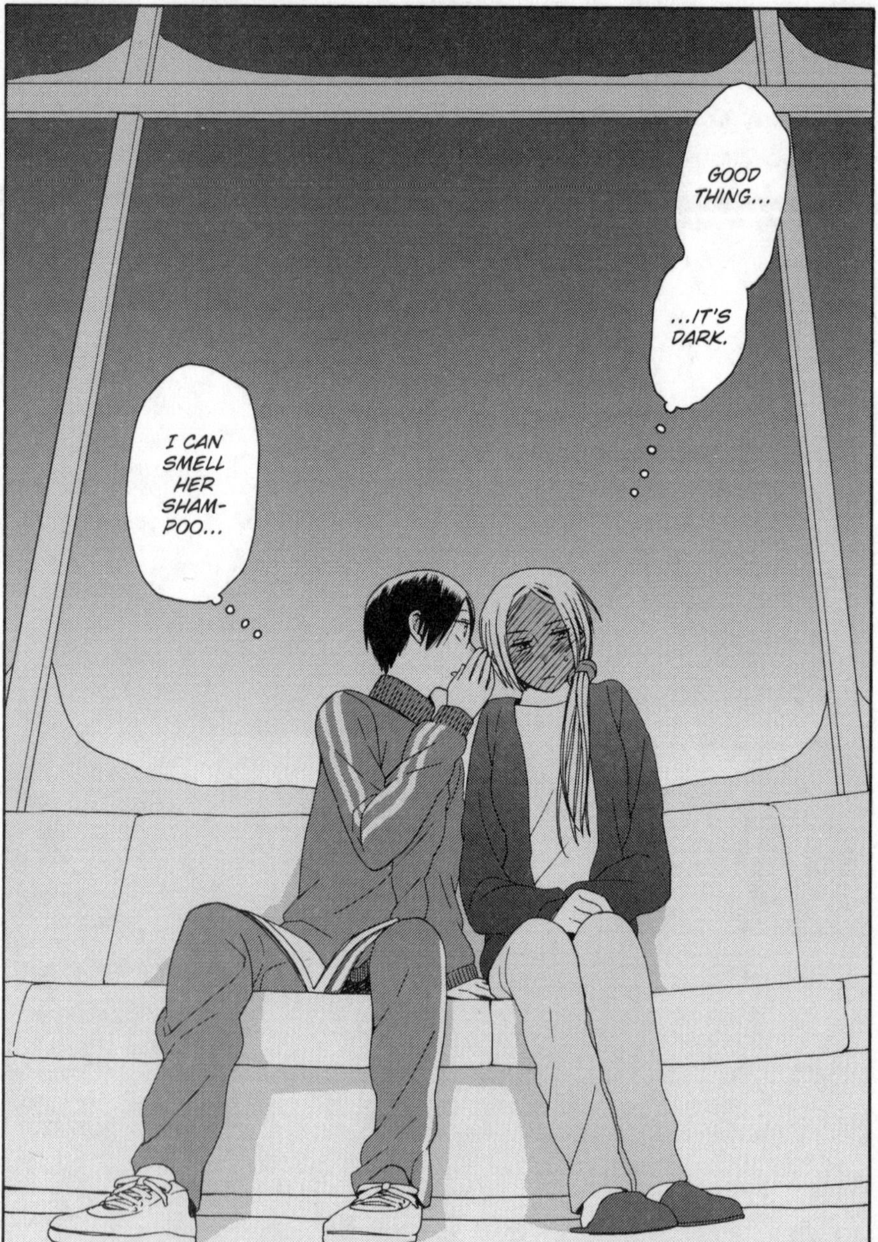
GOOD THING...
...IT'S DARK.
I CAN SMELL HER SHAM-POO...

Fin

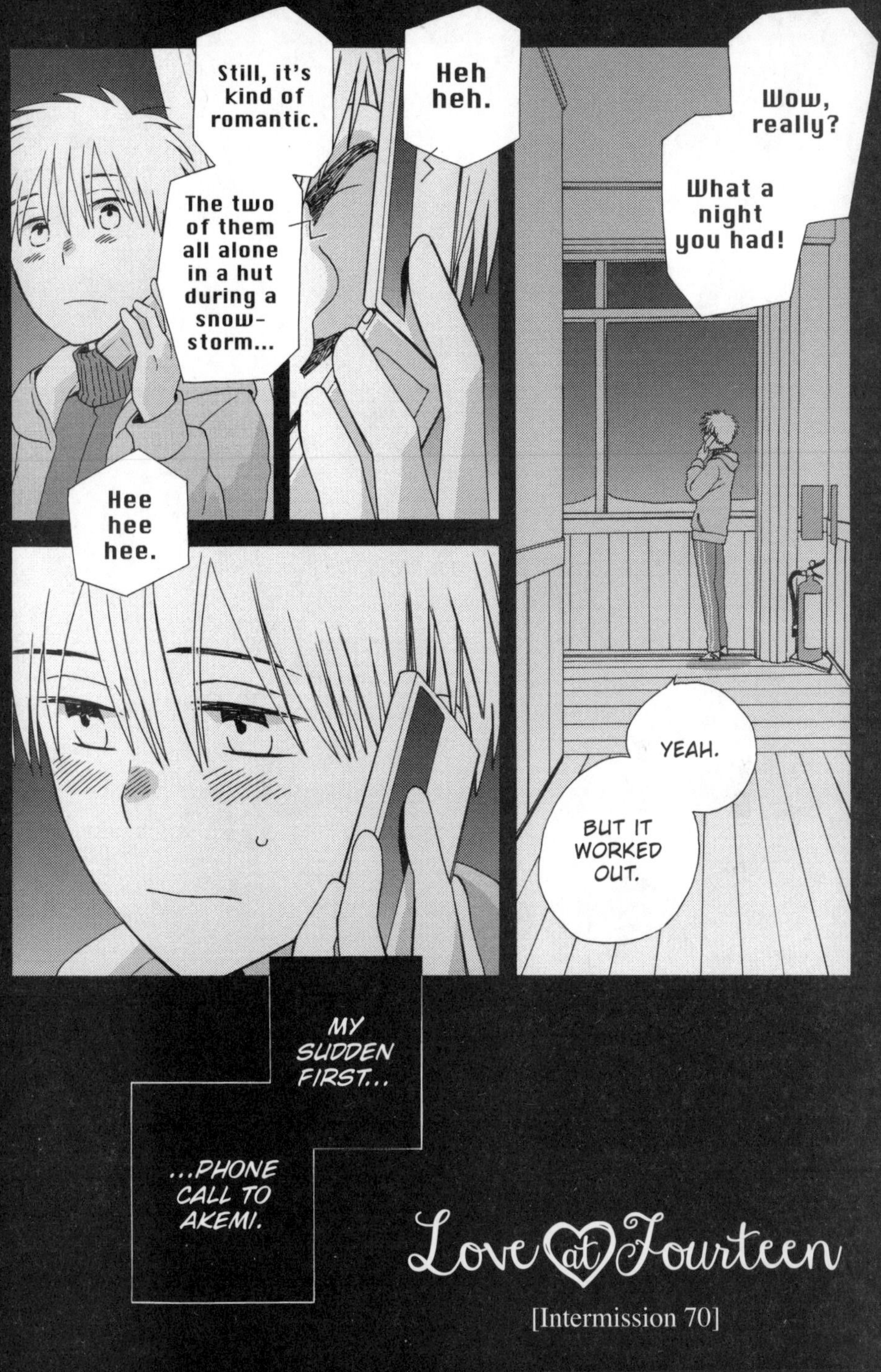
Wow, really?
What a night you had!
YEAH.
BUT IT WORKED OUT.
Heh heh.
Still, it's kind of romantic.
The two of them all alone in a hut during a snow-storm...
Hee hee hee.
MY SUDDEN FIRST...
...PHONE CALL TO AKEMI.

Love at Fourteen

[Intermission 70]

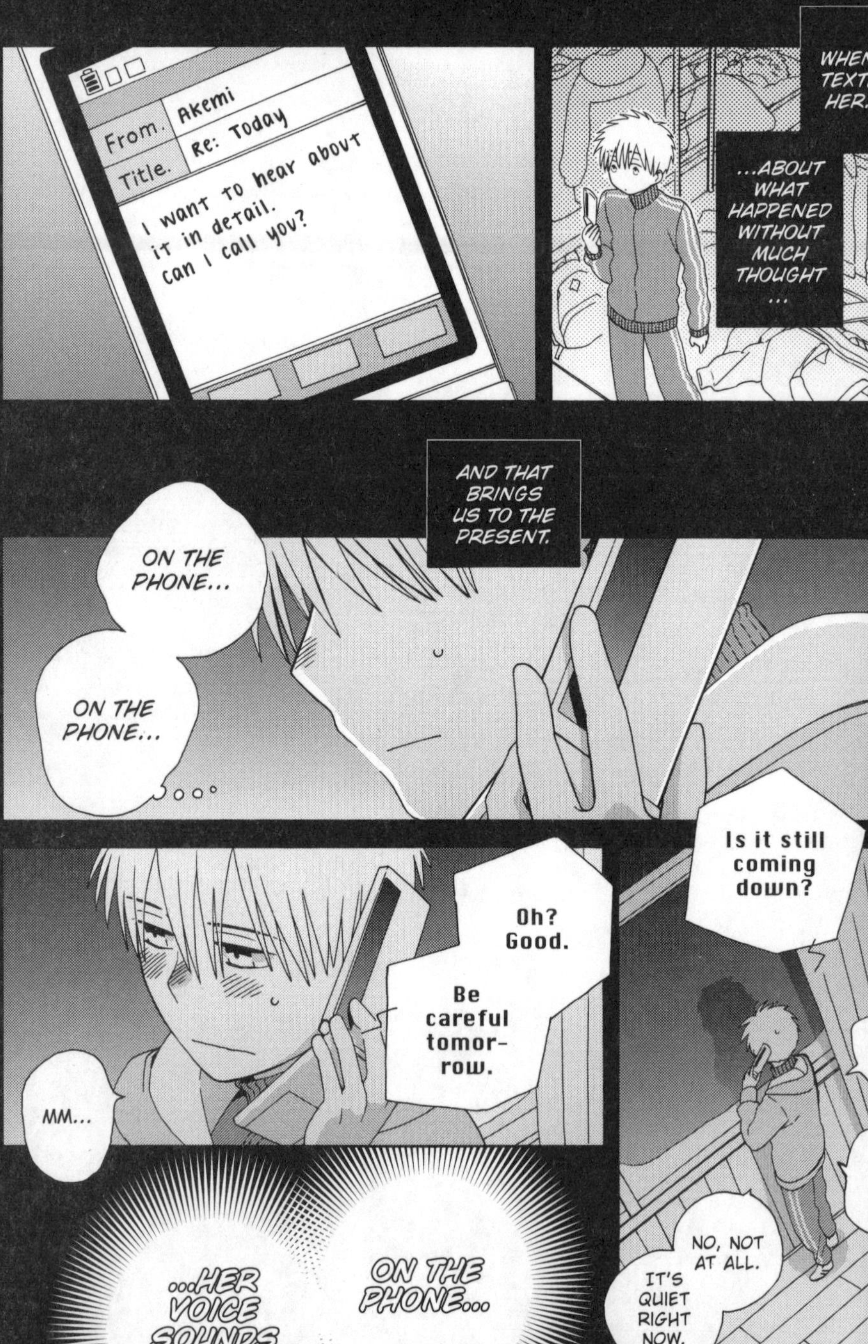
WHEN I TEXTED HER...
...ABOUT WHAT HAPPENED WITHOUT MUCH THOUGHT...
From. Akemi
Title. Re: Today
I want to hear about it in detail. Can I call you?
AND THAT BRINGS US TO THE PRESENT.
ON THE PHONE...
ON THE PHONE...
Is it still coming down?
OH.
UM...
NO, NOT AT ALL.
IT'S QUIET RIGHT NOW.
Oh? Good.
Be careful tomor-row.
MM...
ON THE PHONE...
...HER VOICE SOUNDS SO CLOSE!

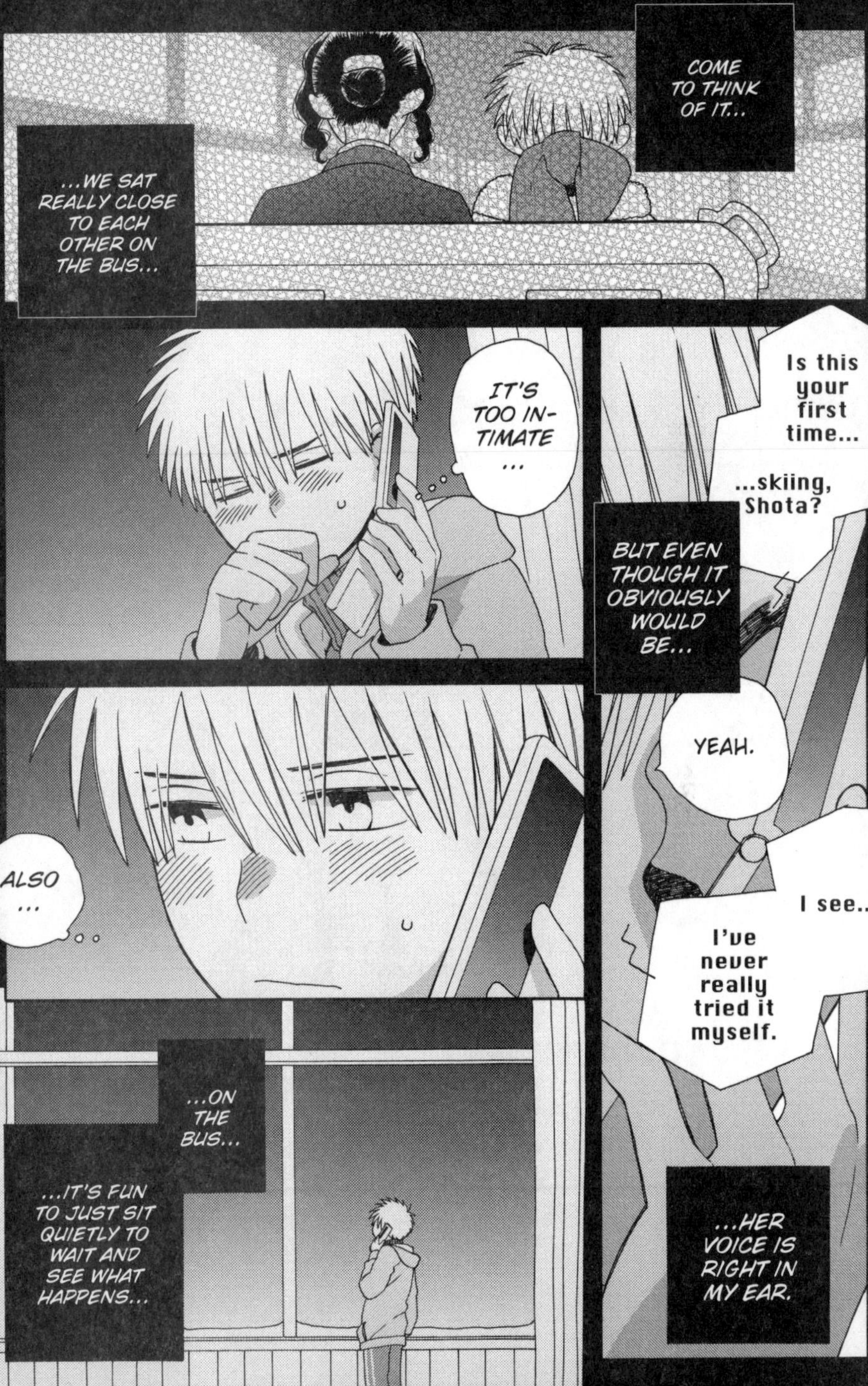
COME TO THINK OF IT...
...WE SAT REALLY CLOSE TO EACH OTHER ON THE BUS...
Is this your first time...
...skiing, Shota?
BUT EVEN THOUGH IT OBVIOUSLY WOULD BE...
YEAH.
I see...
I've never really tried it myself.
...HER VOICE IS RIGHT IN MY EAR.
IT'S TOO INTIMATE...
ALSO...
...ON THE BUS...
...IT'S FUN TO JUST SIT QUIETLY TO WAIT AND SEE WHAT HAPPENS...

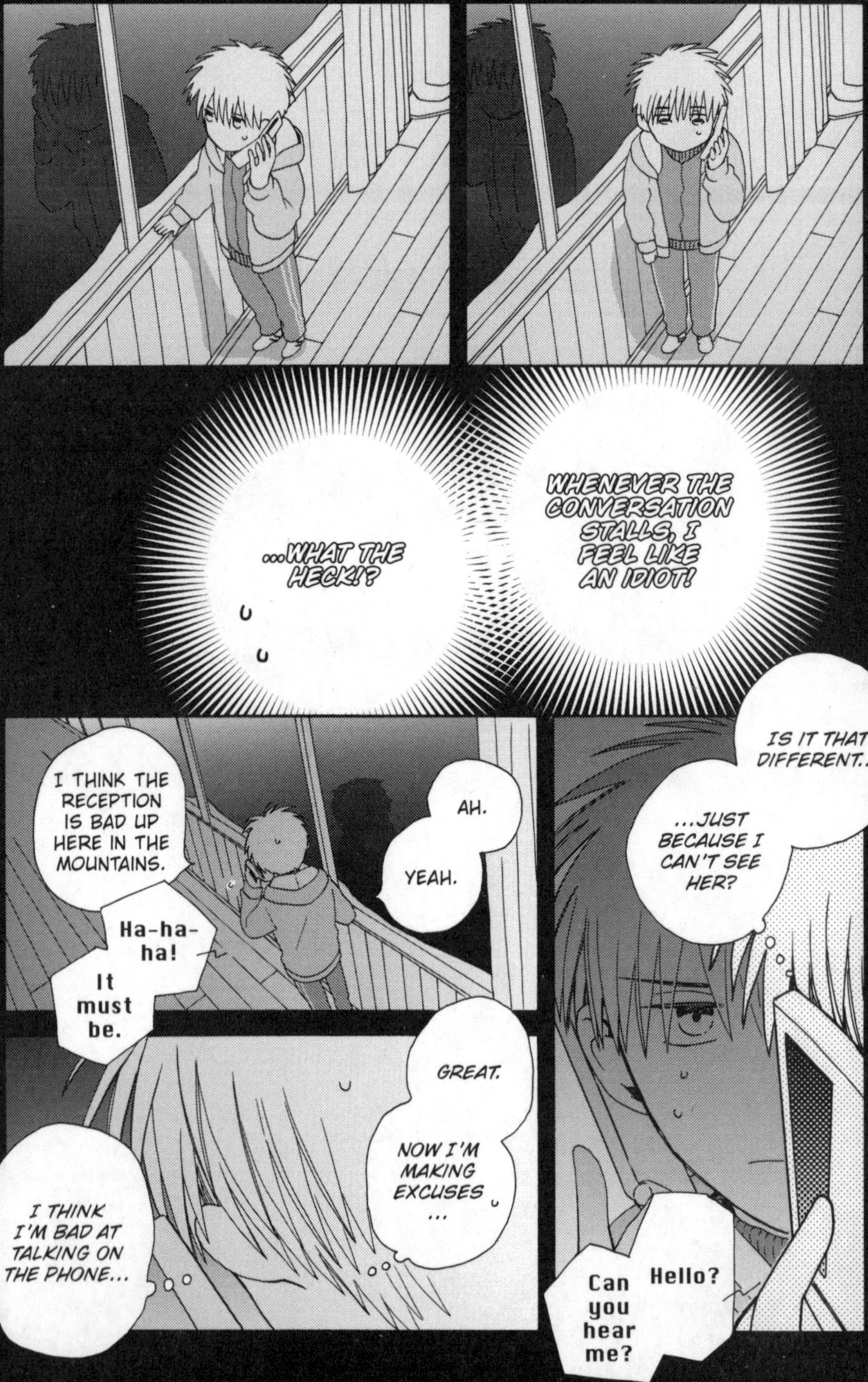
WHENEVER THE CONVERSATION STALLS, I FEEL LIKE AN IDIOT!
...WHAT THE HECK!?
IS IT THAT DIFFERENT...
...JUST BECAUSE I CAN'T SEE HER?
Hello?
Can you hear me?
AH.
YEAH.
I THINK THE RECEPTION IS BAD UP HERE IN THE MOUNTAINS.
Ha-ha-ha!
It must be.
GREAT.
NOW I'M MAKING EXCUSES...
I THINK I'M BAD AT TALKING ON THE PHONE...

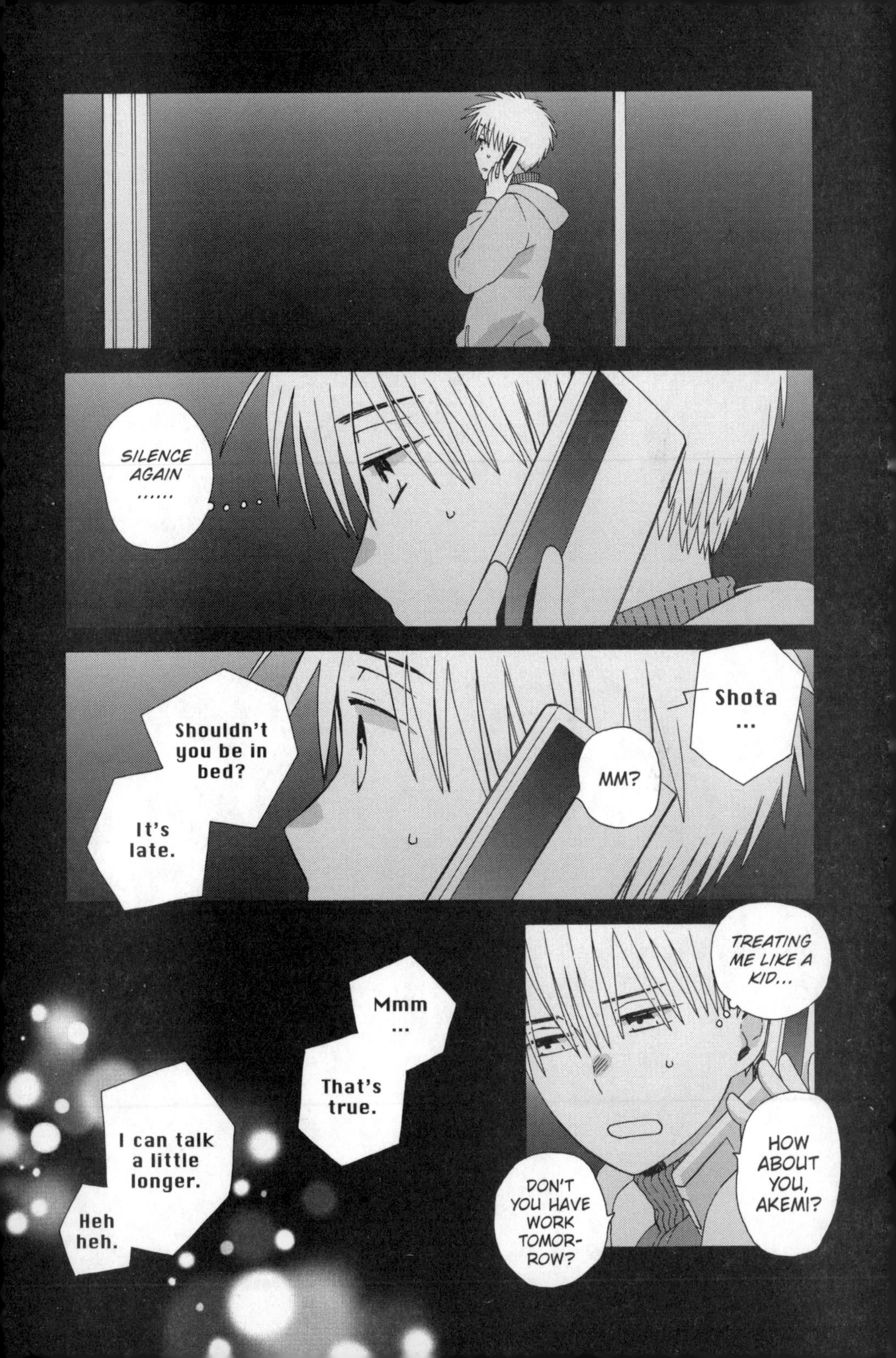
SILENCE AGAIN ......
Shota ...
MM?
Shouldn't you be in bed?
It's late.
TREATING ME LIKE A KID...
HOW ABOUT YOU, AKEMI?
DON'T YOU HAVE WORK TOMOR-ROW?
Mmm ...
That's true.
I can talk a little longer.
Heh heh.

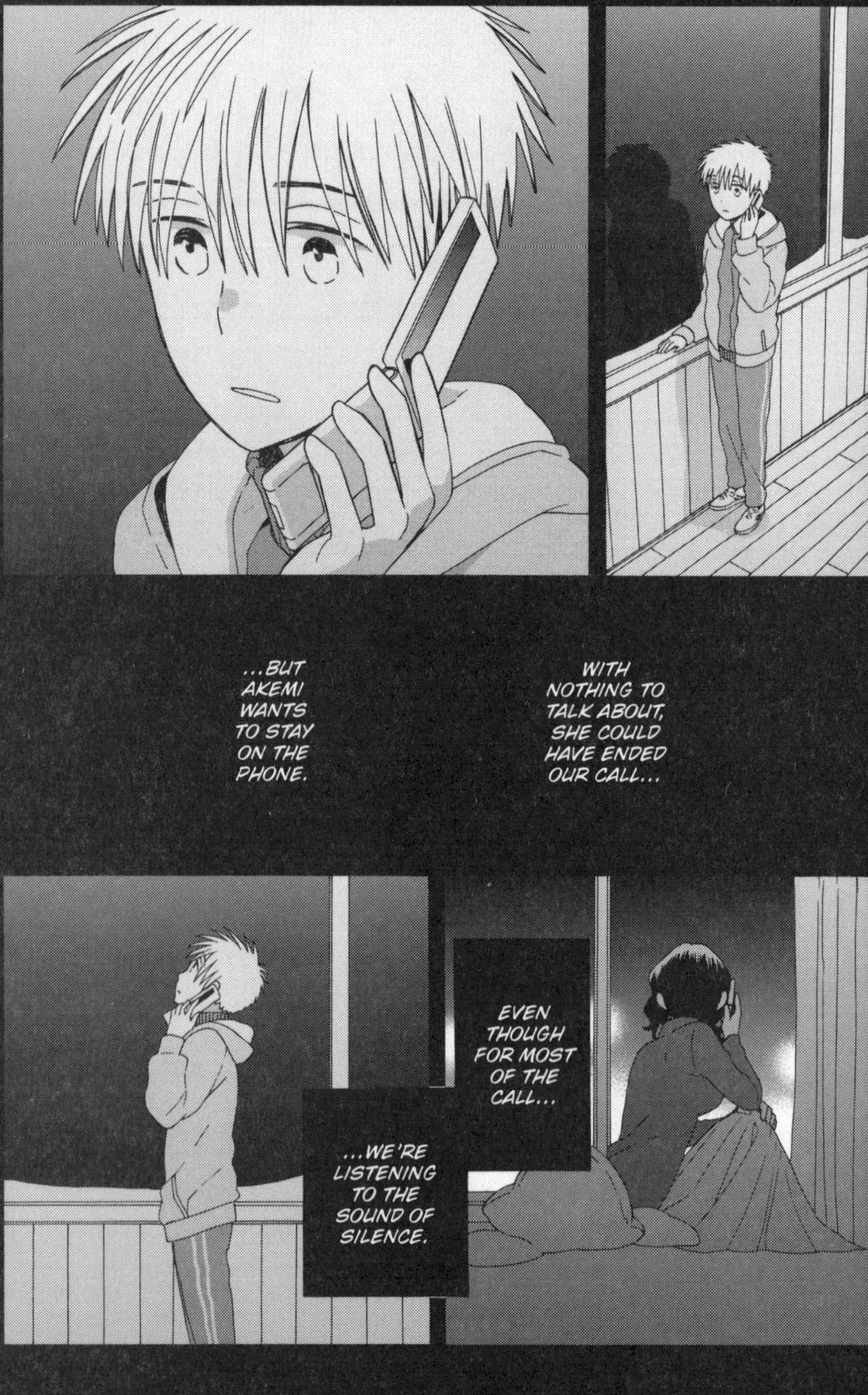
WITH NOTHING TO TALK ABOUT, SHE COULD HAVE ENDED OUR CALL...
...BUT AKEMI WANTS TO STAY ON THE PHONE.
EVEN THOUGH FOR MOST OF THE CALL...
...WE'RE LISTENING TO THE SOUND OF SILENCE.

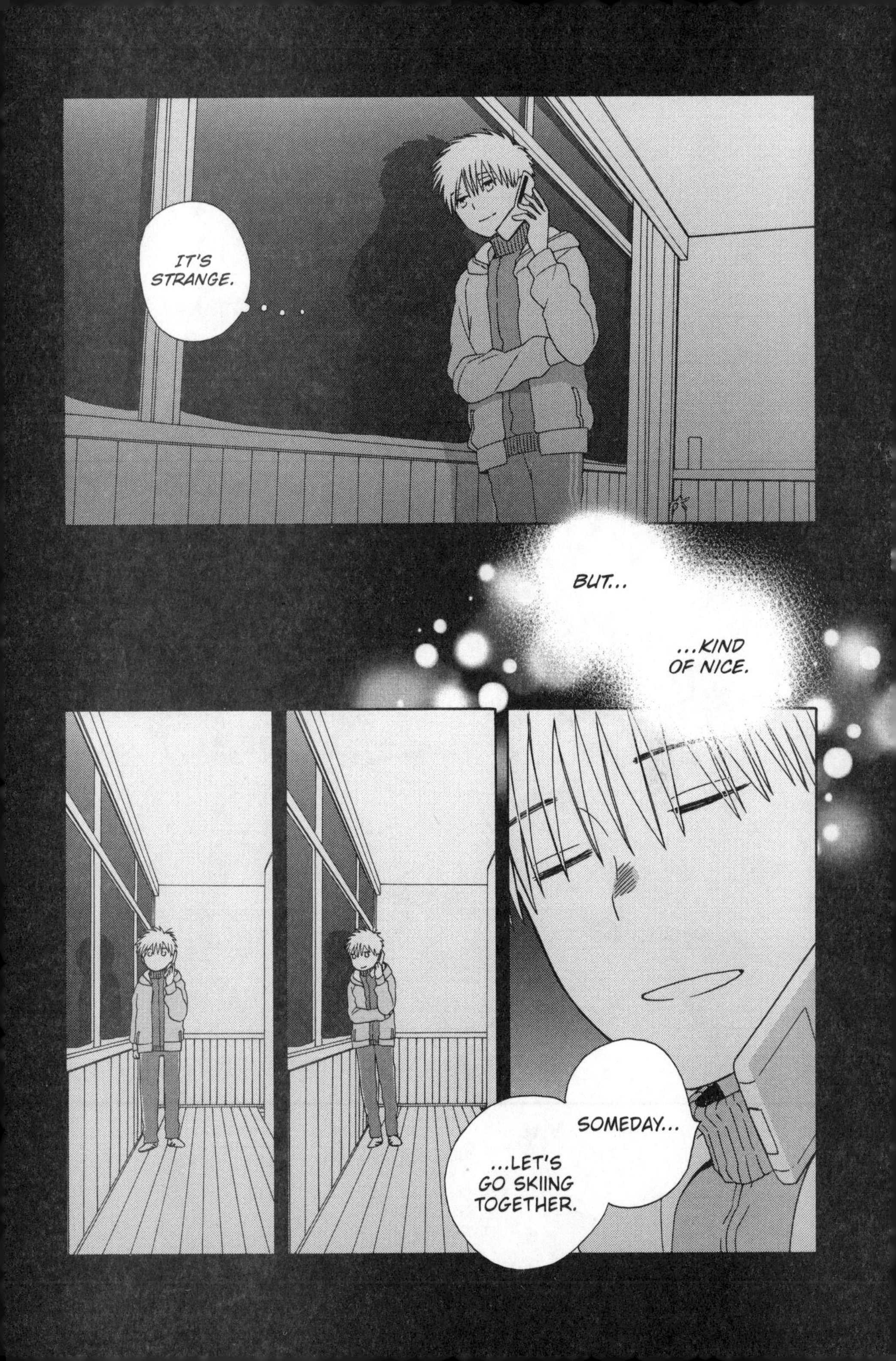
IT'S STRANGE.
BUT...
...KIND OF NICE.
SOMEDAY...
...LET'S GO SKIING TOGETHER.

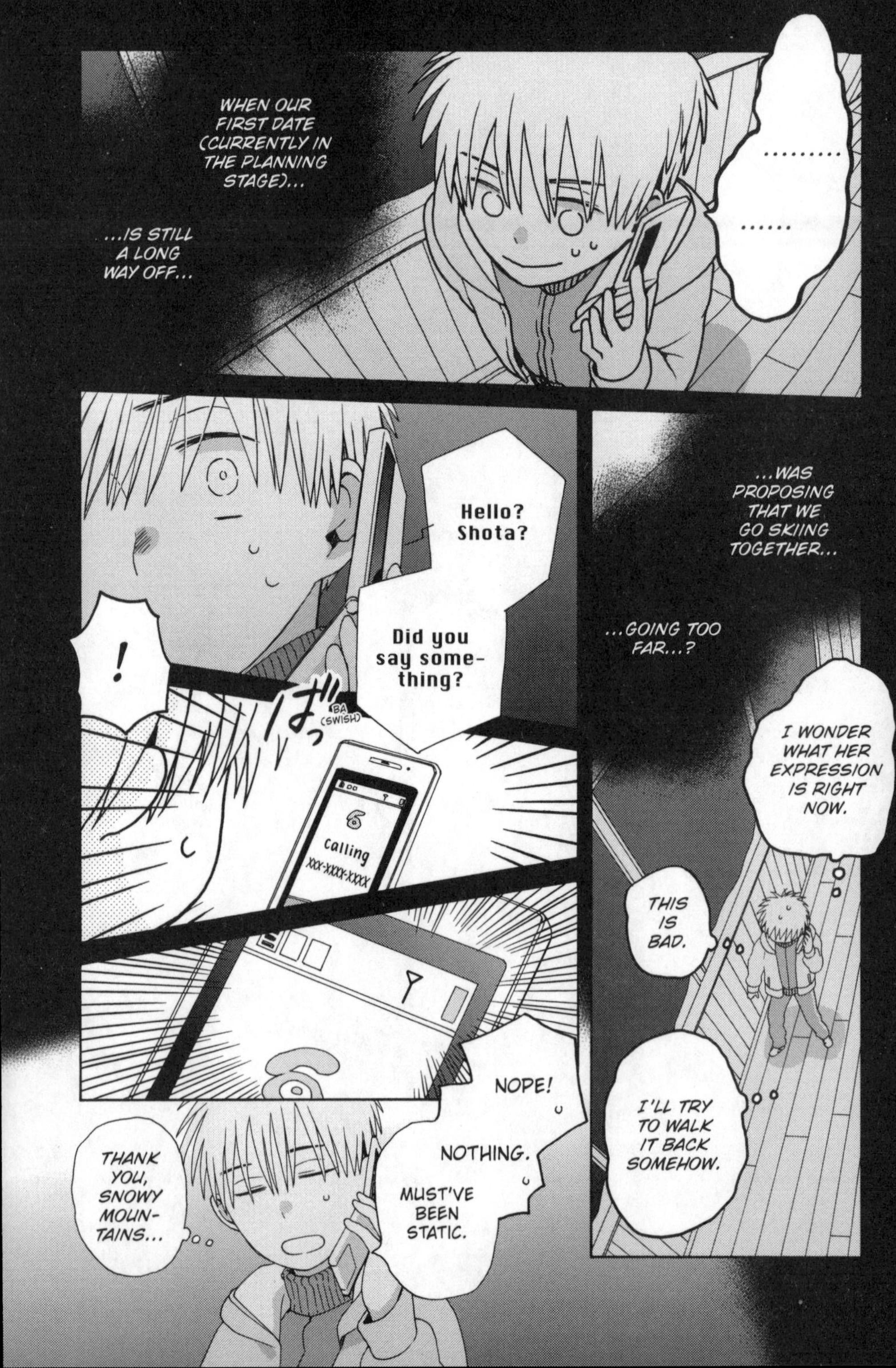

....
......
WHEN OUR FIRST DATE (CURRENTLY IN THE PLANNING STAGE)...
...IS STILL A LONG WAY OFF...
...WAS PROPOSING THAT WE GO SKIING TOGETHER...
...GOING TOO FAR...?
I WONDER WHAT HER EXPRESSION IS RIGHT NOW.
THIS IS BAD.
I'LL TRY TO WALK IT BACK SOMEHOW.
Hello? Shota?
Did you say some-thing?
!
BA (SWISH)
Calling
XXX-XXXX-XXXX
NOPE!
NOTHING.
MUST'VE BEEN STATIC.
THANK YOU, SNOWY MOUN-TAINS...

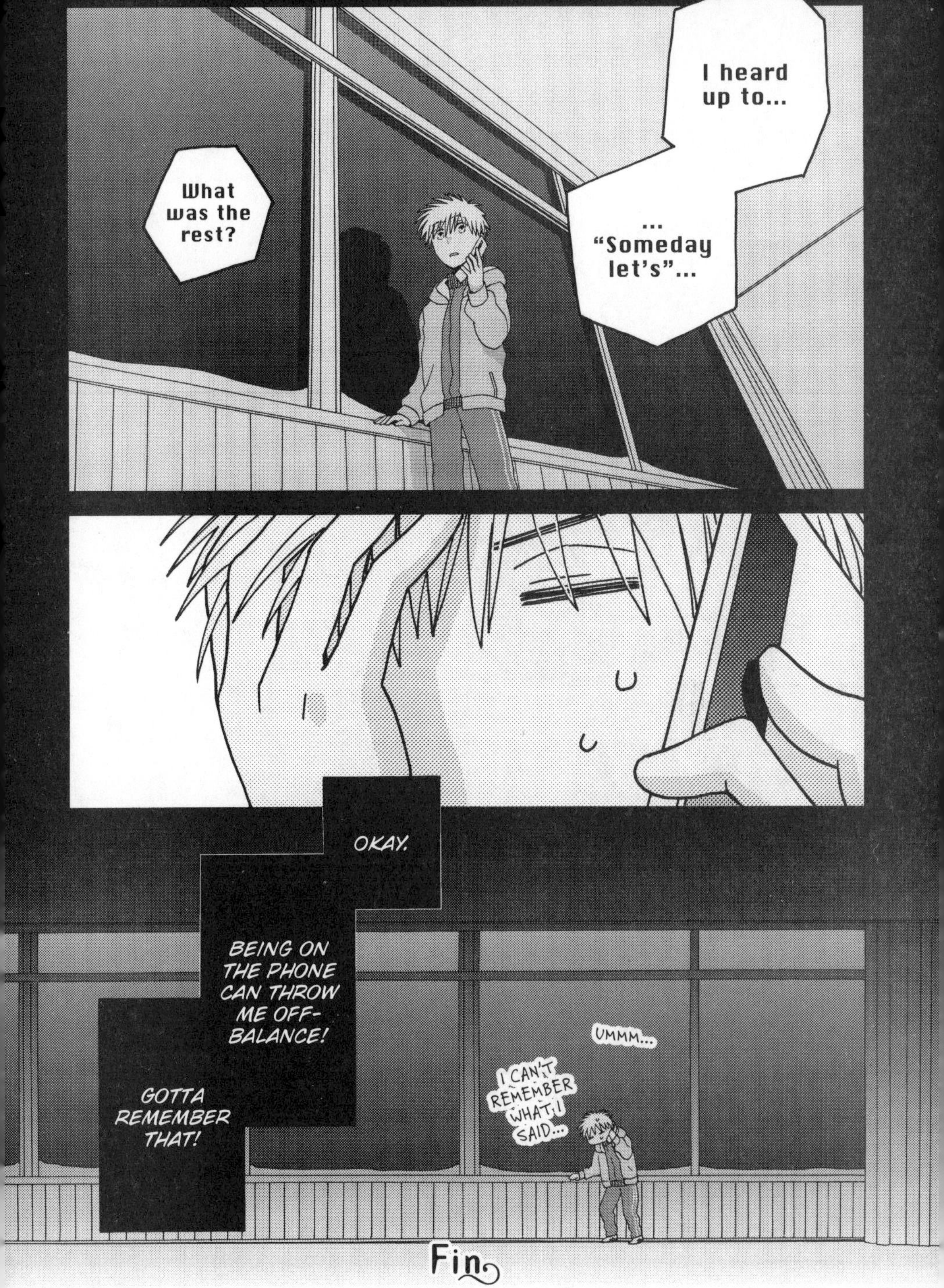
I heard up to...
... "Someday let's"...
What was the rest?
OKAY.
BEING ON THE PHONE CAN THROW ME OFF-BALANCE!
GOTTA REMEMBER THAT!
UMMM...
I CAN'T REMEMBER WHAT I SAID...
Fin

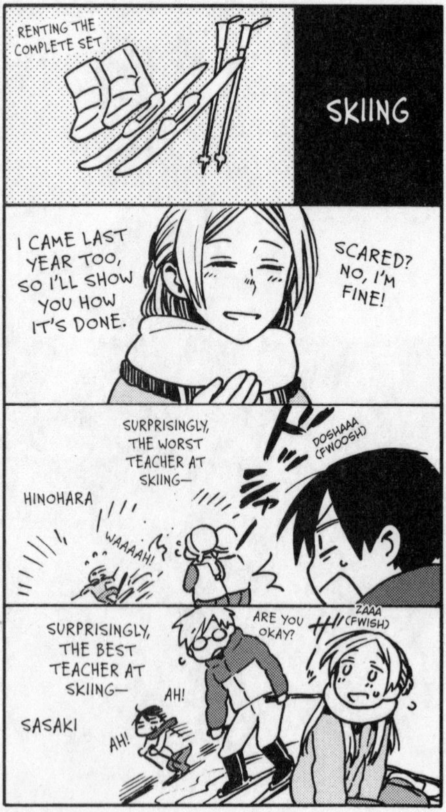
SKIING
RENTING THE COMPLETE SET
I CAME LAST YEAR TOO, SO I'LL SHOW YOU HOW IT'S DONE.
SCARED? NO, I'M FINE!
SURPRISINGLY, THE WORST TEACHER AT SKIING—
HINOHARA
DOSHAAA (FWOOSH)
WAAAAH!
ZAAA (FWISH)
ARE YOU OKAY?
SURPRISINGLY, THE BEST TEACHER AT SKIING—
SASAKI
AH!
AH!

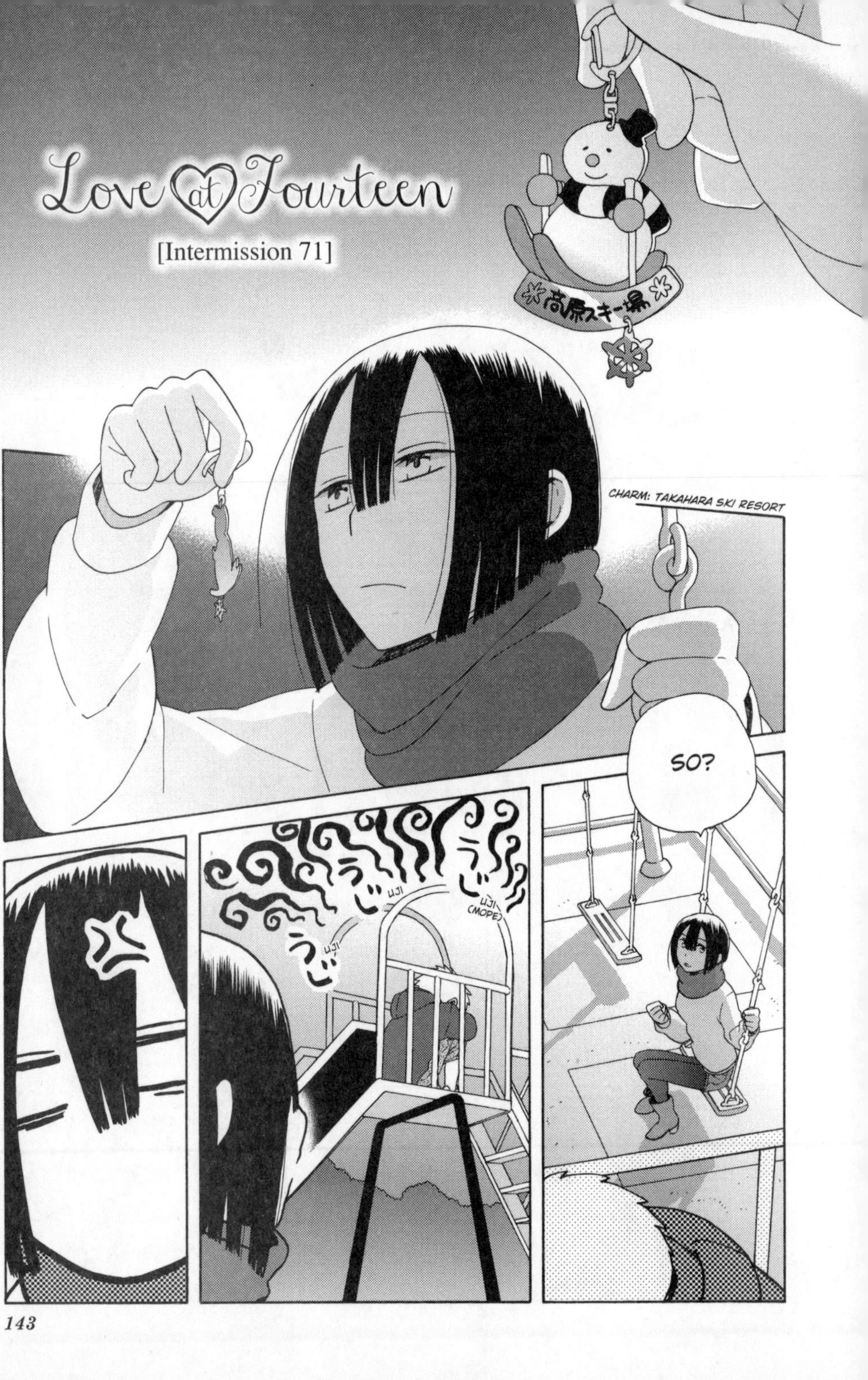
Love at Fourteen
[Intermission 71]
高原スキー場
CHARM: TAKAHARA SKI RESORT
SO?
うじ UJI (MOPE)
うじ UJI
うじ UJI

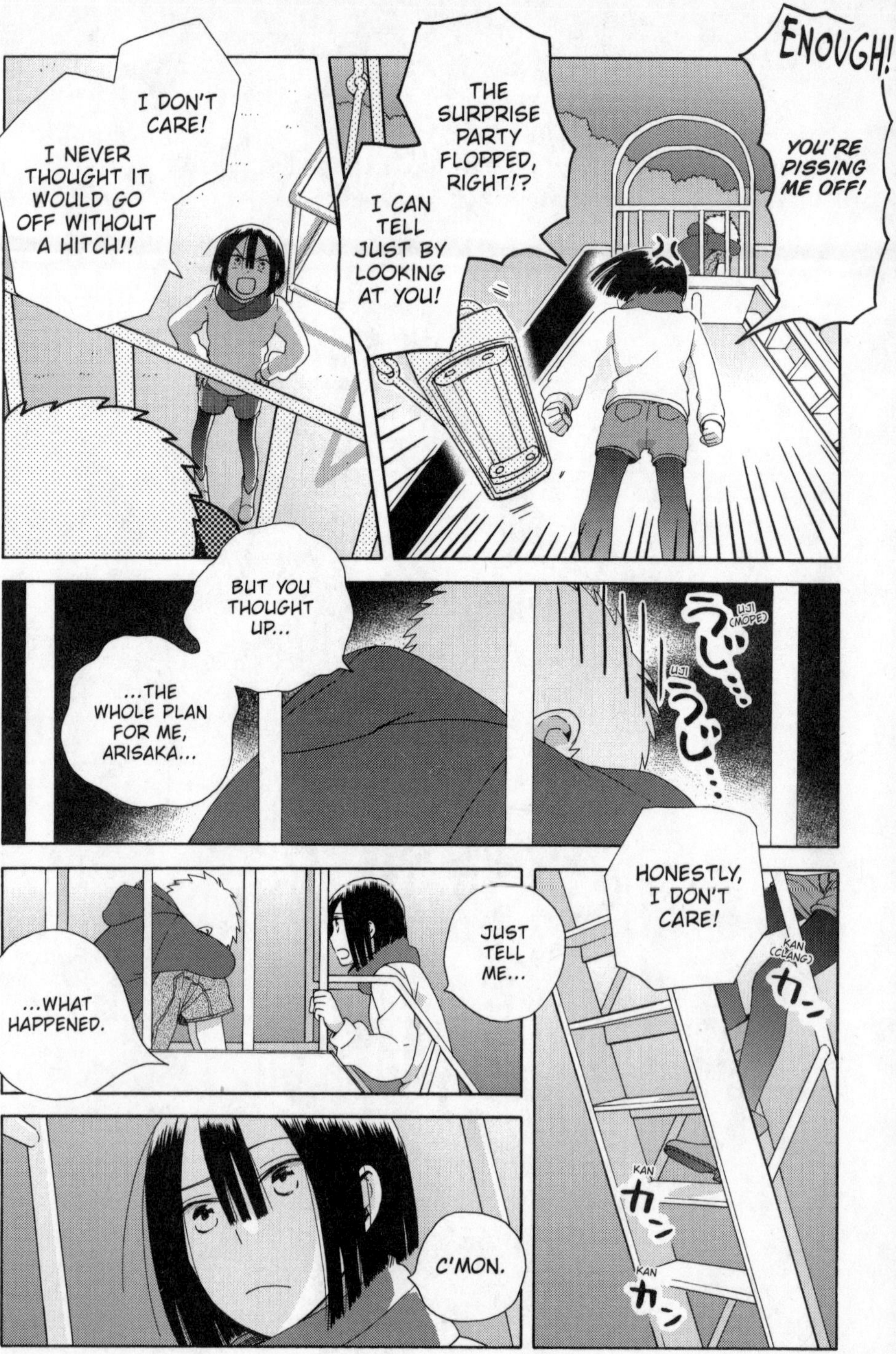
ENOUGH!
YOU'RE PISSING ME OFF!
THE SURPRISE PARTY FLOPPED, RIGHT!?
I CAN TELL JUST BY LOOKING AT YOU!
I DON'T CARE!
I NEVER THOUGHT IT WOULD GO OFF WITHOUT A HITCH!!
UJI (MOPE)
UJI
BUT YOU THOUGHT UP...
...THE WHOLE PLAN FOR ME, ARISAKA...
HONESTLY, I DON'T CARE!
KAN (CLANG)
KAN
KAN
JUST TELL ME...
...WHAT HAPPENED.
C'MON.

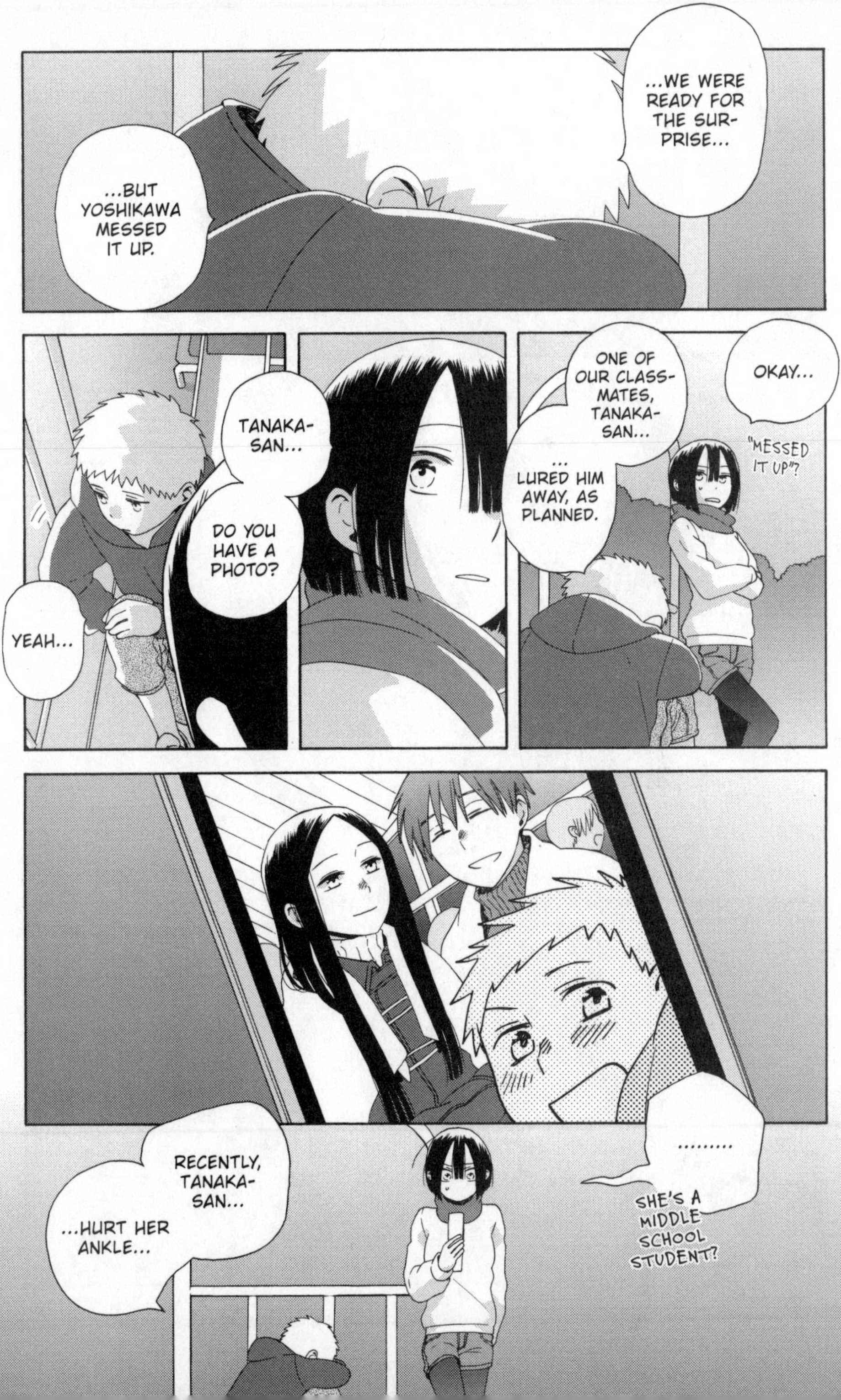
...WE WERE READY FOR THE SUR-PRISE...
...BUT YOSHIKAWA MESSED IT UP.
OKAY...
"MESSED IT UP"?
ONE OF OUR CLASS-MATES, TANAKA-SAN...
... LURED HIM AWAY, AS PLANNED.
TANAKA-SAN...
DO YOU HAVE A PHOTO?
YEAH...
....
SHE'S A MIDDLE SCHOOL STUDENT?
RECENTLY, TANAKA-SAN...
...HURT HER ANKLE...

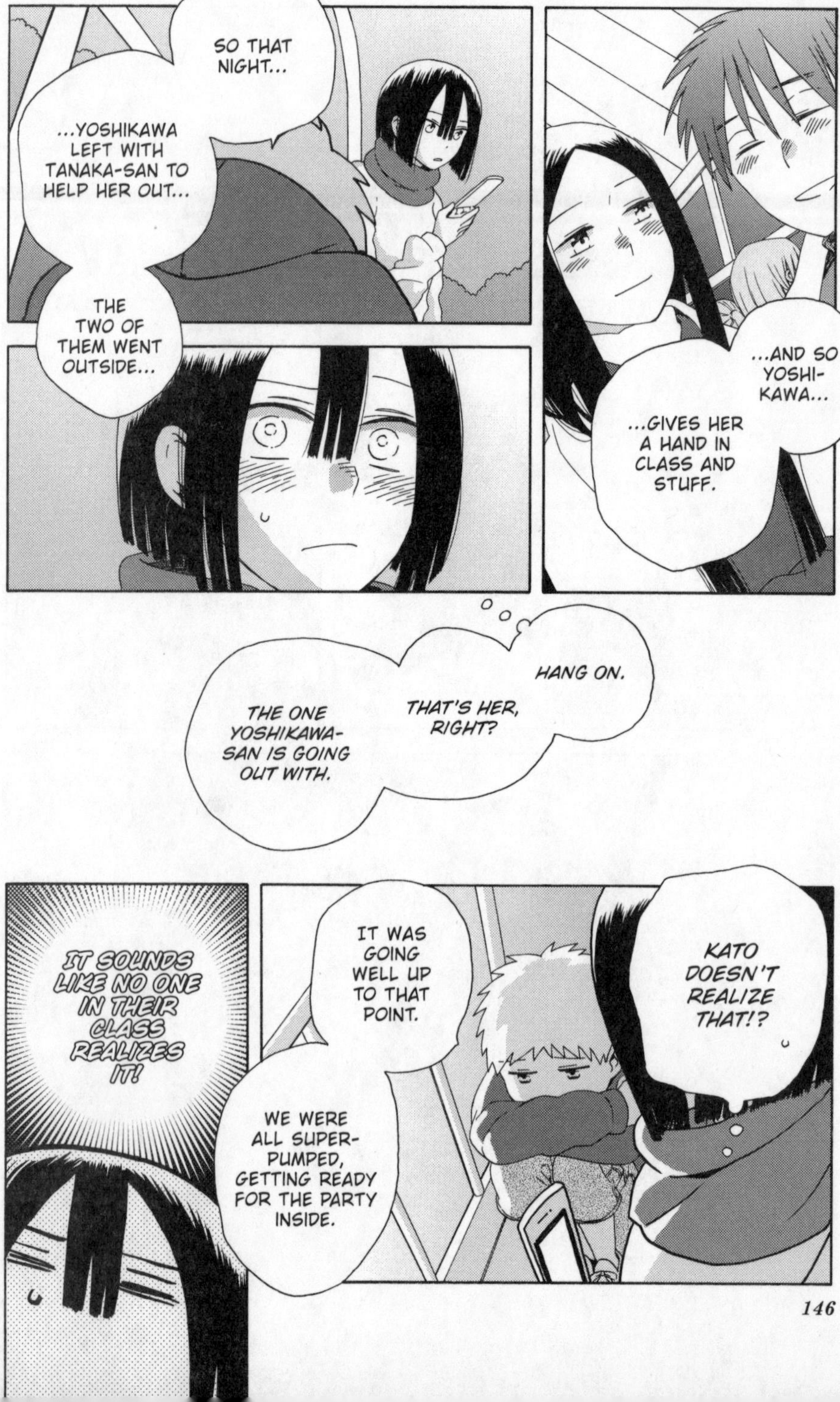
...AND SO YOSHI-KAWA...
...GIVES HER A HAND IN CLASS AND STUFF.
SO THAT NIGHT...
...YOSHIKAWA LEFT WITH TANAKA-SAN TO HELP HER OUT...
THE TWO OF THEM WENT OUTSIDE...
HANG ON.
THAT'S HER, RIGHT?
THE ONE YOSHIKAWA-SAN IS GOING OUT WITH.
KATO DOESN'T REALIZE THAT!?
IT WAS GOING WELL UP TO THAT POINT.
WE WERE ALL SUPER-PUMPED, GETTING READY FOR THE PARTY INSIDE.
IT SOUNDS LIKE NO ONE IN THEIR CLASS REALIZES IT!

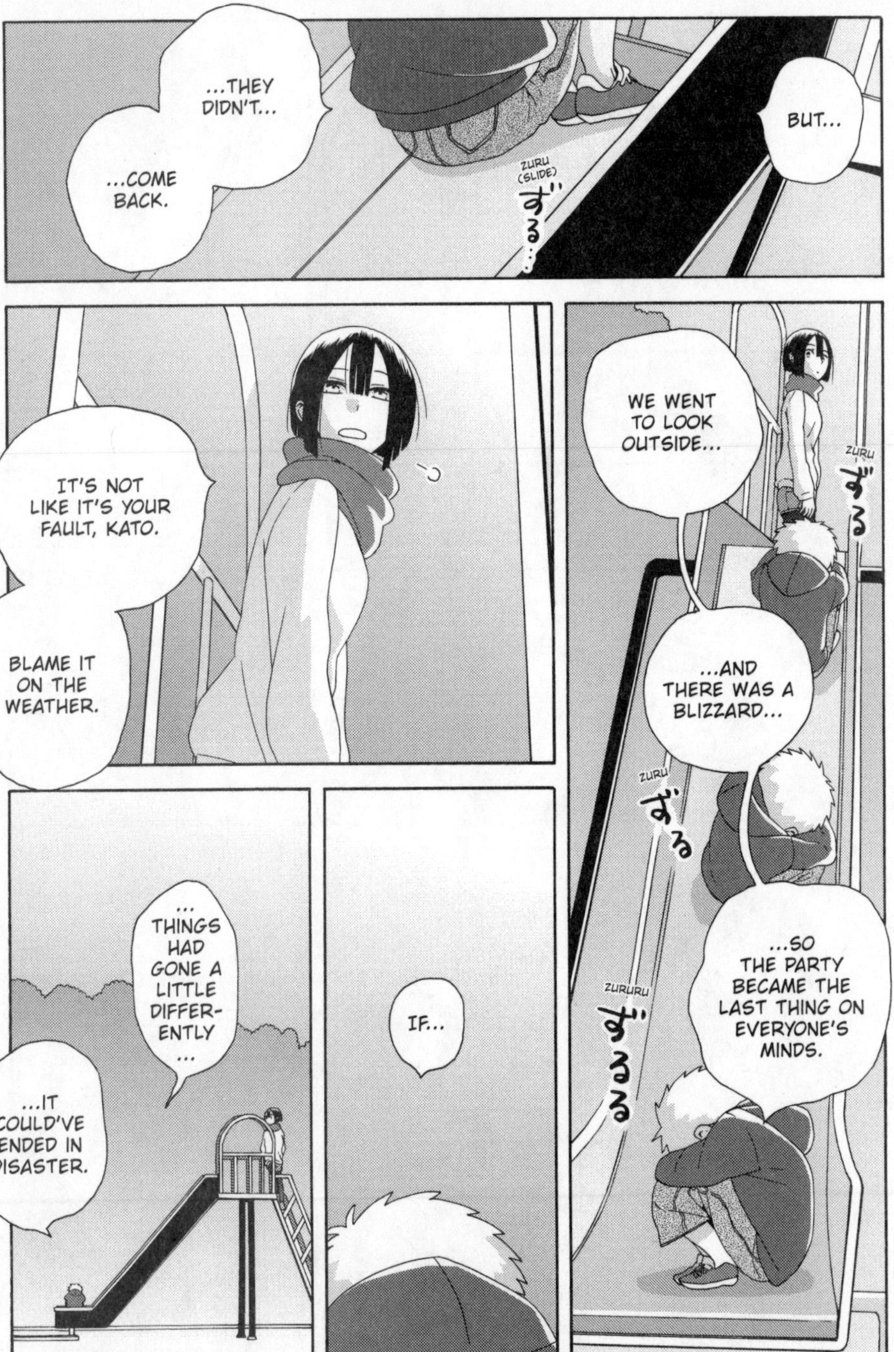
BUT...
ZURU (SLIDE)
ずる...
...THEY DIDN'T...
...COME BACK.
WE WENT TO LOOK OUTSIDE...
ZURU
ずる
...AND THERE WAS A BLIZZARD...
ZURU
ずる
...SO THE PARTY BECAME THE LAST THING ON EVERYONE'S MINDS.
ZURURU
ずるる
IT'S NOT LIKE IT'S YOUR FAULT, KATO.
BLAME IT ON THE WEATHER.
IF...
...THINGS HAD GONE A LITTLE DIFFER-ENTLY...
...IT COULD'VE ENDED IN DISASTER.

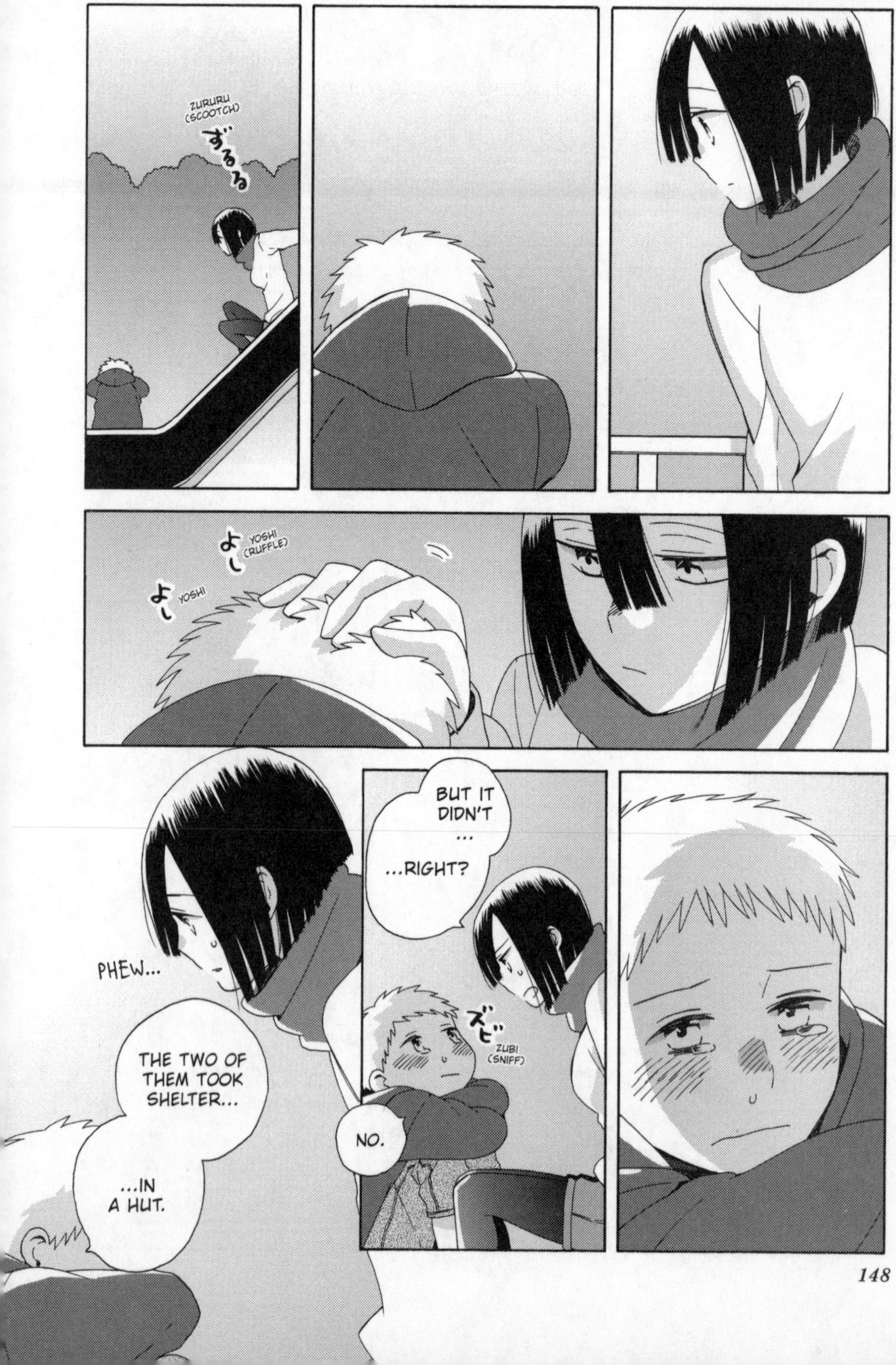
ずるる
ZURURU (SCOOTCH)
よし
YOSHI (RUFFLE)
よし
YOSHI
BUT IT DIDN'T ...
...RIGHT?
ズビ
ZUBI (SNIFF)
NO.
PHEW...
THE TWO OF THEM TOOK SHELTER...
...IN A HUT.

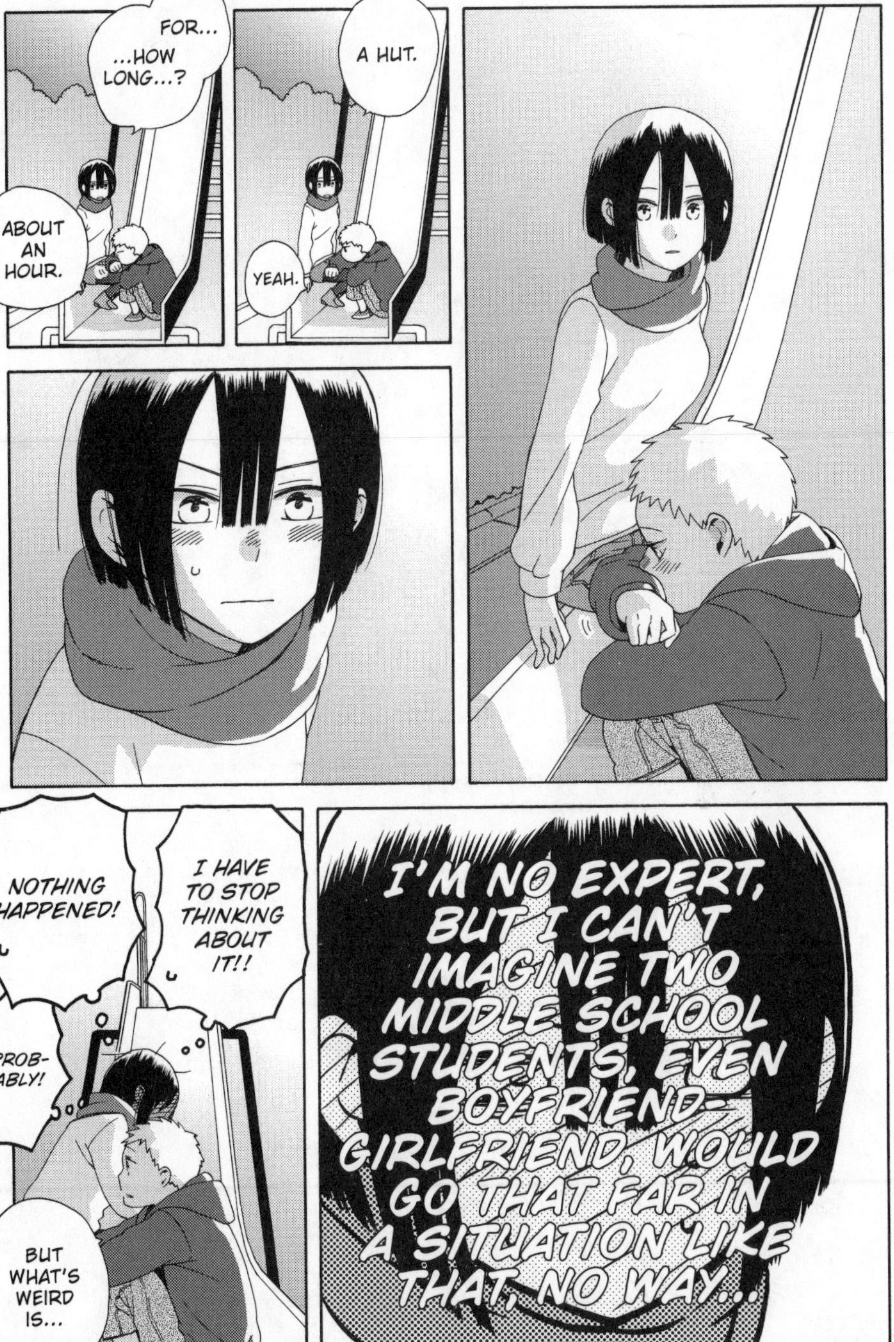
A HUT.
YEAH.
FOR... ...HOW LONG...?
ABOUT AN HOUR.
I'M NO EXPERT, BUT I CAN'T IMAGINE TWO MIDDLE SCHOOL STUDENTS, EVEN BOYFRIEND-GIRLFRIEND, WOULD GO THAT FAR IN A SITUATION LIKE THAT, NO WAY...
I HAVE TO STOP THINKING ABOUT IT!!
NOTHING HAPPENED!
PROB-ABLY!
BUT WHAT'S WEIRD IS...

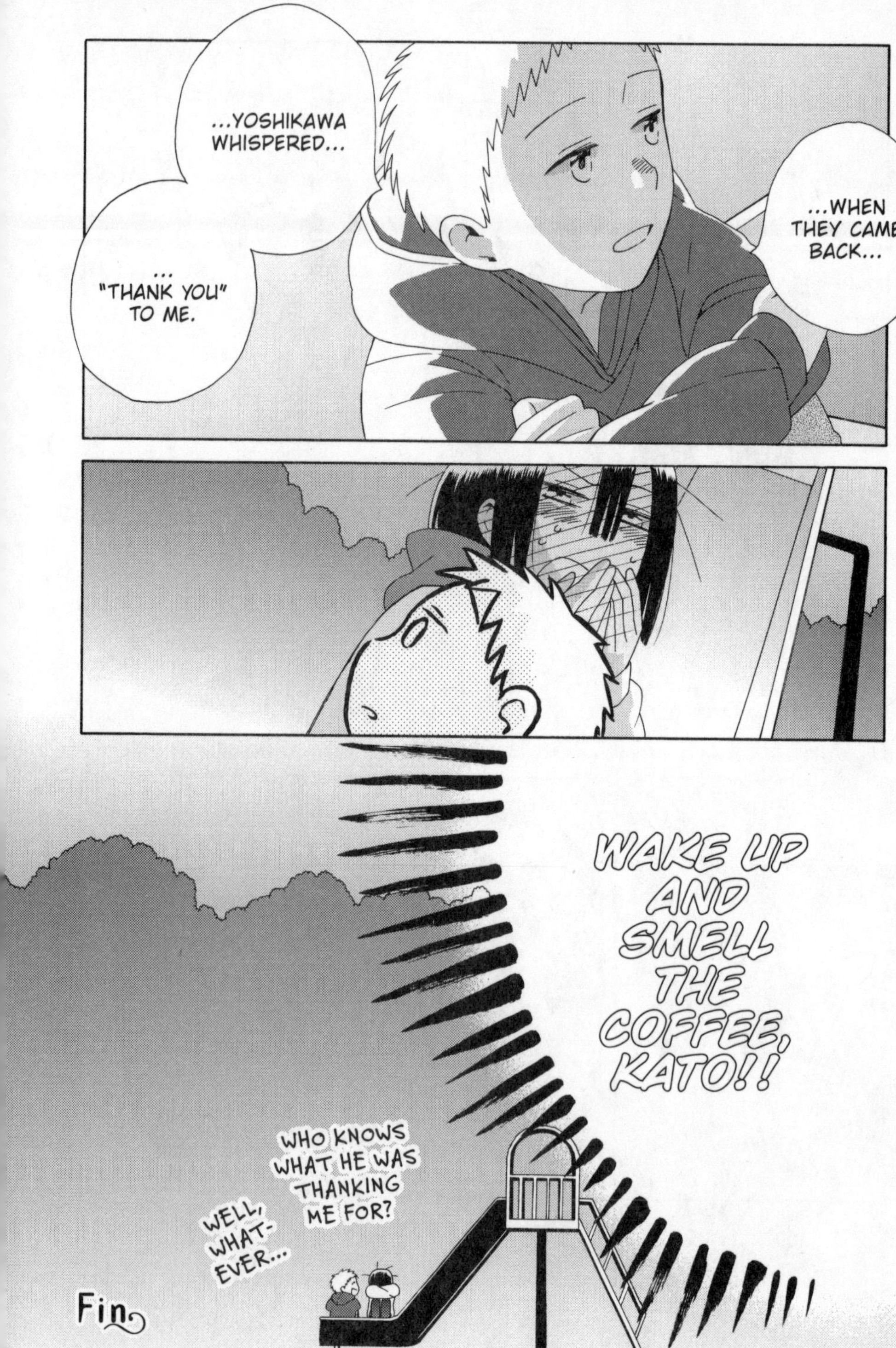
...WHEN THEY CAME BACK...
...YOSHIKAWA WHISPERED...
... "THANK YOU" TO ME.
WAKE UP AND SMELL THE COFFEE, KATO!!
WHO KNOWS WHAT HE WAS THANKING ME FOR?
WELL, WHAT-EVER...
Fin

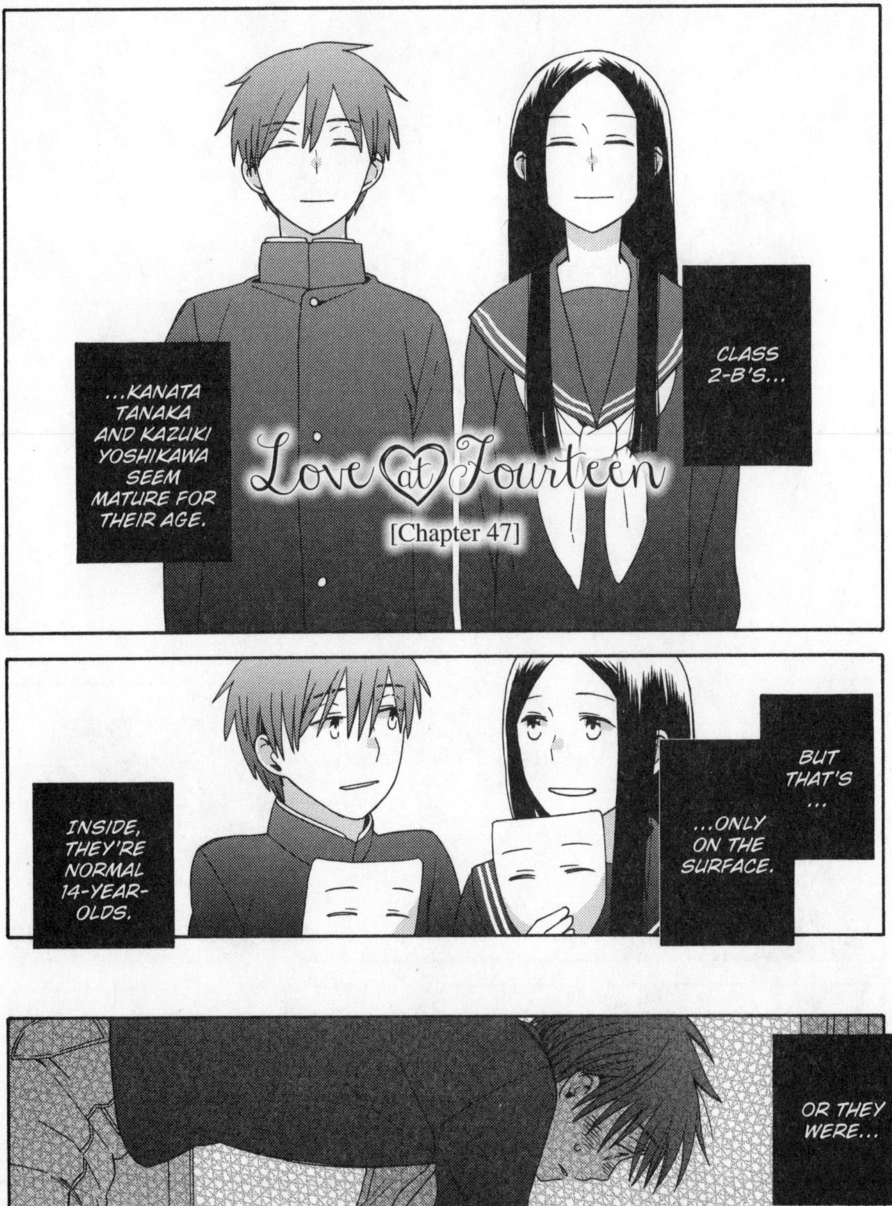
CLASS 2-B'S...
...KANATA TANAKA AND KAZUKI YOSHIKAWA SEEM MATURE FOR THEIR AGE.
Love at Fourteen
[Chapter 47]
BUT THAT'S...
...ONLY ON THE SURFACE.
INSIDE, THEY'RE NORMAL 14-YEAR-OLDS.
OR THEY WERE...

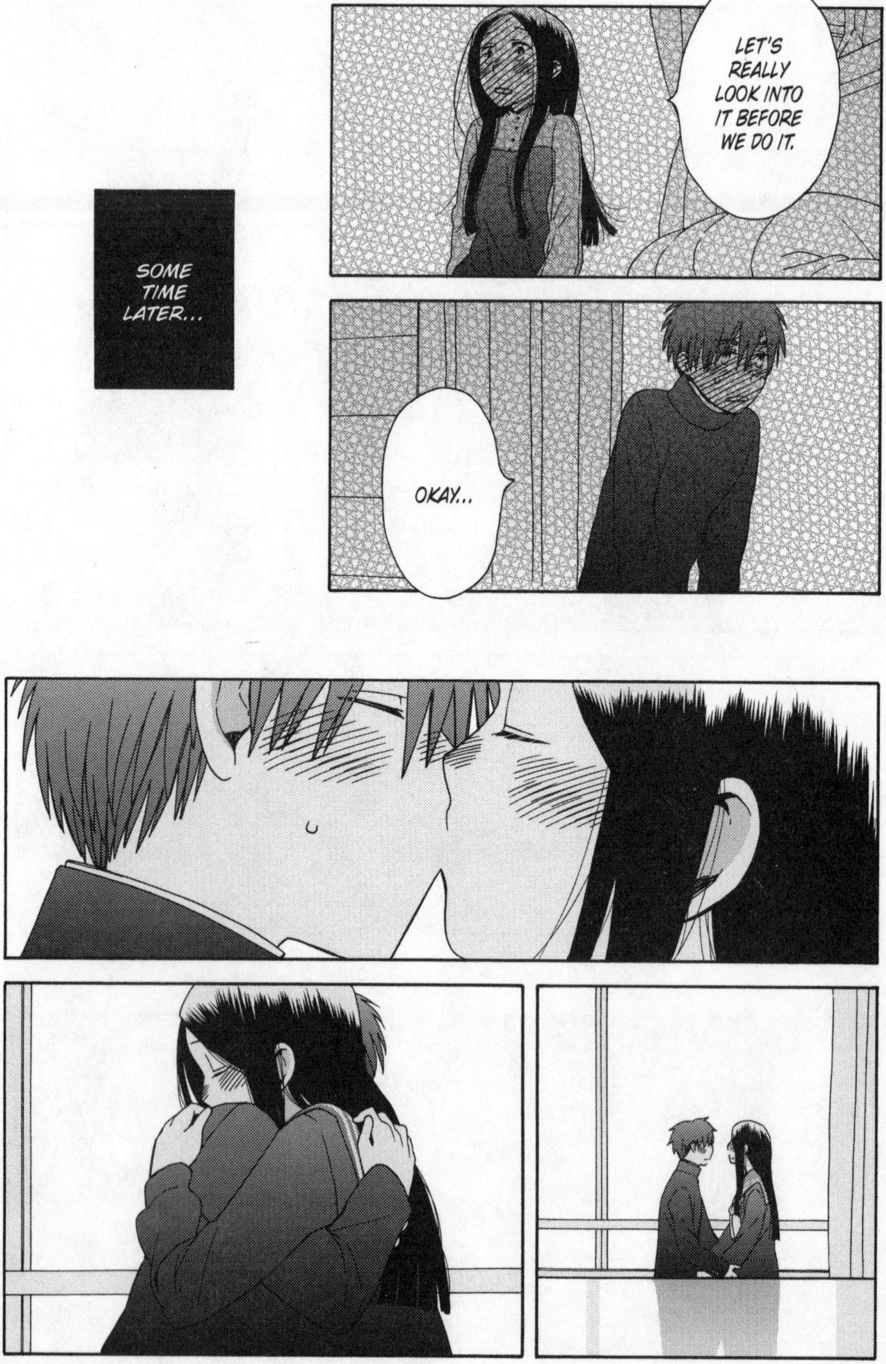
LET'S REALLY LOOK INTO IT BEFORE WE DO IT.
OKAY...
SOME TIME LATER...

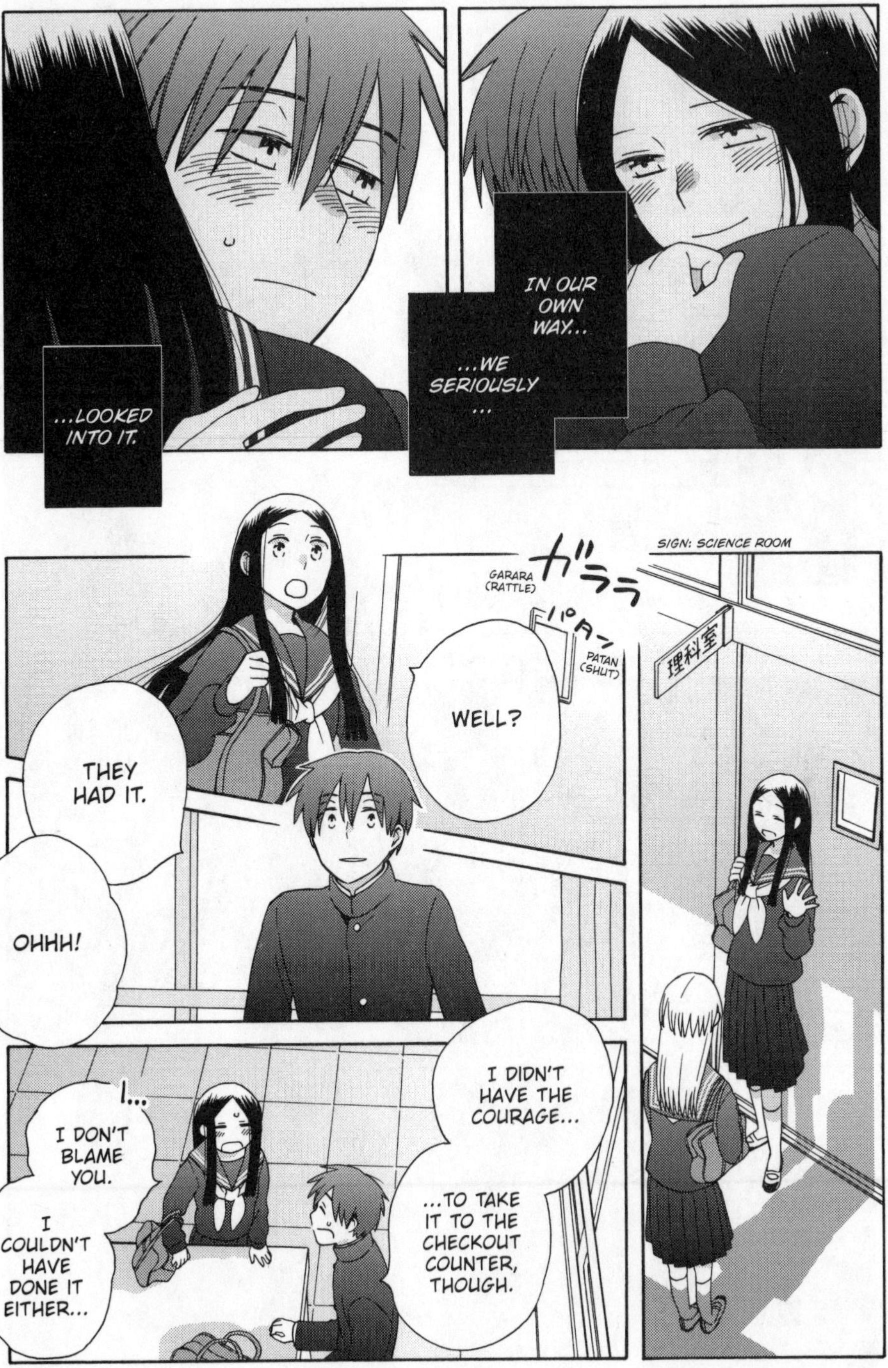
IN OUR OWN WAY...
...WE SERIOUSLY ...
...LOOKED INTO IT.
SIGN: SCIENCE ROOM
ガララ
GARARA (RATTLE)
パタン
PATAN (SHUT)
理科室
WELL?
THEY HAD IT.
OHHH!
I DIDN'T HAVE THE COURAGE...
...TO TAKE IT TO THE CHECKOUT COUNTER, THOUGH.
I...
I DON'T BLAME YOU.
I COULDN'T HAVE DONE IT EITHER...

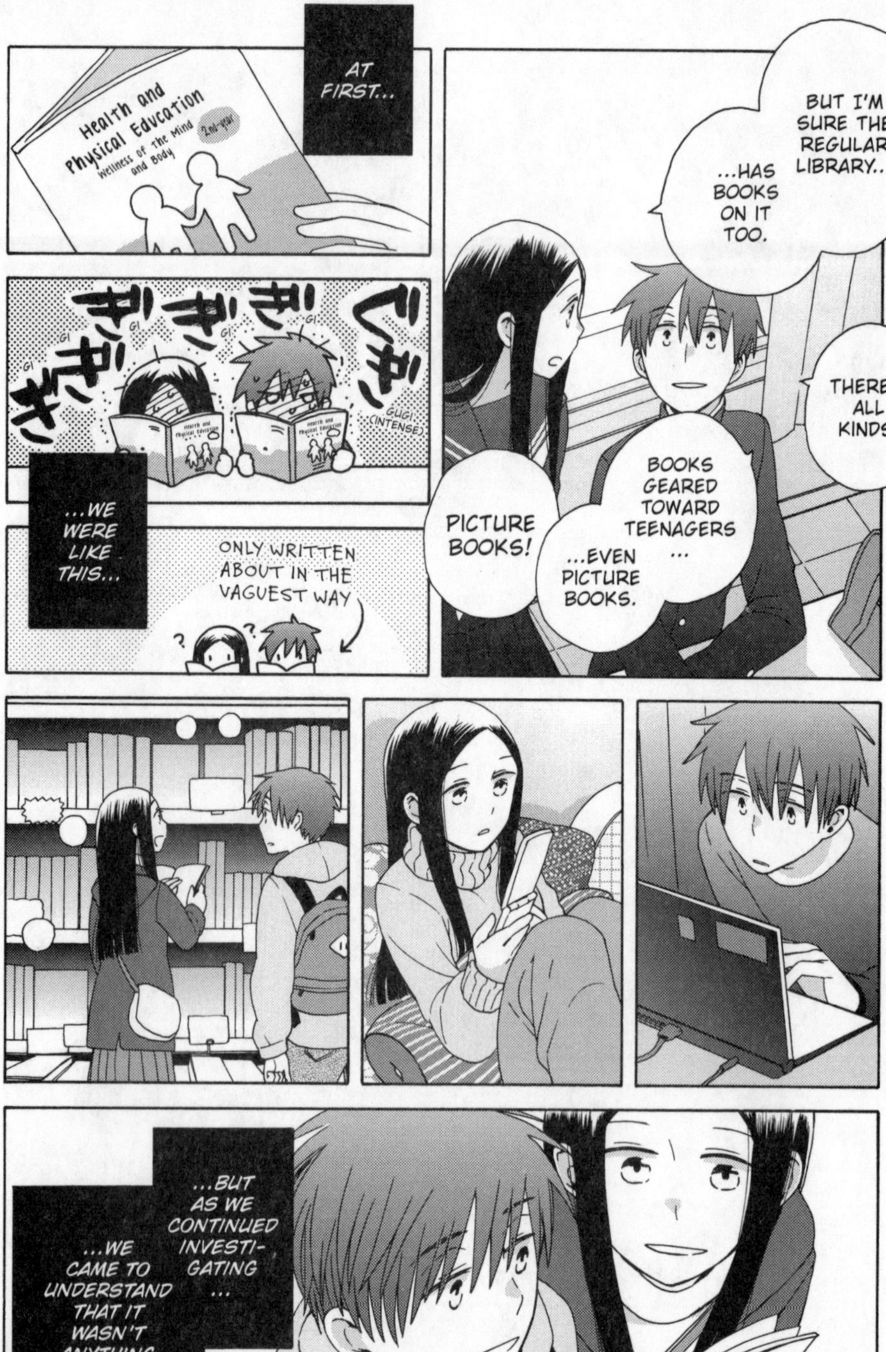
BUT I'M SURE THE REGULAR LIBRARY...
...HAS BOOKS ON IT TOO.
THERE'S ALL KINDS.
BOOKS GEARED TOWARD TEENAGERS ...
...EVEN PICTURE BOOKS.
PICTURE BOOKS!
AT FIRST...
Health and Physical Education
Wellness of the Mind and Body
2nd-year
GI
GI
GI
GI
GUGI (INTENSE)
Health and Physical Education
Health and Physical Education
...WE WERE LIKE THIS...
ONLY WRITTEN ABOUT IN THE VAGUEST WAY
?
?
...BUT AS WE CONTINUED INVESTI-GATING ...
...WE CAME TO UNDERSTAND THAT IT WASN'T ANYTHING STRANGE.

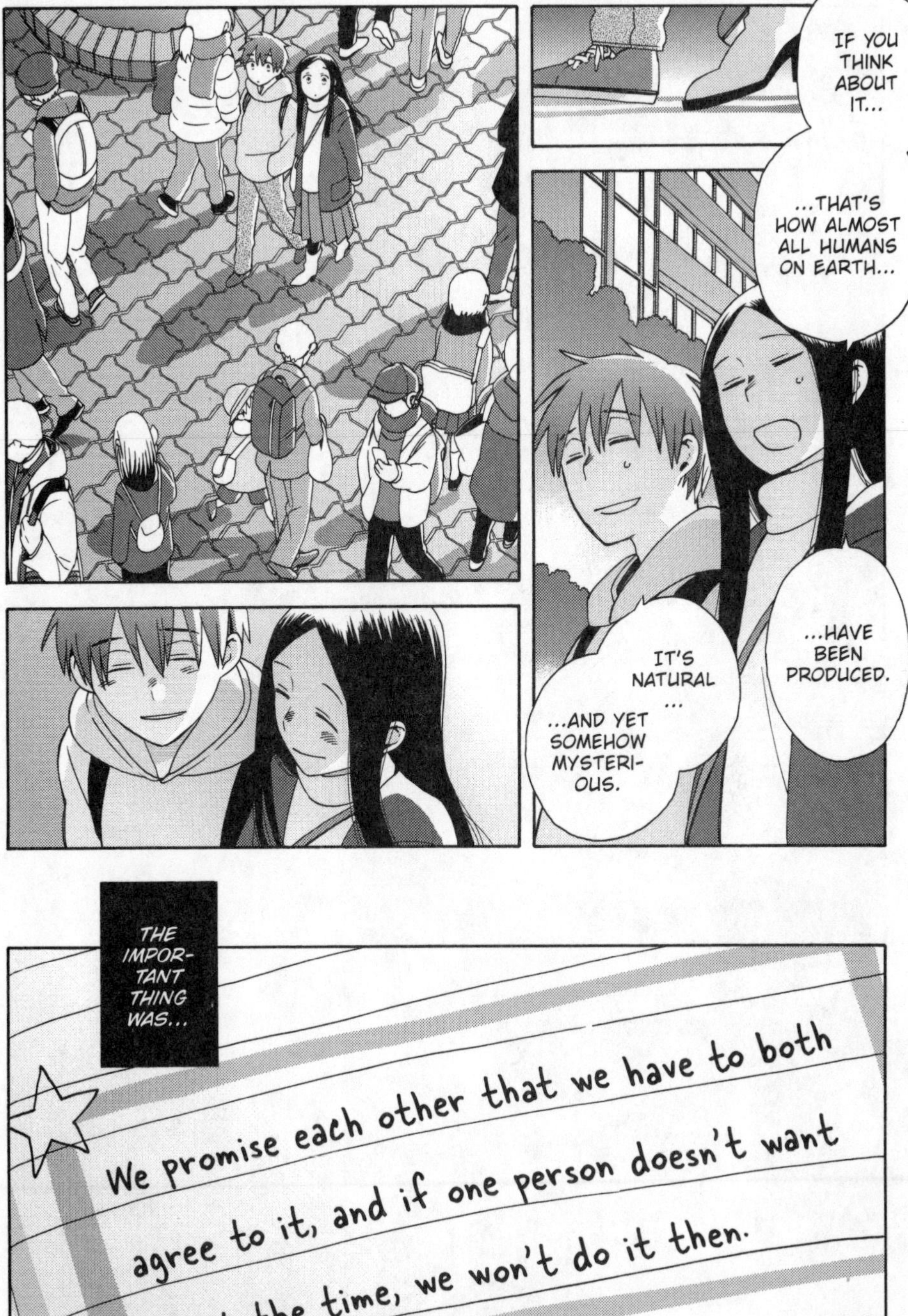
IF YOU THINK ABOUT IT...
...THAT'S HOW ALMOST ALL HUMANS ON EARTH...
...HAVE BEEN PRODUCED.
IT'S NATURAL...
...AND YET SOMEHOW MYSTERIOUS.
THE IMPORTANT THING WAS...
We promise each other that we have to both agree to it, and if one person doesn't want to at the time, we won't do it then.

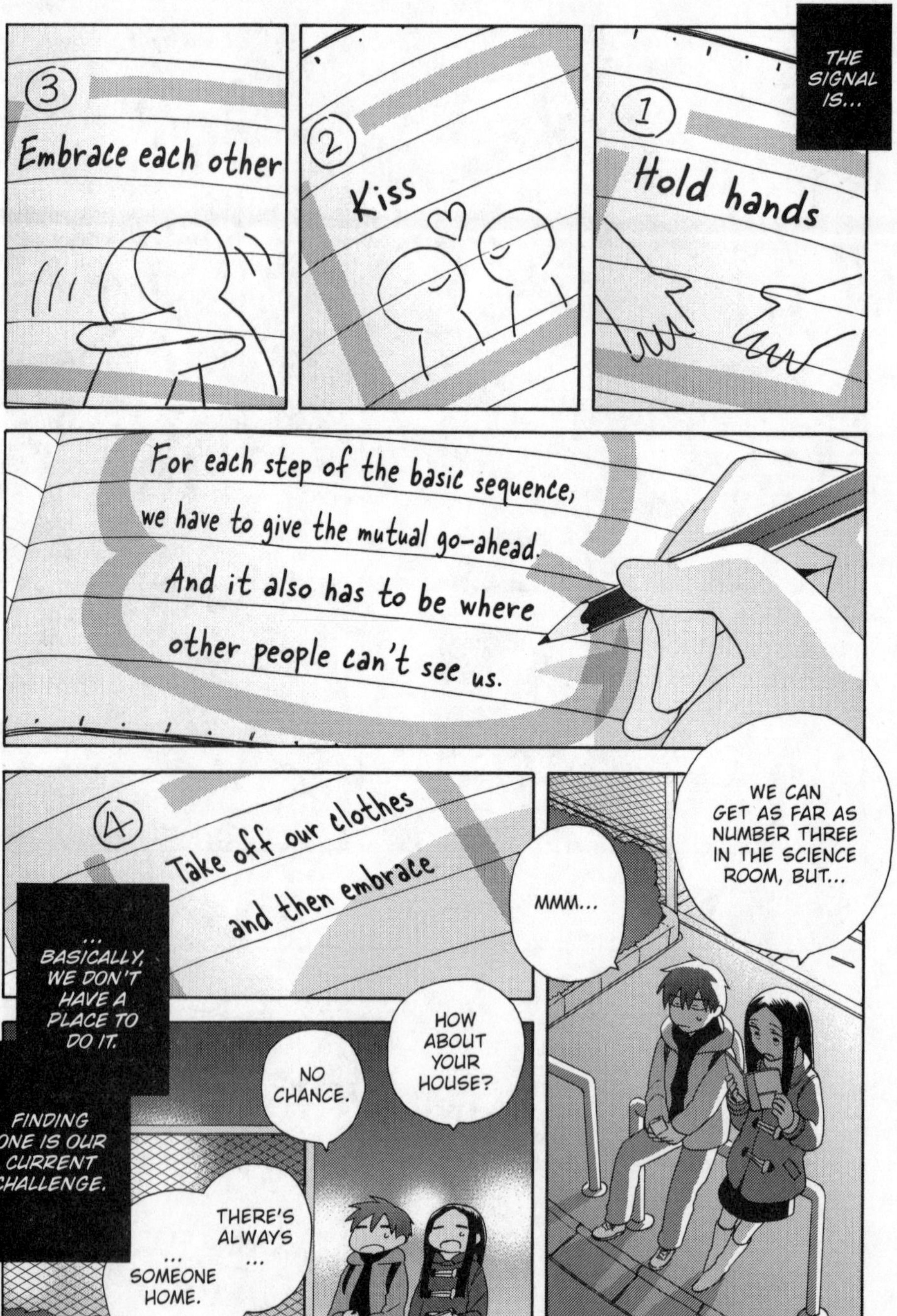
THE SIGNAL IS...
① Hold hands
② Kiss
③ Embrace each other
For each step of the basic sequence, we have to give the mutual go-ahead. And it also has to be where other people can't see us.
WE CAN GET AS FAR AS NUMBER THREE IN THE SCIENCE ROOM, BUT...
MMM...
④ Take off our clothes and then embrace
...BASICALLY, WE DON'T HAVE A PLACE TO DO IT.
HOW ABOUT YOUR HOUSE?
NO CHANCE.
THERE'S ALWAYS...
...SOMEONE HOME.
FINDING ONE IS OUR CURRENT CHALLENGE.

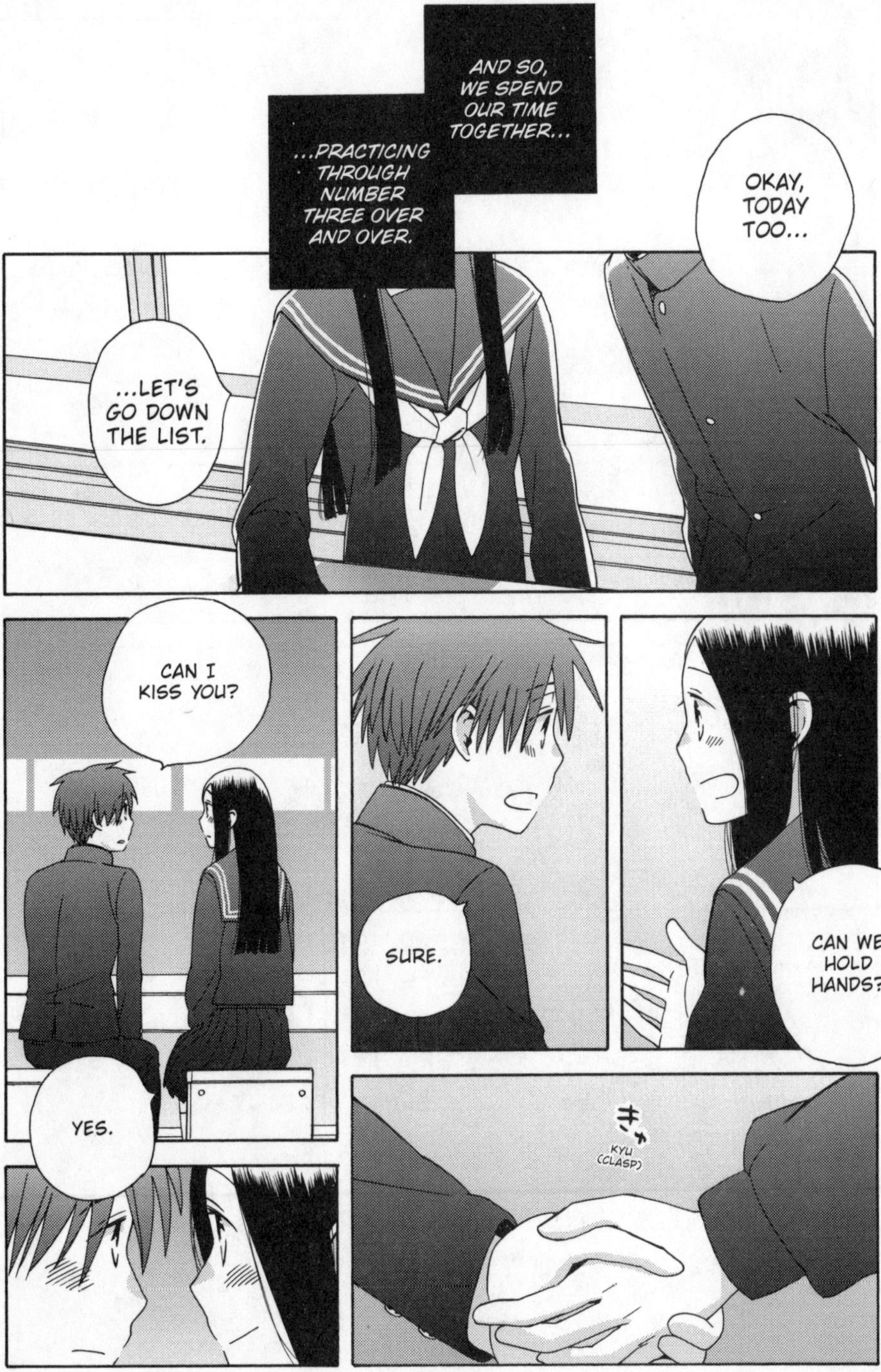
AND SO, WE SPEND OUR TIME TOGETHER...
...PRACTICING THROUGH NUMBER THREE OVER AND OVER.
OKAY, TODAY TOO...
...LET'S GO DOWN THE LIST.
CAN WE HOLD HANDS?
SURE.
CAN I KISS YOU?
YES.
きゅ
KYU (CLASP)

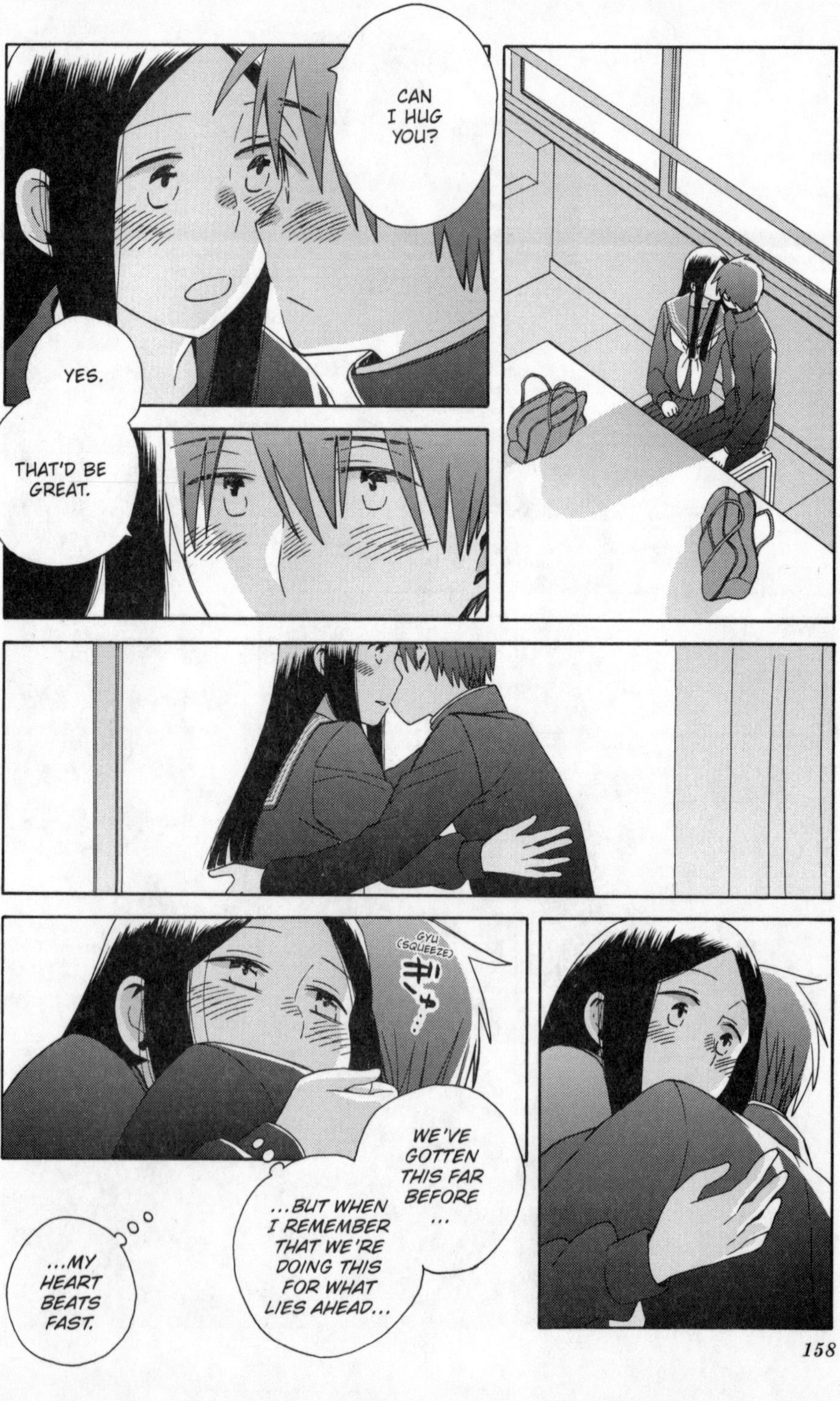
CAN I HUG YOU?
YES.
THAT'D BE GREAT.
GYU (SQUEEZE)
ギュッ…
WE'VE GOTTEN THIS FAR BEFORE…
…BUT WHEN I REMEMBER THAT WE'RE DOING THIS FOR WHAT LIES AHEAD…
…MY HEART BEATS FAST.

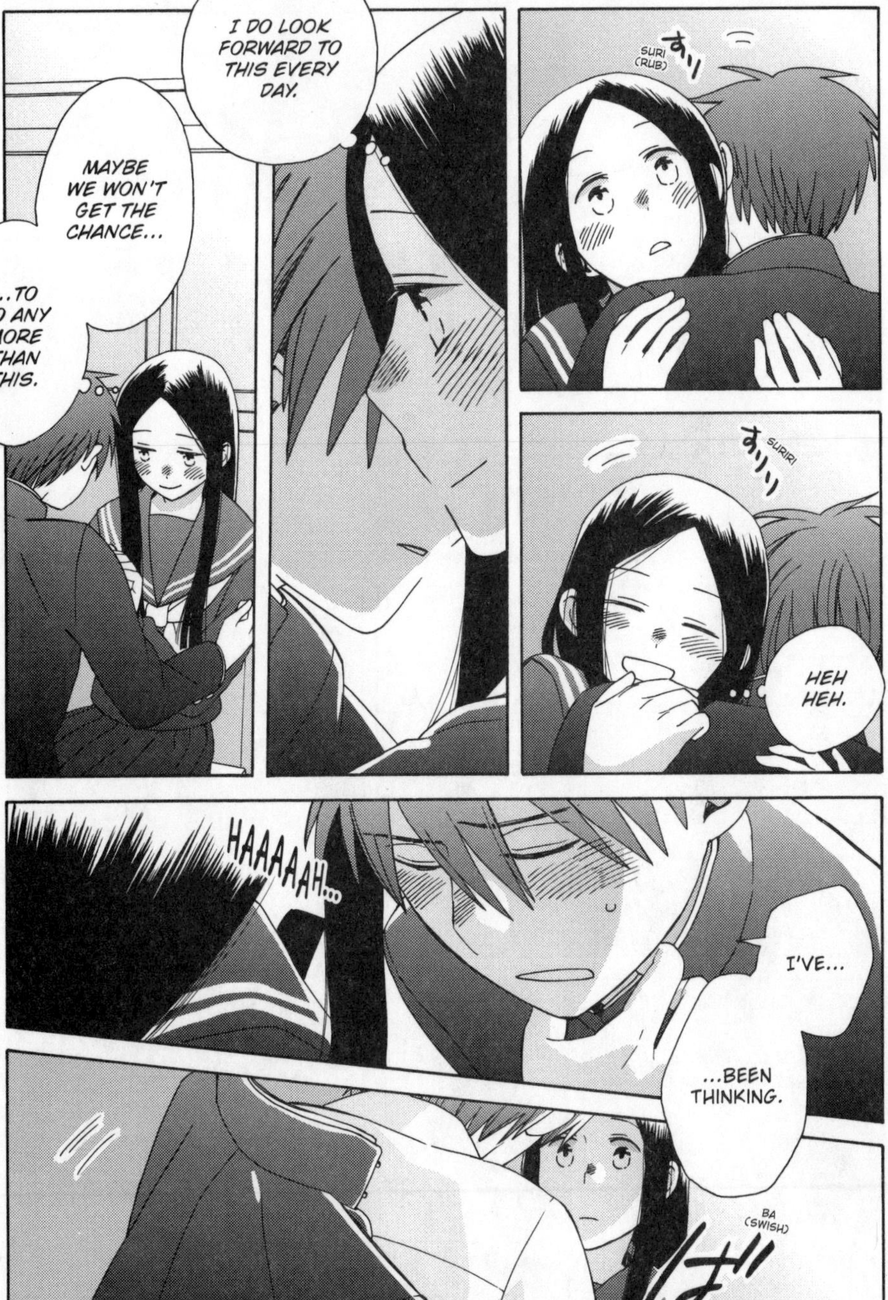
すり
SURI (RUB)
すりり
SURIRI
HEH HEH.
I DO LOOK FORWARD TO THIS EVERY DAY.
MAYBE WE WON'T GET THE CHANCE...
...TO DO ANY MORE THAN THIS.
HAAAAAH...
I'VE...
...BEEN THINKING.
ぱ
BA (SWISH)

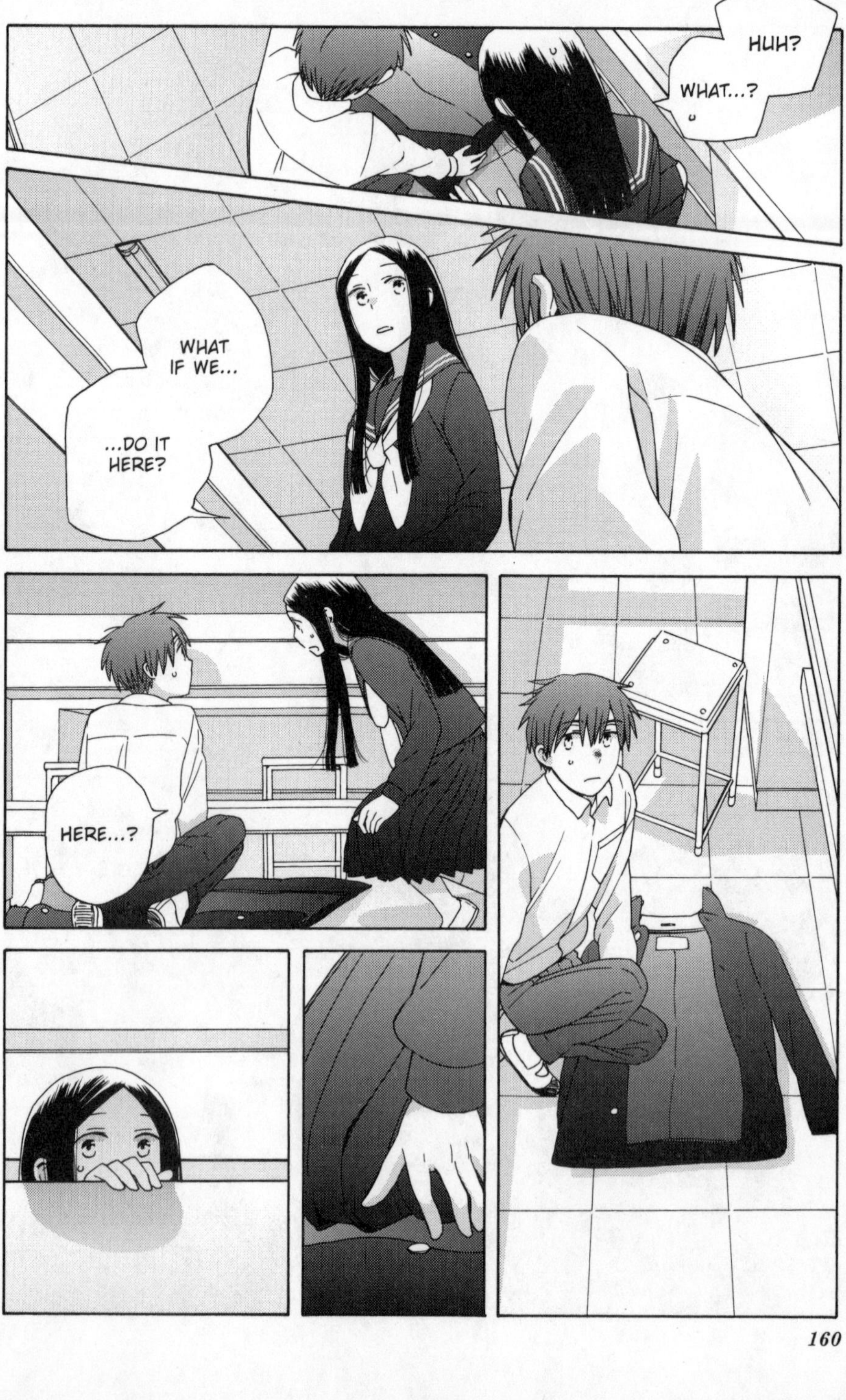
HUH?
WHAT...?
WHAT IF WE...
...DO IT HERE?
HERE...?

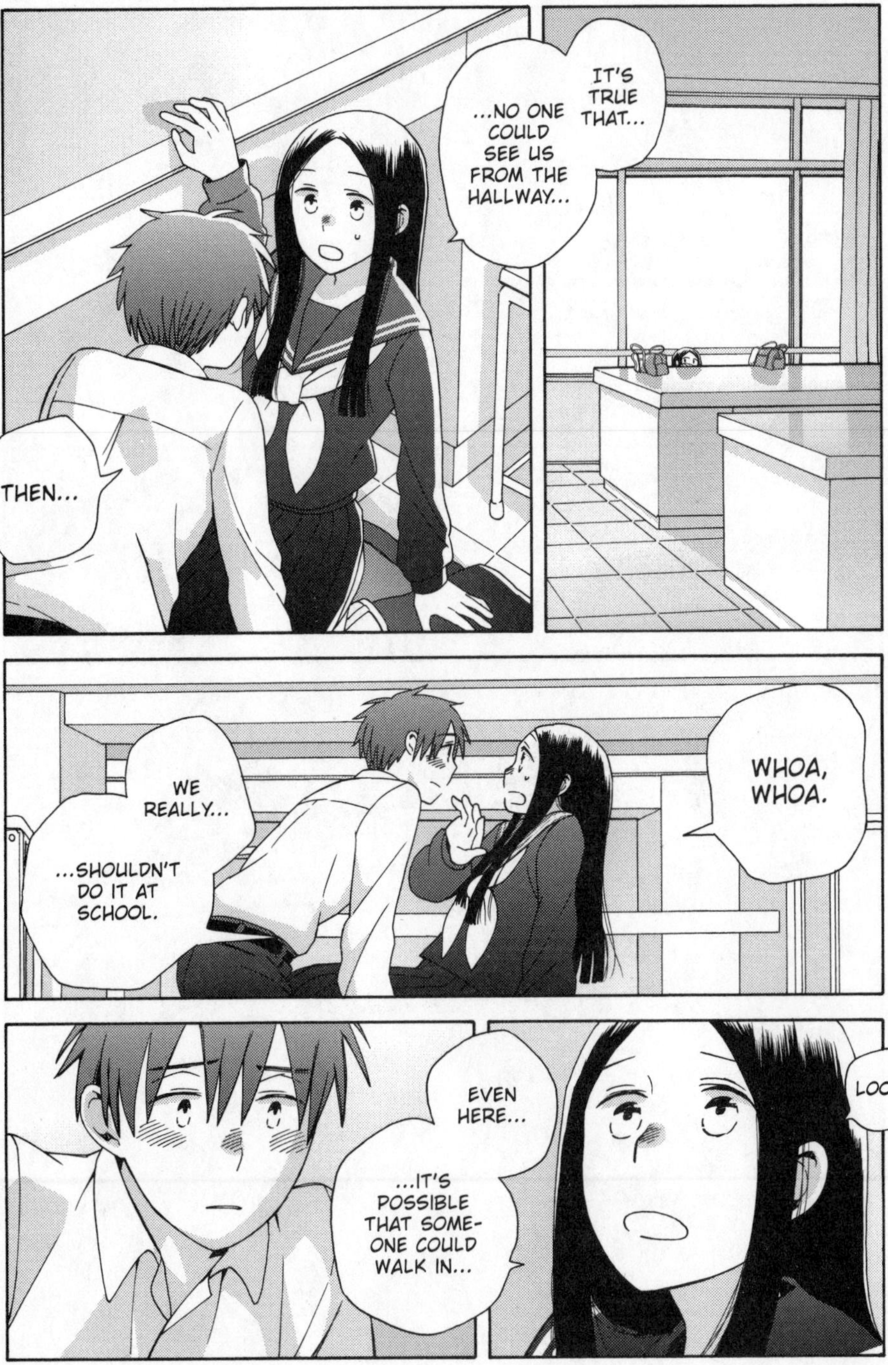
IT'S TRUE THAT...
...NO ONE COULD SEE US FROM THE HALLWAY...
THEN...
WHOA, WHOA.
WE REALLY...
...SHOULDN'T DO IT AT SCHOOL.
LOOK.
EVEN HERE...
...IT'S POSSIBLE THAT SOME-ONE COULD WALK IN...

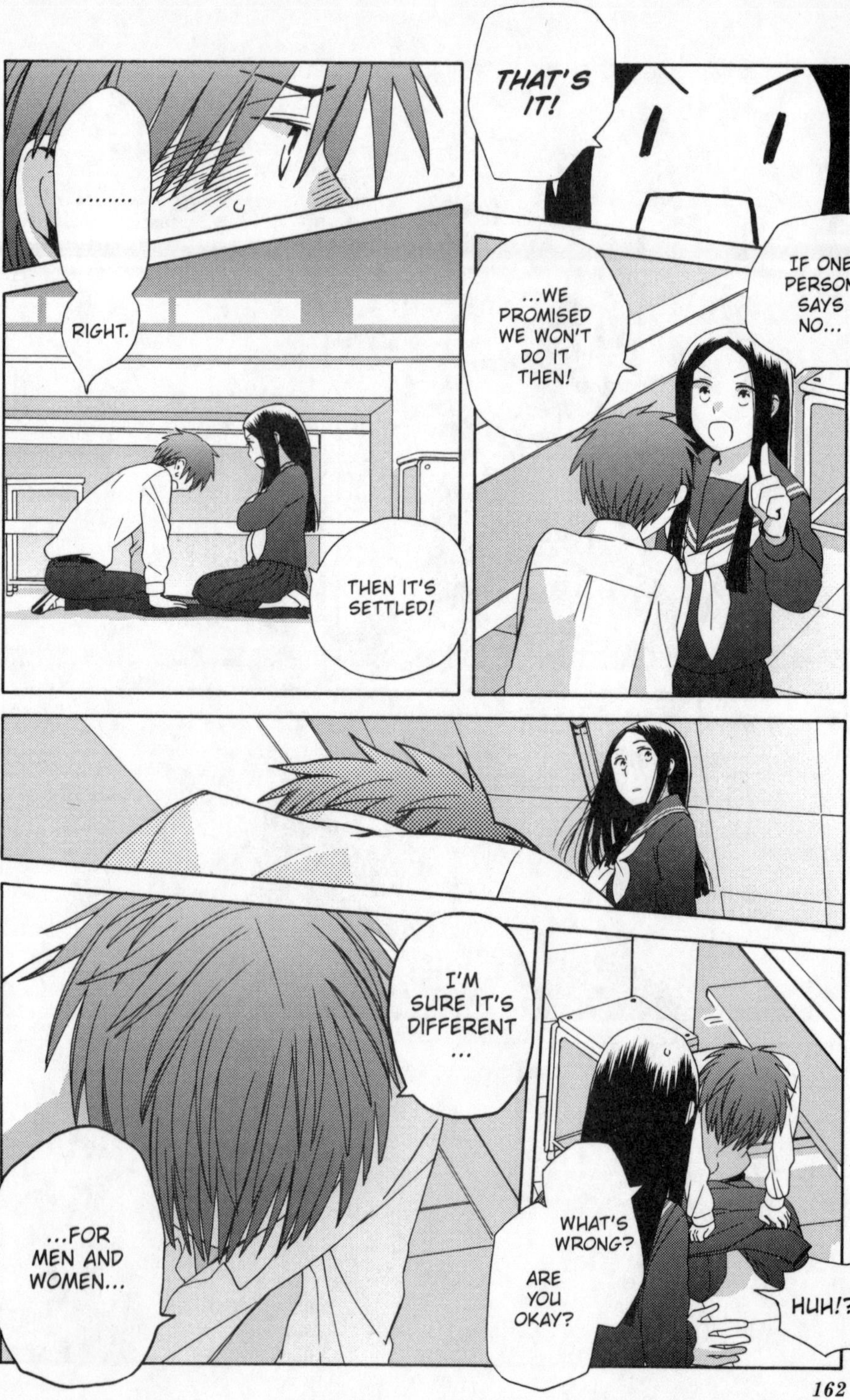
THAT'S IT!
IF ONE PERSON SAYS NO...
...WE PROMISED WE WON'T DO IT THEN!
....
RIGHT.
THEN IT'S SETTLED!
HUH!?
WHAT'S WRONG? ARE YOU OKAY?
I'M SURE IT'S DIFFERENT ...
...FOR MEN AND WOMEN...

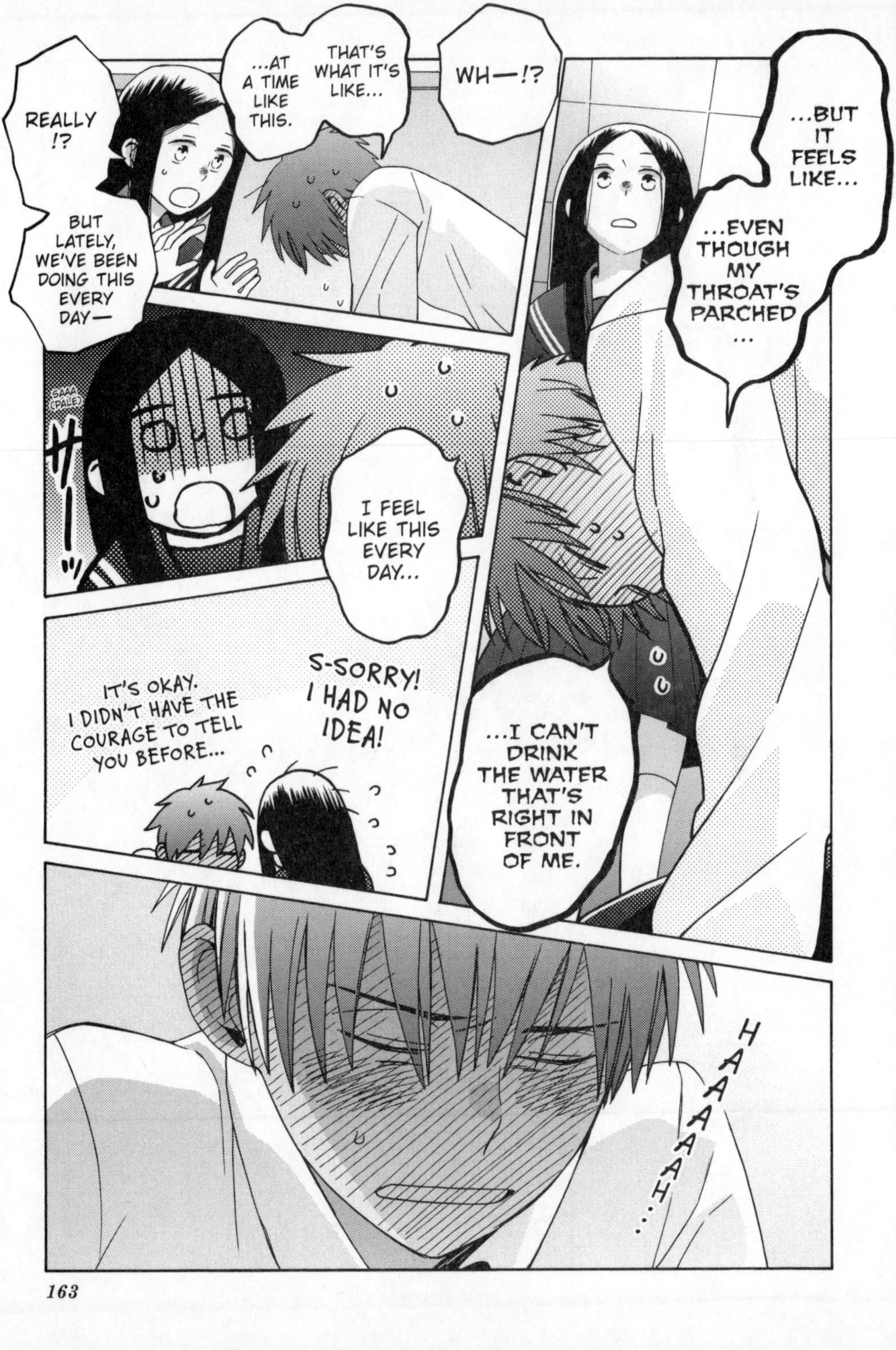
...BUT IT FEELS LIKE...
...EVEN THOUGH MY THROAT'S PARCHED...
...I CAN'T DRINK THE WATER THAT'S RIGHT IN FRONT OF ME.
WH—!?
THAT'S WHAT IT'S LIKE...
...AT A TIME LIKE THIS.
REALLY!?
BUT LATELY, WE'VE BEEN DOING THIS EVERY DAY—
I FEEL LIKE THIS EVERY DAY...
SAAA (PALE)
S-SORRY! I HAD NO IDEA!
IT'S OKAY. I DIDN'T HAVE THE COURAGE TO TELL YOU BEFORE...
HAAAAAAH...

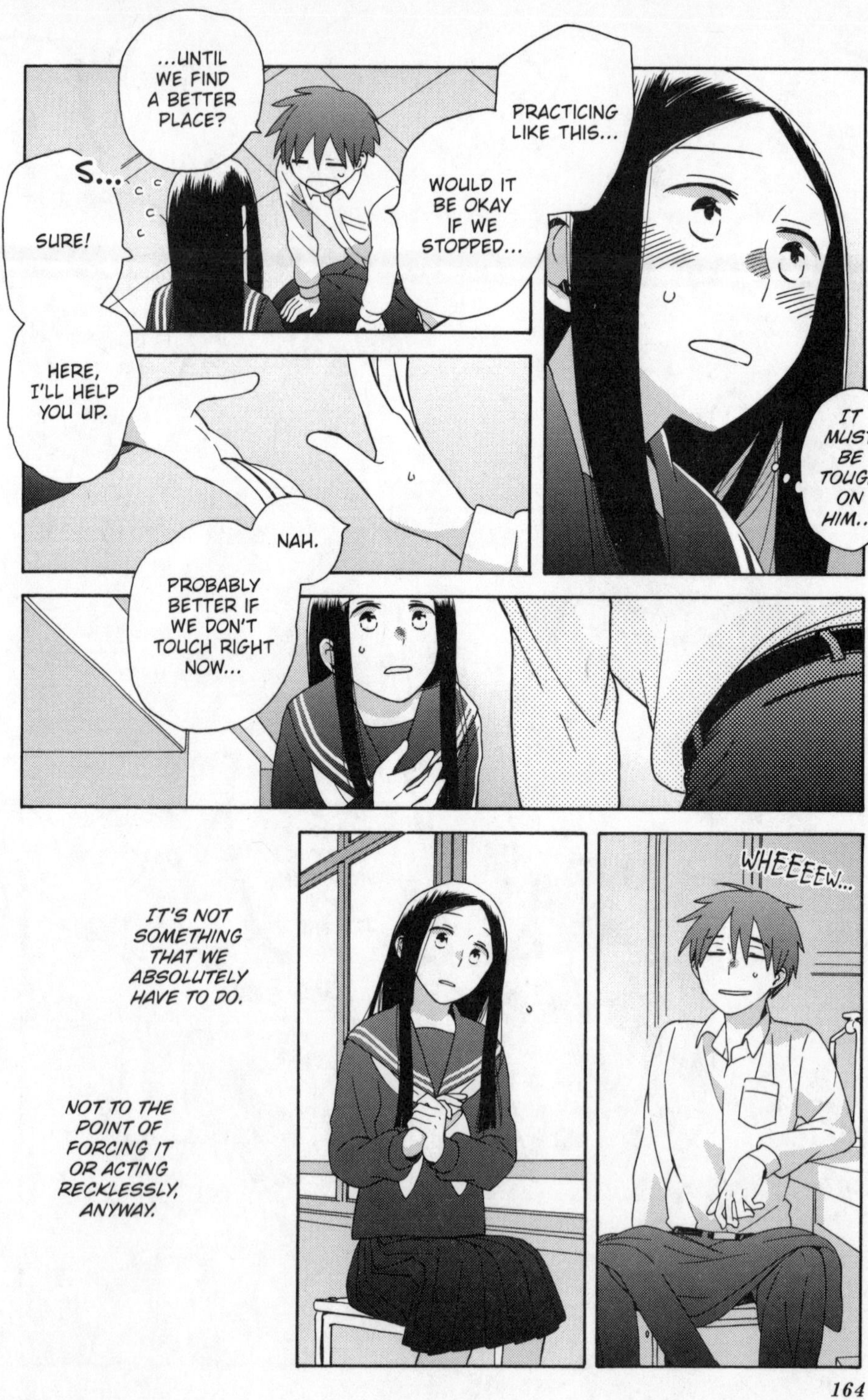
PRACTICING LIKE THIS...
WOULD IT BE OKAY IF WE STOPPED...
...UNTIL WE FIND A BETTER PLACE?
IT MUST BE TOUGH ON HIM...
S... SURE!
HERE, I'LL HELP YOU UP.
NAH.
PROBABLY BETTER IF WE DON'T TOUCH RIGHT NOW...
WHEEEEW...
IT'S NOT SOMETHING THAT WE ABSOLUTELY HAVE TO DO.
NOT TO THE POINT OF FORCING IT OR ACTING RECKLESSLY, ANYWAY.

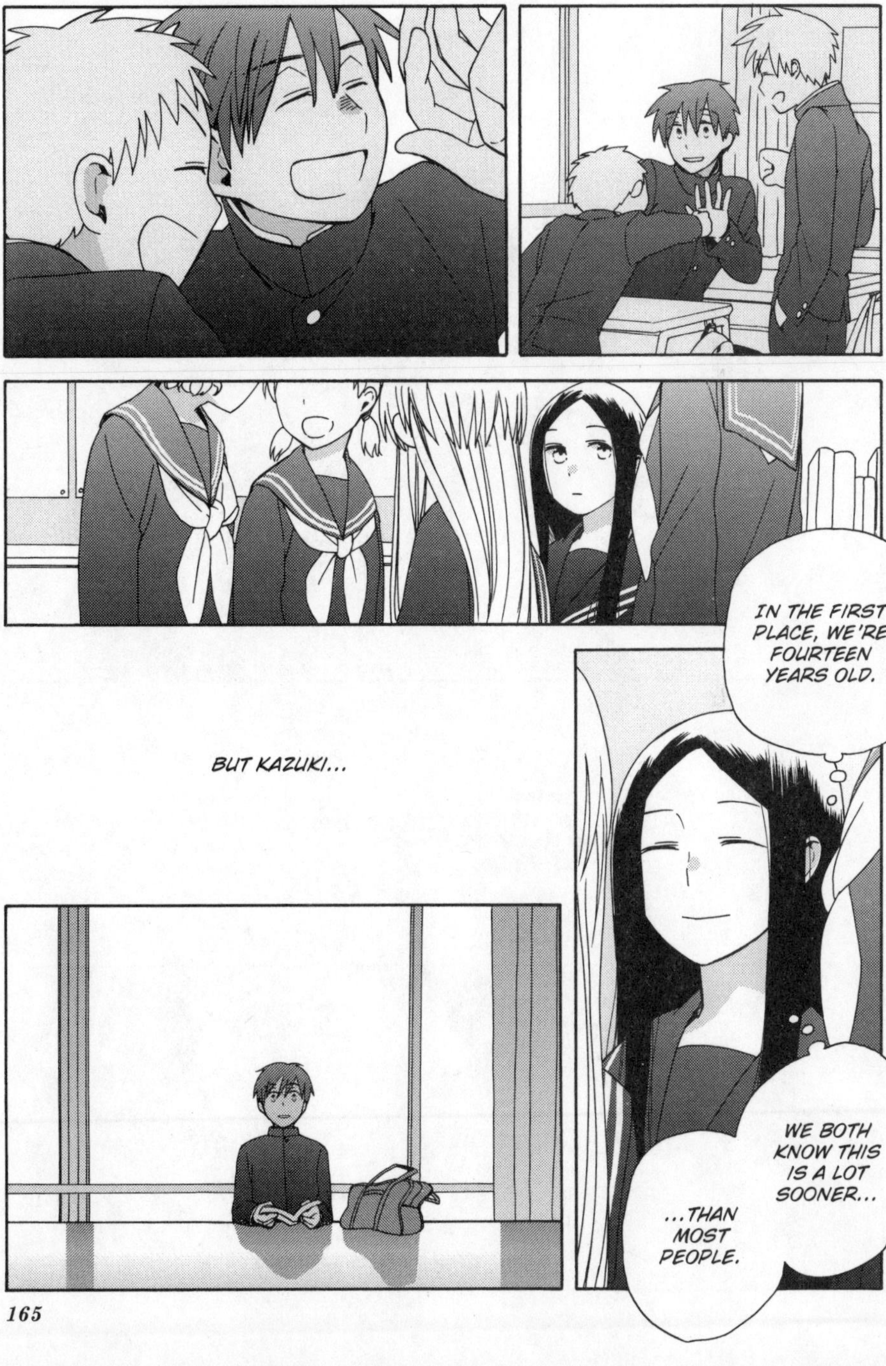
IN THE FIRST PLACE, WE'RE FOURTEEN YEARS OLD.
BUT KAZUKI...
WE BOTH KNOW THIS IS A LOT SOONER...
...THAN MOST PEOPLE.

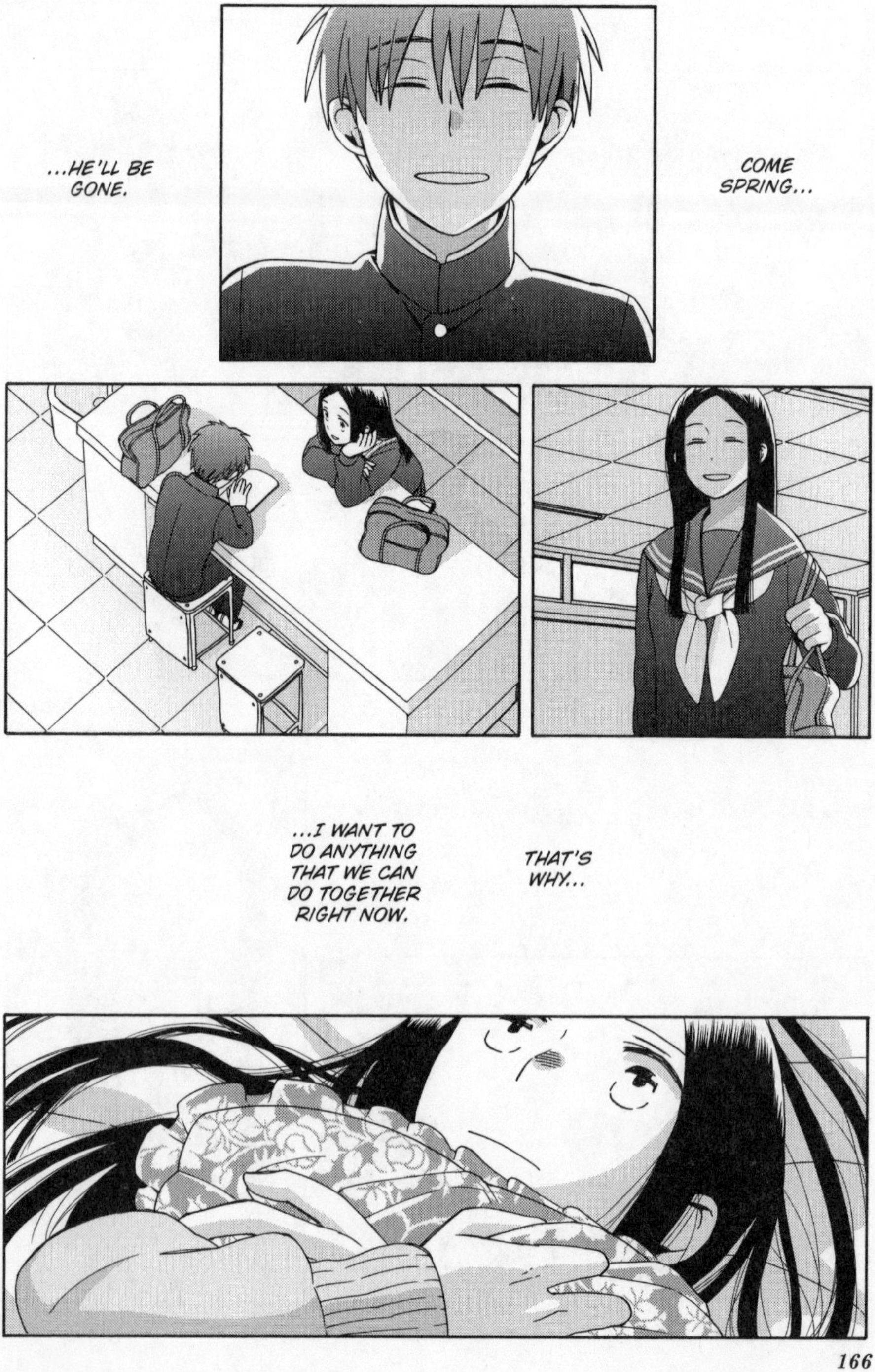
COME SPRING...
...HE'LL BE GONE.
THAT'S WHY...
...I WANT TO DO ANYTHING THAT WE CAN DO TOGETHER RIGHT NOW.

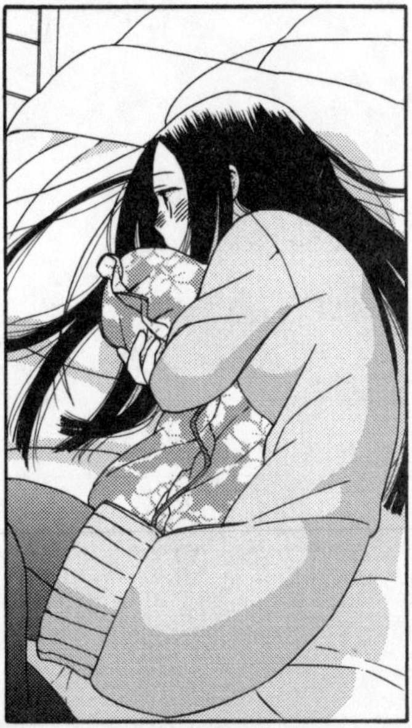

WE LOOKED INTO IT PROPERLY.

WE ALSO PREPARED FOR IT.

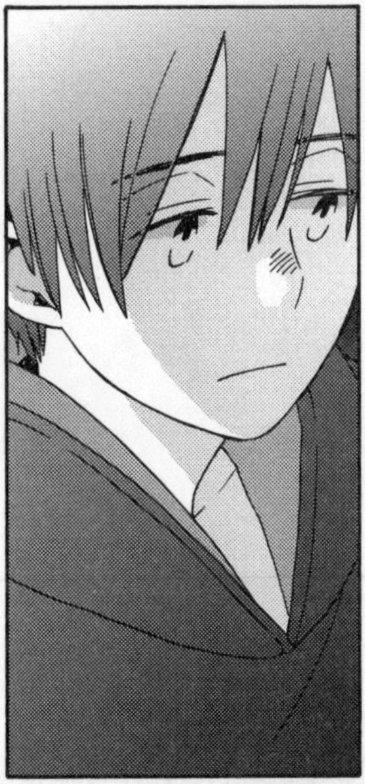

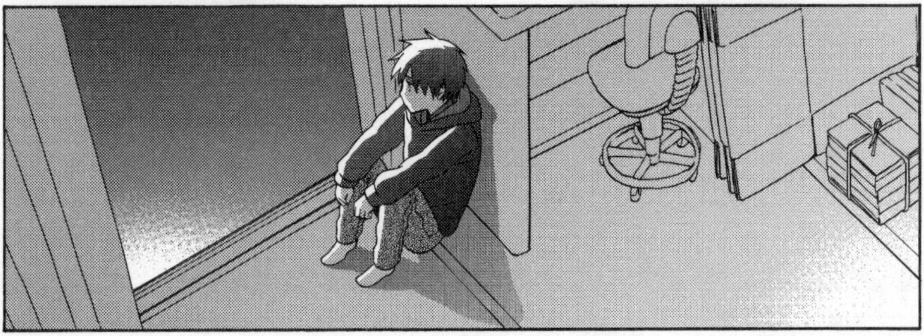

NOW WE JUST NEED A PLACE.

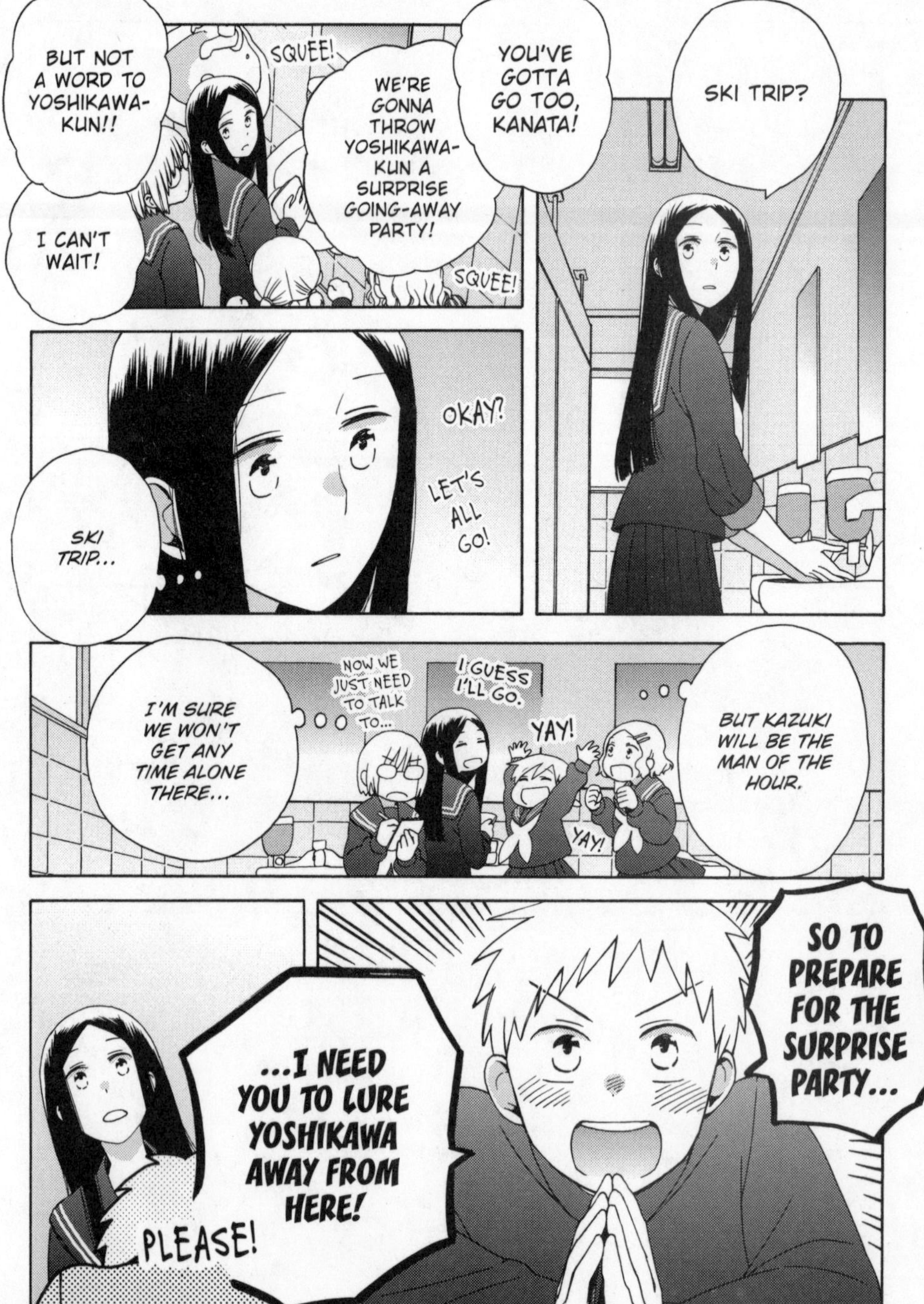
SKI TRIP?
YOU'VE GOTTA GO TOO, KANATA!
WE'RE GONNA THROW YOSHIKAWA-KUN A SURPRISE GOING-AWAY PARTY!
SQUEE!
BUT NOT A WORD TO YOSHIKAWA-KUN!!
I CAN'T WAIT!
SQUEE!
OKAY?
LET'S ALL GO!
SKI TRIP...
BUT KAZUKI WILL BE THE MAN OF THE HOUR.
YAY!
YAY!
I GUESS I'LL GO.
NOW WE JUST NEED TO TALK TO...
I'M SURE WE WON'T GET ANY TIME ALONE THERE...
SO TO PREPARE FOR THE SURPRISE PARTY...
...I NEED YOU TO LURE YOSHIKAWA AWAY FROM HERE!
PLEASE!

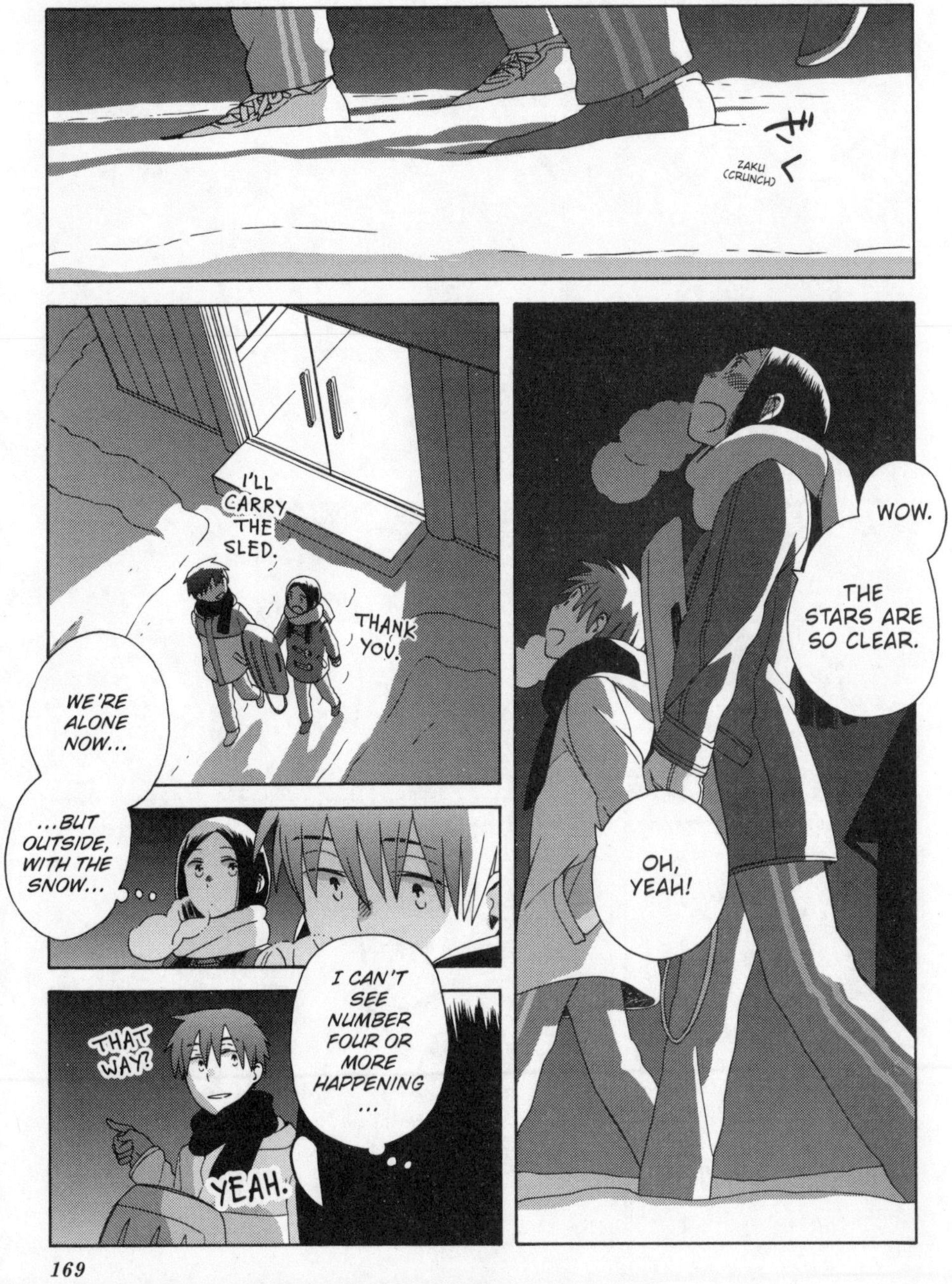
ざく
ZAKU (CRUNCH)
WOW.
THE STARS ARE SO CLEAR.
OH, YEAH!
I'LL CARRY THE SLED.
THANK YOU.
WE'RE ALONE NOW...
...BUT OUTSIDE, WITH THE SNOW...
I CAN'T SEE NUMBER FOUR OR MORE HAPPENING...
THAT WAY?
YEAH.

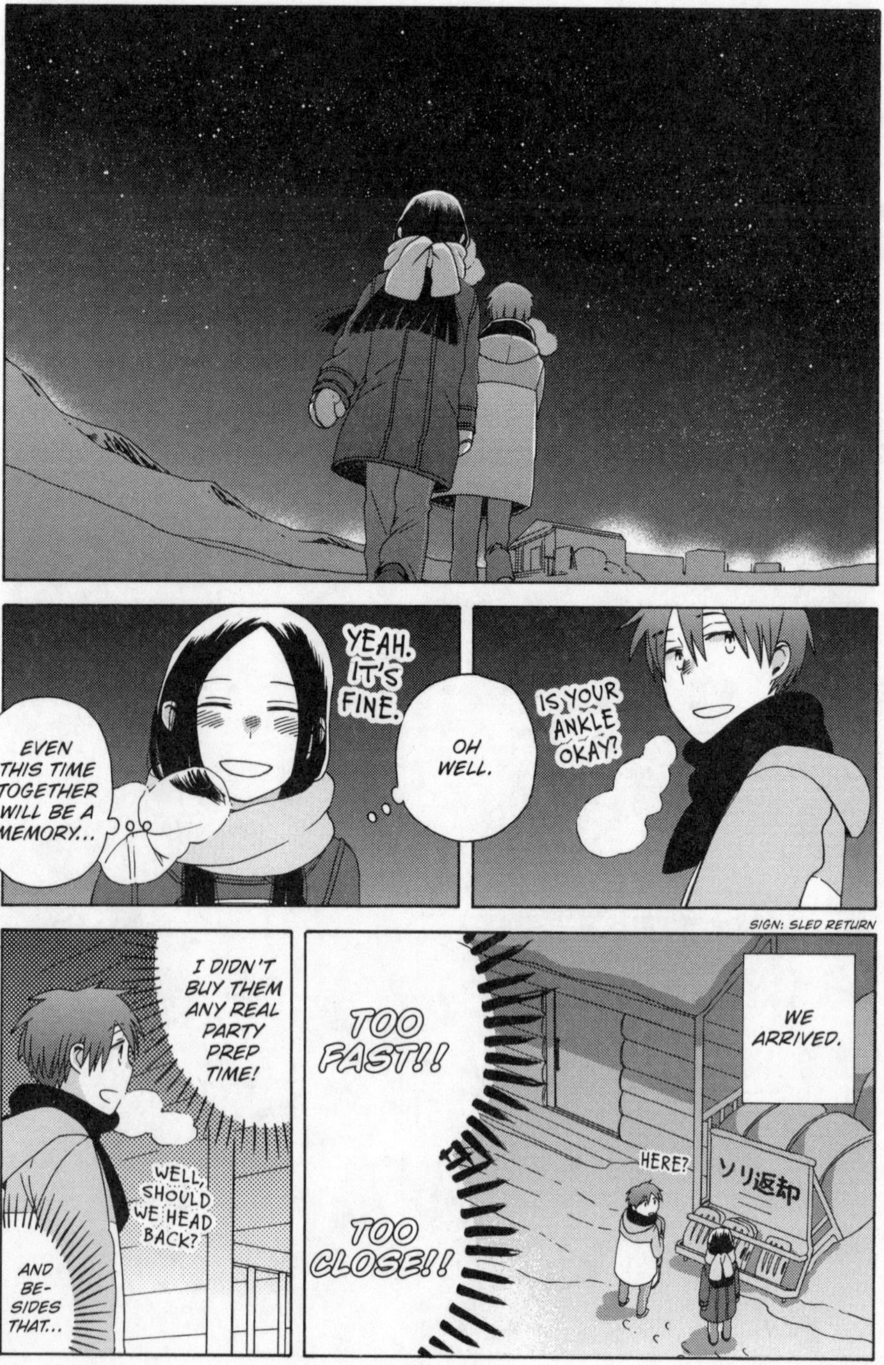
IS YOUR ANKLE OKAY?
YEAH. IT'S FINE.
OH WELL.
EVEN THIS TIME TOGETHER WILL BE A MEMORY...
SIGN: SLED RETURN
WE ARRIVED.
HERE?
ソリ返却
TOO FAST!!
TOO CLOSE!!
I DIDN'T BUY THEM ANY REAL PARTY PREP TIME!
WELL, SHOULD WE HEAD BACK?
AND BE-SIDES THAT...

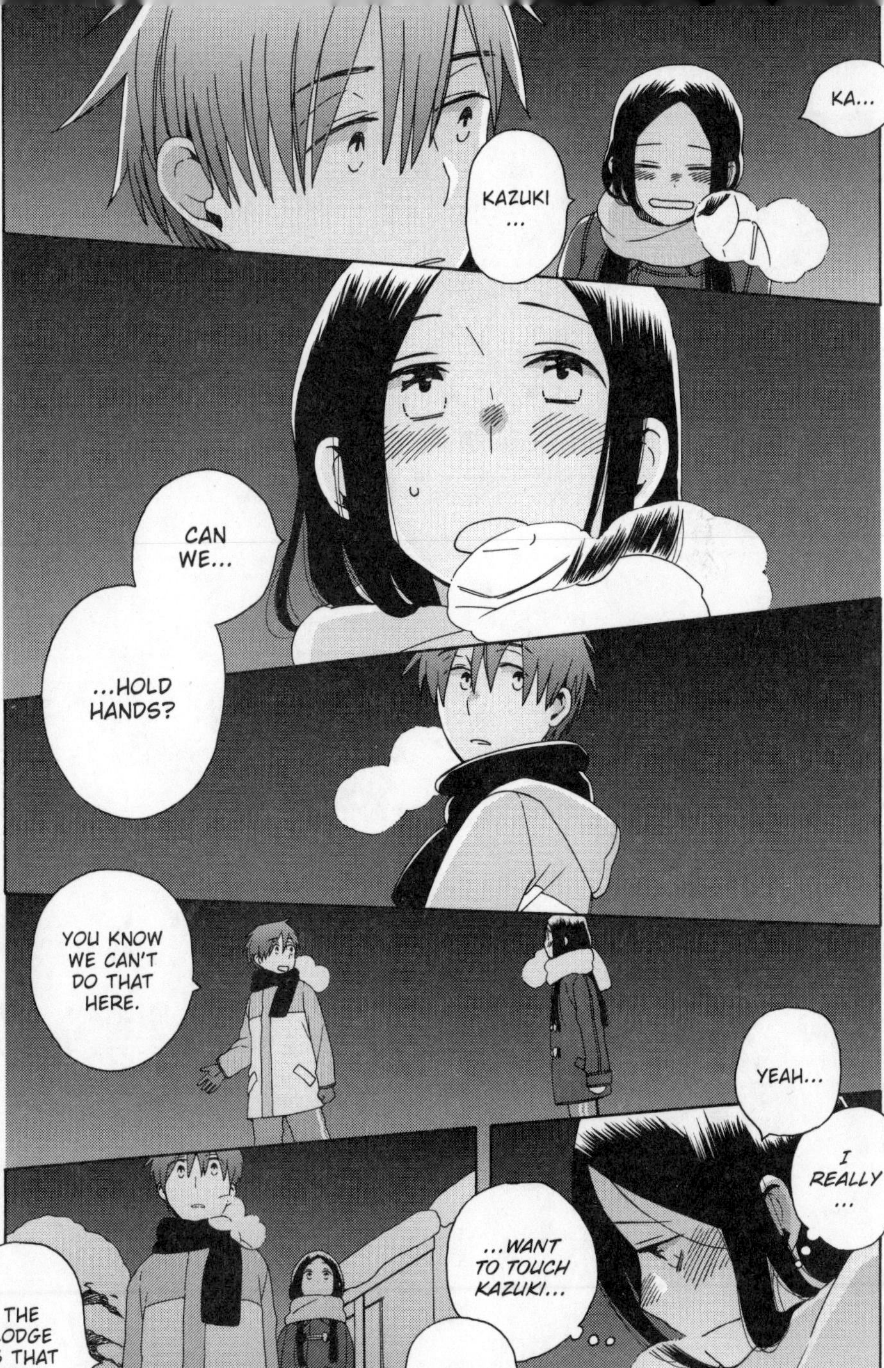

KA...
KAZUKI ...
CAN WE...
...HOLD HANDS?
YOU KNOW WE CAN'T DO THAT HERE.
YEAH...
I REALLY ...
...WANT TO TOUCH KAZUKI...
HUH?
THE LODGE IS THAT WAY, RIGHT?

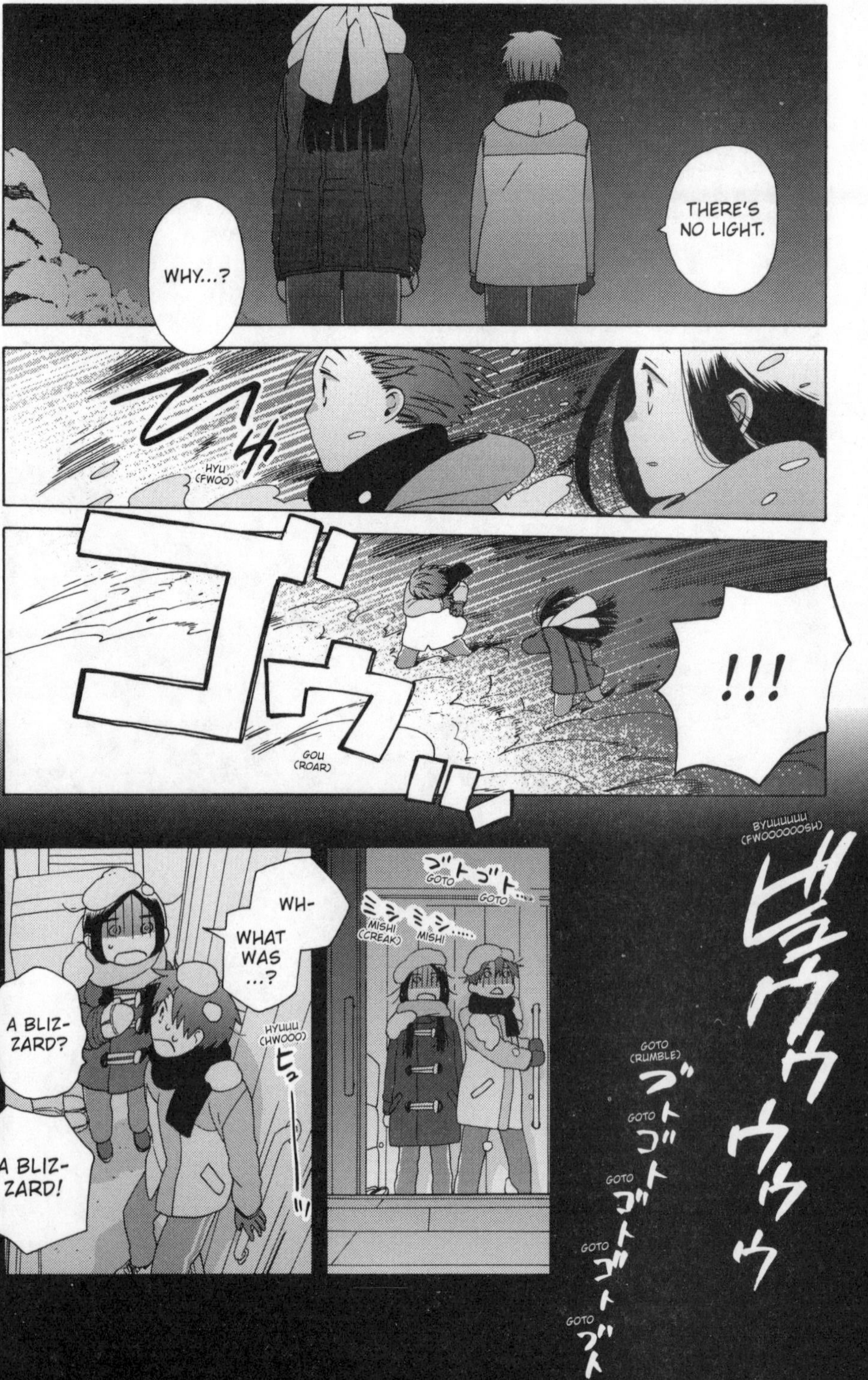
THERE'S NO LIGHT.
WHY...?
ひゅ
HYU (FWOO)
!!!
ゴウ
GOU (ROAR)
ビュウウウウウウ
BYUUUUUU (FWOOOOOOSH)
ゴトゴトゴトゴトゴト
GOTO (RUMBLE) GOTO GOTO GOTO GOTO
ゴトゴト…
GOTO GOTO
ミシミシ…
MISHI (CREAK) MISHI
WH- WHAT WAS ...?
A BLIZ-ZARD?
A BLIZ-ZARD!
ヒュー
HYUUU (HWOOO)

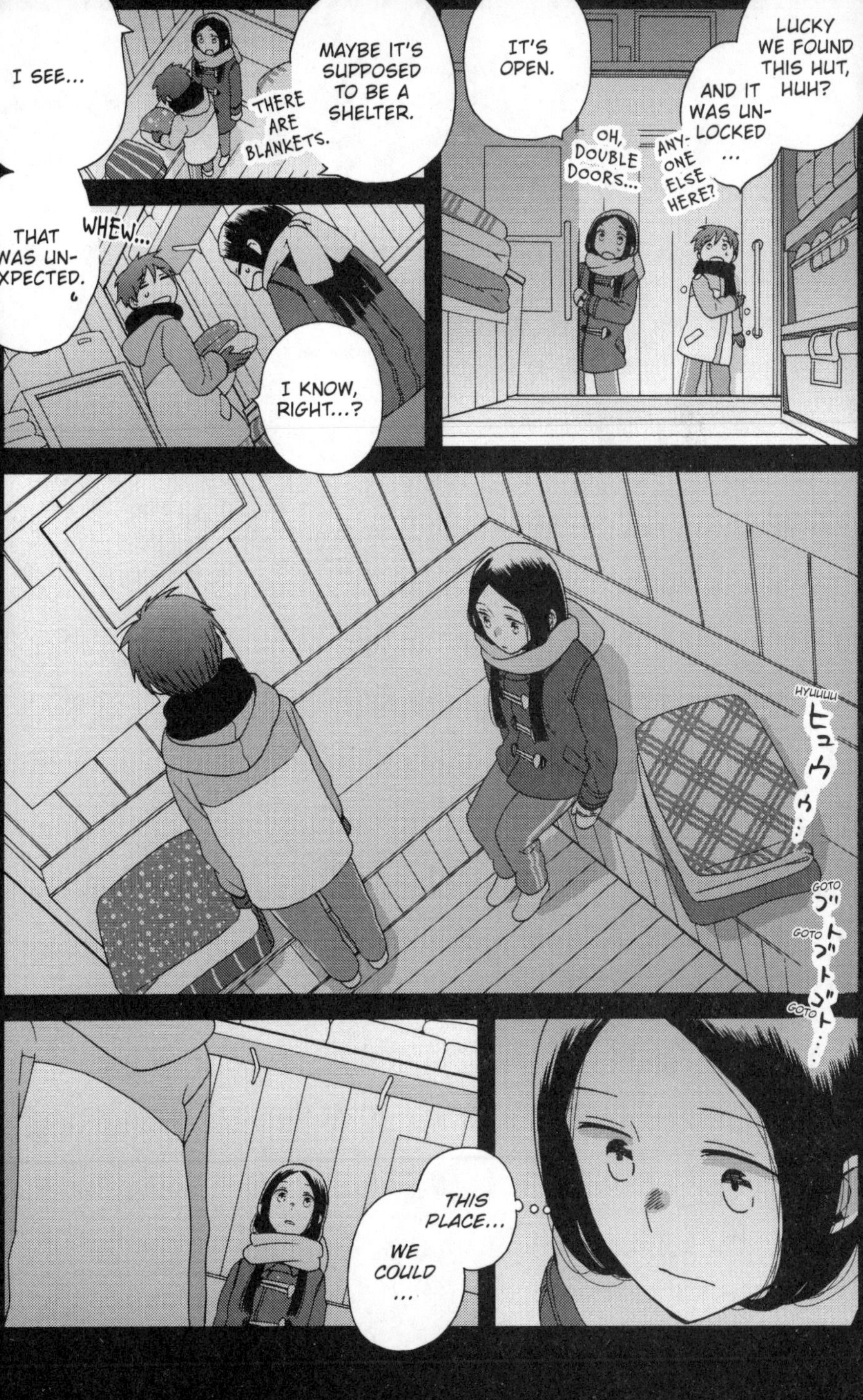
LUCKY WE FOUND THIS HUT, HUH?
AND IT WAS UN-LOCKED...
IT'S OPEN.
ANY-ONE ELSE HERE?
OH, DOUBLE DOORS...
MAYBE IT'S SUPPOSED TO BE A SHELTER.
THERE ARE BLANKETS.
I SEE...
WHEW...
THAT WAS UN-EXPECTED.
I KNOW, RIGHT...?
HYUUUU
ヒュゥゥ…
GOTO GOTO GOTO
ゴトゴトゴト…
THIS PLACE...
WE COULD...

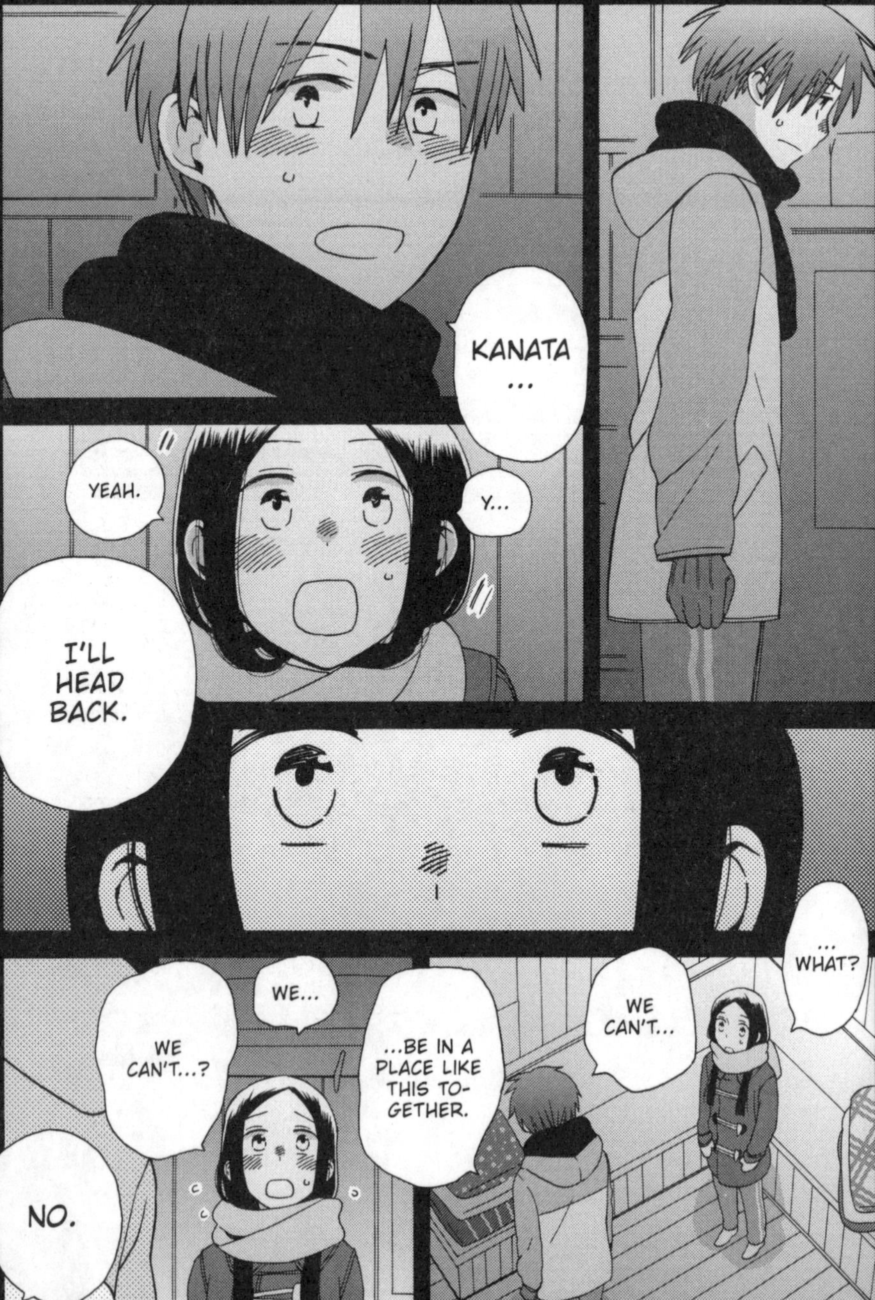
KANATA ...
Y...
YEAH.
I'LL HEAD BACK.
... WHAT?
WE CAN'T...
...BE IN A PLACE LIKE THIS TO-GETHER.
WE...
WE CAN'T...?
NO.

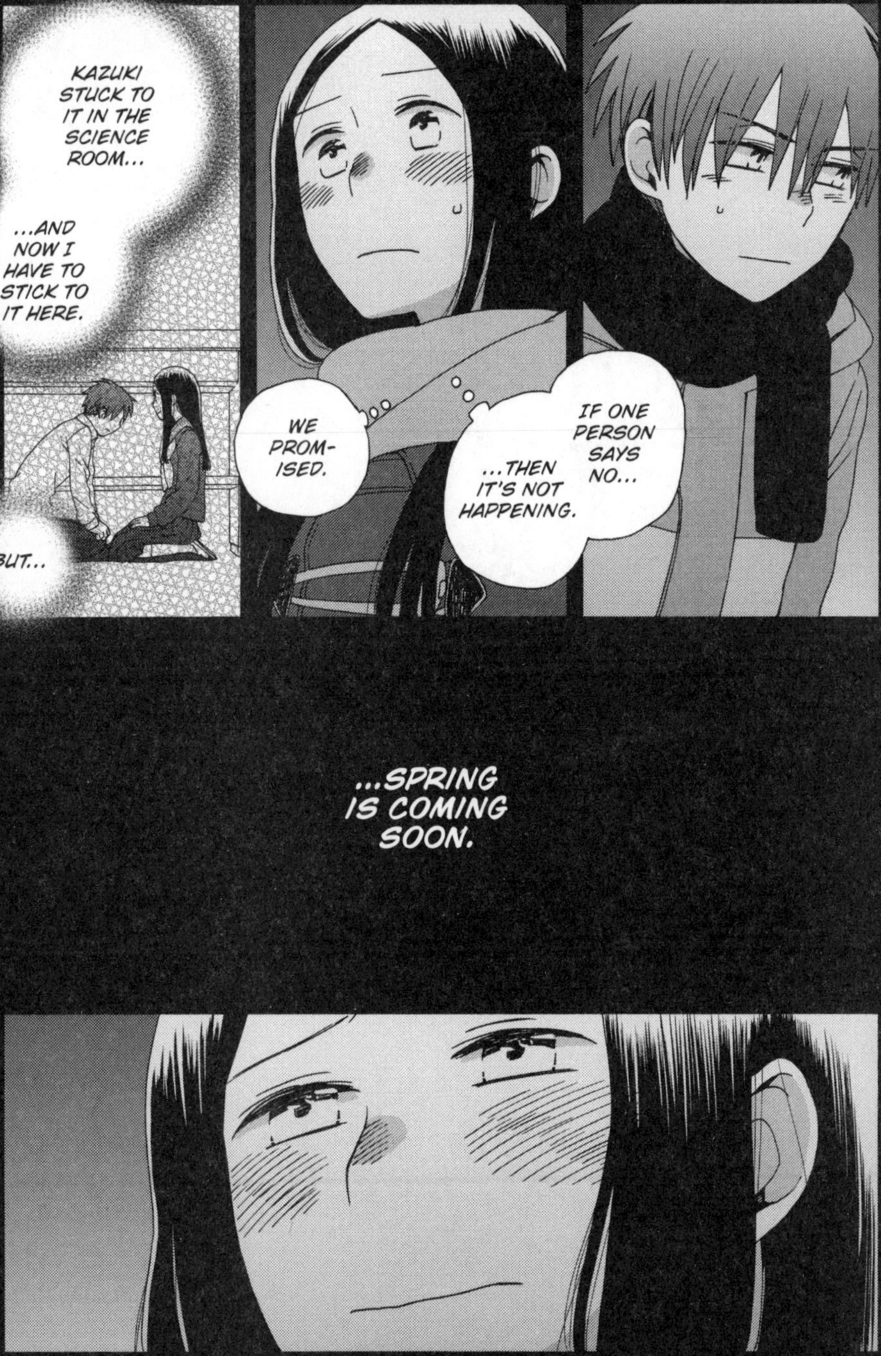
IF ONE PERSON SAYS NO...
...THEN IT'S NOT HAPPENING.
WE PROMISED.
KAZUKI STUCK TO IT IN THE SCIENCE ROOM...
...AND NOW I HAVE TO STICK TO IT HERE.
BUT...
...SPRING IS COMING SOON.

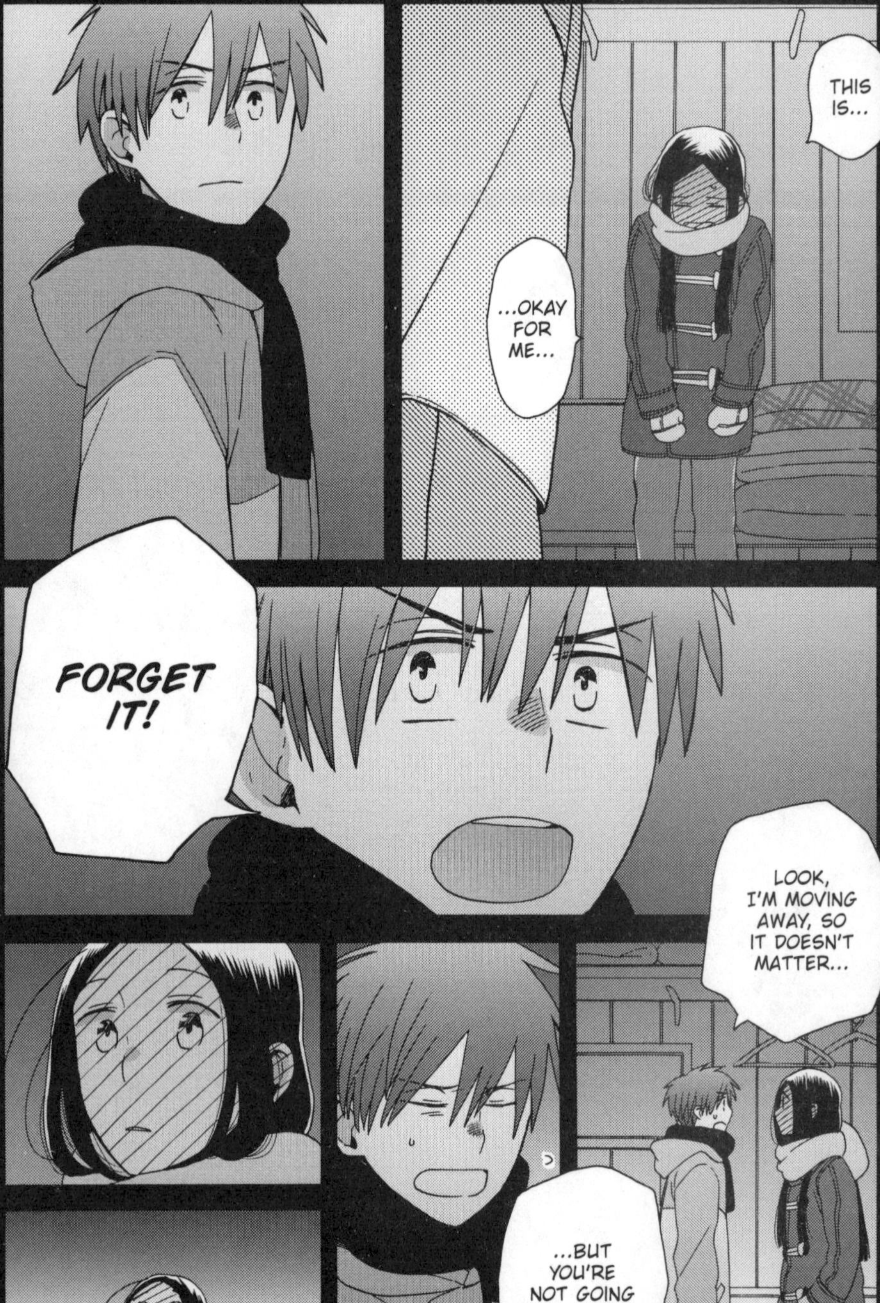
THIS IS...
...OKAY FOR ME...
FORGET IT!
LOOK, I'M MOVING AWAY, SO IT DOESN'T MATTER...
...BUT YOU'RE NOT GOING ANYWHERE.
?

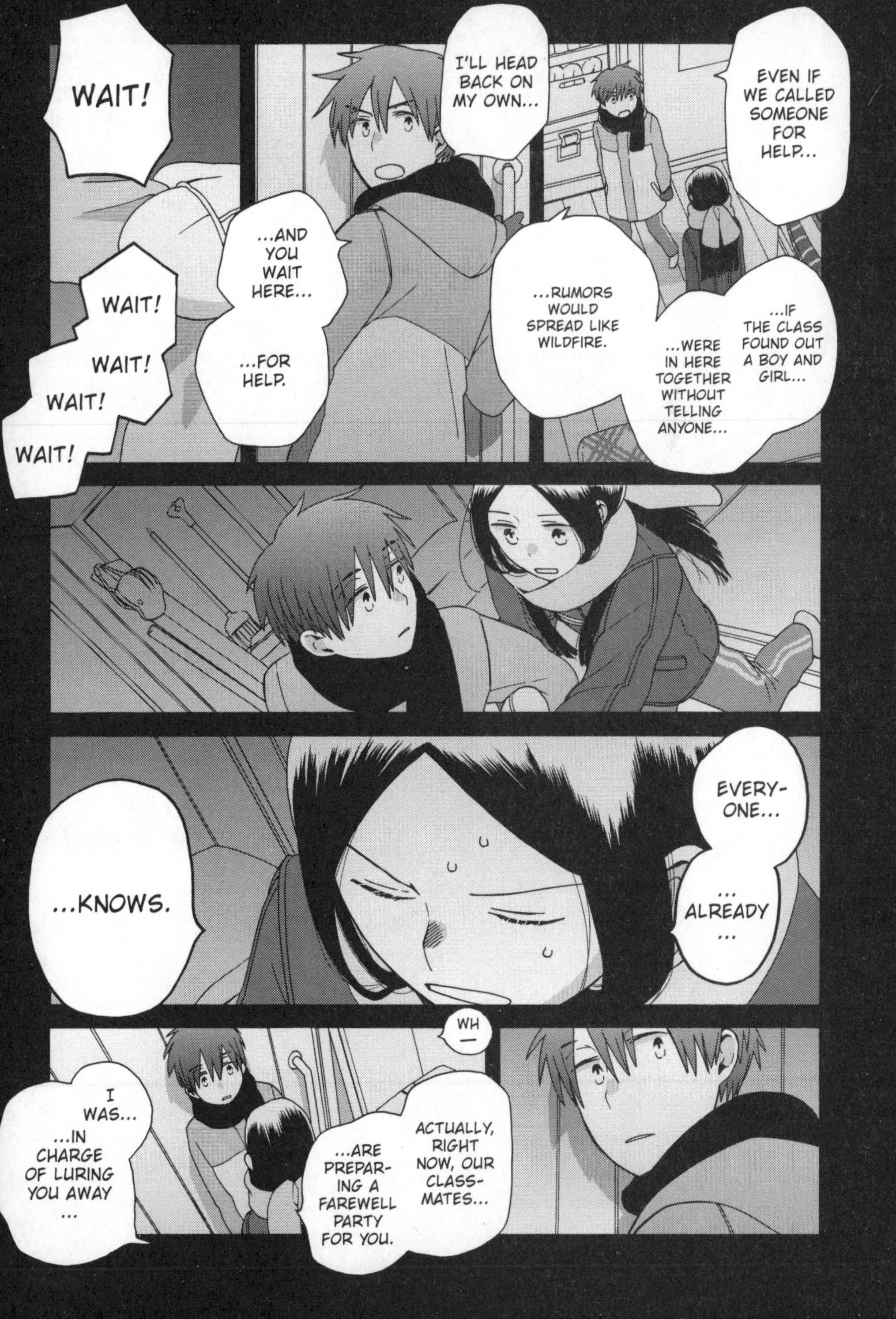
EVEN IF WE CALLED SOMEONE FOR HELP...
...IF THE CLASS FOUND OUT A BOY AND GIRL...
...WERE IN HERE TOGETHER WITHOUT TELLING ANYONE...
...RUMORS WOULD SPREAD LIKE WILDFIRE.
I'LL HEAD BACK ON MY OWN...
...AND YOU WAIT HERE...
...FOR HELP.
WAIT!
WAIT!
WAIT!
WAIT!
WAIT!
EVERY-ONE...
...ALREADY...
...KNOWS.
WH—
ACTUALLY, RIGHT NOW, OUR CLASS-MATES...
...ARE PREPAR-ING A FAREWELL PARTY FOR YOU.
I WAS...
...IN CHARGE OF LURING YOU AWAY...

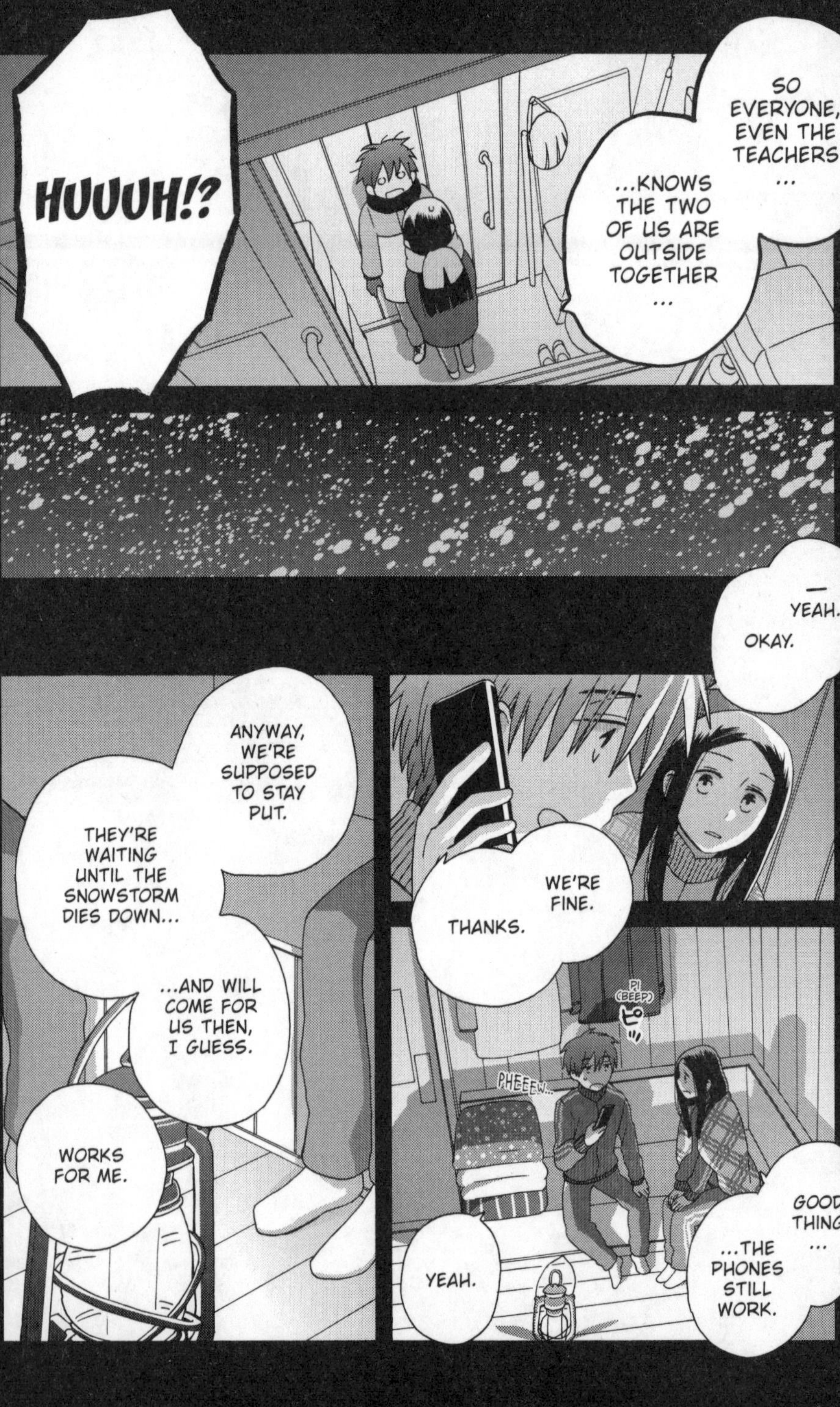
SO EVERYONE, EVEN THE TEACHERS...
...KNOWS THE TWO OF US ARE OUTSIDE TOGETHER...
HUUUH!?
—YEAH. OKAY.
WE'RE FINE.
THANKS.
PI (BEEP)
PHEEEW...
GOOD THING...
...THE PHONES STILL WORK.
YEAH.
ANYWAY, WE'RE SUPPOSED TO STAY PUT.
THEY'RE WAITING UNTIL THE SNOWSTORM DIES DOWN...
...AND WILL COME FOR US THEN, I GUESS.
WORKS FOR ME.

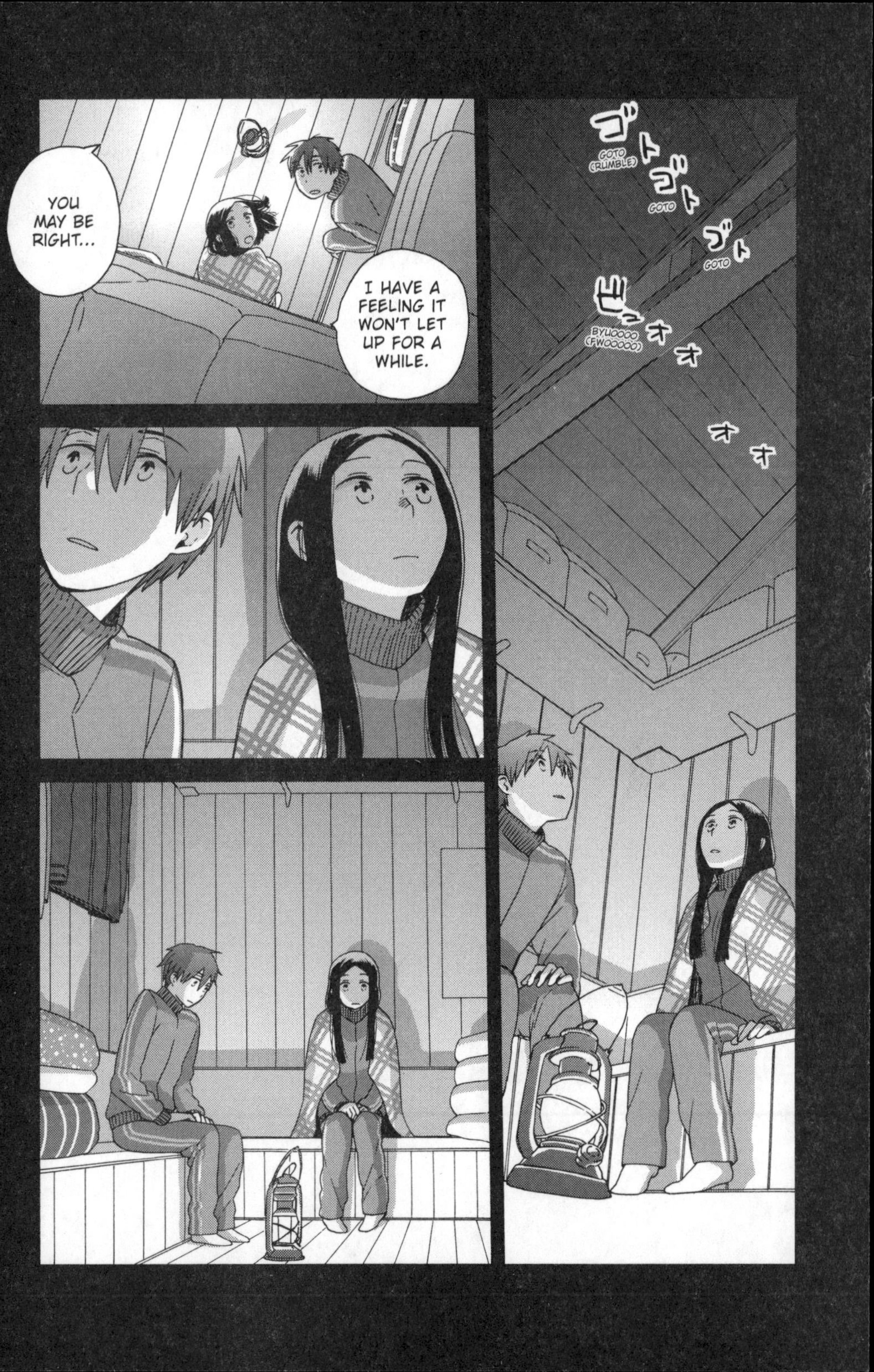
ゴト
GOTO (RUMBLE)
ゴト
GOTO
ゴト
GOTO
ビュオオオオ
BYUOOOO (FWOOOOO)
I HAVE A FEELING IT WON'T LET UP FOR A WHILE.
YOU MAY BE RIGHT...

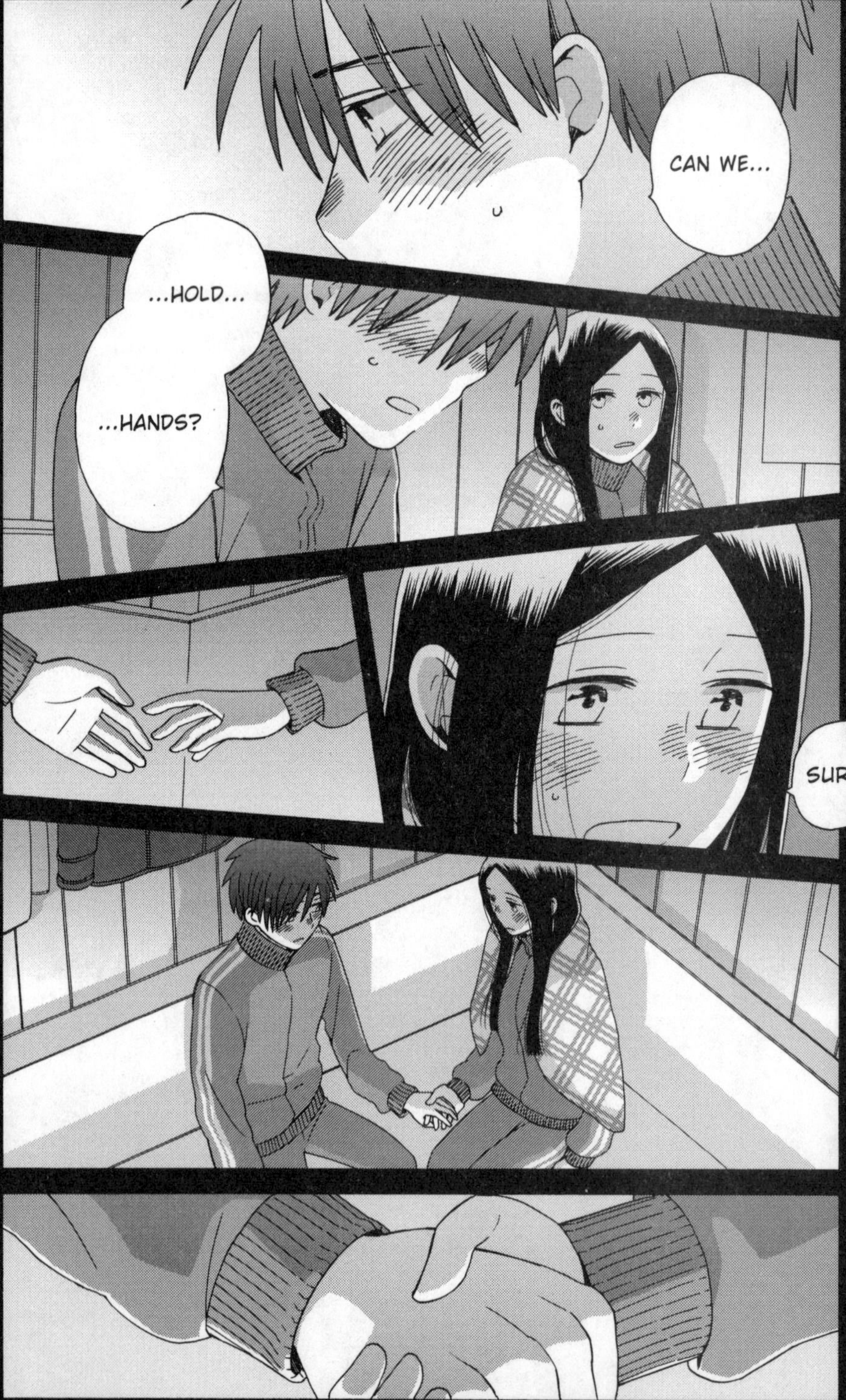
CAN WE...
...HOLD...
...HANDS?
SURE.

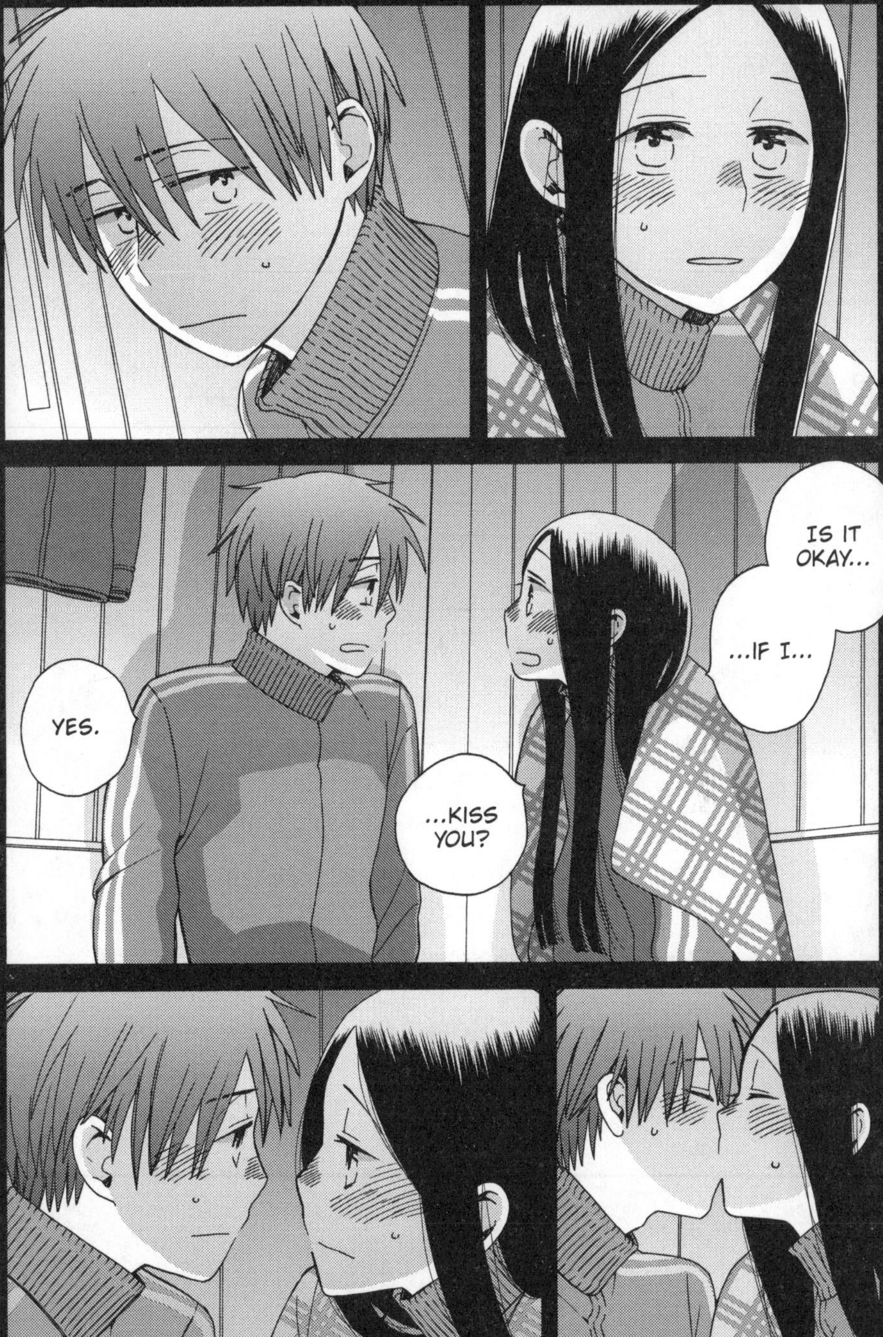
IS IT OKAY...
...IF I...
...KISS YOU?
YES.

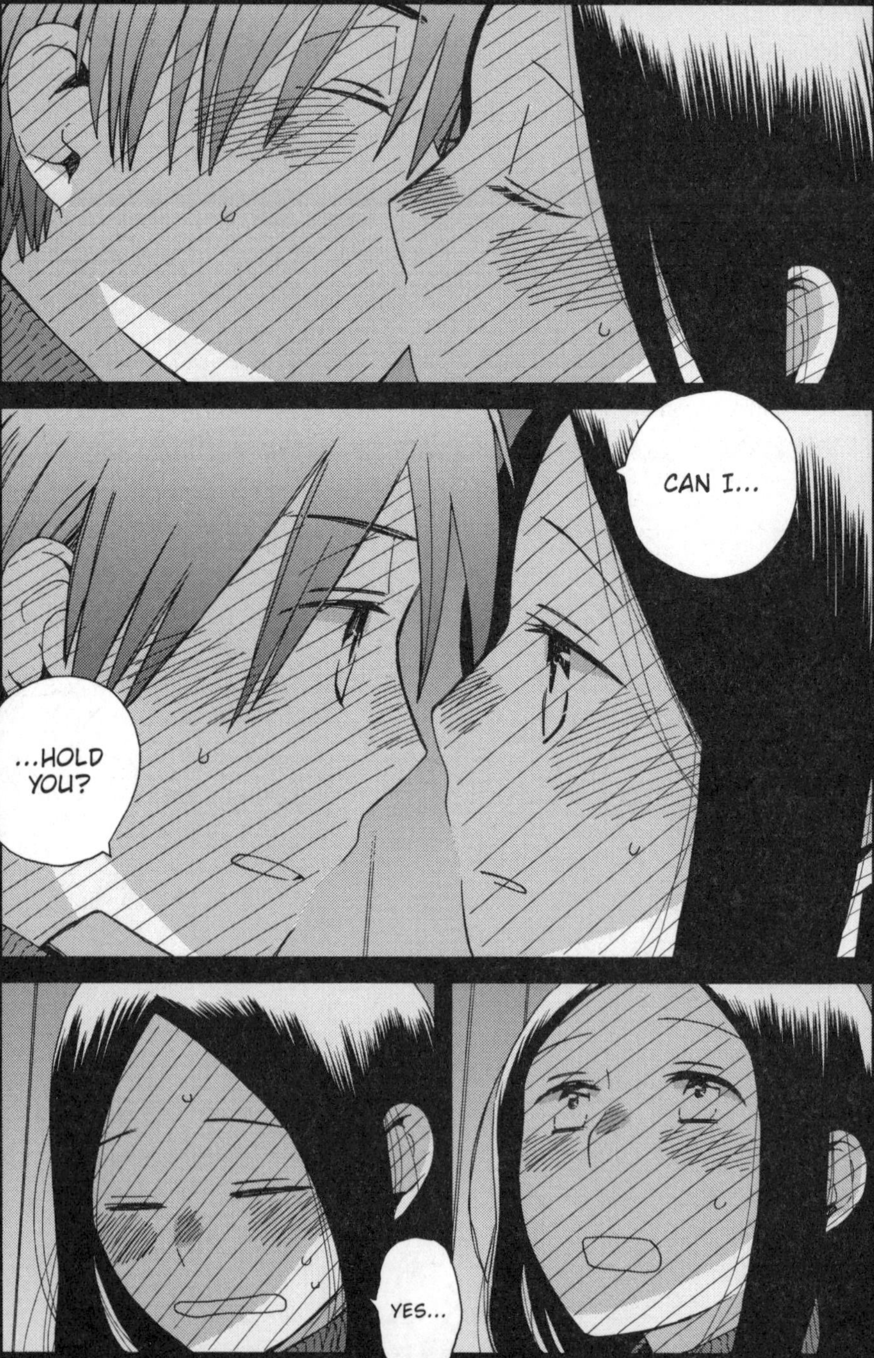
CAN I...
...HOLD YOU?
YES...

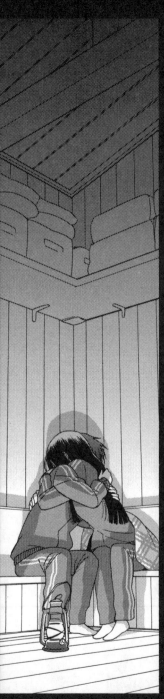

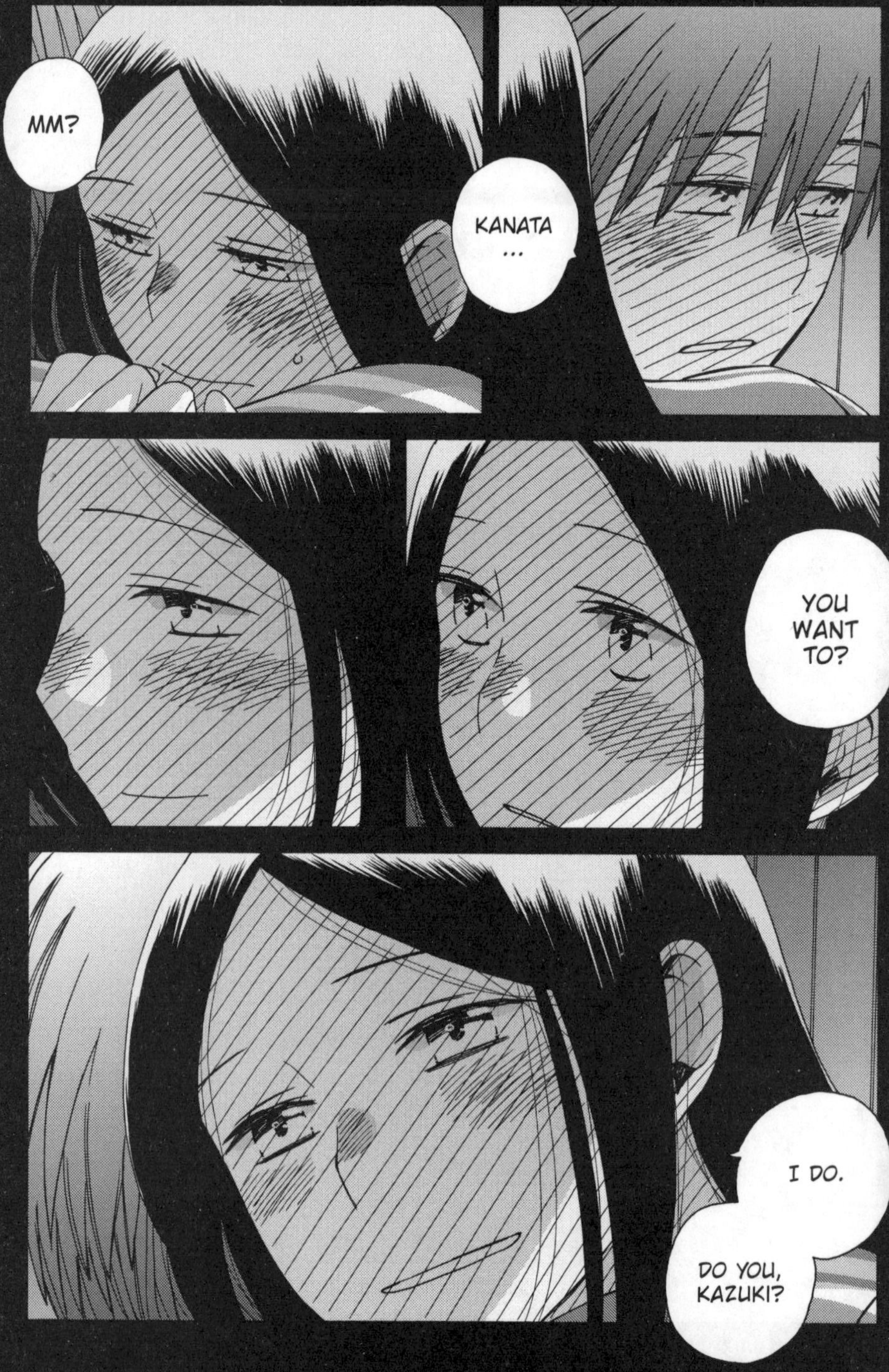
KANATA...
MM?
YOU WANT TO?
I DO.
DO YOU, KAZUKI?

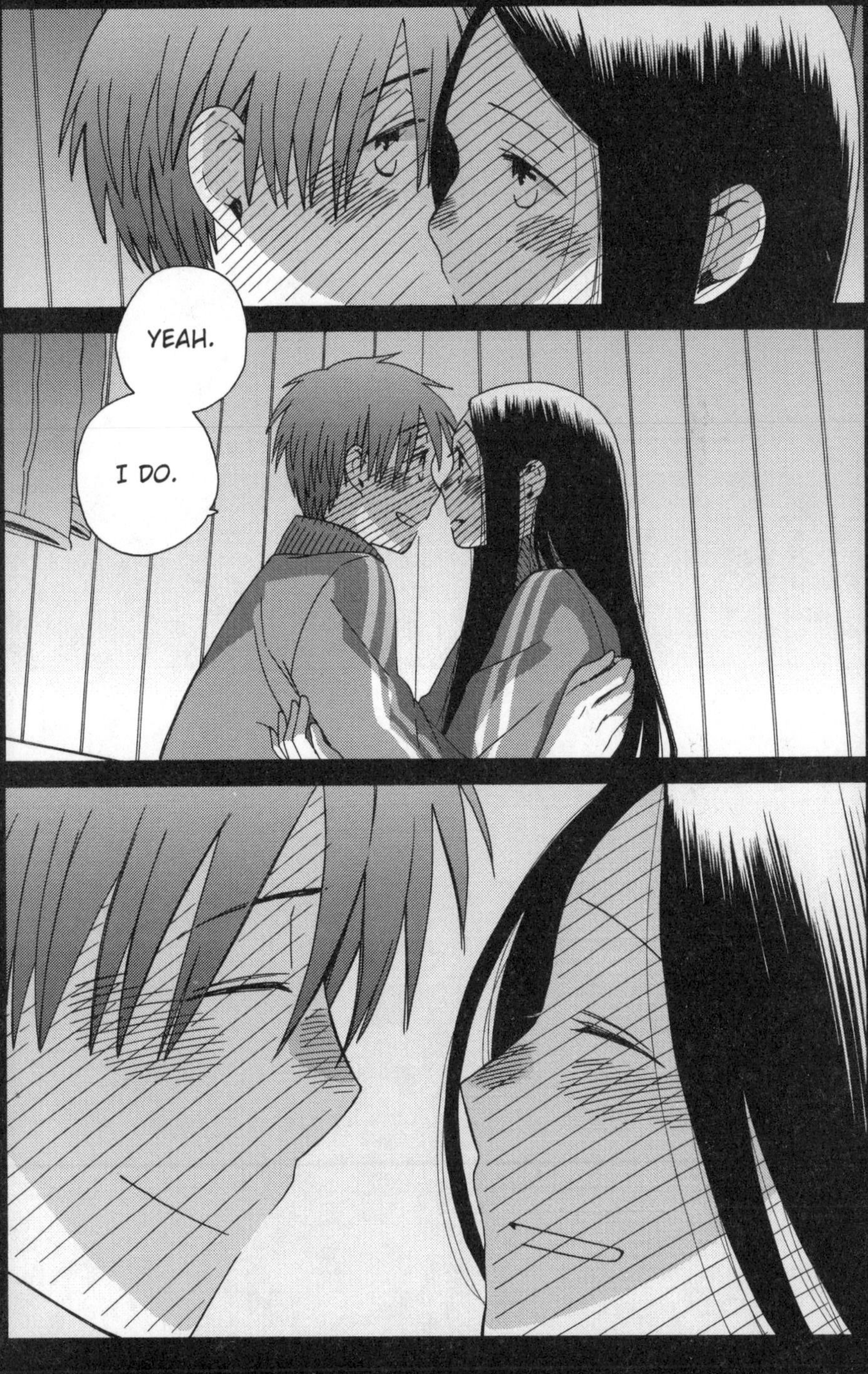
YEAH.
I DO.

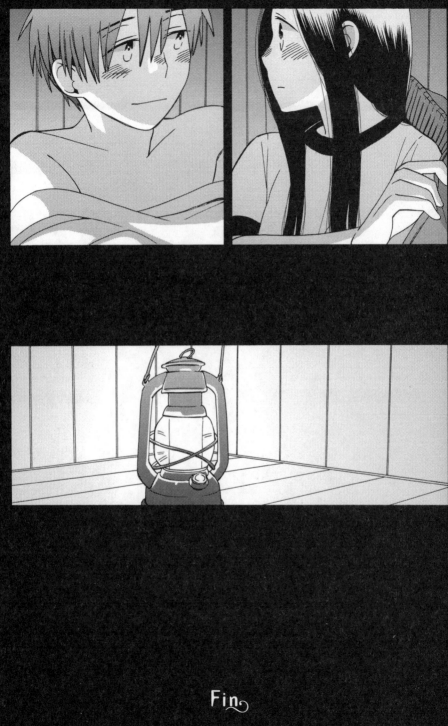

Fin

Love at Fourteen

Fuka Mizutani

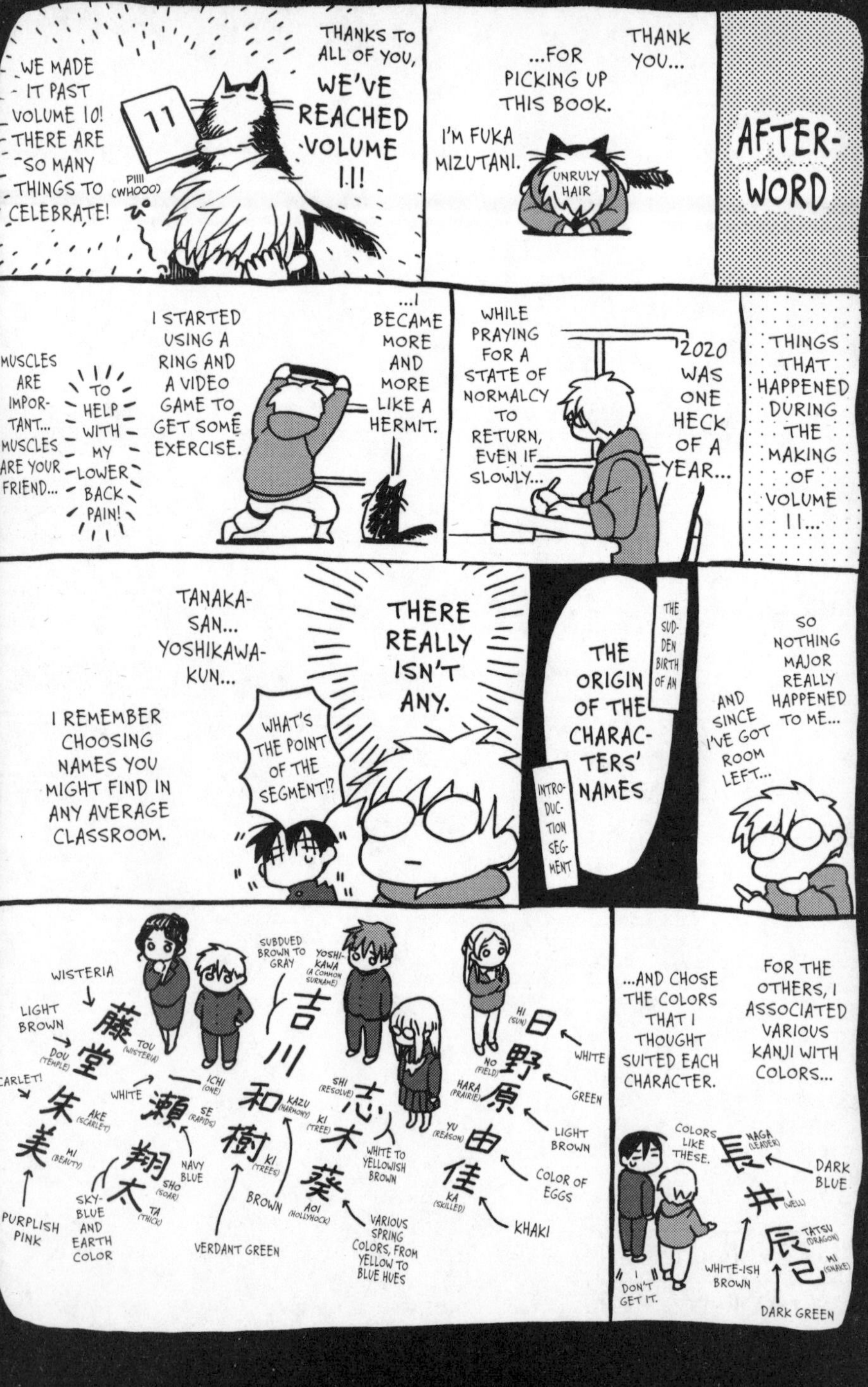
AFTER-WORD
THANK YOU...
...FOR PICKING UP THIS BOOK.
I'M FUKA MIZUTANI.
UNRULY HAIR
THANKS TO ALL OF YOU, WE'VE REACHED VOLUME 11!
WE MADE IT PAST VOLUME 10! THERE ARE SO MANY THINGS TO CELEBRATE!
PIIII (WHOOO)
11
THINGS THAT HAPPENED DURING THE MAKING OF VOLUME 11...
2020 WAS ONE HECK OF A YEAR...
WHILE PRAYING FOR A STATE OF NORMALCY TO RETURN, EVEN IF SLOWLY...
...I BECAME MORE AND MORE LIKE A HERMIT.
I STARTED USING A RING AND A VIDEO GAME TO GET SOME EXERCISE.
TO HELP WITH MY LOWER BACK PAIN!
MUSCLES ARE IMPORTANT... MUSCLES ARE YOUR FRIEND...
SO NOTHING MAJOR REALLY HAPPENED TO ME...
AND SINCE I'VE GOT ROOM LEFT...
THE SUDDEN BIRTH OF AN
THE ORIGIN OF THE CHARACTERS' NAMES
INTRODUCTION SEGMENT
THERE REALLY ISN'T ANY.
TANAKA-SAN... YOSHIKAWA-KUN...
WHAT'S THE POINT OF THE SEGMENT!?
I REMEMBER CHOOSING NAMES YOU MIGHT FIND IN ANY AVERAGE CLASSROOM.
FOR THE OTHERS, I ASSOCIATED VARIOUS KANJI WITH COLORS...
...AND CHOSE THE COLORS THAT I THOUGHT SUITED EACH CHARACTER.
COLORS LIKE THESE.
長 NAGA (LEADER)
DARK BLUE
井 I (WELL)
WHITE-ISH BROWN
辰 TATSU (DRAGON)
巳 MI (SNAKE)
DARK GREEN
I DON'T GET IT.
日 HI (SUN)
WHITE
野 NO (FIELD)
GREEN
原 HARA (PRAIRIE)
LIGHT BROWN
由 YU (REASON)
COLOR OF EGGS
佳 KA (SKILLED)
KHAKI
志 SHI (RESOLVE)
木 KI (TREE)
WHITE TO YELLOWISH BROWN
葵 AOI (HOLLYHOCK)
VARIOUS SPRING COLORS, FROM YELLOW TO BLUE HUES
吉川 YOSHI-KAWA (A COMMON SURNAME)
SUBDUED BROWN TO GRAY
和 KAZU (HARMONY)
BROWN
樹 KI (TREES)
VERDANT GREEN
一 ICHI (ONE)
WHITE
瀬 SE (RAPIDS)
NAVY BLUE
翔 SHO (SOAR)
太 TA (THICK)
SKY-BLUE AND EARTH COLOR
藤 TOU (WISTERIA)
WISTERIA
堂 DOU (TEMPLE)
LIGHT BROWN
朱 AKE (SCARLET)
SCARLET!
美 MI (BEAUTY)
PURPLISH PINK

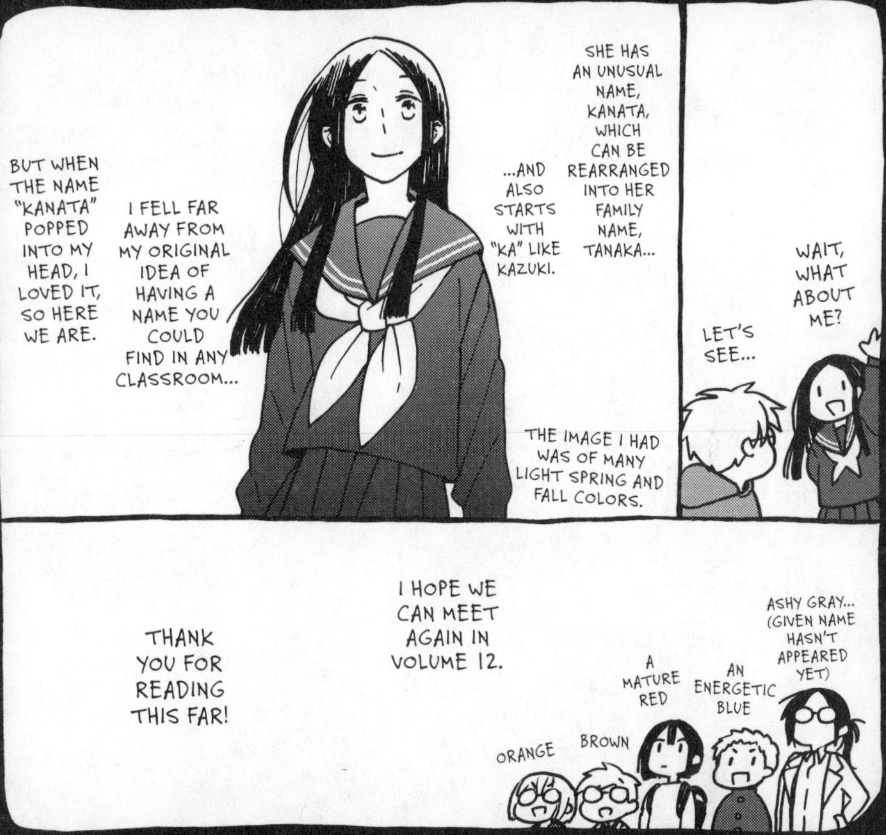
WAIT, WHAT ABOUT ME?
LET'S SEE...
SHE HAS AN UNUSUAL NAME, KANATA, WHICH CAN BE REARRANGED INTO HER FAMILY NAME, TANAKA...
...AND ALSO STARTS WITH "KA" LIKE KAZUKI.
I FELL FAR AWAY FROM MY ORIGINAL IDEA OF HAVING A NAME YOU COULD FIND IN ANY CLASSROOM...
BUT WHEN THE NAME "KANATA" POPPED INTO MY HEAD, I LOVED IT, SO HERE WE ARE.
THE IMAGE I HAD WAS OF MANY LIGHT SPRING AND FALL COLORS.
ASHY GRAY... (GIVEN NAME HASN'T APPEARED YET)
AN ENERGETIC BLUE
A MATURE RED
BROWN
ORANGE
I HOPE WE CAN MEET AGAIN IN VOLUME 12.
THANK YOU FOR READING THIS FAR!

Special Thanks.

Iida-sama

Kohei Nawata DeSign

My family

My great friends

Digital Resources Sangatsu-sama

Sayo Murata-chan

And all of you who are reading this now.

Winter 2020

水谷フーカ.

Fuka Mizutani

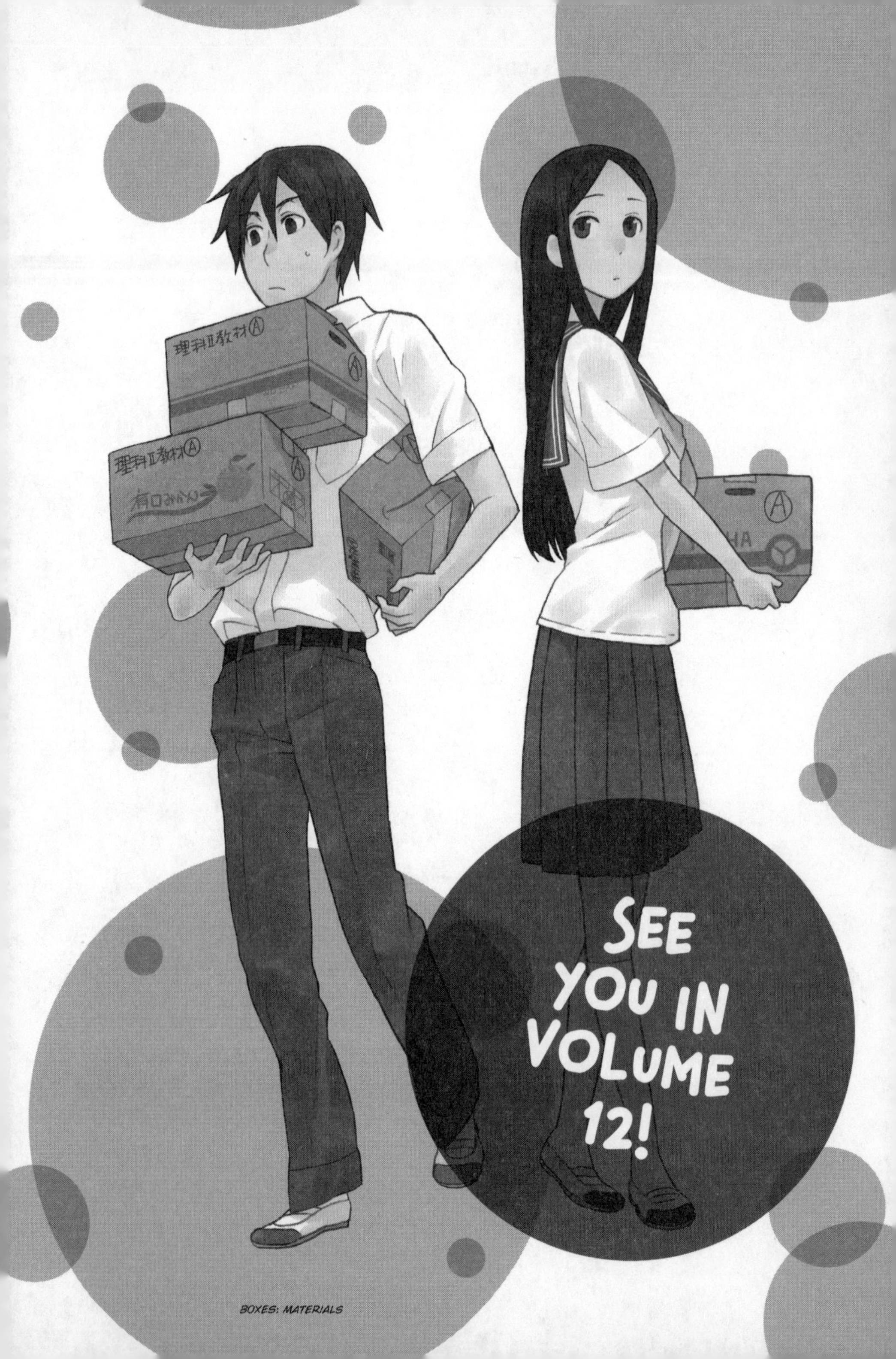
SEE YOU IN VOLUME 12!
BOXES: MATERIALS

TRANSLATION NOTES

COMMON HONORIFICS:

no honorific: Indicates familiarity or closeness; if used without permission or reason, addressing someone in this manner would constitute an insult.

-san: The Japanese equivalent of Mr./Mrs./Miss. If a situation calls for politeness, this is the fail-safe honorific.

-sama: Conveys great respect; may also indicate that the social status of the speaker is lower than that of the addressee.

-kun: Used most often when referring to boys, this indicates affection or familiarity. Occasionally used by older men among their peers, but it may also be used by anyone referring to a person of lower standing.

-chan: An affectionate honorific indicating familiarity used mostly in reference to girls; also used in reference to cute persons or animals of either gender.

-senpai: A suffix used to address upperclassmen or more experienced coworkers.

-sensei: A respectful term for teachers, artists, or high-level professionals.

PAGE 5

New Year's cards: In Japan, people send out annual New Year's postcards, or *nengajyo*, to their family, friends, and acquaintances. They often depict the zodiac animal for the upcoming year, and while store-bought ones are commonly used, many people also design their own. The post office is always overwhelmed by the sheer amount of cards they receive during this time of year and have devised specific procedures to deliver the cards efficiently and on time.

PAGE 10

New Year's shrine visit: Going to a local shrine and praying for a good new year or something more specific is a common custom and can be done any time between midnight of New Year's Eve and early January, preferably before the winter holidays are over. Most people these days go in their regular clothes, but some choose to dress up in traditional outfits.

PAGE 18

New Year's break: While Christmas is now widely considered a holiday in Japan, New Year's is still the day that holds more significance, so winter holidays revolve around the beginning of the year. People usually get a week or so off and spend it cooking elaborate meals and cleaning the entire house from top to bottom.

PAGE 40

Trimester: Most schools in Japan have three semesters as opposed to the two-semester system in America. It is usually broken into a spring, fall, and winter semester with extended breaks in the summer and winter. The Japanese school year starts in April and ends in March.

PAGE 84

First names: When getting to know someone, Japanese people will usually address them by their family name with the honorific -san. Calling someone by their given name or dropping honorifics entirely is a sign that the two people are close, such as two lovers.

PAGE 188

Names: Japanese names are usually created by combining various Chinese characters, known in Japan as *kanji*. Because each character has its own meaning, most people take that into heavy consideration when choosing names.

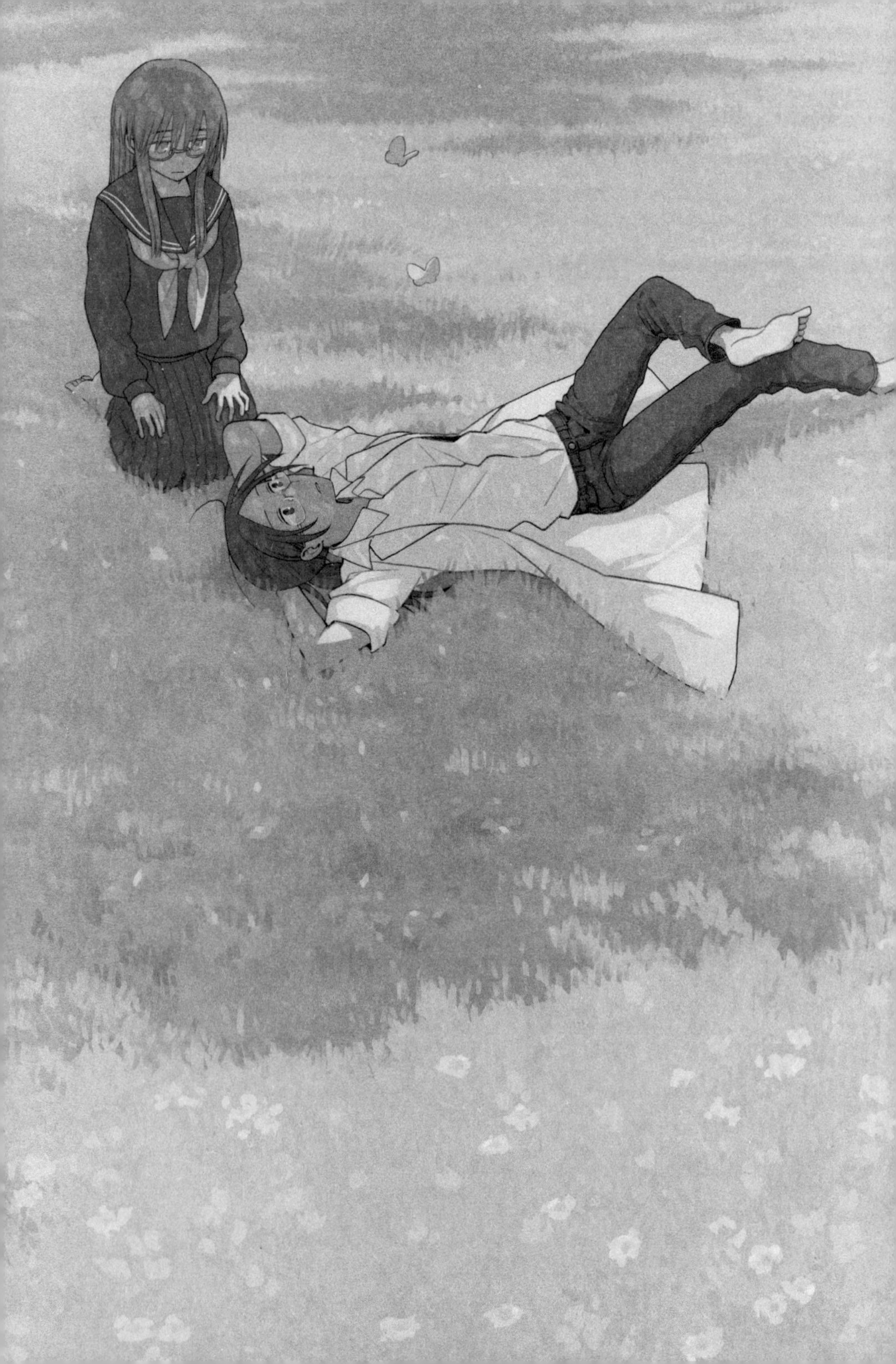

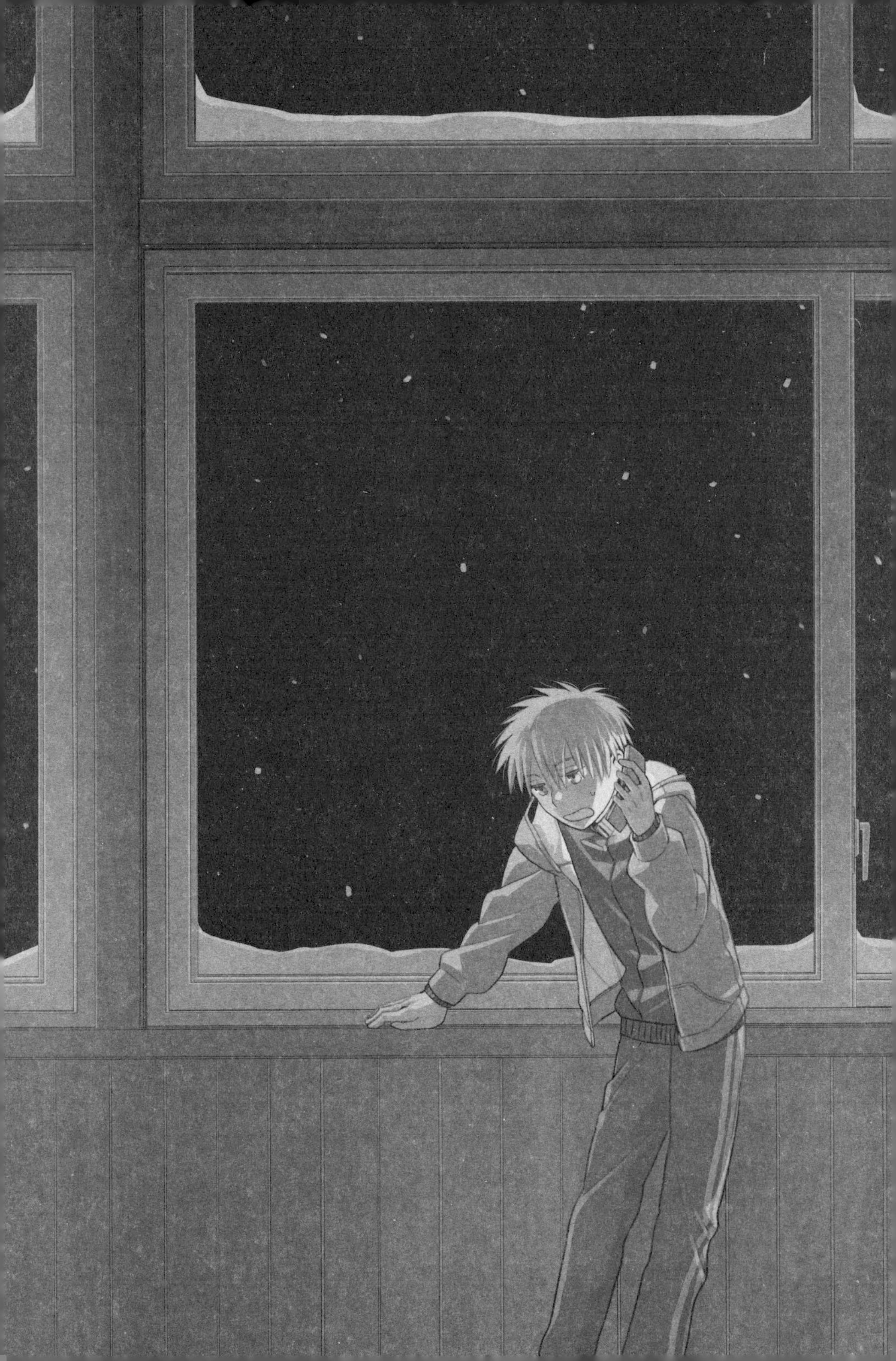

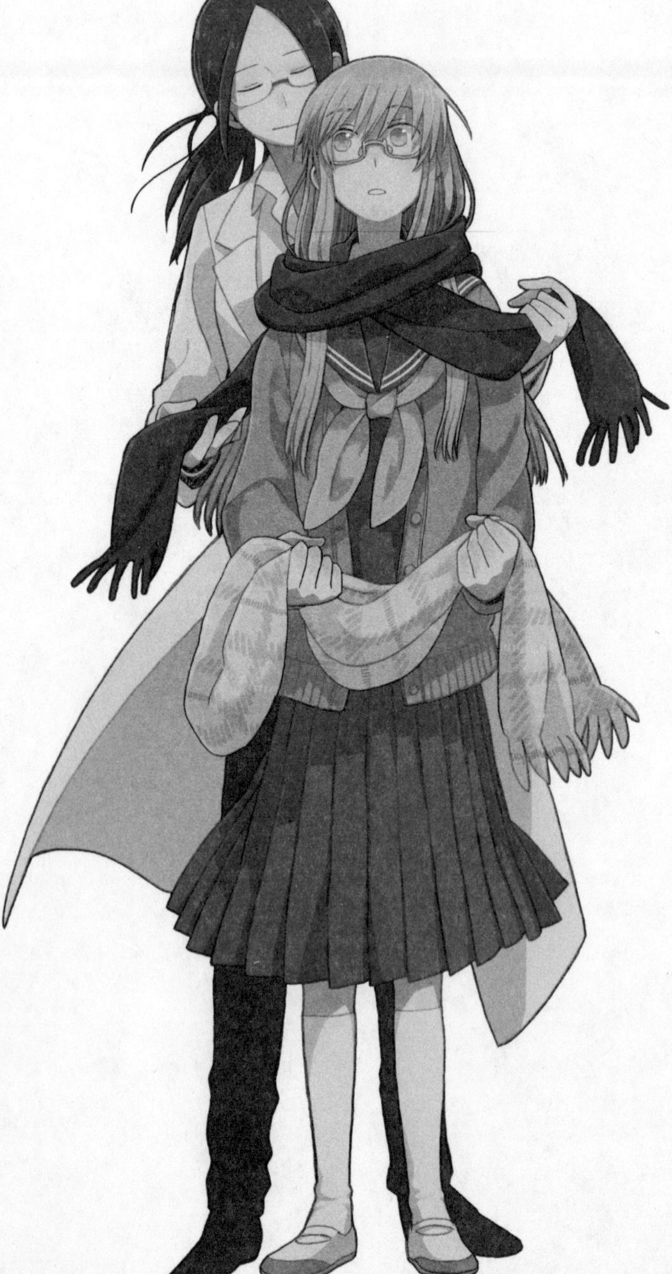

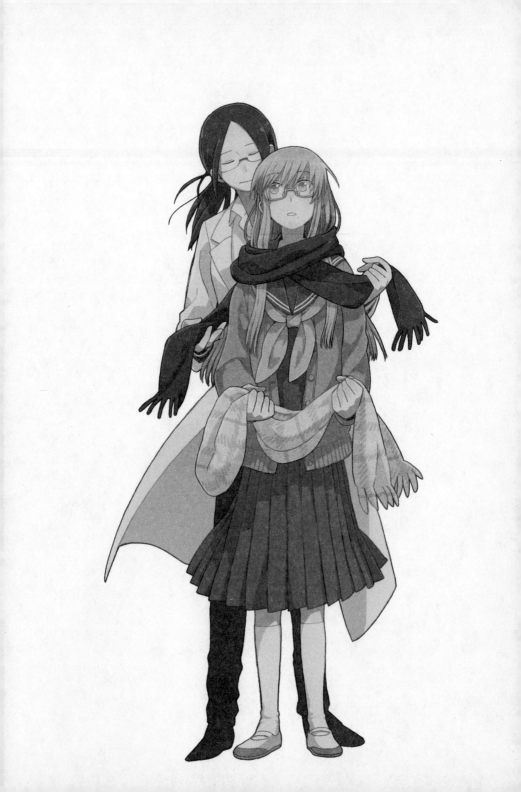

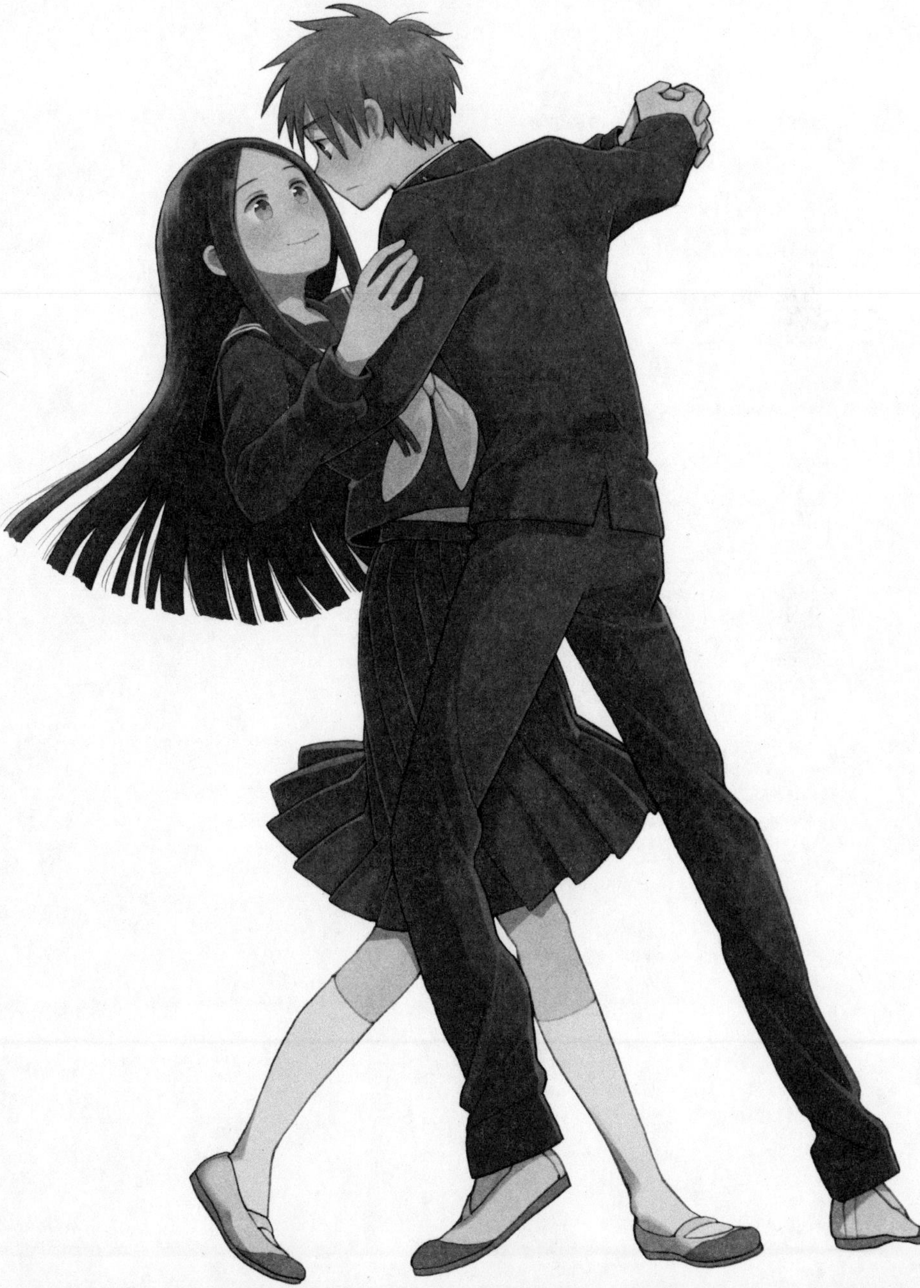

LOVE AT FOURTEEN 11
FUKA MIZUTANI

Translation: Sheldon Drzka

Lettering: Lys Blakeslee

JUYON-SAI NO KOI by Fuka Mizutani
© Fuka Mizutani 2020
All rights reserved.
First published in Japan in 2020 by HAKUSENSHA, INC., Tokyo.
English language translation rights in U.S.A., Canada and U.K. arranged with
HAKUSENSHA, INC., Tokyo through Tuttle-Mori Agency, Inc., Tokyo.

English translation © 2022 by Yen Press, LLC

Yen Press
150 West 30th Street, 19th Floor
New York, NY 10001

Visit us at yenpress.com
facebook.com/yenpress
twitter.com/yenpress
yenpress.tumblr.com
instagram.com/yenpress

First Yen Press Edition: February 2022

Yen Press is an imprint of Yen Press, LLC.
The Yen Press name and logo are trademarks of Yen Press, LLC.

The publisher is not responsible for websites (or their content) that are not owned by the publisher.

Library of Congress Control Number: 2016297684

ISBNs: 978-1-9753-3824-4 (paperback)
       978-1-9753-3825-1 (ebook)

10 9 8 7 6 5 4 3 2 1

WOR

Printed in the United States of America